DUET FOR
THREE HANDS

TESS THOMPSON

booktrope

Booktrope Editions
Seattle, WA 2015

Cover Design by Greg Simanson

Edited by Jennifer D. Munro

*This is a work of fiction. Names, characters, places, brands, media, and incidents
are either the product of the author's imagination or are used fictitiously. Any
resemblance to similarly named places or to persons living or deceased is
unintentional.*

PRINT ISBN 978-1-62015-718-3

EPUB ISBN 978-1-62015-740-4

Library of Congress Control Number: 2015902276

ACKNOWLEDGMENTS

This book came to me in a flash after I attended my mother's family reunion in 2008. It took years to write; the number of eyes on it over the years and drafts are too numerous to mention. I'm grateful to you all. You know who you are. Thank you to my mother's cousin, Arlene, for the letters and essays between my grandmother and great-grandmother; they were a source of great insight and inspiration, as were the stories from my mother of her family and childhood. As always, thank you to my brilliant editor, Jennifer D. Munro, for the final stint in this long journey. To the rest of my team at Booktrope, including Kellie Sheridan, Jesse James Freeman, and Greg Simanson, thank you for your continued excellence. To my early reader group, along with all the fans who write me—thank you for your encouragement on those days when I think surely there must be an easier and more lucrative line of work. To my little girls, Ella and Emerson, thank you for the sacrifices and compromises demanded of you from your unconventional mother. To my gay and lesbian friends who've fought so hard for your right to legally love whomever you choose—your courage inspired many aspects of this book. To historical readers Jack Dwyer and Melody Moore, and to proofreader Margo Paddock, thank you. Finally, thank you to the teachers of the world, who give of themselves every day in the most important job of all.

For Katherine Fye Sears,
Believer in dreams and books and how
they intertwine. Thank you for
suffering this long journey with me.

This book was inspired by my great-grandmother, Beatrice Rains. She plays with the angels now.

"What is the meaning of life? That was all—a simple question; one that tended to close in on one with years. The great revelation had never come. The great revelation perhaps never did come. Instead, there were little daily miracles, illuminations, matches struck unexpectedly in the dark; here was one."

VIRGINIA WOOLF,
TO THE LIGHTHOUSE, 1927

PART ONE

From Jeselle Thorton's journal.

June 10, 1928

When I came into the kitchen this morning, Mrs. Bellmont handed me a package wrapped in shiny gold paper, a gift for my thirteenth birthday. A book, I thought, happy. But it wasn't a book to read. It was a book to write in: a leather-bound journal. Inches of blank pages, waiting for my words.

Mrs. Bellmont beamed at me, seemingly pleased with my delight over the journal. "You write whatever ideas and observations come to you, Jeselle. Don't censor yourself. Women, especially, can only learn to write by telling the truth about themselves and those around them."

I put my nose in the middle of all those empty pages and took a deep breath, filling my lungs with the clean smell of new paper. Behind us Mama poured hotcake batter into a frying pan. The room filled with the aroma of those sweet cakes and sizzling oil. Whitmore came in holding a string of fish he'd caught in the lake, the screen door slamming behind him.

"Tell me why it matters that you write?" asked Mrs. Bellmont in her soft teacher voice.

"I cannot say exactly, Mrs. Bellmont." Too shy to say the words out loud, I shrugged to hide my feelings. But I know exactly. I write to know I exist, to know there is more to me than flesh and muscle being primed for a life of humility, servitude, obedience. I write, seeking clarity. I write because I love. I write, searching for the light.

Mrs. Bellmont understood. This is the way between us. She squeezed my hand, her skin cream over my coffee.

Tonight, for my birthday present, Whit captured lightning bugs in a glass jar, knowing how I love them. We set the jar on the veranda, astonished at the *immensity of their combined glow.* "Enough light in there to write by," I said, thinking of my journal now tucked in my apron pocket.

"They spark to attract a mate," he said, almost mournfully.

"They light up to find love?" I asked, astonished.

He nodded. "Isn't it something?"

We watched those bugs for a good while until Whit pushed his blond curls back from his forehead like he does when he worries.

"What is it?" I asked him.

"They shouldn't be trapped in this jar when they're meant to fly free, to look for love."

He unscrewed the lid, and those flickers of life drifted out into the sultry air until they intermingled with other fireflies, liberated to attract the love they so desperately sought. I moved closer to him. He took my hand as we watched and watched, not wanting the moment to end but knowing it must, as all moments do, both good and bad, light and dark, leaving only love behind to be savored in our memories.

CHAPTER 1

Nathaniel

ON A HOT and humid day in the middle of June, Nathaniel Fye rehearsed for a concert he was to give that night at the Howard Theatre with the Atlanta Orchestra. It was late afternoon when he emerged from the cool darkness of the theatre into the glaring afternoon heat and noise of Peachtree Street. He walked toward the large *W* that hung over the Hotel Winecoff, where he planned to eat a late afternoon meal and then head up to his room for a rest and a bath before dressing for the evening concert. Thick, humid air and gasoline fumes from passing automobiles made him hot even in his white linen summer suit. *Across to Singapore*, starring Joan Crawford, was displayed on the Loew's Theatre marquee. What sort of people went to the moving pictures, he wondered? Ordinary people who had lives filled with fun and love and friendship instead of traveling from town to town for concerts and nothing but practice in between. All the travel had been tolerable, even exciting, when he was younger, but now, as his age crept into the early thirties, he found himself wanting companionship and love, especially from a woman. Lately, he daydreamed frequently of a wife and children, a home. The idea filled him with longing, the kind that even the accolades and enthusiastic audiences could not assuage. But he was hopeless with women. Tongue-tied, stammering, sweating, all described his interactions with any woman but his mother. His manager, Walt, was good with people. He could talk to anyone. But Nathaniel? He could never think of one thing to say to anyone—his preferred way of communication was music. When his hands were on the keys it was as if his soul were set free to love and be loved, everything inside him released to the world. He would never think of taking the astonishing opportunities his talent had afforded him for granted, especially after the sacrifices his parents had made for him to study with the finest teachers in the world. Even so, he was lonely. The disciplined life and his natural reticence afforded little opportunity for connection.

A young woman stood near the entrance of the Winecoff, one foot perched saucily on the wall while balancing on the other, reading a magazine. She wore a cream-colored dress, and her curly, white-blonde hair bobbed under a cloche hat of fine-woven pink straw with a brim just wide enough to cover her face. He caught a glimpse of his reflection in the door's glass window, suddenly conscious of his own appearance. Tall, with a slight slump at his shoulders from years at the piano, dark hair under his hat, high cheekbones and sensitive brown eyes from his father but a delicate nose and stern mouth from his mother. Handsome? He suspected not. Just because you wish something didn't make it so, he thought. As his hand touched the door to go in, the young woman looked up and stared into his eyes. "Good afternoon. How do you do?"

Porcelain skin, gray eyes, perfect petite features, all combined to make a beautiful, exquisite, but completely foreign creature. A beautiful woman. Right here, in front of him. What to do? His heart flipped inside his chest and started beating hard and fast. Could she tell? Was it visible? He covered his chest with his hand, hot and embarrassed. "Yes." He lifted his hat. Oh, horrors: his forehead was slick with sweat. Yes? Had he just said yes? What had she asked him? He moved his gaze to a spot on the window. A fly landed on the glass and went still, looking at him with bulging eyes.

Her voice, like a string attached to his ear, drew his gaze back to her. "It's unbearably hot. I could sure use a Coca-Cola." With a flirtatious cock of her head, she smiled. She had the same thick Georgian accent as all the women in Atlanta, but there was a reckless, breathless quality in the way she oozed the words.

"Quite. Yes. Well, goodbye, then." He somehow managed to open the door and slip inside.

The hotel was quiet. Several women lounged in the lobby, talking quietly over glasses of sweet tea. A man in a suit sat at one of the small desks provided for guests, writing into a ledger. A maid scurried through with an armful of towels. He wanted nothing more than to be swallowed by the wall. What was the matter with him? How was it possible to hold the attention of hundreds during a concert, yet be unable to utter a single intelligible thing to one lone woman?

He stumbled over to the café counter and ordered a sandwich and a glass of Coca-Cola. He allowed himself one glass whenever he performed in Atlanta during the summer. The heat, as the young woman had said, made a person long for a Coca-Cola. But only one, no more or he might never stop, and next thing he knew he'd have one every day and then twice a day and so forth. Sweet drinks were an indulgence, a dangerous way to live for a man who must have complete discipline to remain a virtuoso. If he allowed himself anything or everything he wanted, where might it lead? He could not be like other people, even if he wanted to be.

Waiting for his drink, he heard, rather than saw, the door open, and then the blonde woman sat beside him, swinging her legs ever so slightly as she perched on the round bar stool. "Hello again." She placed her hands, which were half the size of his and so white as to appear almost translucent, upon the counter. She interlaced her fingers, rather primly and in a way that seemed to belie the general forwardness of sitting next to a man she didn't know at an otherwise empty counter. He nodded at her, catching a whiff of gardenia he supposed came from her smooth, white neck.

"Would you like to buy me a Coca-Cola?" She peered up at him from under her lashes. Her eyes were the color of storm clouds.

What was this? She wanted him to buy her a drink? Had she hinted at that outside? What a ninny he was. Of course. Any imbecile could have picked up on that. Walt would have had her in here with a soda in her hand before the door closed behind them. He tried to respond, but his voice caught in the back of his throat. Instead he nodded to the man in the white apron behind the fountain, who, in turn, also in silence, pulled the knob of the fountain spray with a beefy arm.

"I've just come from the Crawford picture. It was simply too marvelous for words. I do so love the moving pictures. What's your name?" She pressed a handkerchief to the nape of her neck where soft curls lay, damp with perspiration. What would it feel like to wrap his finger in one of the curls?

"Nathaniel."

"I'm Frances Bellmont. You from up north?"

"Maine originally. I live in New York City now."

Her gray eyes flickered, and an eyebrow rose ever so slightly. "I see. A Yankee." He thought he detected an excitement as she said it, as if to sit by him were an act of rebellion.

"As north as you can get and still be an American," he said. At last. Words!

"'Round here we're not sure any of y'all are true Americans." She took a dainty sip from her soda and peered at him out of the corner of her eyes. "Now wait a minute. Are you Nathaniel Fye, the piano player?"

"Right."

"Oh my." She turned her full gaze upon him. "That *is* interesting." She had full lips that looked almost swollen. "My mother and I happen to be attending that very concert tonight. I don't enjoy such serious music, but my mother simply adores it. We're staying overnight here at the Winecoff. We live all the way across town, and mother thought it would be nice to stay overnight. Together." She rolled her eyes.

Before he knew what he was saying, a lie stumbled from his mouth. "Party. Later. In my suite. You could come. Your mother, too."

"A party? I'd love to attend. Do I have to bring my mother?" She sipped her soda while looking up at him through her lashes.

"I, I don't know." He stuttered. "Isn't that how it's done?"

She slid off her seat, touching the sleeve of his jacket like a caress. "I'm just teasing. We wouldn't think of missing it. I'll see you then." And then she was out the door, leaving only the smell of her perfume behind, as if it had taken up permanent residence in his nostrils.

* * *

Later that night, before the concert, he stood at the full-length mirror in the greenroom of the Howard Theatre, brushing lint from his black tuxedo jacket. Walt sat across from him in one of the soft chairs, scouring the arts section of the *New York Times* and occasionally making notations in a small notebook.

"I'd like to have a small group up to my room. After the concert tonight."

"What did you say?" Walt, a few years younger than Nathaniel, possessed light blue eyes that were constantly on the move, shifting and scanning, like a predator looking for his next meal. He was once an amateur violinist who had played in his small town of Montevallo, Alabama, at church and town dances before he went to New York City. "Played the fiddle, but I didn't have the talent to go all the way," he told Nathaniel years ago, during their first interview. "But the music, it gets in a person's blood, and I aim to make a life out of it however I can."

Walt closed the newspaper without making a sound, like he was trying not to spook a wild horse. He stood, folding the newspaper under his arm. He had a slim build and wore wire-rimmed glasses. Receding light brown hair made his forehead appear more prominent than it once was. Despite his ordinary appearance, women flushed and giggled when he spoke to them. "Never, in five years, have you had folks up to your room. Much as I've asked you to."

"I know," Nathaniel said, shrugging as if it were nothing important. "You know I can never think of anything to say to people."

Walt's eyes were already at the door. "You want me to bring the music promoter I was telling you about? He's keen to get after you with some ideas."

"Fine."

Walt rocked back and forth on the balls of his feet. "I'll make sure no one stays too late. We leave for the West tomorrow on the early train." He pushed his glasses up to the bridge of his nose. "Why the sudden interest in sociability?" He raised an eyebrow and punched him on the shoulder. "Could it be the young lady I saw you with earlier?"

Nathaniel straightened his bow tie. "How did you know that?"

"I was checking into the hotel when I happened to see the two of you at the bar. I saw her again at the restaurant tonight. Dining with her mother, if I make my guess. They're almost identical."

Nathaniel wanted to ask more but kept quiet. He took his pocket watch out of his trousers and set it on the table. His pockets must be empty when he played. He stretched his fingers.

"You do know who they are, don't you?" Walt's forehead glistened. He took off his glasses and waved them in the air. Nathaniel couldn't decide if he only imagined the movement was in the shape of a dollar sign.

"Last name's Bellmont."

"Yeah, that's Frances Bellmont you bought a soda for, my friend. The Bellmont family's old money. Used to own half of Georgia. He's a vice president over at Coca-Cola."

"I see."

Walt waggled his fingers, teasing. "I know you don't care about such things."

"Just be at my room at ten," Nathaniel said, chuckling. "Before anyone else arrives. I'll need you to do the talking."

"My mama always said I was a good talker," said Walt.

"One of us has to be."

"I'll get hold of some champagne. From what I hear, Frances Bellmont likes her champagne." He slapped Nathaniel on the back.

"What do you mean?" A dart of something, almost like fear, pierced the bottom of his stomach.

"Just rumors. Nothing to worry over."

"Tell me."

"She likes parties. That's all."

"How do you know that?"

"It's my job to know these kinds of things." Walt put up his hand, like a command. "Stop. This is the first time I've ever seen you interested in a woman. Don't ruin it by talking yourself out of it." He left through the greenroom door, calling out behind him, "Good luck tonight."

After the concert, Nathaniel went back to his suite and bathed the perspiration from his body, using a scrub brush and soap he imagined smelled like a woman's inner wrist. He washed his thick, dark hair and slicked it back with pomade so that the waves that sometimes fell over his forehead were tamed. Using a straight blade to shave his face, he scrutinized his looks. Would he ever be appealing to a girl like Frances Bellmont? His eyes were brown and on the small side, if he were truthful. And his lips were thin, now that he really looked at them, although he had straight, white teeth. That was something. People were always telling Walt that Nathaniel came across as intense, and sometimes even the word *frightening* had been used. I'll smile, he assured himself. Easy and fun, like Walt.

He hung his tuxedo in the closet and smoothed the bed cover from where he'd rumpled it during his earlier nap. Then he straightened the sitting room, disposing of a newspaper and moving several music sheets marked with his latest composition to the other room. Would people sit, he wondered? Or stand? He looked about the room. He hadn't noticed much about it upon his arrival. All hotels began to look the same after a while. A crystal chandelier hung in the middle of the room, cascading like fallen tears and casting subdued light across a dark green couch with scalloped legs. A round table stood between two straight-backed chairs with cushions decorated in a complicated red floral design. Would there be enough room for everyone? How many did Walt invite? He should have asked. Despite his recent bath, he began to perspire.

Just then there was a knock on the door. It was Walt, looking newly shaven and dapper in a tan linen suit with a blue tie. With him was a man about Walt's age, whom he introduced as Ralph Landry. "How do you know Walt?" Nathaniel asked him, feigning interest, trying to keep his gaze from wandering to the door.

"Knew one another growing up in Montevallo, Alabama." Ralph's accent sounded like a foreign language to Nathaniel: slow, elongated vowels, twice as many, it seemed, than words usually had, and no "r" sounds. "Moved out to New York together for college, and I went on to med school. Now I'm headed back to Montevallo to start my own practice." Ralph's face, pink and fleshy, looked like the underbelly of a sow, and he had a particularly thick neck that seemed about to pop open his bow tie.

"Best of luck to you." Nathaniel cleared his throat and glanced over at Walt, who was taking bottles of champagne out of an apple crate. He forced himself to look back to his companion.

"How's your younger brother doing?" Walt asked.

"Half-brother," Ralph corrected him. "He calls himself Mick now." Ralph's face turned serious. "He's at loose ends since graduating from high school."

"Send him out to California," said Walt. "Didn't you tell me he lives for moving pictures? He could get a job out there."

"Yeah, maybe," said Ralph.

"We can thank Ralphie here for the illegal suds," Walt said, slapping his friend on the back.

Ralph took a big sip. "Well, let's just say being able to stitch folks up after a gunshot wound in the middle of the night provides some benefits." He laughed and took another gulp of champagne. "Have to get a little wop blood on my hands sometimes, but it's worth it."

Nathaniel felt a blast of revulsion, knowing Ralph meant the New York underworld of organized crime. One of the head crime bosses had asked Nathaniel to play at his daughter's birthday party several years ago. He booked an overseas tour to get out of it, fearing his hands might be crushed if he refused.

"You want a drink, Nathaniel?" asked Walt.

Nathaniel shook his head, no.

"Don't drink, Mr. Fye?" asked Ralph.

"I do not," said Nathaniel, stifling a sigh. This was a mistake. Frances probably wouldn't even show, and he'd be trapped here all night while these derelicts went through the half-case of champagne.

"Nathaniel here is looking for sainthood after his death," said Walt. "All he does is work. So you and I'll have to drink his share."

Before Walt could answer, there was another knock on the door. It was John Wainwright, the music promoter, and his wife. Walt had told Nathaniel the wife's name, but he couldn't remember it. The palms of his hands were damp. His throat tightened. The pulse at his neck was rapid, yet his breathing felt shallow, like he couldn't get enough air. He caught a glimpse of the bed in the other room and felt a sudden, intense longing for the feel of the cool sheets on his skin.

To his relief, John Wainwright came over to him and held out his hand, introducing himself. Mr. Wainwright had the kind of face no one would remember in the morning and a limp, clammy handshake, like a faded, damp cloth on a clothesline. His wife wore a black evening gown that clung to her wide hips and large breasts. Her copper red hair was cut in an unflattering blunt bob above the ears. She stared at Nathaniel with eyes rimmed in charcoal-colored liner, grasping in her gloved hands the program from tonight's concert. "Autograph for me?" She blushed, the fat of her upper arms straining against the elastic of her long white gloves.

He did so, avoiding her gaze. My God, the room was stifling. He reached inside his jacket for his handkerchief and wiped the palms of his hands and then mopped his brow.

"I'm just absolutely thrilled to meet you." Mrs. Wainwright's high-pitched voice reminded Nathaniel of one of those yappy lapdogs he saw with wealthy New York socialites. "Oh, the excitement in the theatre tonight when your hands hovered over the keyboard before those last notes. I thought the woman next to me might faint. How do you do it?" Her eyes bulged as she leaned forward, so close to his face that he caught a whiff of onions on her breath.

"It's just my job." His voice sounded like a rusty gate. He tried to smile, feeling as if his lips were caught against his teeth. "Same as anyone."

Another knock on the door. Walt, setting down his glass of champagne, moved to answer it. Nathaniel held his breath. He wanted it to be her. And he didn't want it to be her.

Walt opened the door, and there stood Frances Bellmont. She wore a pale blue gown with rows of fringe all the way up the skirt, which reminded him of the spikes of sea anemones. Fair hair curled around her face, and her stormy eyes were made up with black mascara. They sparkled even from across the room and were, for an instant, the only things Nathaniel could see. He tore his eyes away from her. Yes, he thought, that's what it felt like to turn away, like a ripping away from something life-giving. Her mother was equally lovely, and Walt was correct, they looked remarkably alike, except Mrs. Bellmont was several inches shorter and wore her hair in longer curls.

The room had gone silent, like an enchanted breeze had woven its way among everyone, rendering them speechless. Walt recovered first, taking the Bellmont ladies' hands in turn and introducing himself. Nathaniel could do nothing but stare at his shoes and wish for a piano where he could play and hide. And then, like walking in a strong wind, he came forward and put his hand out to Mrs. Bellmont. She took it, and he brought her gloved hand up to his lips in the way he'd seen Walt do many times to young ladies after concerts.

"Mr. Fye, I'm pleased to meet you." Mrs. Bellmont's eyes were identical to Frances's, except without any makeup. She was virtually unlined, but her face was thinner than her daughter's, showing evidence of her age. He imagined, for a brief, insane moment, that he saw his future, but then her lovely resonant voice, like a stringed instrument, brought him back to the present. "The concert was simply lovely. What a privilege to meet you in person."

"Mr. Fye, good to see you again." Frances tugged at her gloves as her eyes shifted about the room. "Are more guests expected?"

"I'm not sure. Walt arranged this."

Frances's gloves were off now, dangling in her left hand like discarded snakeskins. "Oh, I do hope so. It's wonderful to be out. You must have such a glamorous life in New York City." She held out her left hand.

He took the offered hand, but instead of kissing it properly as he intended, his shaking hand seemed incapable of bringing it to his mouth; instead of making contact with her soft skin, he kissed the air just above her knuckles, resulting in a smacking from his lips that sounded like a baby suckling. He felt his ears turn red.

Frances smiled at him and removed her hand, which was the texture of a rose petal. Dazzling, that's the only way he could think to describe her smile. It reached him someplace deep inside, stirring feelings he didn't know he had. Was it possible that a man like him could get a woman like Frances Bellmont to love him? If only he were less awkward, less confused.

She stuffed her gloves into the small, black purse she carried. "Do you?"

"Do I what?"

"Do you have a glamorous life in New York City? I imagine you know actresses and singers. Think of that, Mother." Without waiting for an answer, she continued, her eyes bright, "I suppose there are hundreds of parties?"

"I'm unsure. I travel much of the time. In fact, I leave for the West tomorrow. I'll be gone eight weeks."

"The West? Do you mean California?" asked Frances.

"Yes. All the western cities, including San Francisco and Los Angeles."

"Hollywood?" Frances clapped her hands together. "How exciting."

"I suppose." He wanted to tell her how lonely he was, how comforting it would be to have a wife by his side, but, of course, he could not. Even he knew this was not appropriate cocktail party conversation.

Ralph Landry brought champagne to both the Bellmont ladies and then guided Mrs. Bellmont over to the Wainwrights, leaving Nathaniel alone with Frances. For the second time in less than a minute he wished for a piano, and then he simply wished for music, but there was not a gramophone in the room and no piano at which he might sit and transform into the man featured on posters and programs. Instead, in the glow of the beautiful Frances Bellmont he was merely a large, awkward man in an expensive suit.

He remembered then, as if it were only yesterday, standing at the side of the Grange hall when he was in his late teens, home for a brief visit before he left for New York City to begin another chapter in his tutelage, dressed in a suit made by his mother. For days, while he practiced in the other room, he'd heard the stop and go of the sewing machine, between his scales and notes; his mother unconsciously matched the rhythm of whatever he played—relegated, for her son, to seamstress from her own seat at the piano bench.

That night, at the Grange, a band of the variety Walt had once been part of played as entertainment. There was a fiddler, a banjo player, and a pianist who had no feel for the subtlety of music. The singer was a young woman with a clear, crystal voice; thick, shiny, brown hair arranged in a loose bun at the nape of her neck; and round, blue eyes the color of the sea on a sunny day. She wore a cheap cotton dress, loose like it belonged to an older sister, but Nathaniel could see the roundness of her hips and breasts, could imagine what her thighs might feel like in his hands. And the desire for her rivaled even his ambition, so that for nights afterward he thought of her, staring at the ceiling in his childhood bedroom, which was no bigger than a closet, with walls so thin he imagined he heard the wood rotting in the sea air. He prayed for the thoughts to go away, even while imagining himself as the moderately skilled piano player next to her. He wondered, should this be his small life instead of the large one his mother imagined for him, that he, indeed, had imagined for himself?

But he'd gone away, to live with his mentor, and it would be years before he acted on his base desires with a prostitute in New York. While he thrust into the half-used-up immigrant girl who spoke only the romantic, lyrical Italian of her native country, he closed his eyes and imagined the singer. It was only after he was done that he truly looked at the girl's face and saw her humanity. She was someone's daughter, someone's sister. What had he done? Sickened, his lust was immediately replaced by a terrible feeling of regret and shame that lived in his gut for months afterward, like a flu from which he couldn't recover. But he was a man, and there were others from time to time, all women who traded pleasure for money. It shamed him, each one, and yet he was a slave to his desires. Without a wife, he must turn to these destitute women and then repent on Sundays and ask for forgiveness. How lonely it was, this life that was his destiny. The feeling of desolation lessened only when he played. And so he did. Day after day. Night after night.

Now, at this makeshift party, Frances drank her champagne as if it were water. Think of something to say, he commanded himself. Cigarettes. Offer a cigarette. Women liked that. Did they like that? He had no idea what women liked. "Would you like a cigarette?"

"No thank you. Not in front of Mother. She has this ridiculous notion it's bad for a woman's complexion."

He put them back in his coat pocket without taking one for himself and then stuffed his hands in his pockets. Under his jacket, he drew his stomach to his backbone, cringing inside. He caught Walt's eyes and silently begged him for rescue. Walt understood, apparently, because he brought Mrs. Bellmont over to where Nathaniel stood with Frances and offered his arm to the younger woman. "Miss Bellmont, come with me. I'll introduce you to Mr. and Mrs. Wainwright. And my old friend, Ralph Landry."

After they had gone, Mrs. Bellmont smiled up at Nathaniel. "Frances was awfully happy to be invited to a party. We don't have nearly as an eventful life as she wishes." Her accent was slightly different from Frances's, clipped with more distinct "r" sounds.

This was something, he thought. Something to ask. "Are you from Georgia originally?"

"A small town in Mississippi, but I've been in Georgia for more than twenty years now." She paused, glancing over to where Frances was now talking with the Wainwrights. "Frances tells me you're from Maine. I've read it's beautiful there."

"I've never been anywhere prettier." A surge of pleasure exploded inside him. Frances had spoken about him to her mother. Perhaps she liked him a little. "If you can stand the winters."

"How does your father earn his living?"

"Lobster. Worked the cages almost every day of his life, pulling up those crates with his bare hands, often to find only one or two lobsters at a time."

"He's passed, then?"

He nodded, feeling the ache in his chest that had taken a year to subside. "Three years ago."

"He lived to see your success?"

"Yes."

"He must have been quite proud."

"I believe so. He wasn't one to talk much. My mother told me he used to listen to my recordings every single day before he died."

His mother had been his first teacher, but after several years she decided he'd surpassed her ability to teach him and found a teacher of considerable reputation in the next town over. He remembered, vividly, his father taking the boat out on Sunday afternoons, even though it was the Sabbath, to catch additional lobsters to pay for Nathaniel's lessons. "You can't imagine what they gave up for me to have this life."

"I'm sure I can." She played with the collar of her gown, a lovely light green that reminded him of gowns he'd seen in Paris last year. He thought of his mother's one decent dress, ironed faithfully every Saturday night to wear to church the next morning, until the fabric thinned at the elbows and frayed at the hem. "My grandmother did the same for me. And we must never forget those sacrifices." Mrs. Bellmont smiled and took a small sip of champagne.

"Is Frances your only child?"

"No, I have a son. Whitmore." Her face lit up when she said her son's name.

From across the room Walt laughed and clinked glasses with Mrs. Wainwright and Frances. Nathaniel must have sighed because Mrs. Bellmont's kind eyes met his as she touched the sleeve of his jacket. "What's wrong, Mr. Fye?"

He blinked. "Nothing really."

"You don't usually host parties, I imagine?"

"Never." He turned toward her. "I find it difficult."

"Meeting new people?"

"Yes."

"You've had to live a disciplined life. It doesn't leave much time for social engagements." Her voice was sympathetic, understanding. "So why tonight?"

He took his hands out of his pockets. The bubbles in Mrs. Bellmont's glass floated one by one to the top of her drink.

"I suggested the party for the sole purpose of seeing your daughter. I also wanted to meet you properly so that I might ask if I could call on her when I return from the West. But when she was in front of me, I couldn't think of one thing to say."

Mrs. Bellmont was silent for a moment, twisting the stem of her champagne glass with her fingers. "When I married, my husband paraded me in front of people like I was a prize racehorse. I have a nervous stomach, and I'd be sick for hours beforehand. I had to figure out a way to get through those engagements."

"What did you do?"

"You'll laugh."

He smiled, feeling relaxed for the first time that night. "I promise not to."

"I found a book called *The Lost Art of Conversation*, by Horatio Sheafe Krans. I probably should have read Emily Post instead, but I'm one to look to the masters first, so I muddled through each of the essays, and do you know what I learned?"

He put his hand up to his heart. "Tell me, Mrs. Bellmont, and save me from a life of solitude."

She laughed. "It all comes to this." She raised one hand in the air like a preacher. "Ask questions."

"Questions?"

"Precisely. Begin every conversation by asking a question of the other person. It never fails me. People love to talk about themselves." She looked, once again, over at Frances, who was now talking with Mr. Wainwright, and then back at Nathaniel. "Mr. Fye, you must come visit us. This isn't the setting to talk with Frances properly."

"You might think I'm too old for her. I'm thirty-two."

"Frances is twenty. Quite old enough to marry. My husband's ten years older than I am. I see nothing wrong with it. Anyway, her father will like it if you call on her at our home. He'll be delighted that a man of your reputation is interested in Frances." She took another sip of her champagne.

"Do you think she would consider me?"

Her face softened further as her eyes turned a deeper shade of gray. "I didn't raise a fool, Mr. Fye."

"That's kind. Thank you." He forgot himself for a moment, forgot his terrible wanting of young Frances Bellmont and his paralyzing shyness. The room was beautiful and so were his party guests, and, in the company of Mrs. Bellmont, he felt like the kind of man who laughed at parties and thought of questions and answers. It was good, this, to have people around him, and he felt hope, too, for a future that might include the beguiling Frances Bellmont and her lovely mother.

Then, he noticed Frances and Walt across the room in a corner by themselves. Frances leaned into Walt, whispering something in his ear. Walt flushed and shook his head. A moment later Walt left Frances and came to stand next to him. "Excuse me, Mrs. Bellmont, but it's getting late, and our prodigy here needs his beauty rest."

Mrs. Bellmont set her glass on the table behind them. "Oh, of course. It's getting late for us, too." She waved to Frances. "Time to go, darlin'."

Frances stood next to Ralph Landry now; he poured more champagne in her glass. "But we just arrived," said Frances.

"Nathaniel has a busy day tomorrow," said Walt. Nathaniel stared at him. He'd never heard Walt sound so cold. What had happened?

Frances glared at Walt while drinking the rest of her champagne in one swallow.

Everyone else bustled about, getting ready to leave. Goodbyes were made until it was only the Bellmont women left, standing in the doorway, and Walt, gathering the empty champagne bottles.

"Good night, Mr. Fye," Frances said. "It was awfully nice of you to invite us." Behind them, Walt flung bottles into the apple crate. Frances leaned forward, pulling at the lapel of Nathaniel's suit jacket, and whispered in his ear. "Please tell me I'll see you again soon?"

"I would like that very much."

"Mr. Fye's agreed to call on us at the house when he returns from California," said Mrs. Bellmont to her daughter.

Frances gave Nathaniel her hand. "Something to look forward to then, even though it seems terribly far away." She paused, looking up at him from under thick lashes. "I can't remember a better evening."

Nathaniel kissed both women's hands and bid them good night. After he closed the door, he turned toward Walt, grinning. "She wants to see me again. I can hardly believe it."

"I don't think Frances Bellmont's a good idea." Walt went to the table and poured a last bit of champagne into his glass from the open bottle on the table.

"Why? Did something happen between you?"

"Let's just say I know women, and she's trouble." Walt downed the champagne in one gulp and thumped the glass down on the table. "You could have your pick of women, you know, if you could conquer this shyness."

"I tried tonight, Walt. I thought you'd be pleased." He deflated, like a cake just taken from the oven into a cold room.

"I want you to be happy. I know you're lonely, the way we work all the time. Hell, so am I. But you have to be careful of beautiful women. They come at a price."

"They do?"

"The most important decision of any man's life is who he chooses as his wife. Remember that." Walt picked up his jacket from one of the chairs and draped it over his arm. "Miss Bellmont is the most beautiful woman I've ever seen. That also makes her the most dangerous."

Walt was out the door before Nathaniel could think of what to say.

*   *   *

Later, he tossed about in the large bed, fluffing pillows and then flattening them, moving from one side of the bed to the other in an attempt to get comfortable, thinking about Frances. He thought he heard a knock on the door. Surely he hadn't? No one would call this late. The knock came a second time. He sat up. It must be Walt. Perhaps he'd forgotten something. Pulling on his dressing gown, Nathaniel walked to the door. "Walt, is that you?"

"It's Frances Bellmont. I've left a glove."

His pulse quickened. He opened the door a crack. She was in the hall, wearing the dress from earlier, but without shoes. Her feet, beautiful like the rest of her, he thought. The sight of them made him almost light-headed. "Come in." He opened the door wider and searched the hallway behind her, expecting to see Mrs. Bellmont. It was empty.

"I'm awfully sorry to bother you." She raised her voice a half octave and put her hands in front of her like a cat batting a string and backed him all the way into the room. She closed the door behind her. "I'm the little kitten who's lost her mitten."

He looked around the suite. The glasses were stacked neatly on the table, the bottles taken away by Walt. "I haven't seen it."

She made her lips into a pout. "Oh, that's too bad for me, I guess."

"I'll send you a new pair tomorrow."

"How thoughtful."

I'd spend a lifetime buying you gloves or anything else you want, he thought. Anything to please you.

"I wish you didn't have to go tomorrow," she said.

"You do?" He stared at her, a flicker of happiness in his gut.

She looked into his eyes. "I confess I have a schoolgirl crush on you, Nathaniel Fye." She smiled without showing her teeth and shrugged her slender shoulders. "Do I sound awful?"

"It makes me sound like an old man when you say it like that." Why had he said that? He meant to have said something about how nice that was, how much he liked her, instead of another idiotic utterance.

She came closer until she was only inches away. He smelled talcum powder and the now almost familiar scent of her skin. Gardenias. "You're awfully handsome for an old man. Yet you have no idea that you are. Do you see how women look at you like they want to eat you?"

"No, not exactly."

She took hold of the bottom of his sleeping shirt, eating the space between them so his thighs brushed the fringe on her dress. "I haven't thought of anything but you since the moment I spotted you on the street."

He swallowed, trying to breathe away his erection, but it was no use. His hands twitched at his sides, desperately wanting to pull her into his arms. "It's the same for me. How I feel about you, I mean."

She looked up into his eyes. "Please don't make me beg you to kiss me."

"Kiss you?"

"Yes, please?"

He didn't know what he would have done next, but it didn't matter because her mouth was on his by then, her tongue darting in seductive pokes, and her small frame pressed into him. His arms went around her waist as she moved her mouth to his ear.

"You smell delicious, Nathaniel Fye," she whispered.

"You. Gardenias." He could barely speak. It was as if the room had suddenly lost all air.

"It's perfume from France. I had to wait months for it to arrive." She tilted her head backward, presenting her neck to him. "Smell here."

He did as she asked, leaning over to breathe in her scent. Her skin was damp and soft. Like rose petals, he thought, once again. Then, he didn't know how or why, he felt suddenly bold. He moved his mouth to the spot under her ear, and then imparted tiny kisses down her neck until he reached her collarbone. "You're lovely, so lovely."

She sighed as she reached under his nightshirt and touched the skin of his belly lightly with her fingertips. Her touch felt better than it had in his imagination, sure and soft and seductive all at once. He was helpless, unable to move or take his eyes from her, like paralyzed prey in the grasp of a snake. Somehow they moved to the wall; he pressed her into it, his body covering hers. They kissed, and kissed again. If only it could go on like this forever, he thought.

Suddenly, she shifted, creating space between them and then tugging at the hem of her dress and pulling it up, ever so slowly, revealing, inch by inch, her bare skin: first her knees, her thighs, a patch of light brown hair covering her female parts, a creamy, flat tummy, and finally her small round breasts. Then, in one last, quick movement, she pulled the dress over her head and tossed it onto the back of the chair, brushing into him as she did so. "I have to feel your hands on me. Please, Nathaniel." The space disappeared between them once again as she put her arms around his neck, hovering near enough to his face that he caught the sweet smell of champagne on her breath. She looked into his eyes, and he imagined he saw the future, but maybe it was only every moment of his former solitude. She kissed him long and hard. Yes, she kissed him because he'd lost all sense of time or place, a slave only to the sensual pleasure and desire he felt for this beautiful creature. They were breathless. Her narrow hips pressed again his erection, and he knew it was impossible now to stop. She pulled away, moving toward the bedroom. He followed.

It was over sooner than he wished. He regretted it, of course, but he was inexperienced, and it had been so long since the last shameful occasion. He was overcome by his desire, and it made his touches clumsy and grasping. Being inside her felt better than anything he'd ever felt, and he exploded too soon and then felt desperate and unsure and tilted at a precarious angle. "I'm sorry," he whispered against her damp neck.

"Don't be." She guided his hand down to where she was hot and wet. "Use your fingers like you do on a piano." With her slender fingers she moved his to the hot nub and showed him how to touch soft and quick, then harder until she cried out, her back arched like a small cat in the sunlight. To give her this pleasure, to watch her face twist and hear her moans—it was beyond glorious. Nothing would ever be the same. He was sure of this. No other moment could ever compare to the one that held this beautiful girl in his bed. He would do anything to keep her there.

She scooted over to her side of the bed and grabbed his cigarettes from the bedside table. His hand shook as he reached over her willowy body for his lighter and lit her cigarette.

She took a long drag, blowing the smoke upward so that it hovered near the ceiling like words unsaid. "I never imagined you were a virgin," she said.

"What?" he sputtered. "No. Of course I'm not."

"Oh, I just assumed." She paused, taking another drag of the cigarette. "Have I hurt your feelings?"

He stared at her, speechless.

"I'm sorry, darlin'." She slid closer to him, stroking his chest. "We just need a little more time together. Don't you think?"

"Miss Bellmont," he began but then stopped. What did he want to say, exactly? How had he let himself get into this situation? It was his fault. She deserved better. He should have resisted. This was not the way he wanted to woo her.

She smiled, playing with a lock of his hair that had fallen onto his forehead. "I think you can call me Frances. And I'll call you Nate."

"Nate?"

"It has a modern quality to it, don't you think?" She took another drag from her cigarette and then blew it out in small puffs, making rings. He'd never seen a woman do this before. There was nothing ordinary about this girl. Frances Bellmont was special. He would get her to marry him if it was the last thing he ever did. He must have her.

"Tell me about your life in New York, Nate." Her fingers played with the curly hair on his chest. "I belong there, I'm sure of it."

"It's busy. More people than you can imagine. Never quiet. Even at night there are shouts and laughter, honking and car engines, streetcar noise. I wish for quiet there, much of the time."

"Quiet? Oh, it's dreadfully quiet everywhere I go. I long for excitement, for people, for a less conventional life than Atlanta has to offer. There are so many rules here, mostly invented to keep a girl like me from having any fun. Georgia's god-awful. So backward and stifling. I spend nights just dreaming of how I might escape." She looked up at him with eyes the color of smoke. "But I'm a southern girl. I don't get to make decisions for myself. I have to hope that a man will marry me so that I might move from my father's house to his, destined to be unhappy like my mother."

"The right man, perhaps, could make you happy?" He said this lightly, hoping to sound merely playful instead of desperate, which is what he felt at the moment—absolutely desperate that she choose him.

"A man like you?" She stubbed her cigarette out in the ashtray before rolling to her side and propping herself up to look him fully in the face. Her cheeks were flushed pink, and her hair was in wild curls around her face. Was it possible she'd grown more beautiful in the last five minutes?

He smiled. "Yes, a man like me. Will you let me try?"

"I'll be here when you return." She kissed him lightly on the mouth. "I should get back before Mother wakes and finds me gone."

She slid out of bed and stood, picking up his right hand, which lay limp on the bed cover. Pulling on his fingers one by one, her forehead crinkled as if pondering a deep mystery. "These fingers are awfully powerful on that piano." She placed his hand on her bare chest, just above her breasts. "I could grow quite accustomed to them on my body every night of my life." She kissed the palm of his hand and then let it fall onto the bed. "Please call me when you return. I'll be waiting. Don't fall in love with anyone else while you're away."

"Impossible."

"Promise?"

"I promise."

"Good night, Nate."

"Good night, Frances."

He collapsed against the bed pillows, miserable and delighted all at once. Everything in him screamed for her to stay. Why had he met her right before he left for months? Framed in the doorway, she slid her dress over her pale skin and then turned to him, blowing him a kiss and fluttering her fingers. It reminded him of a scene in a play or a moving picture, like he was merely a spectator instead of a participant. Then she was out of the frame, disappearing from his view. The door creaked and shut with a bang. And then there was nothing but the beating of his faint heart in a hollow chest.

CHAPTER 2

Lydia

BY LATE AFTERNOON the flowers had wilted and smelled of death. The sickly sweet scent of their dying permeated the parlor of Lydia Tyler's farmhouse and drifted among mourners eating cake and drinking coffee from her wedding china. Geraniums, sweet peas, and lilies from her garden covered the coffin the men from Sam's barbershop, her husband's friends, had cut and constructed from local pine. Only weeks from summer, the late Alabama spring was warm, and they hadn't much time to wait for burial. News of his death ran swiftly through their small town of Atmore, and Midwife Stone had come at once. There were no babies born that day, only death for William. Lydia could not help but think of the days her daughters were born, delivered by Midwife Stone, as William paced the floor of their parlor. The happiest days of his life, he often said, while telling the girls the stories of their births.

Midwife Stone had prepared him for burial in their very own bedroom, but Lydia had stayed away, lining the newly constructed coffin now in their parlor with their best set of sheets; Lydia had made them only last month from the finest cotton. Every night William had commented on how soft they were as his foot wandered to her side of the bed to stroke her bare calf.

When William was readied, some men came to place him inside, next to those sheets. Lydia had taken one last look before closing the lid of the coffin. His features had softened in death so that he appeared peaceful, as if taking a Sunday afternoon nap after one of the minister's particularly long sermons. She touched his face one last time, expecting him to wake any moment and ask for a glass of sweet tea. Then she turned away, wanting to remember him in motion, in life, not this static sleeper. But it didn't matter, really, if she looked or not. Grief blinded her eyes like blots of black ink on paper, and she saw only the image of William, as if he'd been captured in a photograph during the last seconds of life, waving to her as he came up the driveway for his midday meal. When she told Midwife Stone this truth, the wizened old woman smiled and patted her hand. "That there is a blessing."

As she greeted the mourners, Lydia thought more than once, *if only he might wake.* It seemed everyone in town had come, making the parlor smaller: friends, neighbors, William's customers at the bank. She nodded her head while accepting condolences and pressed back when hands pressed hers, but their voices were dim, like a glass window separated them. *He was a good man. Taken too soon. We're sorry for your loss. Such a shock for you and the girls, but he's with God now. He was fair to us, always.*

Her silent shouts to her husband overshadowed all.

Please sit up, darling. Declare it all a terrible mistake.

And in answer, *I'm feeling right as rain, Lyds. What's for supper? I could eat a small horse.*

Please, climb out between the boards and those awful eternal pillows and tease me about Sunday dinner being late because I practiced too long on the piano and forgot to stoke that blasted old wood stove you refuse to replace.

Better to save than spend, Lyds.

William was frugal; no need for modern appliances, he often said. Regardless of the electric stoves most of her friends took for granted, he felt obliged to wait another year or two before purchasing one. Better to save than spend, he said at least once a week to his daughters. Spoken like a banker, of course, who had seen the near financial collapse of 1927 and predicted that something worse was soon to come.

William had been frugal. Past tense.

Finally the last horrid step in the ritual of burial commenced. The men of Sam's barbershop, acting as pallbearers instead of playing checkers and smoking cigars as they normally would on a Saturday afternoon, took him out the front door like the coffin was an ordinary piece of furniture. The flowers were tossed aside, in various locations, their usefulness done. Later, she recalled nothing of the burial, but there was dirt under her fingernails and mud on the midsection of her skirt. She could not fathom how that had come to be.

When they returned home, her daughters each holding onto an arm because she could not walk alone, the sickly sweet smell of the flowers greeted them. Lydia gagged. Emma, her oldest at fourteen, guided her into a chair. Birdie brought a glass of water. At fourteen and twelve they were little ladies, taught in the southern style despite their northerner mother.

The women from church had cleaned up, but they'd left the flowers, perhaps thinking they would be a comfort. They were not. She hated them, every petal, every stem. They covered her beloved piano, the formal sofa her daughters weren't allowed to sit on, the side table where letters often waited for the post. Had the flowers multiplied while they were away watching William being lowered into the ground?

She sent Birdie and Emma to wash up and put their nightgowns on. "I'll be there shortly to tuck you in."

They didn't argue, knowing when to leave and when to stay, a quality they'd inherited from their father.

The silent conversation with William continued. It was softer now, without the other voices to interfere. *I need to play you one more hymn, William. Your favorite hymn.* But this time he did not answer. Already she was losing him. She collapsed onto the piano bench. But even here, the flowers mocked her. They occupied every inch of the keyboard's closed cover.

She twisted on the bench; her gaze swept the room. Angry energy coursed through her until she was hot and damp. She rose to her feet. The flowers must be removed so she could breathe again. They could not, would not, stop her from playing one last hymn for her William. Every last flower was destined for the compost, if it took her all night. She stomped to the sewing basket and pulled out her scissors. They must be cut to bits, their perky buds slaughtered. They must suffer.

She turned and stumbled on the corner of the braided rug, the scissors like a sword in her hand. Wait. Where to start? The scissors dangled now from her index finger. William would know where to begin, but he wasn't here. She closed her eyes, gripping the scissors. *Please no*, she begged the pain. *Please don't come until I get through this day and into bed.* The pain heeded no pleas. It came in cruel waves, as if someone stabbed her with the benign sewing scissors, but worse because the wound was inside and could not be healed with ointment or pills.

William waving to her from the driveway. Chicken potpie in the oven smelling like love, like life. That grin he always had when he first spotted her, even after fifteen years together.

She'd come to greet him from the porch like most days, anxious to tell him of her morning, of the way the sparrows had seemed to sing harmony with her piano. First the wave, the grin, and then he collapsed onto the red dirt, inches from the green lawn, clutching his left arm. His last breath was of the red dust instead of the cool grass. Even that small comfort was denied her.

Not even two days had passed since that last moment. And now? The house smelled of death.

The flowers must suffer.

The doctor assured her that William hadn't suffered. "Heart failure. It was instantaneous. Didn't feel a thing. That should be a comfort to you." *It*, she wanted to tell him nastily and with emphasis, was not a comfort to her; she knew it wasn't true. His last thoughts would have been of her and their daughters. He clung to life, to them, even in those final seconds.

Now, the clock chimed eight. Four days ago William had read them a chapter from *The Voyages of Doctor Doolittle.* William thought the children should read all the Newbery Medal winners.

Emma's voice from the bedroom startled Lydia from her thoughts. "Mother, are you coming?"

"Yes, right now." Wake up, she ordered herself. Take care of your girls.

They stared up at her, snuggled together in the double bed they shared. Lydia forced a placid smile. No need to scare them with her plans to murder the flowers. She tucked a cool white sheet around their shoulders. Dark smudges under their eyes betrayed grief.

The house creaked, settling in for the night, as if shrinking back to size after holding half the town in its modest rooms. Birdie, still childlike, spoke with a sleepy voice. "Mother, stay with us until we fall asleep."

"Yes. Close your eyes now."

But Birdie's blue eyes remained wide open, steadfast in the study of her mother's face. "Do you think Daddy can see us from heaven, Mother?"

She felt scratchy, salty tears behind her eyes. "I do."

Emma moved closer to Birdie in the bed.

"Are we poor now, Mother?" Birdie asked.

Lydia brushed blonde hair from Birdie's freckled forehead. "Your Daddy took care to make sure we aren't. His daddy's daddy owned this house and property, so we'll always have a place to live. He had some money put aside for us in case anything ever happened to him." Just last week, he'd suggested he teach her to drive, though most women in Atmore, Alabama, did not. She'd agreed, pleased that he would think her capable. Thinking about how carefully he'd planned for them, it seemed to Lydia as if he knew he might die young. There was money and a small life insurance policy, too, that he'd mentioned to her a year ago. She hadn't listened carefully, believing they had many years left together. No one expected a healthy man to die of natural causes at age forty-five. Was there something in him that suspected he wasn't long for this earth?

The worried look disappeared from Birdie's eyes. "So we won't have to move out of our house?"

"No, of course not. What made you think that?"

"One of her friends told her that when your daddy dies you have to move to the poor side of town." Emma pulled her arms from under the sheet, clasping her hands together. "But Daddy took care of things, didn't he?"

"He did. All he ever cared about was taking care of us. Since the moment I met him, he started looking after me."

"You looked after him, too, Mother," said Birdie. "He told us so."

Lydia's eyes brimmed with tears. She brushed them aside. "I've been a very lucky woman. Now go to sleep. This has been a long, terrible day."

The girls nodded. Emma reached under the sheet and took Birdie's hand. Their entwined fingers made a bump in the sheet in the shape of a heart. They closed their eyes, and Lydia watched until their grief-pinched faces turned peaceful in sleep.

Now, the flowers. She tiptoed out of the bedroom to the parlor and slipped her feet into her husband's work boots for the first time.

Only a size too big. Enormous feet and hands for a woman, she thought with disgust. How a man as handsome as William had ever overlooked her feet she had no idea. They were flat and wide, like a duck's.

In the last of the evening light, she pushed the wheelbarrow close to the porch, filled it with flowers, then took the lot of them out to her compost heap near the chicken coop. As she walked, her feet moved up and down in the boots, rubbing against her toes and heels. William's voice in her head: *You'll get a blister, Lyds. Do you have to do this now?*

She averted her gaze from the spot where he'd fallen. Once she reached the compost, she stopped, clutching both handles of the wheelbarrow. The flowers lay atop one another, their blooms bowed in repose, like dancers taking a final bow. They were benign. Of course they were. How had she thought otherwise? They were nothing but innocent flowers that she'd lovingly cared for. What was the matter with her?

She let go of the wheelbarrow and slumped against the side of the chicken coop; all the venom evaporated, replaced by awful pain. The last of the sun peeked through the pines at the edge of her property, making long, slanted shadows. How William had loved those trees. When they first met he'd regaled her with stories of running through the forest, playing cops and robbers and war and other little boy games. He'd spent most of his life looking at the trees sway in the Alabama breezes.

The old barn cat, Piggy, appeared, purring and pressing against Lydia's legs. "Oh, Piggy, I hate this." She knelt and then sat on the hard ground. Piggy climbed onto her lap, resting his rather large head (Birdie said he had the face of a pig, thus the name) on Lydia's knee. Lydia caressed him absently. Piggy purred louder. Something scurried, probably a lizard or mouse, and Piggy jumped as if possessed by the devil and ran toward the sound. Sighing, Lydia rose to her feet and brushed the back of her skirt with her hands.

She left the flowers and the wheelbarrow and William's trees, walking across the yard in his boots until she was inside and seated at the piano. She could play *How Great Thou Art* from memory. Her fingers knew it and so many other hymns, just like her legs knew walking. She didn't sing along like she did when she played at church, but as she played the last refrain, William's rich baritone seemed to fill the room.

Afterward, she whispered the Twenty-Third Psalm and walked over to the shelf where her special things were displayed: a silver vase given to her by her mother when Lydia graduated high school, framed baby pictures of the girls, her mother's formal tea set, and the Tyler family Bible. She turned to the Bible's front page, where William's mother had written:

William Benjamin Tyler. Born December 10, 1882.

Using her best pen, she filled in the date of his death: *June 10, 1928.* She sat in the parlor as night swallowed the last of the light, gripping the Bible between cold hands, unable to think of a prayer to ask of God. She could think only, why, why, why? Then, William's voice:

Sweetheart, go to bed.

She left his boots by the front door. In their bedroom, she slipped into her cotton nightgown and took the pins from her hair, letting it fall around her shoulders, shivering despite the summer heat. The feel of her hair about her shoulders always made her feel young, like the upstate New York farm girl she once was. She'd come to Atmore fifteen years ago to marry William, bringing with her nothing but the clothes in her suitcase and leaving behind the promise of a career as a concert pianist. She was eighteen when she married the thirty-year-old William Tyler. Who she was before she was his wife was a dim memory, like the faded photograph of her at sixteen, put away now in a neglected drawer.

In the mirror, she examined her reflection, wondering if the last several days had changed her. No, it was the same face as the one William kissed only days ago. She touched her cheek, thinking of that last kiss, wishing she'd held his touch for a moment longer, had kissed him properly like when they'd first been married. If only she'd known to say a final goodbye instead of taking for granted his promise to return for lunch.

She undid her dark blonde hair from the braid she always wore and began to brush it. One hundred strokes will keep it shiny, her mother always advised. Thick, it reached the middle of her back and was crimped from being in the braid so that it appeared to have movement, like a wheat field swaying in the wind. It was her eyes, her mother once said, that made her pretty. Framed by thick lashes, they were a light blue that looked like a hazy sky one day and the blue of a tropical sea the next. Her mother had said to her the day before she left for university, "Your eyes are remarkable, Lydia, and make you a great beauty. Use your beauty for good, as it's a great responsibility." A great beauty? This was not true to anyone but her mother. Lydia suspected that women never saw themselves as they truly were, no matter how they stared at their own reflections. And their mothers? They surely did not see their daughters as they truly were, for love distorted their view. At the time, she'd dismissed both her mother's compliment and her advice, knowing her face was long, her lips thin, and there were the freckles—they covered almost every inch of her almost pointy nose. Simply awful. There was the problem of her height, as well. She was tall, way too tall for a woman.

Tall women could not be beautiful, Lydia thought, so she put aside her mother's words and became accomplished and educated instead, not worried over her appearance until the day she met William.

She was in Atmore during a break from college with a friend from school who was born and raised in Atmore. The second evening of her visit they'd gone to a dance at the Grange. There he was, looking at her from across the room, with a slight smile on his face. His name was William, she learned later, and he worked at the bank. But at that moment she knew only that he was tall (taller than she) and handsome in a no-doubt-he-was-of-English-descent kind of way, blond and fair-skinned, with dark blue eyes. He raised his hand in greeting. She quickly looked away but not before she saw him grin wildly at her. A blush started from her toes and ended at the top of her head.

Later, waiting on the porch for her friend, she heard the door creak, and when she looked up he was there again. She watched as his breath caught and he smiled at her once more. He thinks I'm lovely, she thought. How wonderful it was. The way he looked at her, really looked at her, as if she were truly beautiful, made it true. For even with her height and unusually large hands, he'd thought her a great beauty, just as her mother had. During their years together, he'd been a man of a thousand compliments, with a rebuttal to every self-criticism she might utter. Now she would be no one to any man. She would no longer have the privilege of feeling beautiful in the particular way that love brings. *William, who will help me decide which hat to wear?*

She moved to the bed, bone weary. The room consisted of a simple wooden bed frame, a quilt in a pattern of red stars over the bed, and, in the corner, a rocking chair where she'd nursed both her babies. Perching on the side of the bed, she imagined slipping under the cool sheets but somehow could not move. It was the prospect of sleeping alone in their marital bed—impossible. Her fingers traced the outline of a star on the quilt, and she pulled his pillow onto her lap. Had she been a good wife? Please, God, let it be so.

She wept silently into his pillow. After the tears stopped, she made the bed up again, her strong hands halting their work only long enough to breathe in the scent of her husband from his pillow. Tobacco and shaving cream. At the window, she peered into the backyard. Fireflies had come to the dark, sparks of undaunted light. They never ceased to delight her. Often William captured them in a jar for the children, tiny gifts that were really only a loan, for they were let out into the world before bedtime. None of them could keep anything beautiful trapped for long.

William's voice came to her again. *Sleep with the children.* Nodding, as if he were in the room, and holding the pillow close to her chest, she crossed the hallway to her daughters' room. Pushing Birdie gently into the middle of the bed, she climbed in, placing William's pillow under her cheek.

Birdie shifted in her sleep, making the purring noise of a kitten. Lydia snuggled closer. She stayed in the same position for most of the night, the yearned-for yet elusive sleep thwarted by the hollow, fearful pain in her chest that felt like a vise. Outside the windows, the crickets chirped a rhythm that after a time began to sound like: *I'm afraid. I'm afraid. I'm afraid.*

Finally, just before dawn, the crickets ceased, and the emerging day fell silent. She might have uttered a response to fill the quiet, but nothing came, not even the sound of William's voice.

CHAPTER 3

Jeselle

ON A CLOYINGLY hot day in early September, Mr. Bellmont demanded roast beef for his supper. So after breakfast, Mama left for the market, wearing her yellow straw hat and the brown, cotton dress with the bell sleeves that cupped her muscular shoulders. "Jes, wash up the dishes while I'm gone." Almost six feet tall and lean, Mama pushed open the screen door using her backside; it slammed against the side of the house and then came to a close with a bang. Mama powered across the yard, scattering the brown, decaying magnolia blossoms with the force of her rapid gait, and then disappeared around the side of the house.

To the hum of the ceiling fan that swirled warm air around the kitchen and offered little relief, Jeselle scrubbed away the morning's grits stuck to the bottom of a pan, perspiration soaking the collar of her thin cotton dress, where her hair hung in two braids. She was small for thirteen, willowy, with a delicate bone structure. Jeselle looked like her father's mother, according to Mama, with the same heart-shaped face and dimples on either side of her full mouth. Unfortunately, Jeselle would never be able to judge for herself if this were true or not. Her father and his parents were all dead, buried in the colored cemetery on the other side of town. Jeselle was only weeks old when he died coming home from work, killed by white men for the dollar he'd made that day washing dishes. Mama had come to the rich part of town looking for work and through divine providence, there was no other way to explain it, claimed Mama, she'd found Mrs. Bellmont.

While she worked, Jeselle watched Whitmore in the garden, sketching a fallen, forgotten peach, shriveled brown and punctured with holes from a bird's voracious feast. The other peaches, harvested in June, were in jars, canned by Mama and lined in neat rows in the cool basement. He sat on the grass under the shade of the peach tree with his sketch pad propped on his knees. His eyes moved from the peach to the paper and back again, while his left hand sketched, holding the pencil in a way both assured and relaxed. With his other hand, he occasionally swiped at flies and bees hovering near his head.

He was growing so tall, she thought. For years they'd been around the same size, but around six months ago, he'd started to grow tall and lean, and now at fourteen—just a year and one month older than Jeselle—he was a full head taller than she.

"Study of a wounded peach," she thought. She would tell Whit later. It was her job to name his drawings and paintings.

He scrambled to his feet, looking up at the sun, mostly likely estimating the time and what it would do to the light. Then he walked toward the kitchen, stopping on the top step and calling out to her, "Jes, please tell Mother I'll be back for supper, would you?"

"She won't like it." She went to where he stood in the doorway.

He lowered his voice. "I know. But it's Saturday." Mr. Bellmont was home all day on Saturday, and Whitmore did whatever he could to avoid seeing him.

"I think he's still in bed." Sleeping off the booze from the night before, according to Mama, waking only long enough to dictate the menu for supper before falling back to sleep, snoring.

"But he won't be for much longer." He tugged gently on one of her braids. "I'll bring you a caramel from the candy shop. The biggest one they have."

Jeselle washed the plates next, hurrying, pining for the next chapter of Pip and Stella that waited for her on the kitchen table. She was like Pip, she'd decided, even though he was a white boy from England and she was a black housekeeper's daughter in Atlanta, Georgia. They both longed for things they couldn't have. She wiped her face on the bottom of her apron, feeling as hot and wet as a bowl of boiled collard greens. It was impossible to imagine that the season would change in a few weeks, bringing relief to Atlanta from the early September air that felt so thick and moist it slowed your every movement.

Even the garden seemed lethargic, the squash and pumpkin leaves wilted like spent athletes. Dogwood leaves hung from their branches as if they might at any moment unfurl from their precarious attachment and float unfettered to the rust-colored, thirsty soil. Only the sweet, pink-skinned potatoes hidden under the red dirt were unbothered by this relentless summer. She envied them their cool shelter from the sweltering heat.

Mama returned an hour later, flinging the screen door open with her foot, carrying a small package wrapped in brown paper.

Jeselle, at the table, placed her finger on the last sentence she'd read. Mama's dress was wet, clinging to the muscles of her back. Without taking off her hat, she set the parcel of meat on the table, her eyes settling briefly on Jeselle's book, then roaming to the spotless sink and stove, and finally to the hutch, where plates were stacked in their usual places and cups hung from the tiny hooks. Presumably seeing no errors in Jeselle's task, Mama poured a large glass of water from the tap and drank it in one fluid swallow, her other hand squeezing the rim of the sink. Then, pulling the hairpins from her hat, she took it off and fanned her face.

"Do you need me to do something, Mama?"

"Go out to the garden and dig up some of them potatoes. Bring in five or six."

"Yes, ma'am." She closed the book, silently repeating, "Second paragraph, page fifty-six," three times in her head.

Outside, the morning sun was bright in the vegetable garden, and it burned into the middle of her bare scalp where she parted her hair. After she pulled the potato plant from the ground, she used a small shovel to dig several inches into the dirt and burrowed her fingers into the dry ground, feeling for the round, hard potatoes huddled together like eggs in a nest. There were five altogether. She brushed the dirt from them until their pink skin was visible and then gathered them into her apron.

Back in the kitchen, Mama had pulled the yellow curtains over the windows so the room had a yellow glow that made the white walls and hutch seem dingy. Mama trimmed blue-tinted fat from the raw meat but stopped when Jeselle came into the kitchen and pointed to the hutch. A tray with biscuits, peach jam, and a pot of tea sat waiting. "You run that up to Miss Frances."

"Yes, Mama." Jeselle took the tray, walking slowly, like she was in quicksand. She hated to go to Frances's room in the morning, especially the last several weeks. Frances stayed in bed most days.

Jeselle came to the open door of the sitting room. Mrs. Bellmont looked up from where she was writing at the secretary's desk. "Morning, baby girl."

"Morning, Mrs. Bellmont."

"Please see if you can cajole Frances into eating something."

"Cajole, Mrs. Bellmont?"

"Coax, entice, convince. Spelled c-a-j-o-l-e." She lowered her voice to a whisper, pointing to the locked box next to the desk where they kept Jeselle's schoolbooks secret from Mr. Bellmont. "I'll put that on our vocabulary list for next week."

"Thank you, Mrs. Bellmont." Feeling fortified, released from quicksand, Jeselle went up the stairs quickly, holding onto the top of the teapot with one hand, spelling c-a-j-o-l-e under her breath.

Frances reclined on a stack of pillows on the bed, a light sheet covering her. The shades were drawn, but even in the muted light her usual alabaster skin appeared sallow and yellow. One hand was on the covers, limp; the other held a handkerchief to her nose. "Girl, there's the most awful smell in here. I can't stand it another minute. You simply have to find out what it is."

"What does it smell like, Miss Frances?" She put the tray on the bedside table and poured a cup of tea.

"Like awfulness."

"Awfulness?"

"Like something's dead." Frances removed the handkerchief from her nose. "Or wet dog, maybe."

Jeselle surveyed the room. Everything seemed in its usual place: the wallpaper scattered with pink roses; the frilly white curtains with embroidered pink edges; the pink velvet chair; a Bible next to Frances's framed portrait, taken for a debutante party that never happened; and a vase of white daisies, picked by Mrs. Bellmont from the garden. Jeselle went to them and took a big sniff. This was the offender. They smelled like dirty stockings. "It's the daisies."

"Get them out." Frances sat up slightly, her voice a shriek only in pitch, not volume. "Leave it to mother to try and poison me with those vile weeds."

Vile was a good word, Jeselle thought. She put her hands around the vase, carrying it carefully, heading toward the door, thinking of synonyms in her head for vile: revolting, repellent. Another hovered near the corner of her mind. What was it? It also started with an r. Repugnant. That was it.

"Girl," Frances screamed, startling Jeselle so that she almost dropped the vase. "Are you listening to me?"

She turned to look at her. "Yes, Miss Frances?"

"What did I just say?"

"The flowers are repugnant?"

"What?" She wrinkled her smooth forehead, as if looking at a creature, or an anomaly, that couldn't be explained. "No. My God, you're a stupid child. I said, 'Get my hairbrush.'"

"Shall I take the flowers away first?"

"No. Yes. I suppose." Some color returned to Frances's cheeks. "Then come back and brush my hair."

"Yes, Miss Frances."

Jeselle disposed of the daisies in the small compost heap Mrs. Bellmont kept at the far end of the garden, near a raised box where Mama grew various strange herbs for medicinal purposes—always aiming to cure Mrs. Bellmont's bad stomach. When she reentered the kitchen, the scent of browning beef and onions greeted her.

CHAPTER 4

Whitmore

WHITMORE STAYED OUT that afternoon as long as he could, drawing under the shade of an oak at the cemetery. He liked it in this quiet place, amongst the dead, although he didn't walk about, looking at tombstones, imagining the stories of the lives represented there as Jeselle might have. Instead, during his frequent visits, he chose a spot he found beautiful and then either worked on a drawing he'd already started or simply sketched what was around him: a branch swaying, a ladybug resting on a rose bush, the groundskeeper stooping over his work. Now, the sun had settled lower in the sky, and Whitmore knew he must get home for supper or his mother and Cassie would be upset with him. He hated to have Cassie cross with him, and his mother, well, he would do anything to keep her from disappointment or pain if it was at all possible.

He packed his things in his art bag and slung it over his shoulder as he walked out of the cemetery and down the street toward home. He took the long way so that he could stop at the candy shop, which smelled of cooked sugar. The owner—an older gentleman with a handlebar moustache wrapped into circles like cinnamon rolls, which gave him a comical expression no matter his mood—greeted him with a wave of his hand. Without asking Whitmore what he wanted, he reached into the case and pulled out the largest of the caramels.

Whit paid and said a hearty thank you before heading back out, sticking the caramel into his bag between his charcoals and drawing pad, hoping it wouldn't melt given the warmth of the evening. When he returned home, he entered the back gate and made his way across the garden to the one-room cottage Jeselle and Cassie shared at the back of the Bellmont property. It was necessary to hide the treat under Jeselle's pillow, otherwise his sister would find it in his bag, then devour it like a greedy cat with a bowl of cream.

He didn't bother to knock, knowing Cassie and Jeselle would be in the big house putting the final touches on supper. The cottage was compact but tidy, with both of the twin beds neatly made, the small fireplace clean of ashes, and a basket of knitting waiting near the rocking chair. Jeselle slept on the right side of the room, near one of the small windows. He set the caramel under her pillow, knowing she would look there when she came to bed.

He entered a silent house through the kitchen door. An empty kitchen? Where were Cassie and Jeselle? The room smelled of beef roasting in the oven; the platter waited empty on the table. He hesitated at the door, listening, and detected his mother's voice from the upstairs hallway calling out to his father. Often, on a Saturday, his father smoked cigars and drank whiskey with friends in the drawing room while his mother and Cassie talked in the kitchen and his sister sneaked out her bedroom window. Where she went on these Saturday nights he couldn't imagine, and didn't want to. But today, apparently, everyone was home. He sighed.

Whitmore walked up the stairs to look for his mother in her study, stopping in the doorway. Hundreds of books lined shelves covering two walls. Jeselle, standing on a footstool, dusted the top shelf. She wore a thin cotton dress, her braids skimming the collar. Petite, unlike her tall, strong mother, she appeared even smaller next to the masses of books.

"I've returned," he said to her back.

"And what's it matter to me?" She twisted to look at him, holding onto the shelf with one hand, and shook the dust rag at him as if he were a pest with the other. Smiling, dimples appeared on each side of her mouth. All his life he'd wanted to put his fingers inside them. "Did you bring me a sweet?"

He rubbed his forehead as if he'd forgotten. This was their game. "Darned if it didn't slip my mind."

She laughed and turned back to her work. Open windows brought the scent of honeysuckle. White curtains fluttered in the breeze made by a ceiling fan. This room held all the best memories of his life, he thought. Unless his father was home, his mother taught them here, and the room on those days practically pulsated with the energy of their secret learning. That his mother taught Jeselle right alongside him must be kept a secret, always. After she presented their lessons, they studied at the small round table near the window that looked out into the yard while his mother wrote letters at her desk, delicate head bent over the page.

A door slammed from down the hall. Jeselle jumped and turned to look at him. They both froze, eyes locked, listening. He knew it was his parents' door, not Frances having a tantrum. Her door had a tinnier sound than their parents' heavy oak door.

The slamming door always came first, as if his father thought it would keep them all from knowing what was about to happen inside. His father shouted, something incomprehensible except in its tone. Then came a thud. Whitmore's chest tightened. The walls seemed suddenly close. The dust from Jeselle's rag, unnoticed until now, floated through the warm, dense air and seemed to reach him. He gulped the air, feeling as if he might choke. Sure enough, a dry and raspy cough that always accompanied the twitch on the side of one eye began. Tears came to his eyes as he hunched over, trying to catch his breath.

Jeselle, beside him now, touched his shoulder. "It's all right, Whit. She'll get through it. She always does." At the sound of her voice, his coughing stopped. She handed him a glass of water. How had she gotten down from the stool, crossed the room, and poured water from the pitcher without him knowing? She was like a deer. "Drink this."

Whitmore took a sip of the lukewarm water. Then, rage roared through him like the rush of a stormy sea. How he hated him. Whit slammed the glass on the desk, hard, pretending it was his father's fat face—red, bloated, with ugly veins on his bulbous nose. He knew from an old photograph that Frank Bellmont had once been handsome, but drink and gluttony had changed all that. The glass broke. Water puddled on the surface of the desk and then spread until it reached a letter his mother had written but not yet signed—an invitation for dinner to someone named Nathaniel Fye. Water smeared the ink where this Nathaniel's address was written in his mother's loopy handwriting, making the shape of an asymmetrical star cut in half. He gripped the side of the desk with both hands, watching the spilled water drip onto the floor. "Jessie. I can't. This. I can't stand it." His voice cracked.

"Whit."

But he did not stop to listen. He strode toward the door, not knowing what he would do but just that he must somehow take her place. It was time. He was large enough to take his father's beating, the one intended for his fragile mother.

Just a few feet from the bedroom door, he heard his mother cry out. He halted. What should he do? Burst through the door? He imagined coming between his mother and father, taking the fists with his own body. *Courage*, he thought. *You must have courage.* But just then Jeselle reached him and grabbed his hand, forcing him to stop and look at her.

She pushed him against the wall, splaying her hands on his chest and whispering, "Please, Whit, no. There's nothing you can do."

A series of crashes came next: breaking glass, a loud boom, and then splintering wood, and finally, a thud like a body thrown against the wall. Mother cried out, like a scared, hurt animal. "Please, Frank, stop. Please."

"Have you learned your lesson?" shouted his father.

"Yes, Frank. I'm sorry."

"Get out of my sight."

Whit wept without sound, looking down at the floor, his chest heaving with the effort to keep quiet as they listened to the click of his mother's shoes on the hardwood floor. The door opened just wide enough for her to slip out. She shut it gingerly and then jumped at the sight of them. The normally upswept bun at the back of her neck hung loose around her shoulders and made her face seem wan and young. Red welts were scattered on her neck and chest. But it was her eyes, flat, like those in a photograph of a dead person Whitmore had recently seen in a magazine, that hurt him the most.

Mother put her finger to her lips and motioned for them to follow. She moved slowly, walking on the balls of her feet and feeling the back of her head with her fingertips. In the kitchen, she went to the door and opened it, as if she might go out into the garden but then looked back, shaking like she'd come in from the cold in the dead of winter. Jeselle took her arm, leading her to one of the kitchen chairs. "Mrs. Bellmont, sit."

"Mother, are you terribly hurt?" Whit knelt at her side.

Mrs. Bellmont touched the back of her head again gingerly. "I'm fine."

"I'll get you some ice." Whit's voice wobbled.

As he rose to his feet, Cassie bustled through the door, carrying several packages. She came to an abrupt halt when she saw Mother. "Oh, no, Miz Bellmont," she muttered under her breath as she set the packages on the table. She knelt in the same spot Whit had just vacated. "Are you all right?"

"It's just a bump on the back of my head. He stayed away from my face," said Mother. "There's the Winslow party tomorrow night, you know."

Cassie felt the bump with her capable fingers. "What set him off?"

"I took him the wrong drink."

Cassie turned to Jeselle. "Baby girl, fetch me Miz Bellmont's hairbrush and my sewing kit. Then fix some tea."

Mother reached for Cassie's hand. "Don't fuss over me, Cassie. I'm fine. I know the children are probably hungry."

Cassie's gaze turned to the red marks on Mother's chest. "Those'll bruise."

"I have the green dress with the high collar. I'll wear that to the Winslows'."

Cassie nodded, smoothing loose tendrils of hair back from Mother's face. "I'll make an ointment for you to rub on them."

Mother's eyes filled with tears before she brought her hands to her face. "I'm so tired. So very tired."

Whitmore went to the window. The setting sun had turned the sky red.

CHAPTER 5

Nathaniel

DURING HIS TIME AWAY, when not practicing or performing, Nathaniel thought of Frances. He sent several letters but heard no replies. She wouldn't know where to send them, he reassured himself, what with a new city every week. The day before they left California he mailed her a postcard of the beach to let her know he would return to New York in a week's time. He would call her when he got back. He hoped she still wanted him to.

He and Walt arrived in New York late on a Monday night, and he fell into a deep sleep, thankful for his own bed, excited but nervous to call Frances in the morning.

He woke refreshed and went out for a paper and a loaf of bread from the bakery on the corner around midmorning. Upon returning from his errand, there, standing outside his apartment building, was Frances. Startled, and then unsure it was actually Frances, he stopped mid-stride and froze. She was here, now? Were his eyes deceiving him? But no, it was his beautiful Frances in front of his building. He gaped at her, blinking his eyes in rapid succession. His mouth suddenly dry, he walked toward her. "Frances? Is it really you?"

"Nate." She ran toward him and threw her arms around his neck, the bread in his arms a pillow between them. "I'm so glad to see you. I was afraid I had the wrong building."

"What's happened? Why are you here?" He searched her face. Her complexion was odd, almost yellow tinged. She seemed subdued, cowed even. Was she ill? "Frances, are you all right?"

"I had to see you right away." She paused. "I have some rather frightful news. I'm going to have a baby."

It might have been that someone hit him, that's where he felt the blow, right in the middle of his chest. "A baby?"

"It's yours, if that's what you're wondering."

He shook his head, confused. Why had she said that? "I wasn't wondering. Not at all, in fact."

She started to cry and pulled a lace handkerchief from her purse. "There's only one thing to do."

"What's that?"

"We'll have to get married."

What had she said? Married? He floated there for a moment, watching the girl in front of him, who was both a stranger and yet achingly familiar. How often he'd imagined her smooth skin, the way she'd sighed when he kissed her neck. And then, out of his mouth as if they'd been perched against his teeth all the time, came the words, "Yes, right. We'll get married." He smiled and took her hands. "Frances Bellmont, will you marry me?"

"Oh, Nate, I'm so relieved. I'm horrified at what's happened, and I was afraid you might not want me."

He cleared his throat, looking at her hands in his, trying to order his jumbled and confused thoughts into something coherent. "Does your mother know?"

"Yes, she's waiting at the hotel. She gave me no choice but to tell her. It was the only way I could persuade her to bring me here to see you. She thought it inappropriate to call on you, of course."

He felt sick, thinking of the kind Mrs. Bellmont he'd met at the party and how disappointed this must have made her.

"Mother was upset, or shocked might be a better word. She wants you to come to supper tonight at the hotel so you two can discuss the details. This is the way, you see, Nate. A young, southern lady decides nothing for herself." She went on without taking a breath. "The main concern is scandal. Daddy can't have it getting out. So we'll have to hurry everything along."

"I'll arrange everything with your mother."

"Everything arranged. That sounds so final." Her eyes went flat, and she looked suddenly young and vulnerable. "I wanted so many things for my life. I'm not ready to be a mother."

"Frances, this doesn't have to be the end of your life. I'll be a good husband, I promise. We'll have help for the baby. Whatever you need.

Don't worry. There are many interesting people here that you'll enjoy and parties every night if we want to go. I never do, of course, but I could." He paused, searching her face. "If you wanted to, I would. If it pleased you."

She smiled, tilting her face upward and gazing into his eyes. He felt a flutter in his chest and was filled with the possibility of things, of this new start to his life as a family man. "We'll live here in the city, right, Nate?"

"Yes, of course, and you can travel with me if you want. We'll go all over the world together. Would you like that?"

She sighed, smiling again. "Well, that sounds wonderful."

"And there'll be a baby." His chest expanded further. "I've longed to be a father, Frances, for many years now. We'll be happy, the three of us."

She began to cry. "I'm awfully frightened. You won't let anyone talk you out of this, will you?"

"Absolutely not." He pulled a handkerchief from his pocket and dabbed her wet cheeks. "And don't be frightened. I'll take good care of you." Picking up her small white hands between his own, he brought them to his mouth, brushing them with his lips. Gardenias. Frances would be his wife. Could it all have happened, or was it a dream? "I'll go out this afternoon and find you a ring. Something beautiful for your beautiful hand."

Her eyes widened, and she smiled wide, her perfect teeth white against her red lipstick. "It wouldn't sadden me to have something large and sparkly."

"I think I can manage that." He laughed, feeling ridiculously happy that he could do this thing for her. "May I kiss you?"

"I suppose it's only appropriate since we're engaged." Her voice was husky, almost breathless.

He leaned toward her, determined to give her a kiss she'd never forget, to make her forget her fear or uncertainty. Capturing her mouth in his, he gently pressed into her. She put her arms around his neck and sighed into him.

After a moment, he drew back, scrutinizing her face. "Could you ever love me?"

She giggled and placed her fingertips on his mouth. "Nate, I loved you the first time I set my eyes on you."

Soaring happiness like the perfect crescendo in a musical movement. To love and be loved in return? Was there anything finer?

"I will be a good husband and father, no matter what comes our way, Frances Bellmont."

"I know you will."

* * *

After Frances left, Nate sat at the piano in his front room for a moment, staring at the keys. He would have to call his mother. His dear mother. Her discipline and rigidity, brought about from her strict religious upbringing, remained intact despite the changing world. She spent her days caring for the sick or poor in her little town, never tiring, it seemed, no matter how long the day. She walked everywhere in her comfortable shoes with her Bible tucked against her side, in case there was a soul that needed saving before they went on to the next world.

This rushed marriage—she would not approve. She would know straightaway why. He sighed, bracing himself. The truth must be told.

His mother didn't have a telephone, and there was only one phone available in her small Maine town for public use, located at the dry-goods store. He called the owner, Lou, who offered to send his boy over on foot to ask Nate's mother to be at the phone at three o'clock.

"Ma," he said when she answered, immediately falling into the way he used to talk.

"Son? Is that you?" She always talked too loudly into the phone, not understanding that one didn't have to shout to be heard through the wires. He imagined her long neck stretched like an ostrich's, eyes fixated at the mouthpiece while pressing the earpiece into her poor ear hard enough to make a dent.

Lou's store was probably packed with locals, playing checkers, talking about the day's catch, sipping bootleg booze from coffee cups. Everyone listening. He cringed as he spoke. "Ma, I'm going to tell you something, and I don't want you to repeat it. In case there's anyone listening."

She didn't say anything, but he knew she was probably bobbing her head in agreement, one arm crossed over her spare chest.

"I'm getting married."

"You're doing what?"

"I'm getting married. To a girl from Georgia. Her name's Frances Bellmont."

The line crackled.

"Are you there, Ma?"

"Yep, I'm here. When?"

"In a couple of weeks," Nathaniel said.

Silence for a moment. "How long have you known her?" She no longer shouted. He knew what she looked like: mouth clenched, the little muscle below her cheek flexed, her eyes unblinking. She'd given him the same look when he'd been caught at the back of school smoking a cigarette with Billy Bradshaw, or the time he'd lost one of his schoolbooks on the way home. During the entire week he'd been home to bury his father, she had never once loosened her face to betray her grief. The woman could hold her emotions inside better than anyone he'd ever met. Who knew what storms raged within? Her face was like ice covering a lake in deep winter. One knew many things lurked underneath the glittering surface, revealed when spring came in a rush of life. For his mother, spring never came.

"Couple of months." This was true, he thought, if you counted the time he was away in California. He didn't share the fact that he'd spent only part of a day and a night with her. Some things could not be told to one's mother, especially his.

Silence for another moment, and when she spoke again, her voice sounded hollow with disappointment. "Only one reason you'd be rushing into a marriage."

He leaned his forehead against the phone's bell-shaped receiver. "Ma, she comes from a good family. They're part of Atlanta society. It's a good marriage."

"You'll have to make your peace with God, not me."

He let that sit for a moment, feeling the familiar blackness of guilt and shame, like a hole he couldn't escape from. "Ma, maybe you could come down for the wedding? I'll send money for a train." Even as he said it he knew it was impossible. Not only did he know she would refuse on her principles, there was no way she could get there in time, given how quickly everything must be done.

"Impossible to make that kind of trip without your father."

"I'll bring her to see you. Later." He almost said, *after the baby comes*, but he held back, some part of him hopeful that she didn't know the truth.

"Write to me, son, and let me know how you're doing." The line went silent.

*   *   *

The hotel restaurant bustled with life. Well-dressed patrons ate and drank and toasted one another. Ladies in short dresses of every color wore cloche hats, some beaded, some with ribbons, perched deftly over bobbed hair. Men wore gray, brown, or black suits and striped ties in shades of wheat, their hair slicked back with pomade. Optimism, he thought, a sense that life could and should go on like this forever. Silver and glasses clinked above the low hum of laughter and voices. Servers moved about efficiently in black pants and crisp white shirts as the scent of baking bread, cigarettes, coffee, and roasted meat mingled. Nathaniel spotted Mrs. Bellmont at a table toward the back. She sat alone, tracing a circle with her finger on the white tablecloth. As he wove his way between tables he felt like a young performer before a concert, nauseous and sweaty. What could he say to this intelligent and trusting woman that might make her forgive him and maybe someday like him once again? There was nothing. That was the bitter truth. He had betrayed her trust. Would there ever be a way back? *Please, God, let it be so*, he prayed silently.

When he arrived at the table, Mrs. Bellmont looked up, smiling in a way that didn't reach her eyes. She was dressed tastefully, a gray gown with a modest scoop neckline falling at her collarbones and ash-blonde hair arranged perfectly around her pretty face were in direct contradiction to her red and puffy eyes. He'd made her cry. It was almost too much to bear.

The waiter pulled out his chair, and Nathaniel sat. His throat tightened. Could he speak? But right away something came out of his mouth. "Mrs. Bellmont, I'm sorry we have to meet under these circumstances."

"Yes." She sounded tired, like she hadn't slept for nights. "It diminishes our last delightful encounter somewhat."

"I know." He looked at his hands. "I'm ashamed and can only say in my defense that I fell in love with her at first sight. I'm powerless to resist her."

Her face softened. "Yes, I can see that."

"Mrs. Bellmont, I'll spend a lifetime trying to make her happy."

She cocked her head to one side. "Frances can be difficult. She expects a lot. I hope it won't prove too much for you."

"It won't be, Mrs. Bellmont. We'll be a family. There'll be a baby. Think of that."

She looked down at the table and then up at him, her eyes alive for the first time since he'd sat down with her. "I hadn't thought much of the baby, only how it came to be, but yes, there will be a baby. A baby to love."

"Mrs. Bellmont, please say you'll forgive me someday. I'll do anything to win your affection."

Her eyes went wide. "Oh, Mr. Fye, yes, I forgive you. I'm married to Frank Bellmont. I understand how these things happen."

What did this mean? Had they married under the same circumstance?

She twirled her knife in a clockwise motion—once, twice, three times. "The force of his personality has a way of making life turn in unexpected directions. Frances is the same. Anyway, we'll all be the better with you in our family, no matter how you've come to us."

He felt a lump developing in the back of his throat as he pulled from his pocket the ring he'd purchased earlier and handed it to her. "I've bought this for Frances. Do you think she'll like it?"

She held it between her thumb and finger. The round diamond sparkled in the overhead lights like rays of sunshine as she handed it back to him. "It's beautiful. Frances will love it." She straightened the knife so that it was in the correct position before meeting his gaze. "It's important we keep the details of Frances's condition from Mr. Bellmont. I'm not sure what he would do." She shivered and hunched forward as if cold, folding her arms over her chest and causing the neckline of her dress to shift momentarily, revealing her neck and chest just below her collarbones. He stifled a gasp. A purple bruise hovered just below her left collarbone. He blinked, unsure if he was correct. Was it a bruise the size of a fist? Yes, and she'd tried to cover it with powder, but it was no use. Oh, Mrs. Bellmont, he thought. What hell do you live through? But he knew. Mr. Bellmont was a violent man. Had he ever hurt Frances?

She must have caught him staring because she straightened and tugged at the neckline, smoothing it across her collarbones.

He felt sick to his stomach. The worry he'd caused her from his lack of restraint was unforgiveable. He leaned forward. "I can marry her tomorrow."

"No, that won't do. Frank will assume the worst unless we have a real wedding. When the baby comes, we'll all pretend he came early. It's an old trick. People have done it for centuries." The waiter came to take their order. "Nathaniel, will you order something for me? Anything's fine."

Nathaniel asked for two roast beef specials. When the waiter left, he turned back to Mrs. Bellmont. "Can you arrange something quickly? Tell him I'm leaving for another tour and want to take her with me?"

She appeared to think for a moment, folding and unfolding her napkin. "Yes, that will work, I suppose." She paused as the waiter brought them a basket of bread. "We'll do the wedding at the lake house. I'll tell Frank you want only a small affair. Just the family."

"Whatever you want, Mrs. Bellmont. Anything."

She looked at him long and hard, with searching eyes. What did she look for, he wondered?

CHAPTER 6

Jeselle

THE DAY AFTER Mrs. Bellmont and Frances returned from New York City, Jeselle finished up the morning dishes while Mama sliced onions at the kitchen table. Mama worked in silence, her mouth still set in a hard line, squinting at the door into the hallway every minute. Sometimes she held the knife, suspended between chops, and cocked her head, obviously listening for something. The juice of the onions was potent enough that Jeselle's eyes watered, but not Mama's. She was impervious, it seemed, to crying. Not even an onion could do it.

Mama looked over at her, pointing the knife toward the pantry. "Jes, stop daydreaming and concentrate on what're you're doing. I asked you to look in the pantry for the dried thyme."

She hadn't actually asked her, but Jeselle kept that to herself. No need to poke the bear, as Whit would say. In the pantry, Jeselle climbed up the stepladder to look on the topmost shelf. There were a half-dozen dried herbs in canning jars. The jar of thyme was all the way in the back. She'd have to move the stepladder over a foot to reach it.

Before she could do so, Jeselle heard a clicking sound on the hardwood floors of the hallway—Mrs. Bellmont's shoes. She stepped down from the ladder and peeked through the crack in the slightly open door. A moment later Mrs. Bellmont entered the kitchen, closing the kitchen door behind her. She'd changed into a beige linen dress with white lace around the bodice and a sweetheart neckline. Her fair curls were damp and stuck to the sides of her face and back of her neck. She spoke softly to Mama, "Well, it's done. He's agreed to the marriage."

Mama put down her knife, glancing at the door. "You all right then?"

"Frank was calm. None of the nonsense." Mrs. Bellmont brushed her flaming cheeks with the tips of her fingers. Nonsense? It bothered Jeselle to hear the way Mr. Bellmont hurt Mrs. Bellmont described as nonsense. The word was cruel. C-R-U-E-L. The way he hurt his wife, sometimes enough that she had to hide for weeks inside the house for fear someone would spot her bruises, could not be described any other way. Frank Bellmont was a cruel beast.

"What did you tell him?" asked Mama.

"I said, as simply as I could, that after the incident last year at Flora Waller's coming-out party, Frances didn't exactly have many opportunities for securing a good marriage. I went on to say that this man, Nathaniel Fye, while older, is wealthy and famous, a musical genius, and apparently so in love with Frances he wanted to get married right away and without any fuss, given his upcoming European touring schedule."

"He didn't guess there was a baby coming?"

"Not a word about it. I don't think it's occurred to him." Mrs. Bellmont's voice broke, and she took a deep breath, pinching the bridge of her nose between her thumb and forefinger.

Jeselle stifled a gasp. Frances was going to have a baby. That was why she'd been sick.

Mama pulled a handkerchief out of her apron pocket and pressed it into Mrs. Bellmont's hand, leading her over to the table. "Set for a minute, Miz Bellmont. No reason you can't cry. It's been a shock for you." She made a clucking sound with the tip of her tongue against the roof of her mouth. "I'll get you a cup of tea."

Mrs. Bellmont sank into a chair, dabbing under her eyes. "Frank agreed to have the wedding at the lake house, away from Atlanta society. Then, we'll just announce the marriage. People will talk, but it's the best we can do. It'll help that Nathaniel's so esteemed."

"This Mr. Fye ain't heard about that Waller girl's party?"

"He doesn't run in society. Doesn't have to worry about such things. His talent excuses him from that, I suppose. He's what my grandmother would've called painfully shy. But he's humble and intelligent. Has these eyes that seem to take everything in at once."

Mama took a cup and saucer from the hutch and poured a cup of light green liquid that smelled of fresh mint from the pot on the stove.

"This here's the tea I made for you." Mama set it in front of her. "Mint leaves and a new herb I heard about that's good for bad stomachs."

"Thank you, Cassie." Mrs. Bellmont sipped from the cup. "Oh my, such a refreshing taste." She rested her forehead in her hand and closed her eyes for a moment before looking back at Mama.

"It's all so rushed. I can't tell how Frances feels about him, other than she's talked of nothing but moving to New York since we came home. I hope she'll be happy, Cassie. As difficult as Frances has been, a mother always wants better for her child than she's had herself."

"There ain't no such thing as a happy marriage, anyhow," said Mama.

"I always thought there might be. For other people."

"No one we know."

"He's a good man. Of that I'm certain." Mrs. Bellmont sipped her tea. Mama scooped a pile of potatoes into a bowl. "Nathaniel's kin are fishing people up in Maine. Poor, like we were, Cassie."

"Except we can't play the piano," said Mama.

Mrs. Bellmont laughed. "We certainly can't."

CHAPTER 7

Whitmore

IN HIS MOTHER'S upstairs study at the lake house, Whitmore sketched Jeselle's face, sitting next to the open window. Above Sequoyah Lake, the northern Georgia sky was the same brilliant blue of the native blue jays twittering and hopping from pine to pine. They sang loudly this afternoon, calling out to one another as if in protest of the changing season. October had brought autumn overnight, it seemed, the air crisp and the leaves beginning to turn. Soon geese would arrive from the north, decorating the sky as Whitmore took his morning rows across the brown lake.

Jeselle sat in the reading chair; light from the window illuminated one side of her face while the other remained in shadow. Her glance skipped furtively between the window and the book on Mother's desk, *To the Lighthouse*, by Virginia Woolf. "I know I'm too young to read it yet because it's—what did your mother say it was?"

"Radical."

The sound of a car's motor drifted in from the open window. His stomach fluttered, knowing it was Martin and Frances back from fetching Nathaniel at the train depot. He looked out the window to the dirt road. The black Rolls Royce, with Martin behind the wheel, made its way slowly, bouncing in potholes, flinging small rocks from under its tires, and coating the short, fat pines with a fine, rust-colored powder.

Mother called to them, the sound travelling up the wishbone stairs. "C'mon down, children."

They stared at one another for a moment. Whitmore shuffled to his feet, plunging his hands into his dungarees. "What kind of man can he be?" he whispered.

"The kind to marry Frances," she whispered back.

"We'll just stay out of his way."

"Same as we do with Frances."

"And Father."

When they reached the wishbone stairs that led to the first floor, Jeselle took the right side, skipping steps, and Whitmore the left, taking them one at a time, so that despite the difference in the length of their legs, they arrived in the foyer at the same time. Cassie and Mother were just coming from the music room, where the French doors were wide open, bringing the fragrance of freshly cut grass and late-blooming honeysuckle. Fred Wilder, their gardener, had spent the morning tidying the flowerbeds and trimming the sweeping lawn so that Mother's beloved lake house looked its best. The house, built in the French colonial style and painted white, had been constructed from cypress wood, with high columns supporting a large awning. Rectangular windows with black shutters ran along the front of the house, with dormer windows in front of the attic spaces.

At the bottom of the stairs, Whitmore gripped the handrail, not knowing where to set his gaze. His heart pounded at his first glimpse of the tall, elegant Nathaniel Fye. Next to him, he heard Jeselle's quick intake of breath. "Mr. Darcy," Jeselle whispered.

She was right, of course. He looked like Austen's Darcy, tall and mysterious, perhaps even brooding, partly due to his eyebrows. Dark and somewhat bushy, they were pushed together by the furrow of his brow, giving an appearance that he was disturbed or angry. But then Nathaniel came forward, standing in front of Whitmore and reaching his hand out like men do before a handshake. He wanted to shake his hand like Whitmore was an adult? His cheeks flushed. No one had ever done that before. In the presence of Father's friends he was either glared at or ignored. He squared his shoulders and looked into the older man's eyes. But what was this? The eyes didn't match the eyebrows or the furrow of his brow. No, they were kind. They were eyes that looked deeply into a person and saw what others couldn't. Eyes like Jeselle's.

"I'm glad to meet you, Whitmore." Nathaniel's voice was surprisingly soft, almost shy.

Whitmore shook his hand, mumbling, "Good to meet you too, sir."

"Please, it's not necessary to call me sir." Nathaniel let go of his hand, chuckling. "That was my father."

"We'll all call him Nate." Frances stood next to Nathaniel, staring up at him with adoring eyes. Who was this soft and seemingly sweet sister? Was it possible love had transformed her? No, it couldn't be. She was charming when she needed or wanted something. And she wanted Nathaniel Fye. This much was clear. Whitmore shivered.

"Nate?" asked Mother.

Frances unpinned her hat and tossed it on the foyer table, knocking a piece of decorative lace to the floor. "Yes, I've decided. Nate."

"Is this a family nickname?" Mother looked over at Nate with a perplexed expression.

"No, I've never had a nickname, Nate or otherwise. Frances says it sounds modern, and if this is what Frances wants, I shall from this point forward be called Nate." He said this looking at Whitmore and smiling as if it were a private joke between them. Then, he turned to Mother. "Mrs. Bellmont, my mother always said a happy wife makes for a happy marriage."

Mother opened her mouth as if to say something but seemed to decide against it and instead gave one of her dazzling smiles. What could she say to that, thought Whitmore, when married to Frank Bellmont?

Martin came into the foyer with Nathaniel's two small suitcases. "Shall I take these up, ma'am?"

"Thank you, Martin," said Mother.

"Leave the smaller one, if you don't mind, Martin," Nate said. "I've brought Whitmore something from New York."

"Let's all go into the music room." Mother took Nate's arm. "We've a present for you as well."

"Mother, how thoughtful of you," said Frances.

"It's a present for all of us, really." Mother's eyes danced. She loved giving gifts.

Frances took Nate's other arm as they all headed into the music room. Behind them, Whitmore watched Frances go onto her tiptoes to whisper something in Nate's ear that made him laugh. Was it possible this man was actually in love with his spoiled, petulant sister?

"Is Mr. Bellmont here?" Nate asked Mother.

"He'll be here anytime," said Mother. "He's driving up from Atlanta this afternoon."

In the music room, Mother brushed her fingertips along the ivory keys of the new piano. "Our wedding present to you." The piano was a Steinway & Sons 1927 Louis XV style Model S. His mother had ordered what she hoped was the best of its kind for her new son-in-law. Father was outraged when he found out how much she'd spent. Whitmore had heard him shouting at her from behind their bedroom door. The next morning Mother had bruises on her neck and walked gingerly, like one of her legs hurt. Whitmore seethed just thinking of it. But what could be done? No one could fight against Frank Bellmont and win.

His mother continued, "This one is for when you stay with us. I've had another sent to your apartment in New York. This way you'll always have something to play, no matter if you're here or there."

"It's too generous." His voice sounded strangled.

"Nonsense, darlin'. All I ask is that you'll play for us when you're here."

"It'll be my pleasure."

Next, Nate opened his suitcase and pulled out a flat, wooden container with a gold clasp and handed it to Whitmore. "Go ahead, open it."

Whitmore lifted the cover. Arranged in neat rows were tubes of paint, along with charcoals. "Thank you!"

"The clerk at the art store told me charcoal makes a mess of your hands." Nate turned back to his suitcase and pulled out something wrapped in tissue paper. "Here, this too."

It was a set of paintbrushes in every shape and size. Whitmore thanked him again, almost too overwhelmed to speak. How had Nate known about his interest in art? Had Frances told him? He doubted that. She never showed any interest in him. Perhaps Mother had mentioned it. This was not the man he'd expected. Not at all.

* * *

Later, after a meal of Cassie's fried chicken, butter beans, and fried okra, they all went into the music room to hear Nate play. Cassie hovered by the open French doors, refusing to sit. Whitmore sat cross-legged on the floor by the west-facing window, with Jeselle next to him.

Mother spoke to Nate. "The salesmen told me it produces a tone so sublime as to make a person weep."

"Take quite a sound to make me weep." Cassie stood near the doorway, as if she didn't want to stay, but Whitmore knew it was because of Father. If he came home and found either Cassie or Jeselle sitting with them, there would be hell to pay. And Mother would be the one to pay it. Cassie protected Mother no matter the circumstance, he thought. Like a sister might.

Mrs. Bellmont and Nate both laughed. "There are several books of music for solo piano there," Mrs. Bellmont said. "I hope there's something in it you might like."

"I'm sure I can find something to play for you." Nate sat at the piano bench, brushing his fingers over the keys without pressing them, as if he was familiarizing himself with a new friend, then picked up one of the books Mrs. Bellmont had left on the top of the piano. "There are some lovely pieces here."

"We'll like anything you pick, I'm sure." Mother sat on the couch and pulled out her latest embroidery.

"Nate, you look like you belong here in this room with us. Aren't we lucky, Mother?" Frances sat in the soft, felt chair in the far corner of the room, crossing her ankles.

"Extremely," said Mother.

Before Nate began to play, he explained to them that classical musicians referred to pieces with both the key and catalogue reference numbers but that he would tell them only the popular names for fear of running them out of the room from boredom, which made Frances and Mother laugh. First he played Schubert's *Wanderer Fantasy*, a gentle, melodic tune that brought the sunset of orange and pink outside the west-facing windows. Chopin's *Funeral March* then ushered in dusk. It began with soft, delicate notes that reminded Whit of his mother's hands and then grew dark and brooding, building into a crescendo as mosquitoes pushed against the screens, trying to get in. Finally, as darkness arrived, he finished with one of the first pieces Nate said he'd ever learned as a young student, Bach's simple but lovely *Minuet in G major*.

The music ended, and the ghost of those notes hovered in the room for a moment. Whit looked over at his mother as she wiped tears from her cheeks. The beauty of it was almost too much to bear. Nothing could be said, or painted, or written, that music couldn't inspire. He thought of his new paints upstairs and of the colors of the sunset that had just played across Jeselle's face, and it seemed to him that nothing was more important than creating something of beauty.

Then, a door slammed, and they heard Father's boots, heavy on the hardwood floor. He glanced over at the doorway, but Cassie was no longer there. She must have heard his car and escaped to the kitchen. A spot under Whitmore's left eye began to twitch. He put his index finger there, willing it to stop. Father hated the twitch.

Jeselle stood, glancing at the doorway with the eyes of someone caught. "Take your dust rag out of your apron," he whispered.

"Yes, right." She pulled it from her pocket.

"Now go."

She headed for the doorway, slipping through just as Father came through. "Girl, wait," said Father.

Jeselle turned. "Yes, sir?"

"Bring me a whiskey. Three fingers."

"Yes, sir."

Nate stood, and Father went to him. They shook hands.

"Frank Bellmont. Good to meet you."

"Thank you, sir."

"Sorry, my boy, to have to meet so informally, but I figure since y'all are getting married tomorrow we'd better not worry too much about that."

"I appreciate it, Mr. Bellmont."

"Now, call me Frank. No need for formal names now that we're family."

Father turned to look at Whitmore. "Son, you paint any flowers today?"

"No, sir."

Father shook his head, looking at Nate. "Whitmore thinks painting pictures like a little girl is a good way to spend his time."

"Frank," said Mother.

Father's face went red. "Now, don't you try and defend him, Clare. You know as well as I do that only pansy boys spend their time painting goddamn flowers."

"Where were you for supper?" Mother asked. "We waited for you as long we could."

"Since when does a wife ask her husband his whereabouts?" He strode toward the door. "Dammit, where's that girl? I need a drink."

"Sometimes it's trees. Or the lake." Whitmore spoke quietly, readying himself for an onslaught.

"What did you say?" said Father.

"Frank, I'd love a tour of the grounds tomorrow." Nate's eyes darted from one of them to the other.

"Sure thing. Although it's my wife knows every blade of grass and pine needle on the place. Must be where my son gets it." Father turned to Frances. "How's my little bride?"

She smiled her Daddy smile. "I'm simply perfect, Daddy." She meandered over to stand by Nate and slipped her hand into his. Nate smiled down at her.

Jeselle came in with the whiskey. Frank motioned for everyone to sit. "Nathaniel, you need a drink?"

"No, sir."

"Nate doesn't drink," said Mother.

"Well, now, we'll have to do something to change that," said Father. "All Bellmont men drink."

He isn't a Bellmont, Whit thought. And he prayed he never would be.

*   *   *

After everyone else retired for the night, Whit sat at the kitchen table, eating a piece of Cassie's apple pie and gazing at a sliver of moon framed in the window. He was about to take his last bite when Nate came through the door, nodding politely at him.

"Evening," Whit said, feeling nervous.

Nate went to the butler's pantry and came out with a glass of milk and a piece of pie. "Your mother said to help myself." Nate sat across from him at the wooden table.

"Sure." Whitmore moved his fork around his now empty plate. Looking up, he saw Nate watching him, a crease between his dark eyebrows.

"Your mother tells me you row across the lake every day."

"Yep. I'm trying to get stronger."

"Why's that?"

"Might need to protect someone someday."

Nate nodded and continued gazing at him, as if there were words written on Whitmore's forehead. "You ever fish in the lake?"

"Sometimes. They stock it every spring. Catfish mostly."

"In Maine everyone fishes or catches lobster. For a living. Out in boats."

Whitmore wasn't sure what to say, so he just nodded his head and then looked back at his pie.

"You want to go tomorrow morning? Before breakfast?"

"I'd like that, sure." Whitmore picked up his plate and took it to the sink, trying to hide the pleasure he felt. "I'll get us some night crawlers before I go to bed."

* * *

Slightly before dawn, at the lake's shore, they strung the fat, wiggly night crawlers on hooks and then dangled their poles from the edge of the Bellmonts' pier. The morning air had the crisp, cool feel of autumn. Occasionally a fish jumped, causing ripples in the smooth water.

"Are you really famous?" Whit asked. His mother always told him to ask someone a question if you wanted to start a conversation.

"In certain circles, I suppose. That's not why I do it, though."

"What do you mean?" Whitmore sat still, waiting for the answer. He wanted to hear every word, to memorize it for later because he was about to hear something important, of this he felt certain.

"I love to play. The pay and the accolades are gratifying, but all that is not a good enough reason to work as hard as I do."

Whitmore remained quiet, thinking. "Why do you work as hard as you do?"

"Ah, well, that's simply pure love. I love to play music. It's all I've wanted, until recently."

"I love to draw and paint. I could do it all day and not get tired. Is that how it is for you?"

Nate looked over at him, his eyes serious now but not unkind. "Most of the time."

"Father says art's ridiculous. No money in it."

"Not necessarily true, but yes, it can be difficult. Doesn't mean you shouldn't do it."

"Yeah, yeah, it doesn't mean that."

They sat in silence for several minutes, holding their poles, the dappled October light between the scarlet and yellow leaves in the oaks that surrounded the lake. "I'd like to capture the way the light is this morning, someday, in my paintings."

"Keep painting. You will." Nate's line lurched. "Ha! Got one."

After Whit also caught one of the prehistoric-looking catfish, they agreed they were hungry and ready for breakfast. They gutted and cleaned the fish, carefully scooping the remains into a pail at the side of the lake, and headed toward the house, their feet crunching in the thick layer of fallen pine needles the color of brown bread. Nate stopped when they came to the rose garden. The last of the season's blooms, reduced to rosehips and a few straggling petals, fluttered in the breeze. Below each bush, like injured soldiers scattered on a battlefield, fallen petals carpeted the ground.

"Mother keeps the rosehips for the birds instead of cutting the dead blooms. But she won't like how untidy the ground looks." Whitmore knelt and picked up one of the stray petals. "She thinks the gardener, Fred Wilder, is lazy. She won't get rid of him though. Says he has a family to feed."

"Your mother's a kind woman."

"And gentle."

"Her generous spirit reminds me of my father."

He sighed, thinking of Father. What would it be like to have that kind of father? Whit would never know, of course.

Nate put his arm around Whit, briefly, in an almost embrace. "I realize, of course, I'm not your father. But perhaps I could be someone you rely upon. A confidant. A champion of sorts."

Whit glanced over at him, but Nate didn't meet his gaze. There was a red flush on the older man's cheekbones. "Thanks. Yes. I'd like that." Whit dropped the petal from his fingers. It cascaded to the ground, joining her fallen sisters.

"We're kindred spirits, you and I."

"Kindred spirits?" asked Whit.

"We understand one another. Both of us artists, for example."

"Right. We're both artists." His throat ached with pride. Nate considered him a kindred spirit and a friend. How was it possible that this man had come and filled an empty portion of his heart in less than twenty-four hours? How Frances had gotten this man to agree to marry her he could not say. But it didn't matter. Nate was here now. He would be theirs from now on. Family.

"Come on, let's eat," said Nate. "I'm ravenous."

"Ravenous. That's a Jeselle-type word."

"That right?"

"Mother's always teaching her new words, and Jeselle spends all day using them in a sentence."

They arrived at the house and stomped the mud from their boots before they walked into the kitchen. "You want me to fry these up for breakfast?" Nate asked.

"Cassie won't allow that."

Nathaniel grinned, looking suddenly like a boy. "We'll clean up after ourselves. She'll never know. I'm not afraid of Cassie."

"Well, I am. And you should be, too."

Just then Cassie came out of the butler's pantry. "Y'all should be afraid."

"Ah, we've been caught," said Nate.

"This is my kitchen. No one, and I mean no one, messes with my kitchen.

Cassie seemed different around Nate. What was it exactly? Indulgence, like he was a naughty but loveable puppy. Her words were stern, but her eyes sparkled as if amused. Had Nate charmed even Cassie?

"Sit down." She pointed at the table. "I'll fry 'em up for you."

While Cassie melted lard in a frying pan and coated the fish with cornmeal, Nate sipped coffee, gazing out at the garden from the breakfast-nook window. Whit pulled out his sketchbook. Using his new charcoal, he sketched Nate's profile using quick darts and then smearing the lines with his fingers. The room filled with the aroma of grease and frying fish.

Capture the moment, Whit told himself, so that he might have it later to pull out and remember the peace he felt.

Kindred spirits. Was there anything better than this? What had Jes said to him once? Love is all there is and all there ever will be. Surely she was correct.

PART TWO

From Jeselle Thorton's journal.

March 2, 1929

Seeking truth, I listen behind closed doors. I peer between cracks.
I capture memories with words.
Six years old, dust rag in my hand, I stood behind the door to the study watching Mrs. Bellmont teach Whit to read.
Sensing my presence, her face in the soft light from the lamp went still. "Jes, are you there?"
I came out from behind the door, standing before her, my eyes turned downward.
"What are you doing?"
"Nothing. My chores."
"Look at me, Jes."
I lifted my head. She put down her pencil and peered at me, those gray eyes of hers kind, discerning. "You want to study here with us?"
I nodded, unable to utter my greatest desire. To give a desire words makes it real and therefore subject to ridicule, rejection, heartbreak. I was careful then, before education rendered me bold. Before education gave me a voice.
She rose from the desk, striding to the kitchen with a purposeful gait reserved for times when Frank Bellmont was not present. I hovered behind the door, peering through the crack.
It was canning day. Steam and the sweet smell of cooked peaches. Mama peeled the fruit's skin at the sink with her sleeves rolled up to her elbows. Sinewy strength.

"Cassie, Jeselle wants to study with us. I could teach her right alongside Whit."

Mama took her hands out of the steaming bowl, bits of peach skin clinging to her fingers. Her eyebrows went up, causing two creases in the middle of her forehead as she wiped her hands on the front of her apron. I held my breath, sure she'd say no, that I should be learning how to help with the chores instead of schooling.

"What about Mr. Bellmont? No harm can come to you because of this. I can't have that."

"He won't know," said Mrs. Bellmont.

"Fine, then." She made a little nod with her head and then turned away, back to peeling the hot flesh of peaches. When Mrs. Bellmont turned to leave, a wide smile on her pretty face, she did not see Mama fall to her knees with her hands grasping the sink as she bowed her head, praying gratitude. But I did. I will never forget.

Later, when I was eight, Mr. Bellmont discovered Mrs. Bellmont and me with our heads together over an open book. Mrs. Bellmont paid dearly for it with bumps and bruises, but she would not stop. Her eye still black from his fist, she said to me, voice so soft I had to lean close to hear her, "Here's something you must know, Jeselle, given your particular situation on this earth. There will be many times in your life you'll have to pretend to be something you're not, just to keep peace. But make no mistake, there are still ways to do what you want, what you believe is right. You have to be brave, though. Some things must be done in secret. Behind closed doors." And so we did, the teacher and the student in covert alliance for my education.

And what has this clandestine education given me? We cannot measure it, capture it—even with words. I tried to explain it to Mama once so that she might be convinced to let Mrs. Bellmont teach her to read. But she would have none of it, said she's too old to learn to read and that if God had wanted her to, he would've arranged it when she was a child. She tells herself that kind of thing. It keeps her from going crazy with remorse and anger. If only she understood that reading leads to freedom. You can go anywhere or learn anything inside a book. You are liberated inside those words, free to live another's life.

CHAPTER 8

Lydia

AT DAWN Lydia Tyler dressed in a ratty flannel shirt and a pair of William's old pants, cinched at the waist with his leather belt she'd gotten in the habit of wearing after his death. She braided her hair as she slipped her feet into his work boots, pausing only long enough to start a fire in the kitchen's woodstove before going out into the March morning.

At the chicken coop, she tossed some feed to the squawking masses that reminded her of gossiping ladies flocking outside church after Sunday services. She both despised the chickens with their beady eyes that looked at her from either side of their lumpy heads and revered them at the same time, knowing how reliably they gave her eggs and how the fryers fed her and many of her neighbors.

These protesting, pecking chickens were the only animals she raised on her place now, having long ago decided the pigs and milk cow they'd had when William was alive were too much trouble, given their yield and her needs. It was enough, the hundred chicks she bought every spring and raised into chickens: a dozen layers, the rest fryers. She sold the eggs every Friday; her customers knew to stop by before nine to pick up their allotment for the week. After her paying customers, she had just enough for her family and several neighbors who had come on hard times.

Lydia gathered the eggs, placing them carefully into a tin bucket. After setting the eggs near the gate, she went back into the barn, looking for her old cat Piggy. He came out at night to catch mice and then usually fell asleep on a bale of hay. Sure enough, there he was, reliable as always, curled in a ball, his white paws tucked under his black coat. She called to him, but instead of stretching and yawning disdainfully to jump from his perch to rub against her ankles, he didn't move. "Piggy," she called again. "Breakfast time." Again, nothing.

She placed her hand on his back. Stiff. She stepped back as a sob came from her chest. "Piggy," she whispered.

She scooped Piggy into her arms, placed him in the wheelbarrow, and grabbed a shovel, wheeling out beyond the fence to where a wooden cross was forever above Lady's grave. In life Lady had been an orange and white striped mouser and was actually a boy. But Birdie, only four when they found him wandering down the dirt road, refused to believe it, insisting they call him Lady.

Lydia dug into the soft ground next to Lady's grave until she had a hole big enough for Piggy. She placed him inside and quickly covered him with dirt, patting the mound with the back of the shovel. She gathered a dozen rocks in various sizes and placed them over the grave to keep predators away. If Birdie were here, she would give Piggy's eulogy. But she wasn't, Lydia thought, pitifully. The girls were out of town visiting Lydia's father and his wife. They wouldn't be back for another week. She would have to give the eulogy herself.

It was still today, no breeze or rain. Just a thick cloud layer that felt close. "You were a good cat, Piggy," she said out loud. "You never gave up, even when you were old and could've spent your days sleeping. Instead you just kept along, killing mice like a young cat, which is to be admired. I'll miss you."

She went inside the house and sat at the piano. Most days she played three hours in the morning and another two in the afternoon, but now she could not focus, thinking instead about William. Every death, whether a cat or a neighbor down the road she hardly knew, brought grief to the surface.

Around nine, there was a knock on the front door. Startled, Lydia dried her eyes and opened the door. It was Midwife Stone. "Mornin', Mrs. Tyler. Just coming from the Warrens'. She had them twins this morning."

Midwife Stone was nearing sixty, scrawny, with gnarled hands and several missing teeth, known to smoke a corncob pipe on the porch of the general store. She'd helped almost every poor baby in Atmore come into the world. She looked Lydia up and down. "You having yourself a cry, Lydia Tyler? That ain't like you."

Lydia smiled, feeling foolish. "My old cat Piggy died."

"That ole mangy cat? I thought evil lived forever."

Lydia laughed. The last time Midwife Stone was over for a visit he'd hissed and snarled at her before running like something possessed out the door and into the barn, appearing hours later with an accusatory stare in Lydia's direction. "He just didn't like you. He was a grand judge of character. Come on in now, and I'll fix you something to eat."

"Don't mind if I do."

In the kitchen, Lydia set some biscuits, butter, and honey on a plate in front of Midwife Stone. "I'll fix you up a couple of eggs."

"That'd be mighty fine. I came by to see if you'd fry up a chicken for Mrs. Warren. She's feeling poorly, and her kin is surely about to starve to death. These twins make six kids. Nary a crumb of food in that house as far as I can see."

The Warren family lived a ways down the road from Lydia in a two-room shack, trying to make a living growing cotton on a small, overused piece of land. "That's a shame. I'll send them up some eggs, too. And I've some canned beans and peaches I can spare. We don't eat nearly what we did when William was alive."

"That what got you boohooin' here in the broad daylight?"

Lydia smiled as she tied on her apron. "I guess. Just feeling mighty sorry for myself. It's embarrassing." She scooped some lard into a frying pan. "My mother always told me if you're feeling bad to do for others."

"Good way to live, surely." Midwife Stone chewed the biscuit on the left side of her mouth, where she had more teeth. "All them Warren kids need shoes. Anything you could do for 'em?"

"I can put it on our list at church." Lydia cracked two eggs into the frying pan, hot lard spattering over her clean stove. "Sometimes we can scare up some money from a few of the wealthy folks."

"Those same ladies that pray for me?" asked Midwife Stone.

Lydia laughed and flipped the eggs. "Well, you're quite scandalous. Rumor has it you're making voodoo dolls out of corncobs."

"Don't seem to recall that when they're sending for me to birth them babies."

"You're giving them something to pray for," laughed Lydia. "They don't have a thing to do without praying over some misguided soul."

Midwife Stone buttered another biscuit and chewed noisily for a moment. "You should find yourself a new husband. Someone to keep you company."

"I'll do it the minute you do."

Midwife Stone chuckled and sliced into the eggs Lydia set in front of her. "No need for a husband if you can take care of yourself."

"I can't imagine living with another man. William was my one love. I was lucky that way. Most women don't even get that."

"Ain't that the truth." Midwife Stone scooped up the rest of the egg yolk with her biscuit. "Look at me."

Lydia sat in the chair across from Midwife Stone. "Truth is, I've been wondering what to do next. I hate feeling so useless. I can't just be Widow Tyler, the Methodist church piano player and Emma and Birdie's mother for the rest of my life."

"People in town think other things about you, too." Midwife Stone's eyes twinkled.

"I know people think I'm odd."

"In here all day playing your piano." She slapped the table with her hand and grinned her half-toothless smile. "It gives 'em all fits."

They both laughed. Lydia poured them both a cup of coffee. "What do they expect? For me to just sit here waiting to die?"

"Well, it's true that someone's always being born or dying. I guess it's in the years between we have to do something that either helps others or makes us happy. You got a few good years left in you. I feel sure of that. Just keep doing something. Play that piano. All good things come when you do something you love."

CHAPTER 9

Nathaniel

FRANCES'S LABOR PAINS began in the early morning hours on the second day of March. Nathaniel remembered nothing of the journey, but somehow they arrived at the hospital just ten blocks from their apartment in New York City. Frances was whisked away, and his long wait began. He paced the floor for hours, more anxious than he'd ever been in his life. Finally, a nun beckoned to him, her face grim. "Follow me, please, Mr. Fye. The doctor wishes to speak with you."

They walked down a long hallway until they came to the doctor's office. The doctor, whom Nathaniel had never met, sat behind the desk. He looked up when they came in and pointed to one of the chairs. "Please sit. I've some distressing news."

Nathaniel suddenly couldn't feel his feet. The nun steered him into the chair. His heart beat wildly. His stomach churned. Behind the doctor's head, the clock ticked off the seconds, one by one.

"I'm sorry, Mr. Fye, but there's been a complication."

"Are they all right?" Nathaniel said.

"Frances is fine. She lost a lot of blood and needs to rest."

"And the baby?"

"It's a boy, but I'm sorry, Mr. Fye, he isn't going to make it."

"Isn't going to make it?"

"He won't live for more than a few hours. He weighs only a couple of pounds and, well, he was born with severe abnormalities."

"Abnormalities?"

He spoke in one note, methodical, like reading from a textbook. "An oversized head, which usually indicates excess fluid, and clubfeet.

We don't know what his insides look like; we only know from the past that these kinds of babies don't live longer than a couple of hours."

"But why? I mean, how?"

"It's just something that happens. We don't understand it. A freak of nature, so to speak."

A freak of nature? On the wall behind the doctor's head was a painting of Jesus on the cross. "May I see him?" That was all. He wanted to see him. To hold him, no matter the outcome.

"We don't recommend it." The doctor moved a medical journal from one side of the desk to the other.

"Why?"

"He's deformed, Mr. Fye. It's a shock to most people. Something you don't want in your mind when you try for the next baby."

"But he's alive?"

"Yes." He nodded. A concession.

"Then I want to see him."

*   *   *

A nun took him to the nursery. Four or five healthy babies in bassinettes were lined up in neat rows. His son was in the corner bassinet, set aside from the rest, like something discarded. My God, Nathaniel thought when he leaned over to get a better look at him, he's no bigger than a kitten, his face shriveled like an old man, and his eyes scrunched shut. Should he touch him? Was it all right, or would it hurt him? He was so still, so small. But wait. Was he breathing? He felt panic rising in his chest. "Is he alive?"

"Yes." The nun made a sympathetic sound with her mouth, like the cluck of a hen. "It's shallow, but see there, how the blanket moves."

He fought tears, gulping down air to try and stop them. "How could this be?"

"I'm sorry, Mr. Fye. Many newborn babies don't make it." She hesitated, and when she spoke her tone sounded regretful. "I'm sure that's no comfort to you."

It was not. He didn't care about those other babies. He didn't care about the statistics. He cared only about this mite in front of him. His son. Whom he loved. Whom he had loved without knowing him in the flesh for the months he formed in Frances's body. He'd lived an entire imaginary lifetime with his son when he daydreamed at the piano and as he walked the streets of New York and even when he was awake in the night. In those invented moments, he'd taught his son to play piano and listen to music, carefully like a musician, on the gramophone. They'd walked together through every color of fallen autumn leaves in the Maine woods near his mother's home. Later, they'd caught lobster, and he'd told him stories of his grandfather in heaven. He'd taken him to the lake house and watched Clare bounce him on her lap and read him books. They'd sat with Whitmore on the dock and put their poles in the brown water, swatting at mosquitoes, waiting for fish to bite and talking of nothing and everything at once. He'd walked behind his son and Whitmore as they held hands crossing the yard and into the house where Cassie fried up catfish while his boy grinned and stuffed biscuits into his mouth with pudgy fingers. He'd imagined Frances rocking him in the early morning hours, her face peaceful in the dim light of dawn. And now his son was before him, not his imagined fair-haired boy, but just his sweet soul delivered into the wrong body.

And yet, how he loved him. Beyond anything he'd imagined—this love that he had not fully understood until now. He loved him regardless of the way he was made. Regardless of the fact that he would not live. He understood for the first time: this was how his father had loved him.

An image came to him of his father's red, chapped hands folded on his lap in the evening firelight. "Play just one more for me, Nathaniel."

"I'm naming him John," he told the nun. "After my father."

"Do you want to hold him?" She had a round face and wore thick glasses that made it seem as if her eyes protruded unnaturally.

"Will it hurt him?"

"No, Mr. Fye, it will only give him comfort as he waits to meet our Lord in heaven."

He felt a helpless sliding under, like a drowning man. "I don't know how."

"Sit in the chair here and hold out your arms." He did so, and she picked up the baby from the cradle and put him in Nathaniel's arms. He peeked under the blanket. John's scrawny body was purple, like he was bruised. The nun had put a tiny diaper on him. His legs were no bigger than the width of Nathaniel's thumb, and his poor, misshapen feet twisted inward. After a few moments, he looked up to find the nun gone. It occurred to him that Frances hadn't seen the baby. He must tell the nun. They must go to his son's mother. He rose from the chair, wandering out of the nursery and down the hall, meeting the nun on the way. "My wife hasn't seen him."

"I'm sorry, Mr. Fye. I've just been there. She doesn't want to."

"Are you sure?"

"She doesn't think she's strong enough." She held out her arms. "Let me take him for a moment. You can go see her. She needs you."

Frances was in the bed, her eyes closed. She opened them when he took her hand. "Nate, did they tell you?"

He nodded. "I've just been with him. He's fragile but alive. Do you want me to bring him?" His voice cracked.

Her eyes burned with a strange light, like someone with a fever. "I came to from the ether, and no one would look at me. The doctor was making notes in a tablet. I asked about the baby, and they all shuffled their feet and looked at the floor, but I wanted to know the truth so they told me he's deformed and won't live, and they've taken him away to die and that a mother shouldn't look at him."

He borrowed the phrase from the nun. "Frances, they're wrong. He needs his mother to hold him before he goes up to heaven."

She turned to her side, facing the wall. "No. I can't. Go, and let me sleep."

He stumbled back to the nursery and found himself in the chair holding his son once again. He wept, tears falling upon the blanket. He sang a lullaby. He whispered loving words. He said the Lord's Prayer. And when baby John took his last breath, Nathaniel breathed it with him, until it was done and he had to let go.

CHAPTER 10

Jeselle

AT THE LAKE HOUSE, Jeselle sat on the front porch peeling potatoes, grateful for the cool shade of the awning. Out of the corner of her eye, she saw the gardener, Fred Wilder, wearing his customary overalls and frayed straw hat, come around the side of the house. He carried a hoe and a bucket in his tanned arms. Near the magnolia tree, he paused for a moment, taking a pouch of tobacco from his pocket and setting a pinch of it inside his bottom lip. He leaned against his hoe like it was a dance partner and turned to leer at her.

She swallowed and quickly moved her gaze to the bowl of peeled potatoes in the bowl at her feet.

"You watchin' me, girl?" He moved one side of his mouth in a sneer, marring his handsome face. Blond and green-eyed, his features were even, almost pretty. She guessed him to be a little older than Frances, although the harsh sun had made fine wrinkles near his eyes.

"No, sir. I'm peeling potatoes." She lifted her chin a little to show him she wasn't afraid.

He shrugged and spit into the dirt, mixing it with his boot before pulling a flask from his overalls and taking a long swig, all the while looking at her with those eyes that caused a chill to run up her spine, but she had her task and was more afraid of going back into Mama's kitchen with unpeeled potatoes than staring down this half-stupid gardener. But she needn't have worried. When he was done with his deep swallow of whatever was in that flask, he grabbed his bucket and sauntered back around the corner of the house.

* * *

Later, she arranged lilacs in a vase in the pantry. Mama and Mrs. Bellmont were talking softly, compiling a shopping list for the week's meals; it would require a trip into Jasper, twenty miles away. As Jeselle set the final stem into the vase, the phone just outside the pantry door rang: two short rings followed by a longer ring. This was their ring. They were on something called a party line, which Jeselle thought a strange name since it had nothing to do with parties until Mrs. Bellmont explained that party also meant "a group acting together."

From the crack in the pantry door, Jeselle saw Mrs. Bellmont pick up the earpiece and lean forward slightly. "Hello," she said in her usual lilting, expectant way, as if she assumed it was someone she couldn't wait to speak with. "Nate, is that you? Oh, darlin', it's good to hear your voice. Did the baby come? We've just been on pins and needles here, waiting to hear." She smiled, waiting for good news, but in the next instant her face wilted. Her fingers came to her mouth. "Oh no, Nate. This can't be."

There were a few moments of silence. "Two days ago? Why didn't you call sooner?" Then, another pause, and her hand moved to rest near her heart, cheeks flushing. "You've buried him already? What about the family plot?" Another pause. "Frances said that? Well, it's simply not true. We would've loved him no matter what he looked like. He was family. I hope you know that."

Mrs. Bellmont turned toward the butler's pantry and put the palm of her hand on the wall, leaning over as if she were out of breath. "I see. Well, never mind all that, darlin', you just have to come here for a couple months. Frances can regain her strength."

There was another long moment of quiet. Mama leaned against the sink, facing Mrs. Bellmont, her bare arms crossed over her belly and her shoulders hunched over, as if bracing herself against a cold wind.

"Yes, fine, we'll see you then. Goodbye, darlin'." Mrs. Bellmont placed the earpiece into the phone and turned toward Cassie. "The baby died in Nate's arms. A little boy. Something was wrong with him." Her voice broke. "He could barely tell me. Crying." She put her face into her hands. "Nothing worse than a man crying."

Mama took her over to the breakfast nook and gently guided her into the seat. "Set a bit." She took Mrs. Bellmont's outstretched hand, patting it as she stared up at the ceiling.

Just then Whitmore came shooting into the kitchen from the veranda, hair damp with sweat. He stopped in the doorway. "Mother, what's the matter?"

As if she hadn't heard him, Mrs. Bellmont spoke, "Your sister and Nate are coming."

"Really? That's wonderful news, Mother. But why?"

"To recover from a shock," said Mrs. Bellmont.

CHAPTER 11

Nathaniel

THEY ARRIVED at the lake house four weeks after burying their infant son. "Welcome home," Whitmore greeted them as they walked into the foyer.

"This surely isn't my home, little brother," said Frances. "Pickens County, Georgia, feels awful small now that I'm a New Yorker."

Whitmore shifted his weight from one foot to the other and shoved his hands in his pockets.

"Regardless, we're happy to see you. Y'all must feel ready to drop." Clare's mouth pinched, and wrinkles made creases in the skin above her upper lip. Dark smudges under her eyes marred her perfect skin. She'd aged overnight, Nathaniel thought. Grief and worry had made their marks. "Can I have Jeselle bring you some sweet tea or cookies?"

He was about to decline politely when Frances interrupted, "Mother, we'd like separate bedrooms."

Clare's eyes widened, but whatever she thought of the request was quickly hidden behind her usual placid expression. "I'll let Cassie know to make up your old bedroom for you."

"We're grateful to have a quiet place to come," said Nathaniel. He darted glances at both Clare and Whitmore before looking at his feet. "Truly."

"Wanna fish in the morning?" asked Whitmore

"I don't know," Nathaniel said.

"Well, I'll wait for you in the morning and that way if you decide you want to, I'll be here. All right?"

"All right."

Whitmore crossed the foyer and pulled Nathaniel into an unexpected embrace. Whit's blond hair smelled of sunshine. "Every morning I'll wait." He spoke softly into Nathaniel's ear. "Until you're ready." Whitmore pulled away and ambled down the hallway toward the kitchen.

Nathaniel looked over at Clare. Tears made her eyes glassy. "Nate, none of us know what to do. And there's...there's a party here tomorrow night. It's dreadful timing, and I'm utterly sorry, but I didn't know about—well, the invitations went out months ago."

"Nate can't possibly play at the party, Mother, if that's what you're asking." Frances stood at the mirror and dotted her neck with a silk handkerchief.

"My God, of course not, Frances. Nate knows I'm not asking him to play."

Nathaniel looked over at his wife, catching her eyes in the mirror. "Actually, I'd love to play. I haven't felt like it much since John died, as you can imagine." He turned to Clare. "But it might be good for me. Give me something to work on. How about Gershwin?"

"Only if you want to." Clare gazed at him for a moment before taking his hands. "Oh, my poor boy, you look like you're about to collapse. Go on up to the room you stayed in last time. It's all ready for you."

"Thank you. I'll see you all later for dinner." Then he made his way, one foot in front of the other, hand on the rail, up the wishbone stairs to the guest room where he could be alone. As he closed the door, Frances's voice reached him. "Did you hear him, Mother, talking about it like it was a real baby?"

He collapsed on the bed, kicking off his shoes and placing his arm over his eyes. Not only had he lost his baby son, his wife seemed to have disappeared as well. The woman he'd married had vanished, replaced with a girl he could not recognize—a girl who would no longer share his bed and who seemed to vacillate between vacant and hostile. He suspected she blamed him somehow for John, but he couldn't know for sure because she refused to talk to him about it. All of which added to his grief and sense of isolation.

*   *   *

The next morning, he awakened before sunrise and went to the window. Below, on the veranda steps, sat Whitmore, holding two fishing poles. Nathaniel rested his head against the windowpane. Always, he thought, these choices, these moments, when one decides whether to move forward from the pain or retreat back into it. Life over death. Light over darkness.

He dressed quickly, not bothering to shave or comb his hair. When he arrived in the kitchen, Cassie stood at the stove, stirring something in a large pot, her broad, strong shoulders straight and proud. "There's coffee to take with you." She pointed with her wooden spoon to a large mug on the table.

"How'd you know I'd fish?"

"Two kinds of people. Them that wallow in their own muck and them that keep moving. You and me, we're the keeping moving kind, no matter we're different colors. Terrible thing about the baby, Mr. Nate. Nothin' worse than losing a child." She turned from the stove. "Go on now. The boy's waiting for you. I'll cook something for y'all when you get back."

"Thank you, Cassie." He took the coffee and joined Whitmore on the steps. A glass jar of night crawlers perched precariously on the edge of the top step. Nathaniel picked it up and gestured with it toward the lake. "Think they're biting this morning?"

Whitmore grinned and plucked a blade of grass near his feet. "Only one way to find out. Come on then." He stood and held out a fishing pole. Nathaniel took it, and they crossed the lawn to the lake. The boards of the wooden pier squeaked under their feet. Near the edge, they took off their shoes and socks and rolled up the legs of their trousers before sitting side by side. The April morning light was soft. Slices of early morning sun glimmered through the branches of pines. Unseen birds made a discordant orchestra all around them. They perched their poles between their legs and dangled their legs off the side of the pier just inches above the water.

After a few minutes, Whitmore glanced over at him. "Fish must be sleeping late."

"Guess so."

Nathaniel stuck his pole between two slats of wood and sipped his coffee. Whitmore pulled his line in, checking the hook. The night crawler remained, hanging limp in a picture of defeat.

"I imagined him here, with us, fishing," said Nathaniel.

"Mother, too. She talked about it sometimes. Many times." Water bugs skimmed the lake surface, making rings. "She planted flowers that bloom in the spring. To remember him."

"I figured he'd look like you. I don't know why."

Whitmore tossed his lure back into the water with a flick of his wrist. He held the pole loosely in his hands. "I was going to teach him how to row the boat. Y'know, when he got bigger."

Nathaniel reached over and patted Whitmore's shoulder. "Thank you."

"For what?"

"For not pretending like it never happened."

They were quiet again. A fish jumped in the middle of the lake.

"I'm still here," said Whitmore. "To look after, I mean."

"I know, and I'm grateful."

* * *

After breakfast, Nathaniel bathed and changed his clothes. In the music room at the piano, he spent the morning working on scales and a Gershwin piece he felt appropriate for a gay spring party. The family and servants shuffled by the glass door, but he hardly noticed.

Near noon, Frances came in to ask if he would be joining them for dinner. "Mother says it'll be served at twelve thirty." She wore a light green muslin dress with gathered sleeves and lace around the collar.

"You look pretty. Come sit next to me for a moment." He patted the piano bench.

As if she hadn't heard him, she marched over to the table near the window. "I hate it here. When can we go home?" She picked up a vase, turning it in her hands.

"We just arrived."

She went to the window. "Father isn't coming until later."

Nathaniel returned to the music sheet on the piano. "I'd heard that, yes."

"Well, I don't like it."

"Don't like what?"

"We're just stashed here on the side of this godforsaken mountain."

"It's nice here. I felt terrible at the apartment. It's comforting to be with your mother and Whit."

"I want to go back to New York."

He turned on the piano bench, facing her. "Frances, you need to rest. You've been through a lot."

"I can rest in New York."

"It might help if you found something to distract yourself with. Maybe a book?"

"How dare you! You smug bastard." She hurled the vase at him.

He put his hands up to protect his face but was too late. The ceramic vase hit him in the forehead and then clattered to the floor, breaking in half. He blinked, seeing spots before his eyes as he felt the painful spot with his fingers. Sticky. Blood. "Frances, what's the matter with you? You've hurt me."

She knelt on the floor next to him and began to cry. "I didn't mean to hurt you."

The door to the music room opened. They both turned as Clare and Cassie ran toward them. Frances rose to her feet, retreating to the couch.

"What on earth happened?" asked Clare.

"The vase. Hit my head." Nate dabbed at the wound with his handkerchief.

"Hit your head? How?" asked Clare.

Cassie picked up the two broken pieces. "This here was Mr. Bellmont's mama's vase." Her eyes shot to Frances and back again to the broken vase in her hands.

Frances crossed her arms over her chest. "I dropped it."

"Hold tight, Mr. Nate. I have something I can put on it." Cassie left the room. Clare, using her own handkerchief, dotted at the perspiration on his forehead. "Does it hurt?"

"A little."

Cassie came back with a small jar of white paste. "Made this from some roots and herbs. It'll help it heal up faster." He winced as she smoothed it into the gash.

"Cassie's always digging around in the herb garden in Atlanta and mixing up potions," said Clare. "She's quite clever."

"Like a witch from Macbeth," said Frances.

"Frances," said Clare, "how 'bout you get Nate some sweet tea."

"Because I'm not a maid, that's why." She rose from the couch and walked out the door, slamming it behind her.

He looked over at Clare. She was at the window now, fussing with the tassel that held back one side of the curtains. "Nate, what's happened between you two?"

Shaking his head, he took the cold compress Cassie handed him and put it against the wound. "Since the baby, she's different. I've tried everything, but nothing makes her happy. She's been drinking a lot. I don't know what to do."

"She threw the vase at you, didn't she?" asked Clare.

He nodded. "But she just lost her temper. It's nothing."

Clare held his gaze for a moment before glancing at Cassie. "That's what I said about Frank when it happened the first time."

* * *

Late in the afternoon, resting in his room, he was between a place of wakefulness and sleep when he heard the creak of the door. He rolled over and opened his eyes. Frances stood next to the bed, wearing nothing but a silky dressing gown that clung to her skin. Any remnants of the pregnancy were gone, her limbs slender and frail and her stomach nothing but a cavity between jutting hipbones. "Frances, you've gotten so thin. Try to eat a little today, won't you?"

"I feel sick after a few bites."

His head throbbed. With his fingertips, he felt the gash on his forehead. Darned if it weren't already healing from Cassie's magic potion.

"Nate, are you still angry?" She spoke in her high-pitched, baby kitten voice and knelt at the side of the bed. "I want to make it up to you. It's been long enough since the hospital."

"You mean since the birth of our son?"

She ignored him, but her gray eyes flickered. She untied the ribbon at the collar of her dressing gown.

"I want to talk about the baby, Frances. I think you need to talk about him, too."

"Not now." She untied her dressing gown. It fell to the floor, revealing collarbones so prominent it actually pained him to look at her. He knew she would take the slip off next and let him look at her, before joining him in the bed. Even during the pregnancy this was the way: always a display before the coupling. She loved to have him look at her. He'd become good at lovemaking, too, after a time, learning her body and what gave her pleasure, the same way he had learned the piano all those years ago. He could make her moan with pleasure and beg for more.

He rolled to his side, facing the wall. "I'm resting."

She lifted the sheet off his bare torso and ran her fingertips across his upper back.

"Frances, please, I'm tired. My head hurts."

"C'mon now, don't be that way." Her breath was hot at his ear. She bit the lobe of his ear, gently. "I want you."

He went perfectly still. "Leave me be. Please."

"I'm your wife," she shrieked and dug her fingernails into his upper back, like eight tiny knives. He yelped and rose up out of the bed. She fell like a ragdoll onto the floor. Rising to her knees, she sat in the middle of the braided rug and looked at him with wide, sad eyes.

"We need to talk about what happened—about what is happening, not just numb it with sex." He scooted to the side of the bed, put his feet on the floor, and held out his hands to her. "Talk to me, please, Frances."

"I don't have to defend myself to Saint Nathaniel. All I want is to forget."

"I'm not asking for a defense of your actions, but I damn well deserve more than to be ignored and shunned. I'm in pain too, Frances. This happened to both of us. And today? Throwing a vase at me?"

She buried her face in her hands before looking up at him. "Sometimes I hate you."

He flinched. "I don't even know who you are." It almost sounded like a question, he thought. "I don't even know who you are." He waved his hand toward the door. "Just get out."

Frances's face turned stony. She scrambled up from the floor. "Fine, I have to fix my hair for the party anyway." She left, slamming the door hard enough that the walls of the room shook.

Just get through the party, he thought. Just get through the party. Everything will be better tomorrow.

*   *   *

Later that night it was at the ancient oak near the southwest side of the lake that Nathaniel first believed he heard Frances's throaty cry. The sound might have come from any woman, or it could have been Frances; he couldn't be certain. Questioning whether he'd actually heard the sound or not, he stood immobile for a moment, listening in the way a musician does, hard and carefully. But he heard only crickets, the tinny plops of fish jumping, lake water lapping against the shore. He continued on, his steps unsteady on the round pebbles and dry pine needles on the trail around the lake, his mind alternating between irritation and dread.

No visible moon, and the stars were covered by storm clouds, the only specks of brightness a scattering of fireflies over the water. He held a lantern at arm's length from his body, eyes straining to see any evidence that Frances had been there, calculating how long it had been since he'd seen her in the group that stood under the chandelier while he played at the piano.

It was less than fifteen minutes, he was fairly certain. He'd just finished playing the Gershwin, pleased how it seemed to match the mood of the languorous spring evening. The furniture had been pushed aside in the Bellmonts' ballroom and the piano wheeled in front of the large picture windows. The women were in ball gowns, dripping in jewels and perfume, sipping glasses of vintage champagne brought up from the cellar, huddled together in groups of two or three, listening to the music with only half their attention, reserving the rest for gossip and the keen, cruel vision women had for their counterparts' blunders or physical flaws. The men stood mostly at the bar, watching other men's wives, the music creating an atmosphere of drama and romance in a way the ordinary cadence of language and laughter could not.

Clare floated through the scatterings of applauding friends until she reached Nathaniel where he sat with his toes curled under in his leather shoes, perspiration covering his brow. She said, barely moving her lips, "I saw Frances stumble out the door, toward the lake."

"Drunk?"

"I'm afraid so. Please go make sure she's all right, won't you, darlin'?"

He went out to the veranda. Standing between two kerosene lanterns, he surveyed the garden but saw no one. Taking one of the lanterns, he walked toward the water and looked down the length of the fishing pier. She was not there or anywhere within sight. A zing went up his arm. The hair on the back of his neck stood upright.

The air, surprisingly thick with humidity for April, smelled of sweet, cloying honeysuckle. He coughed and wiped his watering eyes, experiencing an odd sensation that the honeysuckle might choke him, as if it were something sinister, something forbidden, like a desire that must remain hidden. He walked as far as he could around the lake until he came to where the beach ended and it was impossible to go farther. He turned back to retrace his steps, toward the light of the lake house. Again, at the oak tree, he heard a woman's voice. Resting his fingers on the rough bark as if it were a familiar friend, he shut his eyes. The sound came again, fainter this time but loud enough that he knew it was Frances. He couldn't recognize the tone of her voice. Was it conversation? Was it a cry of fear? Or did it ring of pleasure or familiarity? He couldn't be sure.

He shone the lantern toward the wooded crest above. There was a foot-worn path. Heart pounding, he followed it, running, keeping his eyes focused on the rocky and uneven trail to avoid tripping. At the top of the low hill he turned toward the left, searching the dark. The farthest tip of lantern light illuminated a pair of women's shoes. Frances. Frances's shoes. Next to them lay a straw hat, frayed at the edges.

Then he saw two figures, a man and woman intertwined on the ground. In a jumble of thoughts that arranged themselves into a lucid realization, he understood that it was Frances with a man on top of her. He wore a shirt, but his overalls, which even in the dim light Nathaniel could see were dirty, settled around his ankles so that his white backside showed in the lantern light.

Nathaniel cried out, something, perhaps his wife's name, but maybe just a shout of some kind. Later, he wouldn't remember.

Frances turned her head, her eyes surprised and then frightened. She screamed, "Nate, help me."

He heard the man say, "I told you to shut your mouth."

Nathaniel dropped his lantern near the edge of the clearing and lunged toward them, not knowing what he would do, only that he must do something, anything, to get the man off Frances. In that same instant, the man came to his feet, pulling up his overalls and then yanking a knife from his pocket. He waved the knife in Nathaniel's direction, the steel of the blade reflected in the lantern light. Nathaniel hesitated and stepped backward. Suddenly, and with the unsteady movements of a drunk, the man charged at Nathaniel's throat. Nathaniel put his arms up to shield himself, and as he did so, the knife sliced long and deep into his left forearm. He felt a searing pain. Using his good arm, he knocked the knife from the man's hand. It clattered against a rock. Nathaniel called out, "Frances, run home. Get help."

The man came at him again, and this time his hands went around Nathaniel's neck, the attacker's breath smelling of stale whiskey and tobacco. His eyes glinted in the moonlight like a rabid dog's as his hands tightened around Nathaniel's throat, pressing into his windpipe. Nathaniel couldn't breathe. He fought for air, but the man's hands were crushing his neck bones, his windpipe. With all his strength, survival adrenaline coursing, Nathaniel punched quick and hard with the heel of his right hand into the man's ribcage. The man grunted, gasped, and then fell backward, releasing his grip around Nathaniel's neck. Nathaniel didn't wait for him to recover; he ran forward, using every ounce of strength he possessed to kick the man in the ribs. The man bent over double, holding his middle. When the man looked up, he appeared dazed and retreated backward several steps to where the ground sloped downward. Like someone falling off a cliff, he reached into the air for something to hold onto and then staggered toward Nathaniel, grunting like an enraged animal. Nathaniel was readying himself to kick again when the man's foot caught on a large tree root sticking up from the ground. He tripped and fell forward, his head landing on a jagged rock the size of a car's tire. The sound of a sickening crack, and then the man let out a soft moan. Quiet. Nothing but the sound of crickets. Nathaniel moved quickly, grabbing the lantern where he'd dropped it earlier, and knelt next to him. The rock gleamed, covered with blood. The man did not move. Nathaniel felt at his neck with the tips of two fingers. Nothing. No pulse. No breath.

Behind him he heard Frances moving through the dry grass. "Nate?" Her voice seemed unnaturally loud in the darkness.

He pushed himself up, using his right arm. "I told you to get help."

She stood near the oak tree, her hair wild and her eyes wide in a thin face. "I couldn't leave you here. Alone. With him."

He couldn't think, couldn't breathe. "He's dead."

"He forced himself on me." Her voice just above a whisper, she cried, her hands at her mouth.

Nathaniel rose from the ground and grabbed her against him with his uninjured arm, but she moved away from him. Aware of his own ragged breaths, he handed Frances the lantern. Her face appeared almost feverish in the stippled light. "Nathaniel, your arm. It's bleeding."

He looked down and wiped away blood to see the wound, but it quickly filled again. He felt no pain, just numbness that spread from his shoulder to his fingertips. "Frances, I can't move my fingers."

"Let's get Daddy." Frances sounded far away now. "He'll know what to do."

CHAPTER 12

Whitmore

AS THE PARTY hummed along below them, Whitmore and Jeselle perched on the window seat in his bedroom and watched the coming storm rumble toward the house. His room faced the back of the house, with a view of the veranda below (now bursting with party guests), the flower gardens, and expansive lawn. The clouds, smoky purple and fat, were above them now. Without warning, the rain unleashed from the moody clouds in a torrent. Below, on the terrace, the guests froze for a split second and then rushed toward the French doors, crying out in surprise, hands over their heads. Rain pelted the ground, like rapid gunshots against the roof and veranda. Wind blew the curtains aside, bringing the scent of rain on dirt after a long, dry spell.

"Smell that, Jes?" Whitmore touched his fingers to the window screen.

"Rain on red dirt. No other smell like it in the world. It's the scent of new beginnings." She paused, tapping her finger on the screen. "No, that's not quite right. Maybe the smell of second chances? Is that better?"

He smiled, teasing. "I smell only minerals. Metal maybe?"

"Those, too." She smiled back at him. "But I like my description better."

"Me, too. Always."

Lightning lit up the sky. Next came a crash of thunder that shook the house. Jeselle shivered next to him. To Whitmore it made everything seem electric and raw, but he knew it scared Jeselle. With the third bit of lightning, Whitmore instinctively moved closer to her. She held up her arms to him. "Look, goose bumps." Without thinking, he rubbed them, fascinated to see the way her skin returned to smooth under his touch. He moved his gaze to her face, looking at her as if it were the first time. Big, round brown eyes fringed with thick lashes and wide, high cheekbones, then a narrowing at the chin. Heart-shaped, his mother had described it to them once. He'd thought, yes, a heart, of course. What else would she have? Now, she smiled, her dimples appearing on each side of her full mouth. How beautiful she was! A twinge of pain that was almost pleasure throbbed in his chest. Why couldn't he breathe? Was it the air, so thick with humidity, or this lovely girl in front of him? The girl. Always the girl. His heart beat faster, louder. Could she hear it?

"What is it, Whit?"

He shifted, moving his hands from their light grip on her forearms and running the tips of his fingers gently on both sides of her jaw line, letting the feel of her soft face move inside him. So many nights lately he wakened from dreams of holding her, touching every part of her. "Will you marry me someday, Jeselle Thorton?"

She wrinkled her brows and laughed. Why did she think it was funny? Couldn't she see how it was between them? Did she ever dream of him?

"You know that can't ever happen."

His jaw made a clicking sound when he opened his mouth to speak. "I want you to be my wife. You'll write stories, and I'll paint pictures." He closed his eyes, capturing the images, letting them stack one on top of the other like photos in a book. "We'll live in the tree house." He'd just finished his masterpiece two weeks ago. The tree house was meant to be sanctuary of sorts for the two of them. Well, it would be if they could ever get a chance to use it without Cassie calling them back to the main house.

She said, teasing, "Mama says your head's always in the clouds, Whitmore Bellmont." She clicked her tongue like he'd seen Cassie do hundreds of time before.

His chest ached as he gazed unseeing through the screen, fighting tears. "You think Father's right about me? Think there's something wrong with me for liking the things I do?"

Jeselle's full mouth turned up in a smile. "Not wrong, Whit. You're special. I know it, and your mother knows it." She lay back on the pillows of the window seat, pulling her legs up under her.

He reclined on the opposite side of the window seat so they faced each other. "Thanks, Jes."

Jeselle spoke again, her voice soft. "Mama says someday you'll go off to college, and we won't see you again."

"I wish you could come with me. Mother says you're the quickest student she's ever taught, and she taught a lot of them before Father married her."

She tilted her head to one side and looked out the window. Her hands clenched and unclenched. "Mama says not to expect too much from my life. She says I better get used to the idea of serving white folks, 'cause that's all my life's going to be. It's true, Whit, whether we like it or not."

"Doesn't mean it's right." He paused, his heart beating faster, thinking of all the ways in which the world kept Jeselle from the life she deserved. There was much he wished to say, but the feelings of outrage in his young heart were only silent cries, for he couldn't find the words or the ways to express or act upon them. Instead he said, aware that he sounded like a querulous child, "Then why's your Mama always after you to study?"

Her shoulder rose and fell in a quick shrug. "Don't anybody understand Mama, most especially me." She pointed out the window. "Colonel Tate's pink house is all lit up tonight."

"Sure is."

The marble tycoon Colonel Tate had built a dam on Clear Creek, forming Sequoyah Lake. Tate convinced Whitmore's family, along with half a dozen of their Atlanta society friends, to build a summer home on Sequoyah Lake's shores. "Tate's people happened on some marble," Father said to Whitmore, "but our people made something out of nothing, planting those first fields using the sweat of their brows." Whitmore understood, although he would never have dared to comment, that the sweaty brows were really those of the slaves and then the sharecroppers. The days of plantations and agriculture were a thing of the past, but the Bellmont family was considered "old money," the social elite, in a society where that mattered more than anything. Old money begets more money: as a young man, Frank had gone to work for an old family friend at Coca-Cola and subsequently worked his way up to an executive position and was rewarded with stock and a hefty salary to add to the Bellmont wealth. Cotton, sugar, corn, and the land it was grown on had made Frank's antebellum ancestors rich, but a caramel-colored drink had made Frank richest of all.

"Some things aren't right." Whitmore swatted a mosquito that had landed on his arm. How they managed to get inside with the screens on the windows he couldn't explain. Blood smeared his palm.

Her shoulder went up and down in another quick shrug. "I know."

"Because we know better, Mother says it's our responsibility to make changes for the better. I just don't how to do that." He wiped his hands clean on the handkerchief he kept in his pocket.

"Sometimes it makes me tired to think of it. How can one person do anything that matters?"

"Mother says it starts with just one small movement. Like ripples in a lake."

She uncurled her legs so they were now side by side with his. We're like the gingerbread people Cassie baked in the oven, he thought, spreading toward each other until their arms and legs touched.

She sat up. "C'mon, let's go listen in on the party."

"Naw, let's stay here. No one's bothering us for once."

"I want to hear what everyone's talking about."

Swinging his legs from the window seat, he sighed. It was no use trying to deny her anything. He didn't have it in him. "All right, let's go."

They scurried down the hallway to the area directly above the foyer. On the landing of the second floor, a large closet occupied an indentation in the wall. Recently they'd discovered a space at the bottom of the closet big enough for both of them to sit. Intrigued by this secret hiding place, Whitmore had rigged a string that pulled the doors shut from the inside. They had only a limited view through a crack between cabinet doors, but sound carried up clear as day from the bottom of the staircase. They could hear almost everything said from the foyer, much to Jeselle's delight.

"I'm always listening to the world through a crack in a door, Whit," she whispered when they were inside the cabinet. "Mama says no one likes an eavesdropper, but how else am I supposed to know what's going on around here?"

Whit snorted. "I don't know why you want to know everything. I like being oblivious."

"That's because you're a boy. Boys want to know nothing. Girls have to know everything."

His father's immense voice reached them suddenly. "The first sip of this swill tastes like fire, but by the second one, boys, you'll swear it's liquid sunshine right down to the bottoms of your toes." Whitmore buried his face in his hands. They smelled of vanilla. Jeselle. They smelled of Jeselle.

"Amen," one of the men said.

"Best homemade whiskey you'll find from here to Mississippi," Father said. "Damn government telling decent folks how to live; by God, here in the South we have our own way."

Another voice said, "Price of land in Florida doubles every day, boys. Gotta get in while you can."

Whitmore whispered to Jeselle, "That's Joe Harding. He's always talking about things to do to make more money."

"Does he need more?"

"They always want more. Father says that's America."

"Need the cash for that," Dr. Miller said.

"Hell, buy it on margin," said Harding.

"Go with textiles if you're looking for an investment."

"Who's that? I don't recognize his voice," said Jeselle.

"That's Roger Baker, a friend of Father's from his university days."

Colonel Tate said in a gruff voice, louder even than Father's, "Hell, if you boys want something to invest in, I'm building a resort out here, gonna call it a Summer Colony, over in the Burnt Mountain area. A lodge, an eighteen-hole golf course, resort homes on the lake, riding stables, tennis courts. The whole darn place for people like us to enjoy ourselves."

"What does he mean, people like us?" asked Whitmore.

"Rich, white people."

Next, Whitmore heard footsteps coming up the stairs. A pair of fat, lumpy ankles along with a bony, skinny pair that reminded Whitmore of two raw chicken wings in shoes appeared. They halted in front of the railing. Whitmore had a direct view of the women's middles. The skinny one's hand fluttered at her side, pulling at the skirt of her dress. "Oh, I simply despise this dress. The minute I walked in and saw what Clare was wearing I wanted to walk right back out and hide myself under my bed." The hated dress, which was the color of lemons, hung just below the woman's knees. "It looks fine to me," he whispered.

"Not compared to your mother's dress." Her breath smelled like honey. "She always looks the prettiest."

Whitmore heard the snap of a cigarette case and a flick of a lighter, and then the smell of burning tobacco made its way inside the closet. "After all the fuss over bobbed hair it seems everyone's doing it now," said one of the women. Whitmore knew from his sister that only the old ladies still wore their hair long.

The other woman, the one with the fat ankles, spoke next. "What I can't figure is how a man like Nathaniel Fye marries a girl like Frances Bellmont. Did you know he's practically as well known as the president? Clare told me he's going all over Europe next month, playing all the best places over there. He's a Yankee, you know, but still as handsome as they come." She took a drag of her cigarette.

"Well, Frances is pretty as a picture."

"Yes, but that kind of beauty's only skin deep. I've known her all her life. She and my Martha played together when they were young." Her voice lowered, and Whitmore imagined she leaned closer to her friend for emphasis. "She was always trouble. Mean like her daddy."

"I've certainly heard that," said the other one. "Louellen, you know, the dressmaker."

"Oh yes, I know the one. Down on Eighth."

"Right. Well, she told me Frances was practically violent one afternoon when her dress wasn't ready."

The other one answered almost before her friend had finished her sentence. "There were all those rumors during her debutante year. Honestly, bless her heart, I didn't think Clare would ever get her married off after all that."

"Well there's only one reason a girl from this kind of family gets married as quickly as she did. And as far as Flora Waller's coming-out party last year, it is absolutely not a rumor that Frances was found naked in the back of the coat check room with the young man Tuck Waller had picked out for his daughter. The two of them were practically engaged before Frances ruined it. The way she throws herself at men, it's disgraceful."

A snicker, and then, "I'm sure that's true, but still, it's terribly sad what happened to the baby."

"Conceived in sin, I guess God's obligated to punish."

The women moved away then, down the stairs. Whitmore felt Jeselle's hand reach for him, her warm fingers curling around his own. She leaned toward his ear. "Just nasty gossips, that's all they are, Whit."

"Do you think they're right?" he asked Jeselle.

"About what?"

"God punishing Frances for her sins?"

Her voice turned flat. "I don't know anything about God."

"What about Nate? He's a good person."

"So was my daddy."

Whitmore didn't know what to say to that, so he kept quiet.

Next came the sound of Clare's voice, breathless and strange. "Frank, come quick. There's been an accident. It's Nate."

CHAPTER 13

Nathaniel

NATHANIEL RECLINED on a cushioned chaise in Frank's study, staring at the faces of his wife's family. They were all here except for Whitmore. "Clare, where's Whitmore?" he asked. "Is he all right?"

"I asked him to stay upstairs. I was afraid all this would frighten the children." Clare leaned over him. "Doctor Miller's going to examine you."

Frank gave Nathaniel a tumbler of whiskey. "Drink this."

"I don't drink."

"You need it," Frank said. "Will help with the pain."

Nathaniel took a timid sip. It burned his throat; he coughed. Why did anyone drink this?

"More," said Frank.

Frances wrung her hands like she wanted to shake something sticky from the ends of her fingertips. The skirt of her dress had a rip up one side. Strands of her hair were fixed to the red lipstick smeared around her mouth.

Clare looked at her steadily, with an expression that Nathaniel could not interpret. Was it distrust or sympathy? Regardless, Clare moved to her daughter and drew her down onto the window seat. "Shush darlin', you're safe now."

"Frances, the man who did this, had you seen him before?" asked Nathaniel.

Frances's voice matched the trembling of her lips. "I'm not sure. I can't remember a thing."

Clare stood and moved about the study. "He's most likely one of the vagabonds that loiter around looking for summer work." Back at the window, she turned toward Frances, her eyes sharp. "What were you doing up there?"

Frances shrugged like a child, staring at the floor. "Taking a walk."

Clare's next words hit the air like shards of ice. "Why would you do that?"

"I don't know." With the same tremor in her voice, Frances's face crumpled as she began to sob.

Frank set down his drink and sat beside his daughter. "Stop it now." He tapped her forearm with the tips of his fingers, once, twice as if he were checking the temperature on a stove.

"I'm telling you it wasn't my fault," Frances whispered. She looked over at Nathaniel. "Nate, tell her."

Clare's voice dipped low into her register, resigned. "He doesn't need to tell me anything."

Frances raised her head. The tears were gone as quickly as they'd come. "Do you think I care what you think of me?" Her tone matched her mother's. In the next second, she turned her gaze toward the door. Her eyes darted to and fro, manic. "No one can know what almost happened to me. Even though it wasn't my fault, people will talk."

"Well, of course," said Frank. "No one needs to know anything about this."

Before anyone could speak, Dr. Miller came in, carrying a black medical bag. He knelt, examining the wound. "Son, can you move your fingers?"

"No."

"The knife sliced through a tendon, I'm afraid." Dr. Miller reached into his bag and pulled out two bandages.

"What do you think, Doc? It'll heal, right?" Frank stood, lurking near the window, his usual authoritative manner replaced with an uncertain tone.

"I don't know. Needs surgery." The doctor began to wrap Nathaniel's arm, applying pressure to the wound.

Nathaniel searched the doctor's face. "Will I be able to play Carnegie Hall next month?"

The doctor rolled the unused bandage into a ball, not meeting Nathaniel's gaze. "Son, not for me to say." He shifted his gaze to Clare, his voice and eyes grave. "Y'all need to get Nathaniel to a hospital tonight. A surgeon needs to take a look at this arm. I'm just a family physician, and this kind of thing's beyond my expertise." He cleared his throat. "I'll go to the kitchen to use your phone and call ahead to a hospital in Atlanta. I have a surgeon friend there."

Dr. Miller gathered his bag and left the room. Frank came to Nathaniel and patted his shoulder. "Now, Nate, everything's going to be fine." He swallowed the last of his drink and moved to the bar, where he poured himself another.

"Clare, we need to call the sheriff. Someone needs to know there's a dead body up there." Nathaniel's voice sounded tinny and unfamiliar inside his own head. Had he spoken this out loud? Had the lights dimmed? Everything seemed to have a gray film over it.

They all stared at him as if he'd said something odd or incomprehensible. "A man is dead. Do you understand?"

"It was an accident," said Frances, small now on the bench. Had she shrunk? Would she disappear altogether?

Finally Frank waved his hand like he was swatting a mosquito. "Don't you worry 'bout that, Son. We'll take care of everything."

CHAPTER 14

Jeselle

JESELLE AND WHITMORE, forbidden by Mrs. Bellmont to come downstairs, watched the front of the house from Mrs. Bellmont's study. The guests left, one by one, either on foot or in cars that lurched and weaved down the dirt road. After they were all gone, Nate, cradling his arm against his chest and followed closely by Dr. Miller, got into the Rolls Royce, where Martin was waiting behind the wheel. "Something's happened to his arm, Whit," she said.

"Has he broken it?" asked Whit.

She didn't answer. The Bellmonts' car disappeared into the darkness just as another car sped up the driveway, parking in the spot just vacated. Jeselle leaned closer to the window, then gasped. It was the sheriff. The car's engine went quiet, and a second later the sheriff got out as Mr. Bellmont approached.

Shaking, Jeselle reached for Whit's hand. His palms were sweaty. Why wouldn't anyone tell them what had happened?

The sheriff was a tall, skinny man with a handlebar mustache. A wide-brimmed hat drooped low on his forehead. Mr. Bellmont shook the sheriff's hand. They spoke for a moment, heads together, until Mr. Bellmont pointed toward the lake. The sheriff nodded and took off his hat, holding it near his chest and gazing toward the ground as if listening intently. Mr. Bellmont looked around, to each side of him and behind him, like Jeselle and Whit when they stole an extra cookie from the jar, and pulled out a wad of bills from his jacket pocket. He handed them to the sheriff, who stuffed the money in his pocket like it was hot and put his hat back on before getting in his car and driving away.

"Why did Father give the sheriff money?" asked Whit.

"To get him to hide something?"

"What did Frances do?" asked Whit. "It has to be Frances."

"I'm going to sneak downstairs. Maybe I can figure out what's happening."

Whitmore turned back to the window. "I'll wait here. I want to be sure to be here when Nate gets back. In case he needs me."

Jeselle had a feeling he wouldn't be back tonight but didn't want to say that. She walked down the hall, passing by the bedrooms. Frances's door was open an inch. She stopped, watching for a moment. Frances sat at her dressing table combing her hair and looking at herself, making pouty lips and examining herself from all different angles.

Downstairs were the remnants of a party: empty glasses, a forgotten sweater on the railing, a dropped earring by the coat closet. The extra servants hired for the occasion collected glasses, emptied ashtrays, and mopped the floors. Nathaniel's piano was still in the middle of the room, the bench askew and the cover propped open like it was waiting for her master to return at any moment.

She found Mama and Mrs. Bellmont huddled together near the kitchen sink, speaking in low voices, with their backs to the doorway. Mrs. Bellmont clung to the edge of the sink as if she might fall over otherwise. Jeselle made herself invisible, hiding behind the open door and watching through the crack.

Clare spoke in a halting voice, explaining everything to Mama. Frances was attacked on one of the trails. Just in time, Nathaniel had come upon them, but the man stabbed him, injuring his arm.

Jeselle held her breath, thinking of Nathaniel cradling his arm. She began to pray silently. *Please, God, let his hand be all right.* But then, Mrs. Bellmont said the most terrifying thing of all—something unimaginable.

"While they were struggling, the man fell and split his head open on a rock. He's dead."

Mama's hands were at her mouth. "Dead?"

"Yes, and Cassie, the worst part is, Frank and Doc Miller went up there, to...to see about the body." She let out a long, shaky breath. "It's Fred Wilder."

"That worthless gardener? He was here this morning, lazy as ever." Mama looked toward the garden, as if she could see Fred Wilder there, pulling weeds. "Lawd have mercy."

Jeselle's breath caught. That very afternoon she had been in Mr. Bellmont's bedroom, tidying and making the bed up with fresh linens, while the rest of the house took a rest. Using the footstool, she dusted above the window frame and along the curtain rod. Like Whit's room, Mr. Bellmont's faced the back of the house, and from up there she could see almost the entire garden. It was then that Jeselle noticed Frances talking with someone behind the large magnolia bush. Jeselle squinted, curious, and was surprised to see it was Fred Wilder. Seeing him always brought a shiver. Now Frances was waving her hand in the air, gesturing at something. Probably giving him instructions on the flowers, as if she knew anything about them, Jeselle thought. They were the perfect pair. He's stupid, and she's mean.

The thought of him dead made her dizzy and weepy and anxious all at once.

Mrs. Bellmont looked out the window too, inching closer to Mama. "I thought it was a vagabond or one of those drifters that come through here. But Mr. Wilder, well, that's a different thing altogether. Have you noticed how handsome he is...was?"

"I suppose, if you think lazy is handsome."

"Frances did, I can tell you that."

"Oh, Miz Bellmont, no. You think it's the same as two years ago? At the Waller girl's party?" Mama, who rarely sounded shocked, did so now. What had Frances done, thought Jeselle? But even as she asked the question, despite her age, Jeselle knew. Nate cradling his arm. Fred Wilder dead. Frances. It all led back to her.

Neither of the women spoke for a moment. In the distance, an owl's lonesome hoot caused Jeselle to shiver as she let out her breath, realizing she'd been holding it for God only knew how long. Finally, Mrs. Bellmont broke the silence.

"I thought we were past all that, what with Nate." Jeselle heard the tears in her voice. "I thought we'd have a baby this summer and it would stop all her foolishness. Nate's a good man, Cassie. As good as they come."

"Yes, I know, Miz Bellmont."

"Doc Miller says he might not play again."

"No, no, it can't be," said Mama. Again, with the tone Jeselle had never heard before.

What was to become of any of them, she wondered.

PART THREE

From Jeselle Thorton's journal.

August 20, 1933

I woke from a dream, one that comes again and again, of men in white hoods and fire. I listen between cracks. My dreams are haunted.

Years ago voices came from the study. I moved behind the door, eavesdropping. Mr. Bellmont sat in his chair by the fire, surrounded by a half-dozen men.

The men were discussing business and the threat of unions. Mr. Bellmont ranted that they were all Communists threatening the very existence of America. He then mentioned something about Catholics, which caused an eruption from one of his friends. "Damned Catholics should be run out of the country."

They talked of this for a moment and then went back to unions. Mr. Bellmont said the unions were targeting Negroes to join, knowing they were vulnerable. Someone began to talk about the Klan, saying that all good southern white men should take the pledge if they wanted to make this country what it should be. Mr. Bellmont balked at that. "Idiots, farmers, and ignorant trash all of them. They helped the damned prohibitionists outlaw whiskey." Then, everyone talked at once, each man defending his own particular position. A few came out against the Klan, others for it. There was talk of lynching and burned crosses used as warnings. All for the name of Jesus, one said, to defend the righteous Christians of the earth.

We sing and worship that same Jesus every Sunday in our black church across town. Can he really think God only loves white people?

I thought about poor white men being more attracted to the Klan than rich ones. I believe it has something to do with the bitter quality of poverty. It seeps into a person's soul, all that worry about where your next meal might come from or how you'll keep the roof over your head. That scratching and suffering makes you see all that others have that you do not and twists around inside your gut like poisoned stew until it spews out as hatred.

Mrs. Bellmont came from poor white people over in Mississippi. Her daddy died before she was born and her poor worn-out mama was dead by the time Mrs. Bellmont turned three, so her grandmother brought her up. They were poor and hungry a lot of the time, but Mrs. Bellmont went to school every day, no matter what. So I guess that even though her skin is a different color than mine, she knows that to be poor is the same all over and that only education can release you. One day when Whit was drawing one of those red-bellied woodpeckers in the margins of his paper instead of writing his spelling words, Mrs. Bellmont told us that her grandmother insisted she go to school instead of going to work taking in laundry or sewing to help out the family. Her grandmother knew Mrs. Bellmont was smart and that the best way for her to get out of her situation was to study hard and pass the teacher examination.

But it's not only education that can change a person's circumstance. One person's kindness can change your life, too. Look what Mrs. Bellmont's done for me.

I wish I could ask Mrs. Bellmont how it feels to be rich after being hungry for so long. I wonder if you still feel like the same person if your circumstances change? Does your character remain the same no matter what kind of house you live in or food you eat? Does all that money make you feel better, stronger, more important than you used to be? Or are you always the same poor waif, thief, slob, or angel you once were, even as your fortunes change? Are you the same to God?

•

CHAPTER 15

Jeselle

JESELLE BREATHED IN the smells of morning. Simple scents of the lake house kitchen held the familiarity of home, of family. Four bowls of grits sweetened with maple syrup and butter sat steaming next to the stove. Bread baked in the oven, oh, that sweet, yeasty smell that was like no other. Mama's latest concoction steamed in a pot on the stove, smelling of mint and rosemary with a hint of rosehip. Mama chopped fresh herbs into flecks, the tea strainer waiting next to a cup and saucer. The morning light came in white slants through the windows, hinting at autumn, only weeks away.

Jeselle was just fixing to call for him when Whitmore came in from outside, smelling of young man's sweat and the air that pushed against him as he rowed his boat in the morning sunshine. Tall and wide-shouldered, with unruly hair the color of autumn hay, his cheeks flushed pink from activity. She felt small and girlish next to Whitmore's brawny vigor, because although she was fully grown at eighteen, Jeselle remained petite, no taller than five-foot-four, a full head shorter than her mother.

Mrs. Bellmont was on the veranda, watering the gold and orange zinnias she'd planted in boxes along the landing. Her wide-brimmed sunhat shadowed her face with mottled squares of light. Jeselle called out to her from the window, "Breakfast's ready, Mrs. Bellmont."

"Jes, do you see the hummingbirds? They've come for my hibiscus."

"Yes, it's wonderful." Several hummingbirds hovered over the hanging hibiscus, drinking the sweet nectar.

"They're beautiful. Just perfection, don't you think?" Mrs. Bellmont emptied the last of the water from the watering can and set it aside before heading toward the kitchen.

Whit didn't sit. He ate his bowl of grits standing by the big table in the middle of the kitchen, his feet shifting as if he stood on hot ground. At the stove, Mama poured hot water over the tea strainer. "Try this, Miz Bellmont. More lemongrass, less mint."

"Thank you, Cassie." Mrs. Bellmont joined Jeselle at the table.

Whit finished his grits and took his bowl to the sink. The spoon clinked against the bottom of the sink as he turned toward them. "Jes needs to learn how to drive a car." No one said anything. Jeselle's eyes darted to Mama, who stared at Whit. A hummingbird flew up to the sink window, hovering with seemingly invisible wings. "I'll teach her myself."

"Too dangerous." Mama pointed her wooden spoon at Whit like a weapon. "Nothing good can come from a girl running around in a car."

"She should know how to drive, Cassie," said Mrs. Bellmont gently. "The child needs to know the ways of the modern world." She gazed out toward the lake, quiet for a moment. "We don't want her left behind like us because she doesn't know how to do what others are learning every day."

"A white boy teaching a black girl to drive?" Mama gestured with the wooden spoon toward the road. "What if someone saw them? What about Mr. Bellmont?"

"He'll never know, as long as the kids are careful," said Mrs. Bellmont.

Whitmore put up a hand, like he was commanding silence. "Listen here, I don't want the three of you up here alone when none of you can drive."

They all stared at him now, not one of them able to think of how to respond to this firm statement from their placid boy.

"I mean it, now." His voice was firmer than it had been the moment before. "What if something happened to one of you?"

"What do you mean, Whit, up here alone?" said Mrs. Bellmont.

He pulled an envelope from his shirt pocket. "It came."

Mrs. Bellmont dropped her teacup into the saucer. Green liquid spilled and pooled around the cup. "Princeton?"

"Yes, Mother. I've been accepted." The muscle at his jaw clenched.

Jeselle's stomach dropped. She pushed away her grits. The hummingbird hovered outside the window by the breakfast nook now, its invisible wings loud like tiny jackhammers.

"Oh, darlin', that's wonderful," said Mrs. Bellmont.

"I won't go without Jes knowing how to drive." He crossed his arms over his chest, his gaze fixed on Mama.

Mama set the wooden spoon next to the stove. "She has to keep up with her chores."

"I'll need mornings," he said.

Mama raised an eyebrow and crossed her arms over her chest and stood taller. "That right?"

"That's right." He puffed out his chest.

Like two peacocks, thought Jeselle.

"Mother, I want you all to have a way to get away from Father. I won't be here to...there's Father, you see, and I need to know you can all leave if you need to."

"Fine." Mama turned back to the stove.

Just then, a thump from the veranda caused them all to turn toward the yard. Mrs. Bellmont rushed to the window. "Oh dear, something's happened to one of the hummingbirds."

Jeselle crossed to look. A hummingbird lay lifeless next to a pot of zinnias.

"Is it dead?" asked Mrs. Bellmont.

By then Whit had reached the veranda and knelt over the bird. He picked it up and carried it into the house. "Something's poisoning them, Mother. I'm finding dead birds all over the yard." He looked over at Mrs. Bellmont. "Sorry, Mother, I didn't want to tell you. Cassie and I can't figure out what they're eating that's killing them."

"It's too awful thinking of all these poor birds drinking or eating something they like that ends up killing them," said Mrs. Bellmont.

"Maybe Mr. Whit can find us another book on plants once he goes off to Princeton," Mama said.

Whit grinned at her. "I'll do my best, Cassie."

Mama smiled back at him in a way that seemed both a peace offering and a warning. "Well, see that you do." She picked up her wooden spoon and pointed at the dead hummingbird. "Now get that nasty thing out of my kitchen. Only dead birds in this kitchen are ones that go in a pot."

"Cassie, you're awful," said Mrs. Bellmont.

But they all laughed as Whitmore headed outdoors to bury the poor little bird, dead too soon.

*   *   *

"I've never been tempted to curse, Whitmore Bellmont, but learning this clutch just might make me start." Stalled on a deserted dirt road several miles from the lake house in the Bellmonts' Rolls Royce, Jeselle felt she might start to cry. "If I ruin your father's car he's likely to skin me alive."

He grinned. "You're much improved. Try it again."

She let the clutch up slowly while pressing down on the gas pedal. It was too much. They lurched forward and then stalled. Rust-colored dust drifted in billows onto the shiny mahogany dashboard. "Ridiculous car." She pounded the steering wheel with her fist. "I can't do it."

"Of course you can. One more try."

She pushed the clutch pedal down to the floor and turned the key. The car roared to life. Again, she let the clutch up as she pushed on the gas. This time they inched forward. Excited, she pressed the gas pedal farther to the floor, and the car leapt forward, fast, the back tires throwing rocks and pebbles in the air. "Oh no!" She slammed on the brake. The car stopped with a heave and a sad, explosive sputter.

Whitmore laughed.

She looked over at him, annoyed, but then a giggle escaped, and she was lost in it. They laughed until they were breathless. "Well, you got the car to move, at least," he said after he caught his breath. "It's a good beginning."

By the end of the first week, she had conquered the cursed clutch. At the beginning of the second week, they ventured farther down the dirt road, between sections of forest thick with pines and oaks and dogwood trees. The car hummed, and the scent of honeysuckle and azaleas wafted in through the open windows. Their breath caught as they realized they'd reached the peak of the mountain. "Stop," said Whitmore. "Let's get out and look."

They stood at the mountaintop. As far as they could see were rolling hills of green meeting the deep blue sky with a couple of clouds floating about like puffs of shaving cream. Whitmore reached over and took Jeselle's hand. "Gives me a lonesome feeling. I don't know why."

"Makes you feel small."

"Are we going to talk about my leaving?"

"What's there to say?"

They drove farther down the road until they came upon a small clearing and a worn footpath into the dark forest. She pulled the car to the side of the road, and they sat for a moment with the windows down. Red-bellied woodpeckers' trills and sparrows' delicate chirps and jays' proud squawks surrounded them. The breeze rustling in the pine needles sounded like the wings of hundreds of fairies moving together in a collective rhythm.

"You want to see what's down the path?" asked Whitmore.

"I don't know. What if someone lives there?"

"What if it's something beautiful?"

So they climbed out of the car and began down the path. They walked into the cool shade of the forest, the smell of pine and moss stronger. Their eyes took a moment to adjust to the filtered light through the branches that made haphazard patterns on ferns and sapling pines. After a short distance, the trees parted, revealing a grassy bank and shallow creek that burbled clear water over pebbles and stones. Across the water several young pines surrounded a tall oak. Knowing at once what the other thought, they took off their shoes, wanting nothing more than to feel the cool water between their toes. It felt as good as she imagined, although the bottom of the creek was slippery as they crossed the water into the shade of the oak. The fallen, dry pine needles made a soft blanket. They reclined against the rough bark of the oak and put their feet back in the stream.

Whitmore had a small leather case with him. He opened it and took out a pencil, his sketchbook, and a book, which he handed to her. "Thought we might have a respite today so I grabbed your book from the table."

"A respite? That's a mighty fine word."

He grinned, rolling up his sleeves. "Yes, it is."

She watched as he began to sketch a wildflower with purple blossoms that looked like falling stars. His forearm rested on the paper, and the muscles flexed as his pencil moved in sure darts and lines and curves.

How she wished for those hands on her skin, to feel how he might mold her into something beautiful.

These yearnings for the feel of Whit's skin next to hers, flesh upon flesh, muscle on muscle, had swooped in and consumed her swiftly and without warning. It was a summer ago now, a June morning on the first scorching day of the season. She stood on the footstool in Whitmore's bedroom at the lake house, dusting cobwebs from the ceiling that only Mama could see. Whitmore was in the rowboat on the lake, nearing the dock with steady, even strokes of the oars. When he reached his destination, he grabbed the rope tied to the bow and jumped to the dock. His shirt and hair dripped from perspiration onto weathered boards as he leaned over to tie up the boat. He pulled his shirt over his head and used it to wipe his damp face, gazing out over the lake. Something caught his attention, and he turned, shielding his eyes from the sun with his hand, watching, motionless, like an animal in the forest might when sensing danger or prey. What he saw, she could not say. Perhaps it was an eagle or a hawk, perhaps only a sway of a tree's branch, or something as small as a butterfly hovering in the midmorning light. But it was something of the natural world that gave him pause, and it occurred to her, watching his tranquility, that he was as much connected to the ebb and flow of the mountain as its natural inhabitants, like he'd come from the sky and soil and water. And the simple beauty of this caused a stirring within her. The real world faded in an instant; she was lost in the imagining. Her hands splayed against his bare torso, feeling his muscles ripple beneath her fingertips. He pulled her to him, smelling of sweat and salt. His mouth hovered over hers for a moment before he kissed her.

The dust rag fell from her grasp. Her hands went to her mouth. Her heart beat hard in her chest. What was this? Wickedness. Devil thoughts. What had she done, letting this into her mind? The nature of their relationship, unexamined thus far in her young life, changed in the instant it took her to envision skin upon skin. And now it was here, in the room with her, this desire for him. He was no longer simply Whit: her anchor in a chaotic world. He was a man. A man she wanted.

All these thoughts blazing in her mind like the hot afternoon sun, she peeled her gaze from the window and hopped to the floor, scurrying to the next task, changing the linens on all the beds and polishing the silver faster than she'd ever done before. At lunch Mama examined her with furrowed brow. "Don't know what's gotten into you today. You're a little ball of fury."

"Why, Mama, because usually I just flit about?"

"Jeselle Thorton, you watch your mouth."

"Sorry," she mumbled and forced herself to eat the bowl of butter beans that tasted like sand. After lunch, she pulled the rug from the music room and draped it over the veranda railing and whacked it like the devil was in the dust particles. With each wallop of her rug beater, she prayed to forget the thoughts she'd had that morning.

And then it came to her, plain as anything. This devil had made his way into Whit a while ago. She couldn't be certain how long. But she understood with new clarity, the furtive glances and the way his lids went half closed when he looked at her sometimes.

Now, here by this creek, he watched her this same way, having taken his eyes from the downward-looking purple flower to her. "Jes, what is it? Is the book no good?"

"Just daydreaming." She glanced down at the book she held between her hands. "Anyway, I finished this last night." The Hemingway novel, *A Farewell to Arms*: a tale of doomed lovers and war and a dead baby. Nate had given it to Mrs. Bellmont the last time he'd visited. For hours last night after she'd finished the book, Jeselle remained awake, thinking of Nate and Frances and of the events on that terrible night.

"It's a heartbreaking story." Her voice caught in the back of her throat. "Don't read it."

"Mother said so, too."

"Why does life have to be so cruel?"

"I don't know." He tossed a pebble into the stream. "I don't want to leave. You know that, don't you?"

"Doesn't matter. You have to go."

"Jes." He held her gaze. A current traveled between them like the lightning that jolted northern Georgia on countless summer nights.

She shook her head, trembling. "No, Whit." And then, as if everything between them was benign, she untangled her legs, which were crisscrossed under her dress, and stood, pointing to the car. "We best be going. Mama will have a fit, we've been gone so long."

*   *   *

Jeselle heard the loud chirp of a cricket from the bottom rung of the ladder up to the tree house. When she reached the landing, Whitmore was there, his long legs stretched out from one side of the small room to the other. The days at the end of summer had ambled and drifted in the midst of the dirt road drives and peach pie and lingering moments on the veranda when the orange and pink twilight was so lovely it made Jeselle ache in the back of her throat. The days that seemed so numerous, that might never end, were now gone, stolen in moments already forgotten. Whitmore would leave tomorrow for New Jersey.

He held up a package wrapped in tissue paper, no bigger than the palm of his hand. "For you."

"A goodbye present?"

"No, just something to keep while I'm at Princeton." The sound of the cricket ceased, replaced by the rustle of pine needles in the surrounding trees.

"I'm supposed to be helping Mama."

"Please, Jes, just come up. Open it."

"I can't be gone but a minute." She climbed all the way in and settled on the floor, sitting cross-legged. She unwrapped the package. It was a small painting: a portrait of her.

"I wish it was bigger," he said.

"But I have to have one I can hide. Isn't that right?"

"From Father, yes."

"From Mama, too. From everyone, Whit."

"You sound angry."

"Everything makes me angry lately." The tissue paper made a crinkling sound as she wrapped it around the painting. "Mama sees how you look at me."

"I know. She's happy I'm going."

Neither spoke for a moment. The three-quarter moon shone brightly between the slats of the tree house roof. A single tear escaped from her eye, falling on the package in her hands, making a hole in the tissue paper. "I'd rather have a painting of you."

He ran a hand through his hair; the spot under his eye twitched. "Not sure I could do a self-portrait."

"Why not?"

"Can't see myself."

"I can see you."

"I know, Jessie." His voice was gruff. "Sometimes it's the only way I know I'm here." Outside the doorway, fireflies glittered, prancing about in the late August air. "I'll write twice a week."

"I'll be sure to get the post before Mama." She hugged her knees to her chest.

"I can tell you everything we do. You and Mother can order the textbooks and study here."

She nodded, resting her forehead on her knees. "All right."

"Don't say it like that."

"Like what?"

"Like this world's already beat you." He took her hand. "Please."

She looked up, almost defiant. "I've never once complained. You know that?"

He nodded. "Yes."

"And I won't."

An owl hooted from a tree close by. Whitmore shifted but continued to hold her hand. "Jes, I have something to say to you."

"Don't." She put her forehead back on her knees.

"I have to. What if something happened to me and I never said it?"

"Please, don't."

"I love you."

She felt the tears coming, the kind that started in her belly and came out as shaking sobs and hiccups. "No good can come of it. You know that as well as I do." They'd never spoken of it, and words gave love a power, a realness that couldn't be drawn back into hiding, like taking a lid off a canning jar full of fireflies. Once set free, they never returned.

He drew her onto his lap like she was nothing but a limp rag doll. "Please don't cry," he whispered, wiping the tears from her cheeks with his thumbs. He looked into her eyes like there was an answer there for him, so close she could almost taste his mouth, imagining the soft plumpness of his lips.

His gaze moved to her mouth, no more than a sliver of air between them. She closed her eyes. He would kiss her, and she would let him. Nothing else mattered more than this.

And then, Mama's voice called from the veranda so that it echoed in the moonlit night. "Jeselle." Just once. But it was enough for her to know that Mama had felt the heat and longing from where she stood on the veranda, searching with an all-encompassing ray like the beam from a lighthouse on a foggy night that surveys and sees every aspect of a landscape.

"I have to go, Whit. I'm sorry."

He loosened his grip from around her waist. She scrambled from his lap, toward the entryway.

Climbing down the ladder, she felt the weight of Whit's gaze as strong as the invisible rope that Mama yanked with all her might.

*   *   *

Jeselle, Whit, and Mrs. Bellmont left for the train station in Tate at midmorning. Whit drove them there; Jeselle, now in the backseat, was to drive home. They pulled out onto the highway, heading down the mountain. The heat felt suffocating. They opened all the windows, making it impossible to converse, but the air felt good on Jeselle's overheated skin. Mrs. Bellmont's perfectly set curls blew this way and that until she tied a yellow scarf around her head. Jeselle wanted to stick her head out the window and close her eyes and let that warm wind take her away until she reached the cool spray of the sea. But instead she peered at the back of Whit's head. The left side of his hair blew up, giving her the idea that those strands were happy to have escaped the heaviness of the pomade he'd carefully combed in, which made those little ridges all along his head. She hated this flattened, slick hair, his going-to-a-new-world hair, and was ridiculously pleased to see that the pomade couldn't hold up against the Georgia wind.

Mama had cut his hair yesterday, so there was a strip of white on the back of his neck where the sun hadn't reached during the hours he'd spent outdoors. That pale section of skin, like the soft underbelly of an animal, made him appear vulnerable to her, instead of the strong, limber athlete she knew him to be. He sat stiffly, upright, the muscles in ropy lines on each side of his neck, as if he were steeling himself for the inevitable farewell. Jeselle's fingers twitched, wanting to touch them. She could simply sit forward an inch or two, she thought, and rest her hand against his skin that she imagined was slightly damp.

Nearing the town of Jasper, Whit slowed the car.

"I do hope your roommate will be pleasant," said Mrs. Bellmont.

"I'm sure he will be, Mother. Don't worry. I'll be fine." His voice was flat, like he didn't care one way or the other.

"You'll write to us right away?" Mrs. Bellmont asked.

"I surely will, Mother."

"I wish that you'd gone to Auburn. Or Duke. A good southern school like your father wanted."

"Closer to home," he said in a tease that sounded miserable.

"I know. It's better this way. Farther from your father." Mrs. Bellmont sighed and adjusted her scarf. Her voice was bright, overly so, Jeselle thought. All of them pretending to be happy. "I'm thrilled about Princeton. Of course I am. I dreamed of it for you." Mrs. Bellmont's face crumpled and tears came to her eyes, her voice quiet now, with a tinge of the grief that always seemed near since that awful summer when the baby died and Nate's career was ruined. "But now, well, I wish you and Jes were still small."

Jeselle looked out the window. Tears were contagious. Stay strong, she thought. Like Mama.

They drove through the middle of town. Several white women, packages in their arms, chatted in front of the drugstore. A small red-haired boy, cheeks crimson from the heat, walked a fluffy black dog on a leash. The Ten Commandments etched on the side of a marble building gave warning to the masses. "Thou shall not covet…" Did God make this proclamation for little black girls who wanted to go to school? Was it a sin to covet what Whit had?

"I'm glad you learned to drive," Mrs. Bellmont said to Jeselle. "Sometimes your mama's so stubborn, I wasn't sure."

"There's nothing to it," Jeselle said. "I could teach you."

"No, no. Frank would never allow it."

They drove ten miles south, to Tate. Whitmore parked around back by the cemetery, and they walked around to stand on the platform. Two other clumps of people also waited on the platform, both groups surrounding young men holding suitcases. They heard the loud, high whistle of the train long before it came chugging down the track, black smoke rising in the air. The conductor waved his hat in greeting as the cars of the train slowed before coming to a loud, horrific stop in front of the platform.

When it was time, Whit hugged Mrs. Bellmont and nodded at Jeselle. "I'll see you both in a couple of months," he said. Mrs. Bellmont's eyes were full again, and she wiped the escaping tears from her cheeks. Jeselle set her gaze on her own shoes. "You both write me now."

"We will," said Mrs. Bellmont.

"You too, Jes?" he asked.

"Of course," she said.

"Goodbye then." He turned, suitcase in hand, and trudged up the stairs of the long, black train.

"I feel like he won't be back," she said to Mrs. Bellmont.

"Nonsense. He'll be back for Christmas. It's hardly anytime at all." But her voice was flat, like she didn't believe it herself.

They were silent, searching the train's passenger car for the appearance of his face.

"Wish we were going with him, baby girl."

"He said he'd send us a list of everything he's doing. Maybe we could get the textbooks."

"Sure." Mrs. Bellmont wiped under her eyes.

"It's not the same," said Jeselle. "I know that."

"No, I suppose not."

Don't say it like that, Jeselle thought. She couldn't bear it, to hear Mrs. Bellmont defeated by this world, too.

Whit was at one of the windows now. He took off his hat and placed it over his chest, watching them. The train began to move, slowly, with a great moan and gusts of steam. Mrs. Bellmont waved with her lace handkerchief. Jeselle stood motionless beside her, never taking her eyes from Whit. His car went around the bend in the tracks and was swallowed by pines. Gone from view, the whistle blew, lonesome in the close, muggy air.

CHAPTER 16

Nathaniel

THE METRONOME on the piano kept rapid time. Nathaniel matched the clicks of the metronome with bobs of his head, standing in the peripheral vision of his student, Sally, as she played Chopin's *Revolutionary Etude, Op. 10, No. 12.* Always a crowd pleaser at the annual Alabama College for Women recital, the piece was based on simple arpeggios and recurring hand movements. Most of his pupils could play it decently after some practice, even with their small, female hands. But poor Sally was hopeless. It was pacing, mostly. A sturdy, blonde, fresh from her family's dairy farm, she had energy like an earnest, rambunctious puppy and short, thick limbs with fingers to match. When she entered his office, he had the urge to put away Frances's photograph and the papers stacked neatly on his desk in case Sally careened unexpectedly and fell over. Sally, hunched over now with her brow furrowed, plunked and pummeled the keys in a haphazard rushing and then slowing so that it felt to Nathaniel like he was on a boat in a stormy sea.

He looked out his office window. It was a glorious September day, blue sky over brick buildings with white pillars. Matching brick paths wound between expansive lawns, scattered with young women chatting or studying under the shade of oaks and pines. Walt, his former manager, had urged him to consider the position as a professor in Walt's hometown of Montevallo, Alabama. This was after Nathaniel had spent a year watching the birds fly outside his New York City apartment while the world crashed below. Black Thursday had come on that dark day in October 1929, and nothing had been the same since. The world slid further and further into despair.

Given that, Walt urged him to consider a steady job in the small college town as a way to move forward. "Alabama College for Women is the place to send proper young ladies to study post high school. You'll teach debutantes how to play the piano while they look for a young man to marry. Just temporary, while you figure out something to do next."

Just temporary had turned into three years. This is the way, he thought. Time tumbles along without any effort at all. What had seemed alien at first was now routine, was now a life. A music professor living in the small, quaint college town of Montevallo, Alabama? Surely he could not have predicted it, yet, here he was.

A few leaves on the oak tree outside his office remained, flapping like the sad wings of a dying butterfly, holding on when the others had fallen and been swept up by the groundskeeper into piles.

"Was it better today, Professor Fye?" Sally asked when she finished, her wide, pale blue eyes hopeful.

"Much better, Sally. Keep up the practice, and you should have it mastered in no time."

She sighed, sliding off the bench. "You're only saying that to be kind. I know I'm dreadful." She swept a section of her hair behind her ear.

He went to the bookshelf, leafing through the phonograph records until he found a collection of Chopin pieces. "Take this and listen to it with your friends tonight. Pay special attention to the pacing."

"Professor Fye, I know we have months left in the semester, but do you think I'll pass? I need this credit to graduate, and I'm supposed to get married next summer."

"It's only necessary that you try. I understand you're not a music major. Anyway, your effort's been exemplary. Keep trying, Sally, and all will be well."

She smiled and clasped her hands over her chest. "Oh, thank you. I'm so relieved. Professor Fye, one of the other girls told me you sometimes play with your right hand." Her eyes skirted to his left hand and then back to his face. "Won't you play the right hand part for me, just so I can hear how it's supposed to be played?"

"If you think it will help."

She slid from the bench and stood by the open window as he took her place at the piano. The breeze brought the smell of camellias as he played the notes with his eyes closed, hearing the left hand in his mind.

There were tears in her eyes when he was finished. "It's awful pretty when you play it."

"Thank you." He rose from the bench. "Now, scoot along. I've two more students to hear before I get to have my lunch."

Tuesday. After Sally, there was Matilda, and then Gertie. She was the best of his students, not particularly gifted except that she adored music and loved playing, and therefore put in the hours of practice that were necessary to improve. After Gertie's lesson, he would have lunch and then teach his music appreciation class, ending the day by grading papers at his desk for an hour before heading home to see how Frances had fared. This was a day in a long string of days so similar to the others it was impossible to remember later almost any detail that would distinguish it.

That afternoon he walked home, enjoying the lushness of the gardens and the moderate temperatures September had blessed them with. Tall oaks lined streets named after trees and shrubs. Homes, a mixture of Victorian, colonial, and modern bungalows in the Craftsman style, sat on small lots with tidy, lush gardens.

They lived on Vine Street in a compact but attractive bungalow. Roses, lilacs, and azalea bushes lined a fenced backyard. A maple in the backyard provided needed shade in the summer months. On a porch covering the front of the house, two wooden rocking chairs sat side by side like a happy couple. He'd had the movers place his piano in the corner by the window that looked out on the front porch.

When they'd arrived from New York, Frances immediately began crying at the sight of the house. "This is where we're living? It looks like one of those Sears kit houses. I can't possibly survive here."

"But it's lovely." It was a kit house, in fact, replete with a sitting room, dining room, and kitchen on the first floor, and upstairs, two modest-sized bedrooms and a bath.

She fell to her knees on the Oriental rug. "Please, Nate, I'm begging you. I cannot live here. I have to get back to New York."

"I'm lucky to have a job. There are so many without work."

"But this horrid little town? My God, do you really hate me this much?"

"The town's somewhat provincial, sure, but it's something. Especially given my situation."

Now, he walked inside. The house felt cool. Calling out to Frances, he heard her moving about the front room. Bracing himself, he went through the kitchen to the sitting room. Frances paced the floor, a half-empty bottle of sherry on the closed piano. She was dressed in an evening gown with a rope of pearls, and red lipstick was smeared around her mouth. He went to her, taking her gently by the arms. She met his gaze with dazed eyes.

"Back from school so soon," she said, slurring. "Did you prepare all the young ladies for a life of utter boredom?"

"Frances." He put the sherry back on the bar. "Let's eat something. There's bread and butter." He wiped the top of the piano with his handkerchief.

"Your precious piano's fine."

"It should never have anything on its surface."

She went to the liquor cabinet and poured another glass of sherry. He moved toward her, like he might with a rabid animal.

"You've had enough. You don't want to be sick."

"I'm already sick. Of you. Of this sad life we're stuck in like two pigs in quicksand."

He let his hands fall to his side. "Frances, please. Let's eat something."

Suddenly, she lurched toward the liquor cabinet, grabbed the decanter of sherry, and hurled it toward the piano. "I don't want something to eat. I want to go home to New York." The crystal decanter broke, spilling sherry over the top of the piano. He ran to the kitchen to get a towel, thinking of the intricate strings within the instrument. When he returned, she lay collapsed on the couch, her gown around her like a mermaid's tail. Sopping up the sherry with the towel, he felt relieved to see that none had seeped under the lid. After he finished, he made a pile of the broken glass.

She sobbed from the couch. "I can't go on this way."

He looked over at her.

She held a shard of glass with a sharp point. "I'm going to end it, Nate, I swear to God, if you don't promise to get me out of this place." She put the glass to her throat.

He inched toward her, his hands in front of him as if she might turn the weapon on him. "All right. I'll start looking for another position. Maybe I can find something in Atlanta or Chicago." He said whatever came to mind. "A bigger city."

She smiled, dreamlike. "Or Los Angeles. I read it's always seventy-two degrees there. And I could become a star."

"Sure. Just hand me the glass." Next to her now, he put his right hand around her wrist, no larger than a child's, and took the glass from her, sighing with relief when the fight seemed to have gone from her as quickly as it had come. "Let's get you up to bed."

She was limp in his arms as he undressed her and tucked her into bed. She fell asleep almost immediately, her hands tucked under her cheek. An angel in appearance. He went downstairs and sat at the piano, practicing easy scales with his right hand.

* * *

He awakened to a sound coming from the washroom and reluctantly got out of bed. The bathroom light was on, and the door was propped open several inches. Frances was bent over the sink, scrubbing her hands. Dressed in a filmy white dressing gown, her hair wet and flat against her head, as if she'd just gotten out of the bath or come in from a rainstorm, she looked up when the door creaked.

"Frances?"

"Nate, is it you?" She blinked. Her gray eyes were now black, their large pupils dilated, like she was in a trance. "I can't stop thinking of him."

"Who's that, Frances?"

"The dead man. I can't get the scent of him off my hands. He smelled of mulch, Nate. Like something rotting." With a glazed look, like a sleepwalker, she spoke in a whisper. "See, no matter how I scrub." She held up her hands for him to see. He gasped. They were red and raw, like his mother's had been after taking in laundry.

Grabbing a towel, he patted them dry, careful not to rub too hard for fear of making the chapped skin worse. He brought them to his nose. "Frances, I smell only soap." When had she stopped wearing the perfume that smelled of gardenias?

"I'm so very tired." She closed her eyes and tucked her head into her collarbone in a way that reminded Nathaniel of an injured swan.

"Come now. It's time for bed." He took her hand and led her to her bedroom.

Once he had her under the covers, she looked up at him with those stormy eyes that had once made his heart beat fast and furiously. "Do you mind terribly?" She spoke with the same strange, vacant look in her eyes.

"Mind what?" He tucked the covers tighter around her frail shoulders.

"Sleeping alone?"

"It's fine. I know I keep you awake with my nightmares."

"I wonder why I don't dream?"

We're just two injured birds, he thought. "Never mind that. Just get a good rest. It'll all look better in the morning."

"Maybe Mother could send some of that soap Cassie makes. It takes out all smells."

He smoothed a lock of her hair back from her forehead. "I'll write and ask your mother in the morning."

Her eyes were closing now, and then she began to breathe in a steady rhythm that sounded so peaceful it was hard to imagine that the moments before were real.

CHAPTER 17

Jeselle and Whitmore

September 10, 1933

Dear Jeselle,

After the long train ride, I've finally made it here to Princeton. It's my first night in the men's dormitory. My roommate is Reginald King, Reggie for short. Apparently his father owns half of New England. Our room's stark and small with two single beds and two desks. I'll start classes in several days, but for now I'm free to wander about and paint. The campus is lush and beautiful this time of year. There's much to capture, many colors and textures.

I'll keep my promise to write twice a week. I realize I'm not as capable as you in remembering all the details of a given situation, especially when it comes to what people say, but I'll try as hard as I can to tell you all the interesting parts with the right details so that it will seem like you were here with me, only this way you won't have to actually experience the boring parts.

Please write soon.

Yours,

Whit

September 18, 1933

Dear Whit,

We're back in Atlanta. We closed the lake house two days after you left. It will take some adjustment, as it always does, to be back with your father. Your mother isn't eating much since we've been back. It's like the sound of his voice makes her feel sick. I noticed a bruise on her forearm the other morning. Mama keeps a close watch on things, but we're both on pins and needles all day long.

Mama announced one morning that I was to get a job. Your mother made a protest, but she was no force for Mama's will in this, telling your mother that it was time for me to earn my own keep.

I found a job working for Mrs. Greer down the street. I've worked only two days, and I'm so tired I can hardly pick up my pen to write. I'm asleep before I hit the pillow.

I'll write another time. Until then, know I'm thinking of you.

Yours,

Jeselle

September 21, 1933

Dear Jeselle,

There are so many smart people here I'm humbled and, dare I say it, intimidated. I was accustomed to being less clever than you, but I was remiss in my understanding of the quantity of other intelligent minds out here in the world.

I'm struggling terribly with my mathematics course. The professors tell me I only have to worry about it this year since I've declared art history as my major. I wish you were here to help me with it.

I've decided Reggie is swell. He invites me on all his adventures even though I'm not exactly the liveliest guy around. The others are always on the search for a party, which they consider any place with girls.

Write soon.

Love,

Whit

September 24, 1933

Dear Whit,

It may sound strange, but everything's dim since you left, the colors less visible like there's a dusting of gray powder on everything. Your mother meanders from room to room, without direction, her footsteps barely discernible and only her deep sighs an indication of where she is. She's lost without the two of us underfoot.

And what do I have without you? I never knew how much there was to tell you until you were no longer here. I have nothing more than this blank page in which to confess all, to explore every detail of my life. I swore I wouldn't complain about my fate, but Whit, sometimes writing is the only thing that gives me pleasure. With each word I can almost feel the gush of something come out of me, making things bearable. I scrub and iron and placate, all the while the words forming in my mind, how I might describe it later on the pages of my journal or in a letter to you. Sometimes I even dream in narrative right along with the pictures in my subconscious mind, like there's a story inside me someone is waiting to hear. That is, when I'm not dreaming of you. Those nights I wake in the morning exhausted, as if I'd walked miles in search of you in my sleep, and dreading another long day at the Greers'.

I don't know if you remember Mrs. Greer. Your mother has had her over for tea on occasion. Her full name is Lucinda Rae Greer, and she has her monograms everywhere. LRG on the towels, LRG on the necklace around her neck, even a pad at her desk with LRG at the top of each page. I thought immediately that it almost spelled LARGE, ironic because she's no bigger than a scarecrow hanging in a cornfield. Regardless, I started thinking of her as LARGE, only seeing the letters LRG when I thought it.

As you can see, some things remain the same. My imagination continues to get me into trouble.

I must close. LRG awaits me in the morning.

Love,

Jes

October 1, 1933

Dear Jeselle,

Mother wrote of your mama's insistence that you get a job. She doesn't understand it, as there's plenty of work at our house. I don't either, although I believe she's hoping to get you out on your own to keep you away from me.

I worry about you working for these women who run in Mother's circle. They are not like Mother in any way, as you know. I wonder why Mrs. Greer hired you instead of a white girl?

Someday we'll have a life together, and I'll take care of things so you don't have to scrub and placate. Jessie, know this: when there is love, all things are possible. Jesus taught us this, did He not?

Love,

Whit

October 8, 1933

Dear Whit,

I believe there were two reasons LRG hired me instead of a white girl. The first is that I come from your mother's staff. The second is that I work for an amount that LRG would be embarrassed to offer a white girl. But a black girl, in LRG's eyes, why, we're hardly better than the savages portrayed in that ridiculous moving picture put out by the Ku Klux Klan years ago. She believes I don't deserve the pay she's giving me. In her view, I'm no better than a trained monkey.

Regardless, I was lucky to find a position when so many go without. Mama and I hear every Sunday at our church that black folks can no longer get even the most menial of jobs because a white man or woman is always offered it first. Before these hard times there were certain jobs a white person wouldn't take, but now they'll do most anything. We're all, black and white, like hungry chickens scratching in the yard, trying to dig up something to eat.

I know Mama and I have been fortunate to work for your mother all these years. Yet I can't help but feel sorry for myself and for your mother. Always there's this yearning in us for something more, for some meaning to our lives that cannot be found in my chores or her life of idleness. I know it in myself, this thirst I have for a life bigger than the one I have, an existence with freedom and intellectual pursuits. I see it in her, too, how she rambles about her big house with nothing to occupy her fervent mind but the daily, mundane nuances of society and fulfilling the requirements of her husband.

It's futile to wish things were different. It's possibly even a sin to want more when I have so much. But still, there it is. A space that needs filling.

Love,

Jes

CHAPTER 18

Jeselle

DESPITE HER DEDICATION to writing Whitmore, there were certain aspects of Jeselle's life she chose not to share with him. She suspected when a man loved a woman it rendered them irrational at the mere hint of any mistreatment. She could not risk Whit doing something rash, therefore she kept the details of her experiences to herself. The truth was uglier than her letters suggested.

The Greers lived one street over from the Bellmonts in a massive Victorian. The morning of her interview, Jeselle had knocked on the back door, knowing it was unheard of for a colored girl to be at the front of anything. Mrs. Greer opened the door at once and motioned for her to come inside. The kitchen, once fine, was now shabby. The wallpaper, a pattern of red apples and frilly red curtains, peeled at the corners, white moldings were chipped and scuffed, and once red curtains were faded to the color of rust.

"Your mother works for Clare Bellmont?" Mrs. Greer, stringy and sharp, made of nothing but bones and dry skin, crossed her arms across a flat chest. "Long time now, isn't that right?" Her front teeth came to a point, like a rodent's, Jeselle thought with a shiver. One of the nasty, greedy ones that skirt out from the bushes on the city streets of Atlanta, waiting for a child's dropped crumb.

"Yes, ma'am. All my life." Jeselle shifted her weight from one foot to the other; the floorboard creaked.

"I see." Mrs. Greer fixed her eyes on Jeselle as if examining her for bruises or hidden worms like a peach in a bin at the grocer. "You work for Mrs. Bellmont, too, then?"

"Yes, ma'am. Since I was small."

"This job's just standard maid duties, along with taking care of my daughter. My husband likes his meals on time."

"I cook, too?"

"Is that a problem?"

"No, ma'am."

"Two dollars a week."

"Thank you, Mrs. Greer."

When Jeselle arrived back at the Bellmonts' she found Mama and Mrs. Bellmont in the garden. Mama knelt in the dirt, tending to her herbs in the corner of the yard. She didn't look up from her task.

Mrs. Bellmont cut dead blooms from a rose bush with a pair of scissors but turned toward her the moment Jeselle was near. "How was it, baby girl?"

"I start tomorrow. I'll be her only help."

"In that big house?" Mrs. Bellmont cut a brown bud from a thorny vine and tossed it into the bucket at her feet. "They're old money, but I've heard rumors they've fallen on hard times." She moved to the next rose bush, cutting a wayward vine. "How much a week?"

"Two dollars."

"What? Why, that's criminal." Mrs. Bellmont threw down her shears. "Cassie?"

"Don't you worry, Miz Bellmont." Cassie looked up from her work. "We can't expect everyone to be as generous as you are."

"Well then, why can't she just work here?"

"Just 'cause that ain't the way it's gonna be," answered Mama.

"You're the most stubborn woman ever born."

"You got that right." Mama plucked a large sprig of rosemary and held it up for them to see. "This'll taste just fine with the pork roast I got at the market."

Jeselle looked over at Mrs. Bellmont and shrugged. They both knew it was no use to argue with Mama.

*   *   *

The next morning Jeselle arrived to the Greer's home at seven. She'd been preoccupied the morning before, nervous about the interview, and hadn't noticed that the garden was as dilapidated as the interior of the house. Weeds carpeted the ground between plants, and brown patches were scattered across the lawn. A birdbath with dirty water, the sides of which were covered in mildew and moss, tilted like it might fall over at any moment. A muddy pond and a gazebo with faded paint and broken steps took up one corner of the yard.

The door stood open. Mrs. Greer sat at the kitchen table, bent over a tablet. Jeselle lingered at the doorway, feeling awkward, and finally cleared her throat. Only then did Mrs. Greer look up. "Well, don't dawdle, girl. Come on in here and get to work." Squinty eyes with bags underneath that looked like uncooked pie dough darted to the paper on the table. She moved her arms over the pad. "Chore list is next to the sink. I expect all of it to be done by the time you leave tonight."

Iron shirts.

Wash clothes in wicker basket.

Give Winnie bath.

Scrub bathroom.

Polish hardwood floor in sitting room.

Prepare supper.

Jeselle calculated how long each task would take. If she used all the tricks Mama had taught her over the years she might be able to accomplish all of it.

A baby toddled into the kitchen. She had fair hair that stuck straight up like she'd had a fright.

"This is Winifred. We all call her Winnie. She's almost two."

Jeselle bent down to the child's level. "Hello, Miss Winnie. I'm Jeselle."

"Me baby." She pointed a chubby finger at her chest, her pale blue eyes never leaving Jeselle's face.

"I have friends coming over later," Mrs. Greer said. "I'll want a cake made before they come. I have to go out." She ripped the piece of paper from the pad and stuffed it in her purse.

"Yes, ma'am."

Winnie stood at the door, crying, watching the back of her retreating mother. Jeselle picked her up and perched her on her hip. Winnie rubbed her runny nose on Jeselle's shoulder. "Me baby."

"Me Jeselle." She grabbed a bowl from the hutch. "And we have a cake to make."

* * *

The days went on, one after the other, a blur of cooking and taking care of Winnie and ticking off tasks from Mrs. Greer's lists. September turned to November with little recollection of October. In December a shift occurred. Additional notes besides the daily instructions began to appear on LRG's stationary. The first was about the fried chicken from the night before.

The chicken wasn't fit to eat. PINK and BLOODY. I will dock your pay 25 cents this week. —LRG

The words *pink* and *bloody* were underlined three times. "I think I know how to fry a chicken, Miss Winnie," Jeselle said.

Winnie was on the floor, playing with an old doll of Frances's that Mrs. Bellmont had sent over. "Baby 'ikes 'icken."

All that week there were notes of criticism, detailing further deductions from her pay. Tuesday, the clothes weren't properly ironed. Wednesday, smudges on the wine goblets. Thursday, Winnie wasn't clean enough before Jeselle put her to bed.

On Friday morning Mrs. Greer stood in the kitchen when Jeselle arrived, obviously waiting for her.

"There's a red mark on Winnie's face." Mrs. Greer's eyes darted to the floor and back to Jeselle. "Did you hit her?"

"I noticed a scratch yesterday. It was there when I came in the morning." Jeselle heard her voice go higher pitched, as if she were guilty. "I would no sooner harm a baby than my very own mama."

"I want you out of my house. You're lucky I don't turn you in to the police. My husband has influence in this town."

"What about my pay for the week?"

"I wouldn't give you a red-dirt cent after what you've done. What'll fancy Clare Bellmont think of you now?"

Jeselle trudged toward home in the rain, wondering how she was going to explain all of it to Mama and Mrs. Bellmont. Instead of going home, she went to the park, where she found a bench and sank into it. Pulling her coat tight, she cried without bothering to wipe her tears from her cheeks.

She carried on this way for a half hour before giving herself a shake and slogging the rest of the way home. It was midmorning by then, the house quiet as she hung up her coat and hat and walked down the hallway. She heard Mrs. Bellmont and Mama talking in the study and found them huddled together at the desk.

"I used two tablespoons for a time, but I think it's better with only one and a half," said Mama.

"All right, so that's one and a half hickory root." Mrs. Bellmont jotted something into a notebook.

Jeselle cleared her throat. "I'm home."

They both looked up. "Jes?" asked Mama.

"What happened?" asked Mrs. Bellmont.

"I was let go." The tears came again.

"Why?" Mama's mouth made a straight line.

"They couldn't afford you," said Mrs. Bellmont. "And she made up a reason, didn't she?"

Jeselle nodded, unable to speak.

"What did she accuse you of?" Mrs. Bellmont rose to her feet.

"She said I slapped the baby."

"Was the child hurt?" asked Mama.

"She had a scratch. But it wasn't from me. I swear." There again— the higher pitch to her voice. Why did she feel guilty when she'd done nothing wrong?

"Well, of course you didn't do anything to that poor baby," said Mrs. Bellmont.

"She refused to give me my wages. There was something new each day this week that she said I did wrong, and she kept docking my pay."

"Why didn't you tell us?" asked Mrs. Bellmont.

"I was too ashamed."

Mrs. Bellmont's cheeks flamed red. "I'll be damned if I let someone cheat you out of what is owed you." She marched into the foyer. Jeselle and Mama followed. Mrs. Bellmont shoved her hands into her white gloves so hard Jeselle expected to see her fingernails push right through the fabric.

From the window, they watched her march down the street with her bag under her arm. "I've never heard a curse word pass her lips in all the years I've known her." Mama shook her head. "That woman never ceases to surprise me."

*   *   *

When Mrs. Bellmont returned an hour later, she launched into her story without even taking off her coat. "I went right on down there to the Greers' home. I knocked on the front door once, loud. But no one answered. I thought I heard footsteps, like someone creeping down the stairs. How I wished I could stick my ear right next to the door so I could hear better, but I showed some restraint, figuring there's always someone looking out a window, hoping for gossip. So I went around back to the kitchen door and knocked again. Still no answer—just a fluttering of faded red curtain at the kitchen window. I had half a mind to wait her out. I'm sorry the Greers are going through hard times, but that's no reason to treat others unkindly." She shrugged out of her coat. "I'm just fit to be tied. Next time I see her I'll be giving her a piece of my mind. You can count on that."

"Here Miz Bellmont, set a bit," said Mama. "I made you some tea."

Mrs. Bellmont did as she was told. But her eyes still had the sharp look. "Jes, you simply cannot work for the Lucinda Greers of the world."

Jeselle looked at her hands. "What other choice do I have?"

"Stay here," Mrs. Bellmont said. "Keep working for us."

"She needs to make her own way," said Mama.

"Why, Cassie? Why, when she has me?"

Mama looked at the floor. "It's the way things are."

"Well then, just until we can figure out what to do next, let her stay here with us." Mrs. Bellmont's eyes went to the crystal displayed on the top shelf of the hutch. "Cassie, how much you think that vase and bowl are worth?"

"No idea."

Mrs. Bellmont twisted her wedding ring on her finger before pulling it off and tapping the diamond in a rhythm on the tabletop. Then she rubbed the indentation left by the ring on her finger. "This ring's bothering me, Cassie. I think I'll leave it off for a while."

"You want me to put it someplace safe?" Mama asked.

"No, I'll just take it upstairs and put it in my jewelry box."

Later, Jeselle and Mama put together a peach cobbler for Mr. Bellmont's monthly gentlemen's club. Jeselle made the crust while Mama mixed three jars of canned peaches with cinnamon and sugar. They were careful not to talk, since Mr. Bellmont was in the sitting room reading the paper and drinking his before-dinner whiskey. Regardless,

Jeselle felt a comfortable silence between them—an unspoken hiatus from worries over her future. Just as they were fixing to stick the cobbler in the oven, they heard Mrs. Bellmont come rushing down the stairs, her shoes click-clacking on the wood. Jeselle expected her to come to the kitchen, but instead she heard the sitting room door squeak and shut. First there was a murmur of voices and then a crash. Mama went still, like an animal in the forest sensing danger. Mrs. Bellmont's cry, though faint, reached the kitchen. Jeselle went instantly hot, scared. Then they heard the sound of Mr. Bellmont's heavy footsteps going up the stairs to the bedroom. Mrs. Bellmont came into the kitchen, holding her arm, her face white.

"What is it?" Mama kept her voice low, but she sighed with an air of inevitability.

"My wedding ring slipped down the drain in the bathroom sink." She sounded faint. Mama rushed over to help her into a chair. "I had to take my punishment."

Jeselle was already at the icebox, wrapping a chunk of ice in a dish towel. "Can you move it, Mrs. Bellmont?"

Mrs. Bellmont shook her head, no. "I think it's broken. He slammed me into the cabinet, and my arm hit the corner just so. We should call Doc Miller. He'll have to set it."

Mama was already at the phone.

It was always Doc Miller they called, thought Jeselle. The secrets that man knew about this family stacked higher and higher like the books in Mrs. Bellmont's study.

Jeselle placed the cold cloth on Mrs. Bellmont's arm. "Just hold it there for a bit."

Mrs. Bellmont flinched. Then she looked into Jeselle's eyes. "Now, you listen here, Jeselle Thorton. You're not to despair. You hear me?"

"Yes, Mrs. Bellmont."

"All those years we studied. They're not going to be wasted, if it's the last thing I do."

*   *   *

A week later Jeselle dusted in Mrs. Bellmont's room. There, behind a stack of books, the wedding ring, newly polished, gleamed in the light of the lamp.

CHAPTER 19

Whitmore

WITH COLD FINGERS, Whitmore painted the image of a bent branch of a birch tree that hung just outside his dormitory window. The bough hung low, burdened with heavy snow. He added a dab of blue to his white paint and mixed it on his palette.

The university had been in bloom when he arrived: wide, flat lawns and lush trees in various tints of green. Late October brought the first frost and turned the leaves orange and red and the lawn yellow. In early November, the temperature dipped below freezing, and the leaves, one by one, separated from their branches and floated to the ground, covering the golden blades of grass. For weeks afterward, the weather was cold and sunny, with the sky blue between bare branches. Then, last night, the snow had come, dumping a full foot while he slept in his skinny dormitory bed, covering everything in a hushed, serene white.

Laughter penetrated the glass windowpane. Reggie and some of the other young men were throwing snowballs, their breath coming out in white clouds. Whitmore put aside his paintbrush and watched the merriment.

Moments later, he leaned under the bed, pulling out a small cardboard box. There were letters inside, all addressed to him in Jeselle's small, looped handwriting, organized in chronological order. The last one was dated October 30, 1933, with an Atlanta postmark. He held it in his hands, not daring to open re-read the words he already had memorized. He put it back on top of the pile and slid it under his bed before going back to the window and picking up his paintbrush.

Later that morning, he trudged in boots to the university mailroom. Under a close, gray sky, brick buildings were stark red in contrast to the white snow. He passed by other students hurrying to class, hats pulled low and mufflers around their necks. When he arrived at the mailroom, he took off his hat and stomped his boots to rid them of snow. The mailroom clerk, wearing glasses attached to a string, pulled them from her face and let them fall upon her ample chest. Pink and plump-cheeked, with tight, white curls, she smelled like the inside of a bakery.

Today, like always, she smiled at him. "Good morning, Mr. Bellmont."

"Anything for me today?"

"Something from your mother."

"Thanks." He pushed his hair from his damp forehead and chastised himself for holding out hope that today would be the day Jeselle broke her silence.

She glanced at his empty hands. "Nothing to mail today, Mr. Bellmont?"

"I'm done with letters for now, ma'am. Thank you." He forced himself to smile. This is how it would be now. He would pretend to be happy, and life would go on as if his heart wasn't twisted inside his chest.

She clucked sympathetically and patted the counter with an ink-smeared hand. "One day you'll find another girl to write, and she'll write back."

He let his face go slack, unable to muster the energy to hold any pretenses that he wasn't suffering. "How do you know that?"

She brushed the counter as if there were dust on it. "I've been around a while."

"You mean in this mailroom?"

She laughed, and he was surprised that it was hearty and from deep in her chest. "No, dear, on this earth. Love always comes around again."

"It's hard to think of ever loving anyone but the girl I do."

"Yes, I know, dear, but believe you me, someday you'll think different."

CHAPTER 20

Lydia

LYDIA ENTERED the chicken coop without a sound, catching the gate with her foot before it slammed. "Sorry, but one of you has to go," she whispered. She chose a fat fryer near the fence and snatched her up, quickly, silently, so as not to alarm the rest of the gossiping ninnies. She held it to her side, cupping its head with her other hand, and went around to the back of the shed. Once there, she moved her hand under its backside and grasped the legs, her thumb pointing away from the body to get a tighter grip. With her other hand, she put her two forefingers and thumb at the base of its head and twisted. She set it on the ground while the thing jerked about as if it were still alive. After it stilled, she hung it by its feet from the rafters in the barn, so the blood would pool in the head. She'd come back with her hatchet after she put water on the stove to boil.

In the kitchen later, Lydia coated the chicken pieces in flour and browned them on each side before turning down the heat and covering the pan. She poured another cup of coffee and sat down to read the paper. It was the usual terrible news, same as the day before. She flipped to the arts section, hoping for something uplifting.

Between articles about the town "singing club" and a play being performed at the high school, an advertisement for a summer piano composition program at Alabama College for Women in Montevallo captured her attention. She smoothed her hand over the page. The chicken crackled and snapped on the stove. She tapped a finger on the words "Acceptance Criteria" and then circled it with a pencil.

A knock on the front door took her away from the paper. Midwife Stone carried a yellow and white kitten in her arms. "Well, look who I found under my porch this morning."

Lydia held out her hands, and Midwife Stone passed the bundle of fur over to her. "She's precious."

"Thought you might be in need of a mouser. Yellow and white ones are the best, from what I hear."

"Come on in here. You want some coffee and a piece of pie?"

"I never say no to pie." Midwife Stone followed her into the kitchen and plopped down at the table, immediately seizing hold of the newspaper. "What's this now? You thinking of going to school next summer?"

Lydia laughed and rolled her eyes as she scratched behind the kitten's ear; it started purring much louder than she expected from such a small animal. "Nothing gets by you now, does it?"

"Well, are you?"

"I don't know. Am I too old for school?"

"Too young for dying."

Lydia put the kitten on Midwife Stone's lap. "Who'll take care of Furball here?"

Midwife Stone held the kitten up to her face. "Well, shoot, I guess I could keep her for you if you got yourself accepted. She might be good company for me."

"I'll apply. I probably won't get in anyway, but at least I'll have tried."

"Better than sitting about here feeling sorry for yourself." Midwife set the kitten on the newspaper. "Now, where's that pie?"

CHAPTER 21

Jeselle

TWO DAYS BEFORE CHRISTMAS, Jeselle cradled the yellow mixing bowl against her chest, stirring together cornmeal, flour, sugar, and salt. A hum and a crunch of gravel coming from the lake house driveway stopped her. She closed her eyes, bracing her shoulders as if for a storm.

Mr. Bellmont and Whit stepped inside the kitchen. Whit set his suitcase down carefully, as if he were afraid to bring any additional attention to himself.

"Where's Mrs. Bellmont?" said Mr. Bellmont.

"In the dining room, sir."

"Whitmore, you think about what we talked about." Mr. Bellmont headed toward the door. "I expect a commitment from you before the school year is over. Understand?"

"Yes, sir," Whit mumbled.

As the door closed, Whit pinched the bridge of his nose between his thumb and index finger and sighed. He came to stand next to her. "How are you, Jessie?"

"Fine. Welcome home." She cracked two eggs and poured a cup of milk and melted lard into the dry ingredients, stirring it hard so that a dollop splashed onto the counter. Whitmore swiped the batter from the counter, wiping it from his finger onto the dishrag next to the sink, and then wrapped his hand around her forearm. She went still. His touch burned, all the way up her arm and into her throat. She turned her eyes to his face. What did she see? A longing so deep she believed it physically pained him. Her breath caught in her throat, knowing then how her silence these last months had hurt him. And yet she could not yield just then, the anger tight in her belly. She lifted his hand off her arm and moved to the other side of the kitchen. "You want something?"

"No, I'll wait for dinner."

"S'pose your mother told you I was let go from Mrs. Greer's?"

He raised an eyebrow, nodding. "Yes. She wrote to me about it." From a nearby shelf, he pulled out a pan for the cornbread. His hands shook when he handed it to her. "Why haven't you written me?"

There was a long silence, her mind blank as to how to answer him. "I don't know. Can't write lately. Not even in my journal."

His eyes widened; he crossed his arms over his chest. "Jes, that's impossible. You've written in that thing every day for years."

She shrugged, spreading cold lard over the bottom of the pan. "I said I don't know."

"Jessie, are you all right?" His voice sounded tender and familiar. He sounded like Whitmore. Her Whitmore. The back of Jeselle's throat ached.

Mama came through the kitchen door, muttering something under her breath. She came to an abrupt stop and folded her arms over her chest. "Mr. Whit. You made it."

"Hi, Cassie. Sure did."

"Your mother will be right glad to see you," said Mama.

"It's good to be here. I've missed y'all something fierce."

"Your mama's in the sitting room with Mr. Nate. They're waiting for you."

"All right, then." He picked up his bag. "I'll see you both later." He left through the kitchen door.

"You best get a move on that cornbread," said Mama. "We've got a big meal to serve up here."

"Yes, Mama." Jeselle opened the oven door; the heat blasted her face. She set the pan on the hot surface, as the heat of the stove seemed to reach every part of her body. Burning.

CHAPTER 22

Nathaniel

ON CHRISTMAS DAY Nathaniel sat with Frank in the lake house study, reclining in twin leather chairs next to the fire, drinking bootleg whiskey straight up. Fog settled over the lake while Frank chattered on about the effects of Prohibition. "The repeal a couple weeks ago is the only goddamned good idea Roosevelt has had to date. Let me tell you, Nate, my friends in the spirit business in St. Louis have been ruined by all the damned teetotalers forcing their opinion on the government. Even Rockefeller agrees, sent a letter out last year saying as how Prohibition hampered the economy and that folks are drinking more than ever. I coulda told you that."

Nathaniel wasn't fully listening, as Frank had given the same speech the night before. He nodded his head, though, as if he were interested. "You don't say?" He finished his drink and felt himself detaching from his body as if he were slipping into the fog, like a ghost haunting a once familiar world.

"The goddamn Communists trying to infiltrate my workers' minds. Trying to unionize 'em right in front of me. Used to be the Negroes were happy for a job." He scratched at the end of his bulbous nose. "Speaking of which, Whitmore's got a job waiting for him once he's done at Princeton."

"That what Whit wants?"

Frank glowered at him. "Sure it is." He emptied his whiskey glass and poured himself another.

"His painting's remarkable, Mr. Bellmont. I could introduce him to some people in the art community in New York."

Frank guffawed. "No one ever made any money off art."

The alcohol made Nathaniel feel bolder than usual, more willing to participate in a fight. He was about to retort that he'd made a small fortune from his own art, but the conversation was interrupted when Frances and Clare entered the study. Nathaniel stood, steadying himself by keeping his right hand on the chair's arm. They were dressed for dinner in evening gowns, with their hair pulled back and jewels around their necks. Frances wore a sleeveless dress with a fitted bodice and low back that displayed her slender frame and matched her eyes. She grew lovelier by the year, he thought, the beauty she had been at twenty now fully blooming at twenty-six, as maturity had hollowed her cheeks and given her eyes a brighter spark. Clare was dressed in lavender silk with a butterfly bodice attached to a long flowing skirt. She'd changed little in the years he'd been married to Frances, her blonde hair scarcely filtered with white, just the slightest of lines around her eyes. Nathaniel moved to take Frances's arm, but she pulled away, flopping into the leather armchair next to her father. Clare sat on the couch. "Where's Whitmore?" she asked no one in particular. "Dinner's in a few minutes."

Nathaniel indicated upward with a nod of his head. "Finishing up a painting."

Frank went to the doorway of the study and hollered into the hallway, "Jeselle, tell Whitmore to get down here for a drink." Back in his chair, he stretched his legs out in front of him. "I'll be goddamned if he's going to stay up there all night painting a sunset."

Clare murmured, "Frank, it's Christmas."

Nathaniel wondered if she meant the cursing or that Whitmore should be allowed to finish a painting on Christmas day.

Jeselle appeared in the doorway of the study. "He'll be right down, Mr. Bellmont."

"Thank you, Jeselle," said Clare.

After she left, Clare turned to Nathaniel, speaking softly, "I'm delighted to have Jeselle back with us. Oh, I miss the kids. Cassie and I just bump around this big house, like two old chickens with no eggs to sit on."

Frances opened a magazine, studying whatever was on the first page. "You mean Whitmore and Jeselle, right, Mother?" She didn't look up.

"I miss you, Frances, but you've been a grown married woman for five years now."

"Speakin' of which, 'bout time you gave us a grandchild." Frank stood, perching near the window, one hand over his protruding belly. "Give your mother something to do besides fussing over the help."

Nathaniel stole a glance at Frances, but her eyes were cast downward, still in the magazine. We had a child, he thought. We had a son.

Clare turned back to Nathaniel. "I just had to insist that Jeselle come home, work for us." She sipped her wine and gazed out the window into the fog. "Oh, that woman was horrid. I begged Cassie not to send her there in the first place, but she had her mind set on it."

Frances stood and rifled through a pile of magazines sitting on the bookshelf. "Mother, why you get involved with the help is beyond me. It's not natural."

Clare's neck flushed red. "We treat all our help as if they're part of the family."

"But must we, Mother? People talk. It's embarrassing."

"You might try it, dear, and perhaps you'll keep a maid longer than a month. And I certainly don't care what people say about me or the way I run my own household."

Grabbing three issues of *Vogue*, Frances raised a saucy eyebrow as she sat back in the armchair. "I'll keep that in mind, Mother."

Frank poured a glass of wine and took it over to Clare. He leaned down, speaking into her ear, softly, but Nathaniel's keen hearing heard every word. "Shut up about the damn help or I'll make sure you can never open your stupid jaw again."

Clare's eyes glittered with unshed tears as she stared at the fireplace, but her voice remained steady. "Is this from the wine block?"

"Sure is. Nate, these bricks come to us from California. To make grape juice, mind you. But on the label there's this note, 'After dissolving the brick in a gallon of water, do not place the liquid in a jug in a cupboard for twenty days, because then it would turn into wine.'" He laughed, slapping his knee. "I put it away for sixty. Won't be long now until California starts making wine like France. I have half a mind to grow some grapes myself." Frank handed Frances a glass of wine.

"Thank you, Daddy." Frances held up one of the magazines. "Do you see this?" she asked Clare. "They've got a color photograph on the December issue of the American *Vogue*. The modern world is simply too much to fathom." A beautiful, dark-haired woman in a white fur stole and a tiara looked forlornly, or perhaps seductively, Nathaniel couldn't be sure, over her shoulder. "This issue has all kinds of ideas for Christmas gifts." She tapped the photo of the fur stole, with a pout in her voice. "Pity you didn't read this before you chose the scarf you gave me."

"I don't have money for a fur stole, Frances." He reached into his jacket pocket and pulled out a cigarette, lighting it with the silver lighter Clare had given him as a Christmas gift.

"We both know that isn't exactly true," said Frances.

He took a long drag of his cigarette and then exhaled. "My fortunes have changed, as you well know."

"So you say." She rolled her eyes, looking at her father. "Nathaniel hoards money like a Jew."

"Frances, don't be crass," said Clare sharply. "Anyway, in this time it's awfully smart to be frugal."

"Especially on a professor's salary," said Nathaniel.

Frances shrugged, opening a second magazine. "It's not like we spend money on anything fun. Living in Montevallo, there's nothing to do, anyway." She held up another one of the magazines. On this cover was a painting of a mansion against a background of stars and a group of people filing through the front door. At the bottom of the page it said, "PARTIES NUMBER" in block letters. Nathaniel wondered idly what that meant but didn't have the energy to ask, as Frances continued her diatribe. "You don't see Montevallo featured in *Vogue*. Mother, did you see this article in the English *Vogue*? It's all about where the parties are in Europe for the holidays. Wouldn't it be wonderful to be in Paris for the holidays?"

Nathaniel put out his cigarette and downed the remaining drops of his whiskey. He glanced over at Clare. "Have you ever been to Paris, Clare?"

"Oh, no. I'd love to go someday, of course. So much history. And art. Wouldn't it be lovely to go, Frank?"

Frank poured himself another whiskey. "Woman, do you ever shut your mouth?"

Cassie, from the doorway, cleared her throat. "Miz Bellmont, dinner is served."

As they walked down the hallway to dinner, Nathaniel made sure to fall into step with Clare. He spoke under his breath, "You would let me know if things were intolerable, wouldn't you?"

She took his arm. "Don't worry, darlin', he's almost never home. Stays most nights with his mistress."

*   *   *

At dinner, like a man succumbing to blindness, Nathaniel's sight was dull, while his musician's ears seemed more attuned than usual. As Jeselle's strong hands poured a new bottle of burgundy into the wine glasses around the table, it made a sloshing sound. The French red wine was from the cellar, stored before Prohibition, and tasted of minerals and tobacco. "The wine is lovely, Clare," said Nathaniel.

"Thank you, Nate. We open our best for Christmas dinner." She smiled widely and looked around the table. "It's wonderful to have everyone home at the same time."

Frances, next to him, smacked her lips each time she took a sip of wine. Nathaniel imagined he could hear Clare's hands fluttering in her lap under the table, but, indeed, it was really only the wavering of the tablecloth that gave her nervousness away. Whitmore, across the table from Nathaniel, was also a silent instrument, staring mutely at his plate, an expression of control on his face, as if he were thinking, "God, just get me through one more family dinner." Frank, on one end of the long cherrywood table, periodically leaned back in his chair so that its front legs were off the floor—each time a creaking sound and then a thump when it touched the wall. Cassie moved in and out of the room, arranging dishes on the buffet table, her shoes squeaking on the wood floor.

The table was set with fine bone china with a pattern of pink flowers and the formal Reed & Barton silver. Between the faint light and the delicacy of the china, Nathaniel felt like an oversized doll in a dollhouse. His left-hand fingers felt stiff and awkward, like a young child's clumsy grasp. He kept it on his lap, reminding himself to be as still as possible so as not to send one of the dishes shattering onto the wood floors.

After pouring wine all round, Cassie and Jeselle served a savory pumpkin soup with a hint of bacon and nutmeg from a large white bowl. The whiskeys had loosened the tightness Nathaniel had carried in his shoulder blades since the ascent up the muddy driveway yesterday afternoon. But the tension seemed to have transferred directly from him to Whitmore. Not only did Whitmore's shoulders appear too close to his ears, his youthful cheeks flushed as if some unnatural heat coursed through his body. He rarely looked up from his plate and, strangely, each time Jeselle passed by with food, his cheeks seemed to grow a deeper shade of pink.

Roast beef and Yorkshire pudding were served for the main course. Nathaniel wondered every time he ate Yorkshire pudding why the traditions of England always involved animal fat—it was simply batter poured into the fat drippings at the bottom of the roasting pan, disgusting if one thought about it too carefully. But the rosemary crusted baby potatoes dripping with butter melted in his mouth.

Frances had an expression somewhere between boredom and disdain, taking small bites of her food as she moved it around her plate.

Clare dabbed the sides of her mouth with her napkin, a faraway look in her eyes. "Whit, tell us about your Renaissance art class this past semester. I hate to sound like a wistful old woman, but I would've loved to learn more about art."

Frank slammed his whiskey tumbler on the table, causing Clare to jump. "Clare!"

Clare's voice quavered, and her neck splotched with pink marks. "Well, right, silly notion, of course."

"What did I take you out of?" Frank boomed, and the rest of the table went deadly still, holding their collective breath. "And I brought you here." He swept the air with his hand. "Art class? Is this what you're whining about?"

"I didn't mean that, Frank." Clare brought the white cloth napkin to her trembling mouth. "I just meant that art is something I'm interested in."

"Don't understand how looking at pictures is considered a study," Frank said, his voice thick from whiskey. "Whitmore, enjoy painting the pansies while you can 'cause once you're back home all you'll be looking at are numbers in a ledger book."

Whitmore cut his meat, the twitch under his eye beating in quarter-time.

Frank slammed his drink on the table again. "Did you hear me, son?"

"Yes," he said, barely audible.

Nathaniel, unable to think of anything to say, felt himself fall further into an alcohol-infused haze. This disgusted him about himself, for he wanted nothing more than to support Whitmore and Clare against Frank's onslaught of criticisms and bullying, but instead he slipped deeper into his chair, his bulk leaning over his plate as if his life depended on the examination of every parcel of food.

Frank cut a large piece of beef and stuffed it in his mouth, pushing it to one cheek like a cow with her cud. "Most important thing about sending you to Princeton is the connections with other wealthy sons of America's businessmen." He swallowed. "Don't you agree, Nate?"

"I suppose." He noticed Whitmore glance at Jeselle. The girl kept her head down and went through the door to the kitchen.

Clare's face was neutral, but her fingers clutched the hem of the tablecloth. "Have you boys read any good books lately?"

"Why, Mother," Frances said, smirking, "how come you don't ask me that question?"

Clare smiled, but her eyes remained dull. "I know you don't have time to read novels, Frances."

"I read a beautiful story in the *New Yorker* by F. Scott Fitzgerald. He went to Princeton," Whitmore said, trailing off.

Frank gave his son a blank look and nodded to Jeselle as she came into the room. "Bring me another whiskey."

"Nate met him once, didn't you, darlin'?" said Frances. She looked at Whitmore, a bit triumphantly, Nathaniel thought. "Did you know that, Whit?" Frances's eyes slithered back to Nathaniel. "Tell them how he was there with his wife, Zelda." She paused for a quick breath. "She's simply one of the most fashionable women in the world."

Nathaniel cut a piece of his beef. "I believe he's a drunk. As I recall they were both more than a little tight the night I met them."

A look of anger passed over Frances's face before she covered it up with a polite, stiff smile. "Not that part, darlin'. Tell how they fell all over themselves to come backstage and meet you. Wasn't that the first night you played Carnegie Hall?"

A silence came over the table, like the fog that crept in over the lake. One didn't see it coming, but suddenly it was there, hovering, encasing everything with a cold, murky chill. Nathaniel felt the familiar constriction in his chest. Whitmore gazed at his hands resting in his lap, the flush on his face gone, replaced with a disheartening paleness. The tablecloth covering Clare's hands swayed. The only sound was Frank chewing what must have been a particularly tough piece of meat.

Finally, Clare broke the silence, her voice careful, light, "Regardless of Fitzgerald's personal problems, the man is a beautiful writer. I'm sorry to hear of his troubles."

Frances tossed her hair. "I saw his photograph in the society section of the *Times* the other day. It was right next to a picture of Ginger Rogers." She smiled at Frank. "One of the girls at the beauty shop says I look just like her. Do you think so?"

"Who's that now?" asked Frank.

"Oh, Daddy, you're awfully funny." Frances giggled.

Nathaniel put down his fork, glancing at his wife. "To answer your question, Frances, it wasn't my first time at Carnegie. But it was the pinnacle of my career."

He spoke flatly, as if simply reporting facts. "I played the Brahms *B-flat* that night. It takes almost fifty minutes to perform, took me six months to learn. The first movement is nearly twenty minutes, nineteen to be exact, and then a difficult scherzo, played appassionato."

Frances brushed aside a lock of hair that had fallen into her eyes. "Yes, but what did they say to you?"

"Who?" he asked.

"F. Scott and Zelda. What did y'all talk about?" asked Frances.

He hesitated, deciding if he should answer or not. "He's a writer, of course, and thus interested in the story of the Brahms piece. He asked me about it, and I told him that Brahms wrote it out of anger, you see, because his previous concerto was performed terribly by a woman pianist. The story goes that Brahms vowed he would write a concerto no woman could ever play. It's believed that a woman's hands are too small for the span and rapidity of the notes." He paused, his voice husky with emotion. Whitmore watched him closely from across the table. "Whether the story's true or not, it's a piece that only the finest pianists in the world can master. Fewer than you could count on one hand."

"But you mastered it, isn't that right, Nate?" asked Whitmore. "No one can ever take that away from you."

"I don't much care for critics," said Nathaniel. "Used to make a practice of never reading reviews. Hated to have them in my head. But Walt, my manager, insisted he read me the reviews from the early edition papers. One of them called it 'flawless' and 'unusual for a pianist only thirty years old.' I've kept those words close over the years, as a consolation."

Clare reached across the table and squeezed his forearm. Whit's face looked both stricken and sympathetic.

"Now, Whit, don't look like that," said Nathaniel. "You must remember, I'll always have the memory to draw upon."

He could recall the night as if it were yesterday, instead of eight years ago. The crowd fell silent, no rustling of programs or stirrings that made chairs creak. He heard them listening, felt them with him at every note. They were at ease, confident in his ability. He'd known then that he was a master of the craft; it was there, unmistakable, in the relaxed silence of a rapturous audience. The months and months of practicing faded from his memory, and he was left with just the feeling of the triumph.

"Sorry darlin'," Frances said now, playing with her necklace, "but that's just about the boringest story I ever heard. You must be the only man alive who can meet the Fitzgeralds and come away with a story about a dead composer."

*   *   *

The morning after Christmas, in the downy softness of the guest room bed, Nathaniel awakened from the edges of a long, familiar nightmare. The man, a knife slicing down the center of a piano, the clanging of bells. He jerked awake, guilty, sweaty. Stifling a groan, he rubbed his eyes. The clock on the bedside table told him it was quarter after nine. How many drinks was it last night, he wondered? He hadn't bothered to count. Frank Bellmont did that to a person.

The room felt cold, which was a relief to his overheated skin. He breathed deeply and rubbed his burning eyes before turning a bleary gaze to the painting hanging on the wall. Frances at two years old smiled at him. She wore a white dress, and blonde ringlets framed an angelic face. Where had that little girl gone?

Dishes clanged downstairs in the kitchen. It smelled like his mother's home on Saturday mornings: bacon and rising bread. He dressed in a freshly ironed shirt and pants, then sat on the wooden chair in the corner of the room, floorboards cold on his bare feet. He bowed his head, as if he might pray, but instead reached for a pair of socks and pulled them over his cold feet and headed out.

All the bedroom doors were shut except for Whitmore's. Downstairs, Cassie worked in the kitchen, her hands and forearms covered with flour. She moved with repetitive efficiency, flattening the bread dough, folding it over on itself and pressing it down again, occasionally adding another handful of flour. She looked at him and nodded. "Mornin', Mr. Nate. Can I make you some eggs?"

His stomach turned as he sat heavily in a chair at the table. "Just some coffee, please."

"Yessir." Her eyes darted to his face before pouring a large cup of dark coffee. She set it in front of him, adding a splash of cream without him asking.

He squeezed the bridge of his nose. "Bit of a headache this morning, I'm afraid."

"'Spect so."

Cassie had the same pencil-straight posture and way of holding her mouth in a line of disapproval as his mother. Rubbing his left arm, he stared out at the fog that hovered over the lake.

An image of his mother came to mind. She knelt on the patch of grass behind their house, her arms deep in a tub of water, washing clothes. It was warm, the smell of the sea drifting through the Maine breeze, her freckled arms moving up and down, the sun shining on her brown hair so that it appeared almost red, the water in the tub making a splashing sound that harmonized with the waves below. She'd taken in laundry all that summer, washing a stranger's shirts so that Nathaniel could study piano.

Cassie's voice brought him back to the warm kitchen. "Your arm ache this morning?" She asked without a hint of pity.

"A little."

"You have the dream again?"

"'Fraid so."

As if she'd softened to him at the mention of the dream, she sighed and poured a thick green liquid from a tin pitcher into a coffee cup. "Drink this before your coffee."

He grimaced. "What is this?"

"Juices of different herbs and roots. It'll cure what ails you."

He sighed and rubbed his eyes. "Even your herbal remedies can't cure what ails me, Cassie."

She put her hands on her hips and shook her head. "Whiskey sure won't cure you, I can tell you that, Mr. Nate."

"Did I ever tell you that you remind me of my mother?"

She shrugged, the corners of her mouth in a half-smile. "Don't change that I'm right."

The green concoction tasted bitter. Earthy? "Cassie, this is horrible."

"You'll thank me in a few minutes."

He got up from the chair. "I'll take it with me into the study. I've got some work to do this morning."

"Composing?" She raised her eyebrows, a hopeful lilt in her voice.

"No, reading through applications for my summer composition course."

"Teaching's fine." She picked up her dough, smacking it and then making it into a ball. "But no reason you can't compose." She buttered the dough and put it into a bowl.

"Ah, Cassie, you think too highly of me. I'm nothing but a sack of self-pity." He paused at the door, gesturing with the glass of green liquid. "Thank you for the coffee. And this. I think."

"Don't bring me nothing but an empty glass."

In the study, thinking how much a whiskey would soothe his headache, he focused his thoughts instead on the papers scattered across the desk. There were at least a dozen applications for his summer musical composition program. Sighing and occasionally rubbing his temples, he looked through the applications and accompanying sheets of original compositions.

There were three decent compositions from the typical applicants at Alabama College: wealthy young ladies from upstanding families. The fourth was from a Mrs. Lydia Tyler. Her composition was technically more sophisticated than the other applicants, and her application letter unusual. He read his favorite paragraph twice, smiling at the Eleanor Roosevelt reference.

I am a middle-aged widow interested in exploring the craft of composition. My life was devoted to my family for almost twenty years, but I now find myself free of obligations. My daughters are grown, and it seems the world would like to discard me as no longer useful. The residents of the small town where I live think I should be content to accompany the hymns at our Methodist church and serve the hungry at our soup mission. However, I rage against the idea that because of one's age one must stop learning and growing. Mrs. Eleanor Roosevelt is a woman I greatly admire. You don't see her in the background of life, meek and quiet.

He wrote the acceptance letters, which included one to Mrs. Tyler, and addressed and stamped the envelopes to ensure they would go out in the afternoon's mail. Afterward, he decided to call his mother. He'd had a telephone installed at her home just for this purpose, to call her on holidays and her birthday. She hadn't answered when he'd called yesterday; he imagined how the ring echoed in the stark, small, seaside house with its brick fireplace, stained black from years of soot, and the twin rocking chairs, empty since his father died.

Nathaniel went to the desk and dialed the operator, asking to be put through to his mother's house in Maine. She answered on the second ring. "Hello." She sounded like she was shouting into the sea's wind, afraid she couldn't be heard.

"Ma?"

"Nathaniel." Her voice softened, sounding pleased.

"Merry Christmas."

"Merry Christmas, son."

"Where were you yesterday? I called several times."

"Ach, well, had to make the rounds with my pies. There are so many folks down on their luck, Nathaniel. I baked a dozen, and Preacher Thompson and I delivered them all yesterday morning."

"You get the money I sent?"

"I surely did. There was no reason to send it. I get along just fine."

"I wanted you to buy something nice for yourself."

There was static on the phone line, and he knew she must be shaking her head. "No, I don't need a thing."

"Something you wanted, Ma." He stifled a sigh. Was that seagulls in the background? "You have the windows open, Ma?"

"A crack. Gotta have some fresh air." Another pause, and then he heard her chuckle. "I gave what you sent to the church, but not before I slipped a little to Earl's wife. I'm making some bread to send up there right now. He's been out of work two years, not a toy in sight for those children on Christmas day if it hadn't been for the money you sent. I was proud to know you had it to send. The people here are suffering, Nathaniel."

He heard loneliness in her voice. "I know, Ma. I'm glad you used it how you wanted. Sorry we didn't make it up to see you again this year."

He imagined she tugged on the front of her apron the way she so often did, her eyes gazing unfalteringly toward the sea from her kitchen window. "I know your wife's family expects you." She always called Frances his wife instead of her name. "How're you feeling?"

"Same, Ma. No difference."

"You keeping up practicing with your right hand?"

He looked longingly at the whiskey on Frank's bar. The phone cord wasn't long enough for him to reach it.

"Yes, Ma. Every day."

"That'll have to be enough to sustain you."

"I know, Ma."

"The folks at the church, they pray for you every Sunday."

A lump developed at the back of his throat. "For what, Ma? What do they pray for?"

"That you'll find some peace, Nathaniel. Just for peace."

"You thank them for me. Merry Christmas, Ma."

"You too, son."

After he hung up he poured a generous whiskey, gulping it down in two swallows, then poured another and stared into the glass. He shook his head, like a horse against the reins, and set the drink on the bar, staring at his hands for a long moment before walking outside to the lake. The landscape was encased in fog and the air bitter cold, giving the whole scene a feeling of misery. He threw a stone into the lake. It made a plop into the water, lost in the mist.

* * *

That evening's party was at a steady hum by eight o'clock. The sounds of the celebration were like those at all of the Bellmont parties Nathaniel had been to: a hum of voices punctuated by the clinks of glasses and an occasional low-toned roar of a man's boisterous belly laugh. Tonight, though, one saw the fragments of a lost world. Many of the women wore fashions that were years old, something no one would have done before the crash. There were several couples missing, too. Roger Baker was dead by his own hand two days after Black Thursday, and his widow "was living with relatives, God knows where," according to Clare. The Hardings, after losing their lake home and most of their other assets, disappeared from society. "The poor bastard had everything in the market, and it was gone, poof, before you could say whiskey sour," said Frank. Colonel Tate's dream of a summer colony had been postponed as well. "Investor money dried up, unfortunately," Clare told Nathaniel. "But he got his resort built anyway. Not that anyone uses it."

The rest of the crowd, as Clare called them, had managed to keep their lake homes, but their demeanors were frayed. The women self-consciously darted their eyes to their own clothing when they came in and saw Clare dressed in an extravagant European gown. Several of Frank's friends seemed a little too jovial, with a pretend optimism about their business ventures or finances.

Nathaniel meandered about the room, feeling unknown and self-conscious at the same time, unsure what to say, wishing to shove his left hand in his pocket to protect it from the inevitable, curious stares.

Clare came up behind him. "Get yourself a drink, Nate. Eat something. Have a good time." She smiled and lowered her voice, almost too quiet for him to hear. "Try not to glare at folks like you're looking right through them, darlin'. It makes people nervous, especially since you're a Yankee," she teased.

He smiled back at her. "I'll try, Clare."

The back of her skirt swept the floor as she walked toward the door to greet a new guest.

He turned to see Frank approaching, cigar between his teeth. "Frances went outside with that Hazel Murphy woman. Haven't seen her come back in." He pointed across the room to a young woman with a flat face. "Hazel came in 'while ago."

The scar on Nathaniel's arm throbbed with a dart of pain. "I'll go look for her."

Outside, the cold caught in his chest. He coughed and pulled his white dinner jacket tighter as he strode across the grass toward the dock. A figured moved in the water. Frances.

"For Christ's sake," he shouted to her. "Frances, get out. It's disgusting in there."

She waved her arms while treading water, calling out to him, "Darlin', come on in."

"Get out of there before you catch your death."

"Ah, don't be such a bore."

"There are water moccasins in this lake." He leaned over the edge of the dock in an attempt to see into the water. "Do you have anything on?"

"Does it matter?"

"Please, Frances." He used a coaxing tone as if she were a frightened child. "Come on out of there before people see you." He sat on his knees on the end of the dock and patted the aging wood of the planks. "Come on now. We can watch the stars together."

She swam closer, and, holding onto the ladder, climbed onto the dock. Naked, she shivered violently in the night air. Frantic to cover her, he took off his jacket and wrapped it around her thin shoulders. She held onto his arm. He noticed for the first time an empty bottle of whiskey at his feet. Before he could think of how to get her inside as quietly as possible, she shook off his coat and began to dance suggestively up and down the dock, as if she performed in a burlesque show, singing *Silent Night* at the top of her lungs. Out of the corner of his eye he saw party guests gathering on the veranda of the house. He ran after her with his jacket, but she was too quick for him. She sprinted to the end of the dock and stumbled, dropping to her knees on the muddy shore before scrambling once again to her feet. He overtook her with three long strides and tackled her so that they both fell into the mud. She flailed at him with her hands, scratching his face. Covering her with his body, he held her arms above her head. A screech exploded from her as she planted her bare feet into the sand and pushed up with her hips. "Get off me. You never let me have any fun."

Speaking through clenched teeth, he kept his voice low, knowing how sound carried over water. "Be quiet. Everyone's watching you."

She went limp under him. "Won't Mother be mortified?" It was like one long word.

"My God, Frances, what's the matter with you?"

"Nothing's the matter with me." She let out a maniacal giggle. "Daddy's going to be real mad."

"Oh, Frances, I don't know what to do with you."

"Nate," she slurred, "was it Juliet's mother that couldn't get the blood off her hands?"

"No, Lady Macbeth." He realized he'd dropped his jacket in the chase and had nothing to cover her with. "How much did you have to drink?"

"Not enough. I can still see your face."

He flinched as though she'd slapped him. Shake it off. Think rationally. Behind him he heard Clare's cashmere voice.

"I brought a robe, Nathaniel. Help her up while I put it on her."

"Mother," mumbled Frances. "Just what I need."

"Nate, is she ill?"

"Drunk." He pulled Frances up and supported her body weight while Clare put her into the robe. "Can you walk or shall I carry you?"

Her eyes fluttered and rolled back in her head as she collapsed against him. "She's out," he muttered, more to himself than to Clare.

"Use the entrance off the kitchen to carry her to her room."

He didn't bother to respond. There was nothing to say. All but the boldest guests had gone back inside the house when they saw Clare on the beach. Regardless, he didn't glance up as he carried his wife around to the side entrance of the house.

CHAPTER 23

Whitmore

FROM THE WINDOW of his bedroom, leaning his forehead against the glass, his breath a cloud of condensation on the window, Whitmore watched Nathaniel carry his sister off the beach. Turning back to his easel, he surveyed his work. It was of the lake that afternoon, gray mist hovering above brown water. Was it finished? Sleep on it, he decided. Sometimes he could tell what it needed after a period away.

He paced about the room, restless, thinking of Jeselle. Everything felt different. The moment he stepped into the kitchen he knew she'd changed. He remembered vividly how she'd been at ten years old, always laughing and moving through life like a dance, so alert and intelligent. How quick she was to learn things, everything absorbed in an instant and portrayed through the snap of her eyes. But now? She seemed old, almost brittle, like her mother, her carriage in a fixed line like Cassie's, with hardness in her eyes. Had his leaving done this, or was it the speed and force of adulthood that could capture your innocence, your brilliance, and bring you to your knees, turning you into your parents? He shuddered, thinking of becoming like his father. How could he get through these several weeks of holiday now, without Jes? All his life he'd felt her by his side, and without her he was left off-kilter and barren.

And his mother? She seemed frightfully thin and nervous, reminding him of a fragile china doll Frances had played with as a child. He couldn't help but think that things were worse since he'd left for school. For all of them.

He wandered outside. The sky had cleared during the party, and the moon was full. Sounds of laughter and clinking glasses floated across the yard as he walked along the path to the tree house, the moon lighting his way through the dense thicket of trees. Rung by rung, feeling in the dark, he climbed the ladder. Almost to the top, he stopped. Had he heard someone sniff? He climbed the last rung and looked in. Jes. Crying. Huddled in the corner.

"Jessie, what's the matter?"

"Nothing." Wooden voice, like they were strangers. "I like to come up here, clear my head, get a little peace and quiet."

A dog howled from one of the neighboring houses. Whit climbed the rest of the way in, watching her in the moonlight. The tree's branches rustled in the breeze.

She sighed in the darkness. "It's not the same here since you left." She said it with a hint of judgment in her tone, like it was his fault.

He sat with that for a moment, fighting against the tickle that started at the back of his eyelids.

"You have any girlfriends up there?" Was that a quiver in her voice? Was she jealous? After all this time she doubted him? She was the one who hadn't written.

"There are no girlfriends." The breeze brought the smell of burning tobacco and the sounds of laughter from the veranda.

"You best find a nice girl to marry. One that looks good sitting next to you at church when you're running Coca-Cola."

"What're you talking about?" She didn't answer. It was silent for several minutes except for the rustle of pine needles. Finally, he said, "Father told me there are a hundred men every day waiting for work outside the gates. How could I walk through the doors and leave them all there, hungry?"

"You know how many men wish they had that problem instead of begging for work?"

"You think I have any say over what happens to me?"

Her voice was soft and sad. "You'll be at one of those fancy parties with all those rich, white girls fawning all over you, and you'll realize you haven't checked for a letter from me in weeks."

He turned to her, horrified to hear the tears in his voice. "Listen to me, Jeselle Thorton. That will never happen. Not ever. You hear me?" A lump in his throat made it hard to swallow. Neither of them moved.

Then he felt her shift so that she was closer to him, her voice husky next to his shoulder. "I've been wondering if you saw the Atlantic Ocean?" She put her head on his arm.

He felt the tears tighten his throat again. "I did. It made me feel small."

"I knew it would."

Her breath came in little shakes. Crying. No, this he could not allow. He wrapped his arms around her, pulling her into his lap. She buried her face in his neck. Tears soaked his skin. He found her hands, brought them to his lips.

"Whit," she whispered against his fingers. "I missed you so much it hurt."

Vanilla and honey. He breathed in her scent as if to bring her mouth to his with the force of a wish, feeling possessed with fever, intoxicated from the nearness of her. And finally, after imagining it a thousand times, he kissed her. She shivered against him as he probed her mouth with the flesh of his lips, the slight tip of his tongue. After a second her mouth parted, and he felt her pressing into him, her small breasts against his chest. A sound in his throat, somewhere between a sigh and a groan, escaped. He spoke against her mouth, "Stay with me." She stiffened. Pulling away so that he might see her face, a chill slid between them. Her eyes, round and frightened. "I've asked too much. I'm sorry." He pulled back, trying to steady his ragged breath.

"No." She tightened her arms around his neck. "Whit, no matter what, tonight, don't stop."

"I'll never stop when it comes to you." He whispered against her mouth before crushing her to him.

CHAPTER 24

Lydia

"MOTHER," EMMA SAID, her face flushed, the beginning of tears in her voice. "You're too old to go to college. I mean, what will people think?" She dropped the knife on the table and stared at Lydia. A loose piece of apple fell to the floor. Birdie, her eyes wide, picked up the wayward fruit and plopped it into the bowl.

Lydia smiled. The week between Christmas and New Year's, having both the girls as well as Emma's new husband home, had come and gone too quickly. Tomorrow they would leave. "What people think doesn't matter to me. Your father's been gone over five years now, you're married, Birdie's off at college. I have some time to spare. You two have no idea how lonely it is here without you." She turned back to the ball of pastry on the table, rolling the piecrust into an even circle. What she didn't say was that if she liked it, she might stay for several years and complete the bachelor's degree that she walked away from to marry William all those years ago.

The acceptance letter that came just before New Year's Eve had been from Professor Fye himself. Before dancing a jig in her kitchen, she looked at the letter a second time just to make sure it was true. He must be old, she thought. His writing was messy, like his hands wobbled.

"I'll only be gone for a short time. You and Jack are busy this summer with his residency, anyway. You told me yourself you didn't think you could get home but once or twice this summer. And Birdie's going to summer school. There's no reason, really, for me to stay."

Emma's eyes darted back and forth. "I've only been married a few months. I wanted to be able to come home when I needed to."

Birdie picked up the knife and held it thoughtfully in her hands. "I think it sounds wonderful, Mother. They say it's beautiful up there in Montevallo. I'll bet you'll be the best one up there. Better than the teachers, even. But where will you live?"

"I'm staying in the ladies' housing."

"Mother." Emma put her hands on her hips. "You can't stay in the housing with girls. Why, they're all our age."

"I'll be used to it then, won't I?"

Birdie tucked her blonde hair behind her ears. "Plus, Mother's so young looking, they'll think she's one of them."

Lydia smiled, pleased at the compliment. "I was thinking about getting my hair cut like you girls."

Emma's eyes filled with tears. "But you've always had your long braid. Papa loved it so, remember?"

Lydia moved a sheet of crust into the bottom of the pie pan. "Change can give you a lift sometimes. I think I could use a lift."

"I think you should do it," said Birdie.

"Cut my hair or go to college?" Lydia asked with a laugh.

"Both." Birdie squealed and clapped her hands.

"But you'll have to sleep in the same room with those girls," said Emma. "It's not dignified."

Lydia laughed. "It's only ten weeks. Surely nothing terrible could happen in that amount of time."

*   *   *

By the next week, half the town knew of Lydia's summer plans. Everywhere she went, someone asked her about it. As she left the drug store, plump, bossy Rachel Stevens cornered her. Rachel widened her flat, brown eyes and rested her fingers on Lydia's forearm. "Now, I hear," pronouncing it *heeah* like they all did. Lydia, even after almost twenty years, still noticed the accent. "Now, I hear you're going up to Montevallo for a college course." Rachel paused and took a big breath into her cheeks. "Leavin' your home and family for two whole months. Why, I'm just amazed you'd think to do such a thing. Now I thought you already knew how to play the piana." She smiled, revealing her upper gums.

Lydia stopped herself from correcting her pronunciation of piano, remembering her mother's advice, that you must meet incivility with grace and politeness. "I'll be studying composition, which has been my interest for many years. Now the children are out of the house I have time to devote to further study." She paused and straightened her hat. "Now you'll have to excuse me, Rachel. I'm off to get my hair bobbed." And then she smiled in her most polite manner and turned to go, but not before noticing how Rachel's mouth was open like the bass that swam in the weeds and shallows.

PART FOUR

From Jeselle Thorton's journal.

May 13, 1934

Before the lake house was built, Whit and I swam in the creek near our home in Atlanta. It was a deep swimming hole, discovered during one of Whit's journeys into the woods. His job was to look for snakes and warn me if one was near. I was deathly afraid of their evil heads sticking out of the water, moving with a swiftness that left barely a ripple on the water. He'd yell out to me, "Snake!" Most times it was a harmless garter snake, but I would move from the water just the same. I never went all the way in, anyway, as my fear overwhelmed any wish for relief from the heat. I couldn't take the chance that I'd be submerged when one happened along.

Whitmore was afraid of nothing, plunging deeply into the water with no thought of snakes, jagged rocks, or hidden creatures. One day he rigged a rope swing from a tall oak and never tired of swinging over the water in a big sweeping loop, like a pendulum on a clock. He held on with both hands and feet, whooping like a wild animal as he swooped past his destination and then back. At just the right spot he'd let go and jump in, a look of sheer joy on his face. He'd disappear under the water for several seconds, during which time I was sure he would not reappear, before popping up and out of the water with a triumphant grin. "You should try it once, Jeselle, just one time," he always called to me where I sat with my toes in the water.

But I never did. Now I wish I had.

I used to daydream about what it would be like if my father were still alive. I imagined that Mama wouldn't be so tough and brittle if he were around to love her. One time I asked her if she and my daddy were an epic love story like Darcy and Elizabeth Bennett in Pride and Prejudice. She laughed hard, her brittle laugh that sounded like the breaking of a tree branch. "I don't know what kind of things you're reading, but real life ain't like a book. Best you know that now."

CHAPTER 25

Jeselle

MAMA KNITTED in the rocking chair near the woodstove in their cottage. Their servant's cottage, a front room and a bedroom that she and Mama shared, felt chilly. "Will you make a fire for us, Jes? Had a chill in my bones all afternoon, like someone walked over my grave." Unusual for May in Atlanta, rain had come in an unexpected gust that morning, and the temperature plummeted to the fifties. Mama picked up one of Jeselle's stockings. "Mercy, how do you get a hole in every one of your stockings?"

"Sorry, Mama." Jeselle knelt in front of the stove and wadded up an old newspaper, making a triangle of kindling around it, then lit the paper with one of the matches they kept on the shelf with Jeselle's books. The dry wood caught easily, but it would take a few minutes for the room to warm.

"Will you read to me from the newspaper?"

"Yes, Mama." Jeselle went to the window, her stomach turning. Rain fell in a steady stream, making mud puddles in the yard. She must tell Mama the truth tonight, or soon she would guess. Blood pounded between her ears so that it almost hid the sound of the rain tapping on the roof and the wood crackling in the stove. She crossed her arms against her swollen, tender breasts and leaned against the wall, trying to muster courage. She'd checked her undergarment after dinner, one last time, for blood—one last desperate hope before she had to face the truth. She hadn't had a cycle since Christmas. There was a strange ache in her midsection. A baby was coming. She'd known it for weeks now.

"Mama." She turned from the window.

"What is it, child?" Mama didn't look up from her knitting.

Jeselle crossed the room and stood before her, knees shaking under her dress, opening her mouth to speak, but no sound came.

"Were you fixing to read to me or not?"

"I'm going to have a baby."

The needles went still. Mama looked up at her, her face like stone. "Lawd. No."

"I'm sorry," Jeselle whispered.

"Who?"

The lie came out of her mouth fast. "You don't know him."

Mama stood. The back of the rocking chair bumped against the wall. "Tell me the truth, child."

"Someone I met when I worked for Mrs. Greer."

Mama stepped closer, peering into her face. Jeselle looked at the floor, feeling like the fires of hell might pull her under. Mama's rough, hardened palm struck her cheek. Jeselle yelped with surprise. "How dare you lie to me? After all I've done for you."

A blaze of anger overtook Jeselle, like a sudden sickness in the middle of the night. She raised her voice in mock deference, imitating Mama's vernacular. "Yep, you raised me up good and proper to take it from white folks. Taught me how to cook and clean instead of using the intelligence God gave me for something better."

"What kind of life did you think you was gonna have? Just 'cause you can read and write? You think Mrs. Bellmont was gonna send you off with Whit to Princeton like you was the same as him?"

Now Jeselle's voice was calm and quiet. "I am the same. You're the only one too ignorant to know it."

Mama raised her hand to strike again, but Jeselle blocked it with her forearm. Mama sputtered, her eyes black with anger. "Baby, you think you're the same as rich white folks? Well, I'm here to tell you that you ain't. You're the same as me, not them."

"Whit knows it, and God knows it. That's enough for me."

Mama went still. A look of understanding moved across her face. She fell into the rocking chair, bringing her hands to her neck. "Whit." Her face crumpled like a punctured ball. "Jessie, what have you done?" She clutched the arms of the rocking chair. "Did he make you?"

Was there a hint of hope to the question? "No, Mama, of course not. I went to him willingly. As his equal." Jeselle felt her chin lift in defiance as she uttered the truth out loud for the first time. "I love him, and he loves me. We've loved each other all our lives."

"You really think love is what that boy has for you? I know what boys think about, and it ain't love. You're a fool if you think he wants anything other than for you to spread your legs for him. Meanwhile, where is he? Back at Princeton. He finds this out he'll run for the hills. Mark my words."

"You're wrong."

Mama's face went from anger to distress. "Do you realize what will happen if Frank Bellmont finds out the truth? He'll throw us out on the street. Did you think of that?"

Jeselle began to cry. "I didn't, Mama. I'm sorry."

"The baby will come at the end of the summer. Maybe early September," said Mama, counting on her fingers.

"Yes, Mama."

Mama pulled Jeselle into her chest, hard. "Oh baby, what have you done?"

Jeselle sobbed harder, soaking the bodice of Mama's dress, but even as she did so she felt Mama's mind turning, working out a solution. After a time, she smoothed Jeselle's head and then led her to the bed. "I'll figure what to do."

Jeselle pulled the bedcovers up to her chin. Her eyes ached with fatigue. All she wanted to do for the last month was sleep. Mama paced, her brow furrowed in concentration. After a few moments she sat on the edge of the bed. "Reverend Young and his wife, they've been wanting a baby for years now. I'll tell them our situation and see if they'll take the baby. We can write to Mr. Nate and see if you can work in his house up there until the baby comes. I have a cousin Bess that lives out near Montevallo. You can stay with her." She wiped her hands together like she did when she'd finished shaping a loaf of bread.

Like I'm flour on her hands, thought Jeselle. She stared at the ceiling, feeling a part of her die. "Just like that, Mama?"

Mama's eyes were hard again. "What other choice do you have? You think Mrs. Bellmont won't figure this out? She's seen plain as I have the way that boy has looked at you all these years. A half-Negro grandchild is not in their plans, I can tell you that."

She turned on her side, pushing her face into the pillow, wanting only to be left alone to think. "Can I sleep now, Mama?"

"You best do that. We'll get everything settled in the morning. You'll have to write the letter to Mr. Nate for me. I'll tell him you need a job. He'll be glad to get you, be my guess, given Frances."

* * *

Jeselle was passing the sitting room when Mrs. Bellmont called out to her from her secretary desk, flushed and breathless like she'd just run up the stairs. "Will you shut the door, baby girl?"

Jeselle did as she asked. What made Mrs. Bellmont's face so queer? "Is everything all right? Is it Whit?"

Mrs. Bellmont waved her hands in the air. "Oh, no, nothing bad. In fact, quite the opposite. I've been practically beside myself, waiting to hear. And now, here it was in today's post." She took a deep breath, picking up an envelope from the desk. "I'm going to try and say this slow, so I don't scare you." She held the envelope between two hands. "This is a letter from Oberlin College. They're in Ohio, and they've been accepting black women for almost one hundred years—there are many black women graduates since the 1800s with bachelor's degrees, and Jes, even a few doctorates. I have a friend whose brother is a professor there. I wrote to him and sent samples of your writing and told him of our studies together. He was terribly impressed with one of your essays. Your analysis of Macbeth. Remember?"

Jeselle nodded, holding her breath.

"We've corresponded, and this morning I received a letter from him. They want you, Jes. They want you to come study there."

Jeselle's legs wobbled. Her eyes followed the second hand on the clock beside the desk. A crow squawked outside the window. "How would I pay for it?"

"I have it figured." Mrs. Bellmont waved her hand dismissively.

"Oh no. You sold your wedding ring to do this." How could she? How could Mrs. Bellmont risk her husband's wrath? For her? Especially after what Jeselle had done. She glanced at Mrs. Bellmont's left arm, healed now, but her bones were easily broken again. Or worse.

Mrs. Bellmont rose from her chair and paced in front of the window. "I have enough for four years, and no one will ever know where it came from."

"Lord. Oh, Lord."

"Please don't be horrified by my lie. Jes, there was no other way I could think of to get the money together."

"Mama will never allow it."

"I've thought about this. We're to tell her that you received a scholarship. Which you would've been granted, I'm certain of it, if it weren't for this rotten Depression."

"When would I go?"

"Not until mid-September. So I can have both you and Whit home for another summer."

Jeselle sank into the nearest chair.

"I feel like I'm going myself, I'm so excited. This is your destiny. You'll be a learned woman, Jeselle."

Jeselle jumped when Mama knocked on one of the glass panes in the door. Mrs. Bellmont waved her in. "Shall I tell her, or you?"

"You, please."

"Cassie, we've wonderful news."

Mama's expression did not change as Mrs. Bellmont told her the details of Oberlin College. "A scholarship?"

"Yes, Cassie. Tuition's covered, and I'll help with books or whatever from my household budget so Frank will never know."

Mama's expression remained unreadable. "She could be a teacher afterward?"

"Or a writer. Or lawyer. Anything she wanted to be. She's smart enough for any profession, Cassie."

"I never heard of such a thing. A black girl going to college." Mama sank into the chair next to Jeselle.

"Do you understand what this could mean?" asked Mrs. Bellmont.

Mama looked at Mrs. Bellmont. There were tears now, leaking from the corners of her eyes. "I know what it means, Miz Bellmont. It means no more Mrs. Greers. It means she could go to the colored parts of town and help people. It means freedom."

Jeselle wept, too, silent tears into her hands.

Mrs. Bellmont kneeled in front of Mama and handed her a handkerchief from her dress pocket. "Cassie, in all the years I've known you, I've never seen you cry."

"I'm a silly fool." Mama wiped her eyes. "Miz Bellmont, there's a letter from Mr. Nate there for you, too." She pointed to the unopened mail.

"Oh, yes, thank you, Cassie. In all the excitement I forgot to open it. I hope it isn't bad news about Frances."

Using her silver letter opener, she sliced open the envelope. She read, her eyes moving over the page quickly. After a moment, she looked up. "Well, it's strange, the timing of it. Nate asked if Jeselle could come help them out for a couple of months. He says Frances is worse, and he's beside himself half the time."

"Can I go, Mrs. Bellmont?"

Mrs. Bellmont's eyes were troubled as she folded the letter and put it back in the envelope. "Well, of course you can't go, Jes. You'll be getting ready for school all summer. You'll need a new wardrobe, and we'll have to shop for books and get everything in order. I'll have to think of something else for Nate." Her eyes skirted to a stack of brochures of resting places for the ill and insane on the desk. Jeselle had seen her looking through them last night.

"But I'd like to go, Mrs. Bellmont. It would give me the chance to earn additional money for school. For clothes and books and all."

"We can't take your charity, Miz Bellmont," said Mama.

Jeselle's eyes went to Mrs. Bellmont's bare hand.

"Yes, but surely there's a better way than working for Frances," said Mrs. Bellmont.

"But think of poor Mr. Nate," said Jeselle. "He needs help."

"Yes, we saw that plain as day at Christmas. Jessie would be a help to them, and she knows Miss Frances's ways," said Mama.

Mrs. Bellmont looked back and forth between them, her eyes glittering. "The two of you—always worrying about someone besides yourselves. I'm humbled." With a flourish, she pulled a piece of stationery from a desk drawer. "I'll write and let him know. It'll just be for the summer, Jes. I'll make certain he knows you have to be back in time to get ready for school." She shook her head, clapping her hands together. "This is one of the happiest days of my life. All your hard work will finally be rewarded."

CHAPTER 26

Lydia

ON THE LAST DAY of May, the hum of men's voices hushed when Lydia came through the door of Sam's barbershop. Half a dozen old men littered the room, three by the window reading newspapers, several playing checkers. A younger man, around the age William would be if he were alive, sat in the barber's chair getting a shave. She reached for the door handle and turned back to look at the street, her resolve of bravery diminished with the smell of men, cigar smoke, and talcum powder, all of which reminded her of the days William had spent here with these men. He was gone, and they were still here—fully present to disapprove of her decision.

She gripped the door handle tighter. What do I do?

Who cares what they think? Ah, William's voice, so distant now, suddenly there in her mind.

"I'm here to have my hair bobbed," she announced, stepping into the middle of the room. Everyone looked at her at once. Someone cleared his throat.

"Have a seat," Sam said. "I'm almost done with George here."

She did so, pulling her long braid over her shoulder and holding it between her fingers, remembering. She thought of her mother's soft hands braiding it when she was a child. On their wedding night, William had taken out the braid, his eyes hungry as the long locks fell around her bare shoulders. Finally, an image came of her babies, pulling on it with their pudgy fingers while they drank from her breast.

When it was her turn, she scooted into the barber's chair, smoothing her dress to avoid looking at Sam, fearing she might lose courage if she detected disapproval in his eyes.

"How short?" He held the braid in the air like it was a piece of meat at the butcher shop. Behind them the men were back to their activities but silent, listening.

She took a deep breath, staring at her reflection in the mirror. "To my chin."

He raised his eyebrows. "Thought you were the old-fashioned type, Mrs. Tyler."

"Perhaps I am. Perhaps I'm not."

He reached for his scissors. "Best thing to do is cut the whole braid off at once. Then I can trim around the edges."

"Fine."

He pulled the braid out from her neck, until it was straight like an angry cat's tail, and then without any announcement or formality, cut it. The remainder of her hair fell in uneven sections just below her chin. He held the braid up for her to see. "You wanna keep it?"

"What for?" What would she do with a braid of hair, for heaven's sake? "Should I hang it next to the dead chickens in my barn?"

He stared at her for a moment before shrugging. "Heard you're leaving town for a time. Someone keeping an eye on your place?"

"Smitty and June across the creek."

"Good," he said, without taking his eyes from her hair. His voice was a touch stern, almost like a warning. "Wouldn't want anything to happen to William's place while you're off running around. His mother would turn in her grave anything happened to that ole place."

Lydia didn't think William's mother would have cared two cents about her old home or the piece of red dirt it sat on. She was most likely in heaven with her husband and William, singing with the angels. But she didn't say anything, knowing it was useless.

He trimmed around her neck and face until her hair was even. When he finished, she looked at herself, surprised. The shorter style made her face look rounder and younger. Her eyes seemed more prominent. It was like looking at a stranger. Her head felt weightless. So did her spirit. Time to move on, she thought.

* * *

At home Birdie had left a note that she was visiting a friend and would be back for dinner. Birdie had come home for the weekend to say goodbye to her mother. Lydia's train to Montevallo left in the early morning. Birdie would head back to summer school with friends after Lydia was gone.

Lydia covered the furniture and piano with spare blankets. In her bedroom she picked up the photo of William in his WWI uniform. Survived the war, she often thought, and died on his own dirt road. She leaned over to place it in the satchel, but hesitated, her hand poised in midair. No, she thought, William would stay. He belonged here. She put his photo back on the dresser.

She'd sewn two new dresses for the trip: one in yellow linen with a white collar and belt, the other in a soft blue cotton that matched her eyes. She splurged by buying a new hat, a pink straw with a yellow ribbon, which she took out of its box and tried on in front of the mirror, strangely satisfied at the effect of the hat with her newly shorn hair.

After she finished packing, she took the kitchen shears and cut some yellow roses from her yard, pricking her index finger on a thorn as she gathered them into a bouquet. It had taken a good two years before she could look at or smell flowers without thinking of death, but finally one day she saw them again for their beauty instead of being reminded of pain.

She headed out Whitaker Road on foot, sucking her finger. When she arrived at the cemetery she went to the family plot and laid the roses on William's grave. "Going away for a while." She wiped a bit of dirt from his tombstone. "Don't worry. I'll be careful."

He didn't answer back.

*   *   *

The next morning she was up before the sun. The train north to Montevallo would leave at six a.m., and she had no intention of missing it. She moved quietly through the house, careful not to wake Birdie, as she washed and dressed in her yellow linen dress and new hat. Examining herself in the mirror, she hoped her homemade clothes didn't look too "country."

She decided not to wake Birdie. No reason to; they'd said their goodbyes last night before bed. The girl needed her rest, Lydia told herself.

She left a note on the kitchen table. "Goodbye, my love. I'll miss you and will look forward to our reunion at the end of the summer. No one could ask for a better daughter than you, my little Birdie. Don't forget to eat. I want you plump by the time I see you again. Love, Mother."

Lydia sniffed a little, walking to the station, dabbing her eyes with a handkerchief, feeling ridiculous for her sentimentality. At the station she boarded the train and chose a seat next to the window. She wanted to see everything on this, her first trip in twenty years. After several minutes, two young men dressed in Navy uniforms took the seats opposite her. They tipped their hats politely, and she managed a small smile before looking out the window at the brick wall of the train station. The smell of oil and cigarettes made her feel nauseous, and she took off her hat, leaning her cheek against the cool glass window. The train squeaked as it began to leave the station, and she spotted a figure in her peripheral vision. She turned. It was Birdie, running along the platform, waving her hat, grinning. Lydia stood, yanking down her window. Birdie yelled, "Mother, you'll be the best up there, I just know it." The train was almost out of the station, and Birdie stopped, still waving. Then the train picked up speed and rounded a corner.

Lydia suddenly remembered the day she'd left for college. Her mother, as they'd waited for the train, had dabbed her eyes with a white handkerchief. She'd seemed so feeble and sad that Lydia hadn't wanted to go. "I should stay home and take care of you."

"No, no, I'll be fine," her mother answered. "Your papa's going to take me to Florida for the warm weather. It's supposed to do wonders for tuberculosis."

"But, Mother," Lydia started.

Her mother put up her hand to shush her. "No. Your heart's made for adventure, Lydia. I want you to have everything the world offers. Go. Go have wild, grand escapades."

Lydia stumbled toward the train, her vision blurry from tears. At the last moment her mother grabbed her and pulled her into an embrace. "Don't forget to stand up straight," she whispered in Lydia's ear. "Stand up tall, the way God made you."

Those were the last words Lydia's mother had ever said to her. She was dead by Christmas.

CHAPTER 27

Jeselle

IT WAS a mighty swell and push at the train station, a swarm of people hustling to find their platforms, lugging satchels and children in grasping palms. Jeselle, Mama, and Mrs. Bellmont huddled together, waiting for the boarding call for the train headed to Montevallo.

"Listen, you come on home if anything goes wrong," said Mrs. Bellmont.

"Yes, Mrs. Bellmont." Jeselle stared at the floor, feeling the shame creep through her until she wanted to fall upon the floor and surrender to the devil himself.

Dressed in her new blue cotton skirt and blouse and matching jacket, she felt hot and bloated. Mrs. Bellmont had presented the new outfit to her as a gift.

"A travelling suit for a young lady," said Mrs. Bellmont.

In her new satchel were two everyday dresses, along with several sets of underclothes and oversized aprons Mama had made with large ruffles to try to disguise her stomach for as long as possible.

Mrs. Bellmont lifted Jeselle's chin in her hands. "No shame in changing your mind."

"Hogwash," said Mama. "She don't wanna let Mr. Nate down now."

"No, I want to go. It's a chance for me to thank you for all you've done for me."

"Oh, baby girl, it's all been selfish on my part. You'll understand, as you get older. But, thank you. Thank you for your gratitude. Grateful people are more content. Did you know that?"

"Yes, Mrs. Bellmont," she whispered. "And I am grateful to you. Please don't ever forget it."

"You're acting like you're going away forever." Mrs. Bellmont squeezed Jeselle's hand. "You'll be back before you know it."

Jeselle glanced over at Mama. "I'm thankful for you, too, Mama. I know everything you've done to make sure I made it through this world safe." She tuned to Mrs. Bellmont. "Will you tell me the story of when we came to you? Just once more as we wait for the train?"

Mama examined calluses on the palms of her hands as Mrs. Bellmont began the story they knew so well: Mama, her husband buried only days before, arriving at the back door holding infant Jeselle, with no job, no place to live, and no more than a quarter in her purse. Mama told Mrs. Bellmont flat out that she needed work, that to find a live-in position with a wealthy family was her only chance. Mrs. Bellmont, weary from caring for thirteen-month-old Whitmore and precocious Frances had welcomed them inside and after only a few minutes offered Cassie a job and the cottage to live in.

"And Cassie's been taking care of me ever since," said Mrs. Bellmont, finishing her story.

"Other way round, Miz Bellmont."

Mrs. Bellmont smiled. "Nonsense, and you know it."

Just then a porter in a black and red suit called for the white passengers to board the train. After a few moments, the man nodded at Jeselle and a few of the other black passengers. He didn't speak to them, just waved them toward the last passenger car.

Mrs. Bellmont took Jeselle in her arms. She smiled, her gentle smile that Jeselle had loved all her life. "Time to go, I guess."

"Goodbye," she said, trying not to cry.

"Tell Nate to call us when you get there," said Mrs. Bellmont.

Mama patted her arm. "Do good now."

"I'll do the best I can."

Once inside the train, Jeselle crouched low in the seat and let the tears flow, watching Mama and Mrs. Bellmont standing together on the platform. Mrs. Bellmont waved a white handkerchief and dabbed her eyes. Mama stared at the train with a blank expression. It was the last time, Jeselle thought, that she would ever see them again.

In the dark night when she hadn't been able to sleep, she'd come up with a plan. To go to college was her dream, but inside her a tiny somebody, a unique person made of her and Whit and Mama and

Mrs. Bellmont, grew. Nothing mattered more than her child. No one would take her baby. She could not possibly give her baby to strangers and go off to college as if she had not brought a life into this world.

She would work for Mr. Nate until a month before the baby was to come; by her calculations the baby would come in the middle of September. She had until August to save enough money to take the train west, where she could disappear forever.

Whit could not be a father to this baby. She knew his life would be ruined if it came out he fathered a Negro child. He would not be able to control himself and would go up against his father, acting impulsively and declaring that they must be together, no matter what anyone thought. Even if one of them weren't mobbed and killed in the street, Frank Bellmont, worried about scandal, would devise a scheme to keep them apart.

That left only one solution. She must disappear.

The train began to move, like a monster waking from the dead. The pace was slow through the busy streets, dingy buildings, and rundown dwellings of industrial Atlanta. Once outside the city, the wheels moved faster and faster until it felt like they were slicing through air. The chugging motion relaxed her as green pastures and farms appeared in her window. She leaned her head against the glass and sobbed silently into her handkerchief that smelled of Mama.

CHAPTER 28

Nathaniel

NATHANIEL TAUGHT his last class of the spring term. He assigned final grades by noon and tidied his office of paperwork, but it was still too early to leave for the train station to pick up Jeselle. He didn't want to go home to Frances. Not yet. But he didn't feel like staying at his office, either. Or fiddling at the piano with his compositions. Nothing was right today. Nothing sounded appealing. What did he want? If he could start all over again, would he even know? The days piled one on top of the other, filled with Frances, always Frances, until, here it was, the start of June already, and summer term would start in a few days.

He would leave early and watch the trains come and go, he decided. Nathaniel drove with his windows down, the scents of spring, mowed grass and gardenias, drifted inside like old friends. The sky was blue with only a few puffball clouds low on the horizon. As he approached the station, he heard the faint whistle of the first afternoon arrival. This would be the train from southern Alabama, he thought, remembering that Walt had come in on it the last time he visited.

In the parking area, Nathaniel tugged off his jacket and necktie and rolled up his shirtsleeves. A cigarette. Just one? Yes, just one. He wanted to quit, having noticed they made his breathing harder when he walked, like he couldn't get enough air inside his lungs. But so far he'd been unsuccessful in quitting cigarettes or whiskey. His mother would be appalled at his new vices. He took one of the cigarettes from the pouch and lit it, taking a deep drag that he blew out the open car window. Near the depot building, the azaleas were in their full spring glory, God's beauty standing in stark contrast to the men in tattered work clothes and boots lined up outside the coal mining office. Waiting. Always waiting. Waiting for work that never came.

The train whistle blew. Trains. How he'd loved them as a boy. As an adult they'd represented adventure and acclaim as he went from city to city on tours. He smoked a second cigarette, staring out the window. Of course there was no such thing as just one. Cigarettes and whiskey, same problem. To think there was a time when he wouldn't have touched whiskey. But that was before. Before the accident. Everything was divided like this. Life before the accident and life after.

Lavender grew next to the fence, and bees swarmed over the fragrant flowers, so many that he could hear their faint, collective buzz. He smoked the second cigarette until he could no longer hold it without burning his fingers and tossed in on the ground. A walk, perhaps? Would that clear his mind? He got out of the car, stomping the cigarette butt with the toe of his shoe, and walked toward the station's office.

The chug of the train's engine was like the low notes of a cello, the whistle punctuating in a high note as if from a flute, the clanging of the wheels against the tracks the percussion. He leaned against the station's brick wall, his hands in his pockets. The arriving train came to a stop. He wondered what the train's arrival meant for each of the passengers: a new beginning, a quest, a reunion with a loved one? All possibilities that no longer existed for him.

It was in the release of that thought that he saw her for the first time. She stood at the exit of the passenger car, a small suitcase in one white-gloved hand and a handbag in the other, surveying the station with squared shoulders and an anticipatory expression on her refined face, like she was embarking on a splendid journey of some kind, perhaps a safari or a visit to the pyramids. She wore a yellow dress the color of lemon pie and a faint pink straw hat with a wide brim and pale yellow ribbon the same shade as her bobbed hair. Without thinking, he moved closer to the train, his eyes upon her. She surveyed the platform, and then her gaze came to rest on his face. She smiled in a hesitant way and then stepped from the train, moving with an athletic grace, as if he were there to meet her. She was unusually tall for a woman, almost like she'd been stretched from head to foot, elongating every aspect of her. Even her face was long and skinny, with a small pointy nose that perfectly matched the elegant tip of her chin. She radiates energy, he thought, transfixed.

By then she was upon him. "Excuse me, sir, would you be so kind as to point me toward Alabama College?" Her voice was low-pitched, almost husky, with a northern accent.

He felt himself go hot at the neck. "That way." He pointed east.

"Oh, thank you very much." Her eyes were light blue and alive, full of humor. "I've just arrived, as you can see, from Atmore, Alabama. Have you heard of it?"

"I'm not from here, but that's near Mobile, isn't it?"

"Right. I'm not from here either, the South, I mean. Well, I've lived here for twenty years, but I'm from upstate New York originally." She set down her suitcase and adjusted her hat. "I was suddenly almost too frightened to get off the train. I haven't been away from my home in, well, in a long while." She peered at him from under the brim of her hat in a way that made him uncomfortable. Women's gazes still did that to him, even after all the years with Frances. "Were you waiting for someone?"

"No. I mean, yes." He tried to think of how to explain his presence, but his mind was blank. He might not remember his own name if she'd asked that. "I'm here to meet someone, but she's not on this train. She's coming from Atlanta." To his surprise, another truth tumbled from his mouth. "I suddenly couldn't bear my own life so I came here to look at trains come and go, wishing I could be on one of them. But I can't." Flushing, he cleared his throat. "That sounds ridiculous, doesn't it?"

"Not at all. I understand perfectly."

The way she looked at him! It felt as if it might pierce through to the center of his brain.

"There are times in every life when we must dig in and stay rather than fly, no matter how much we might want to."

The scar on his arm pulsed. "Quite so."

She picked up her suitcase. "I should get on, then. Thank you for your assistance."

He felt the air go out of him. "Of course. Have a lovely day."

She smiled, revealing a row of small, shiny teeth. Her smile was like sudden sunshine on a dark day and made her as beautiful as any woman he'd ever seen. "Wish me luck. I'm quite terrified."

"I imagine you're the type of woman who makes her own luck, but I wish you some just the same. Good day." He tipped his hat and turned away, feeling her eyes still on him.

CHAPTER 29

Jeselle

NATE WAS WAITING when the train pulled into the station. She almost cried at seeing his familiar face. He rushed to greet her, taking her satchel. "Jeselle, good to see you. How was your trip?"

"Fine, sir."

They drove through the main part of town, passing a downtown area with a café and movie theater. Several brick buildings lining the streets housed various shops: drugstore, grocery store, fruit and vegetable stand, and a lawyer's office. A block from Main Street the streets turned residential: neat homes with green lawns and flowers and dipping, moss-covered oaks. They passed a large, brick church with stained glass windows. Nate pointed across the street from the church. "There's the college." It was a clump of brick buildings arranged around a water tower and wide, grassy lawns and brick paths. Beautiful. Jeselle turned away, focusing on the tips of her shoes.

They turned down a street called Vine. The houses on this street were more modest than others they'd passed: modern Craftsman homes with front porches and small lawns. At several of them, white women sat on rocking chairs, snapping green beans or knitting, occasionally calling out to one another.

Inside the house, Nate and Jeselle sat at a small table in the kitchen to discuss her duties. "Just standard cooking and cleaning."

"Where's Miss Frances?"

He rubbed his eyes. "Resting. She has a lot of sad days. It's best to stay out of her way if you can." He paused, looking at her. "But I suppose you know that."

"Yes, sir. I've known her all my life."

"If you have any questions, save them until I get home."

"Yes, sir."

"I'm looking forward to some decent cooking," he said with a smile. "Come on, I'll take you out to your cousin's. You can start tomorrow."

"No, sir. I'm here. I'll fix your supper before I leave. And I'll walk to Bess's." Mama had given strict instructions on this: Nate was not to see where and how Bess lived. "It's no more than a quarter mile out of town." This was a lie. From the directions Bess's husband, Ben, sent, Jeselle knew it to be at least two miles out of town, down a dirt road on Pierson's farm.

She fixed Nate and Frances's supper: slices of leftover ham, collard greens, and some biscuits. Nate insisted she eat as well before setting out to walk to Bess's farm.

Jeselle carried her satchel in one hand, feeling a blister developing in the palm of her hand. The heat of the day had dissipated some with the setting of the sun, but it was still muggy and warm, and Jeselle was weary and emotionally numb. She felt the additional girth of her growing baby; she was breathless, and her feet ached.

She walked past a creek, over a crest of a low hill, and then along a paved country road until the she saw a dirt lane marked with a sign that said, "Pierson." Ben had written that the house was about 200 yards down the dirt driveway, but it felt like she might never see another sign of humanity. Pines, unusually tall, enclosed the road so that Jeselle felt alone and frightened. Dark shadows between the trees reminded her of a children's fairy tale, as if something frightening might jump out any moment. She told herself it was ridiculous to think this way. It was nothing but a hot and dusty road.

At a bend in the road, Jeselle rounded the corner and saw the cabin—a ramshackle heap of boards tossed together, leaning to the left, and the roof and front porch sagging into the shape of a crooked smile. No front door and two windows without glass, so that Jeselle could see right through the house to the other side.

A young couple stood on the porch. Jeselle assumed they were her cousin Bess and the husband, Ben. Holding onto Bess's skirt were two small girls. An older boy, around ten, stood next to his father. Bess held a baby in her arms.

The little girls came running toward her. "Cousin Jes. Cousin Jes," they shouted. She realized she had no gifts for them as they tugged on the skirt of her dress, pulling her toward the house. The boy took her satchel, his eyes on the ground.

"Thank you for having me," Jeselle said straightaway.

"You talk like a white girl." Bess, tall, stooped-shouldered, and with a protruding midsection, narrowed her eyes, looking Jeselle up and down.

"Bessie, that ain't polite." Ben was a clear-eyed, large man with skin the color of dark brown leather. He put out his hand. "Glad to meet some of Bess's family."

Bess's eyes hadn't left Jeselle's face. Jeselle felt her assessing her character in a way that reminded her of Mama. "Hardly family." Bess turned to her husband as if Jeselle were not there. "She's a distant cousin ain't no one heard of 'til they needed something."

They all went inside the house: two rooms, with only a thin wall dividing them. "We all sleep in there." Bess pointed to a double bed, cot, and an apple cart with a baby blanket. "You'll have to sleep on the porch."

The boy handed her two blankets, still with his eyes cast toward the floor. "Made a cot for you from some old scraps of wood." He pointed toward the porch. "It can be a bench, too."

"What's your name?" asked Jeselle.

"Tom."

"I have a friend who made things from scraps of wood when he was a boy, too," said Jeselle.

"Ain't nothing but couple boards I nailed together." He glanced up this time and gave her a slight, shy smile.

"Good Lord gave Tom a gift for making things," said Ben. "He built that table for us with nothing but his bare hands." He pointed to a wooden table in the corner of the room.

"Made it from wood from Pierson's old barn," said Tom.

Jeselle peered more closely at the table. The legs were peeled pine trunks or branches, as big around as a man's forearm. The tabletop was made of thin slabs of wood with peeling red paint, like a snake shedding its skin. "It's beautiful," said Jeselle. "Pierson?"

"He's the landowner," Ben said. He went on to explain to her that as sharecroppers they were given seventy-five dollars' worth of supplies for the cotton season, and whatever profit they made at harvest time was theirs to keep.

"But at the end of the season, there never seems to be any left, and we owe more than we borrowed," said Bess.

"Who keeps the books?" Jeselle asked.

"The boss," said Tom.

"You want me to look at them for you?" asked Jeselle.

"Boss never allow that," said Ben.

"Tom can pick like a man." Bess pointed at a stack of picking bags near the doorway. "He fill two of those a day."

"Joy and Lizzie as fast as me," said Tom. "Only they can't last as long, being little." He paused, looking over at his mother. "I can go twelve hours in hundred-degree heat."

"He sure can," said Bess.

Twelve hours? "How old are you, Tom?" Jeselle asked.

"Twelve," said Ben. "Lizzie and Joy are five and seven. They pick with two hands, sacks so heavy they can't carry 'em by the end of the day."

"Pluck, pluck, drop-it-in-the-bag," said the older girl, Joy.

"Me and Bess do the chopping," said Ben. "It's harder, and the boss always staring at us to go faster."

"Chopping?" asked Jeselle.

Bess made an impatient sound. "Clearing weeds. With a hoe. Cotton can't grow with weeds taking from the dirt."

"Do the children go to school?" asked Jeselle, ignoring Bess's glare but feeling the heat of embarrassment. She must seem like a spoiled dolt to her cousin, not knowing something that was a rote part of their lives.

"They closed the Negro school 'cause there ain't money to keep it open. Don't matter," said Bess. "Pickin' season lasts all through the summer and into November so they don't got time anyway. By time winter comes it turn cold, and they don't got shoes."

"I went to school a couple of years," said Tom. "I can read."

The little girls continued to stare at Jeselle. They pulled on her skirt and looked up at her with round brown eyes. "Did you come here on the train?"

"Yes," said Jeselle.

"Was it fast?" the older one asked. "Tom told us it's like a bullet shooting from a gun."

"It was. Faster than a car for sure."

"You been in a car?" said Joy.

"I know how to drive a car," said Jeselle.

"You do?" said Tom, his eyes big.

"We start work at dawn," Bess said, her features turning from flat to hostile. "During pickin' season we work from when we can see to can't see."

"Of course. I'm sorry to be a bother to you," said Jeselle. "Is there anything I can do to help while I'm here?"

"Your mama sent us some money," said Ben. "We're mighty glad for it."

"Um, where's the bathroom?" asked Jess, flustered. She hadn't known that Mama sent money.

"Outhouse around back." Ben lit a new candle from the one on the table and handed it to her. "But we left a bucket for you by your cot. It's best to use a bucket this time of night. Snakes and such after dark."

Jeselle shuddered as she said goodnight and went outside. It was dark now, and the light from the flickering candle made shadows. The cot was a flat piece of lumber stacked on bricks. She put one of the blankets down in place of a mattress and then pulled one of her work dresses out of the satchel and changed in the light of the candle, too tired to care if anyone saw her. She squatted over the bucket and urinated, throwing the waste off the side of the porch. Shivering from fright rather than cold, she blew out the candle and climbed onto the cot. The air felt heavy with moisture. She used the blanket for a pillow, lying on her back and cradling her belly with both arms.

The night was a pool of black ink. A cloud layer, low in the sky, allowed no stars or moon to give Jeselle any relief from the despair that was beginning to seep inside her. She closed her eyes, thinking of Whitmore, wondering if there were stars where he was tonight.

A rustling, scratching sound penetrated the quiet night. Rodents, she realized with horror, scampering about on their tiny feet around the porch and up the walls. "Please, God, don't let the rats get me while I sleep." The crickets began to chirp. They were loud, drowning out the clamoring scuttle of critters' feet, and she drifted off to sleep. She dreamt of her cousins' little hands, grabbing at that cotton, pluck, pluck, drop-it-in-the-bag, their brown eyes hungry, and they were singing:

> Trouble comes, trouble goes,
> I done had my share of woes.
> Times get better by-n-by.
> But then my time will come to die.

*   *   *

She awakened to the sound of a bell ringing from some distance away. Loud like a church bell except that it was a dull, relentless clanging. Inside the house, the baby cried. Floorboards creaked, and voices, low, called out to one another. Flatware clanked against tin plates. Jeselle got up, folding her blankets into neat squares before going inside. Bess was in the rocking chair, nursing the baby.

"Morning," said Jeselle.

Bess nodded but didn't say anything. The children sat at the table, eating biscuits that crumbled in their hands. They wet their fingers with their tongues and scooped up every crumb, leaving nothing but the sheen of the tin plate.

Jeselle hovered a few feet from the table. The children, intent on their measly breakfast, didn't look over at her. Ben came in from the other room. "Mornin', Jes. There's a biscuit saved for you."

"No, it's all right. I'll have something once I get to work."

"Best be getting on then," Ben said to his family. The children rose from the table and gathered their picking sacks from a corner by the door, slinging them over their shoulders. Bess tied the baby to her back using something that resembled a horse harness. The children trudged out the door, with Bess and Ben behind them. From the doorway Jeselle watched the children head toward the fields, walking behind their parents, abreast, in birth order like stair steps. She put her hand on her belly. "No," she whispered. "No."

CHAPTER 30

Nathaniel

NATHANIEL KNELT to smell the lilacs that hung in fragrant abundance near the back gate of his house, the late afternoon sun hot on his shoulders. He felt preoccupied, bothered by a comment the dean had said to him that morning. "Saw a woman coming out of the tavern the other day, midafternoon, who could've been your wife's sister." Nathaniel had peered at him closely afterward, to detect either malice or insinuation, but saw nothing. It was only a genuine, innocent remark. Yet, it agitated Nate all morning, and he'd decided to walk home and simply ask Frances if she'd been there or not. He couldn't imagine that she would set one dainty foot in the joint, rumored to be full of old drunks and women of ill repute, but he would ask just the same, he decided, to ease his mind.

Using his pocketknife, he clipped a bunch of the lilacs. It was then he heard a screech through the kitchen's open window. "What have you done?" It was Frances.

Dropping the bouquet, he ran toward the kitchen door. He heard Jeselle say, "I'm sorry, Miss Frances. It was an accident."

"This was silk from India, you stupid girl," Frances said, loud and shrill. Jeselle screamed.

He burst into the kitchen, tripping over the top step. Jeselle stood at the ironing board clutching her right arm, her face twisted in pain. Frances, her eyes wild, waved a dress with a hole the size and shape of the iron through the bodice. In the other hand she held the electric iron, its cord dangling at her feet.

"She burned me," Jeselle whispered.

Nathaniel felt bile rise to his throat. He grabbed the iron from Frances. "Get out of my sight." Frances opened her mouth as if to protest, but Nathaniel put up his hand. "Get out." She ran through the door to the living room.

He guided Jeselle to a kitchen chair, and she buckled into it, gazing at him with big, scared eyes.

"Will I have to go now?"

He didn't answer as he opened the door to their electric refrigerator, searching for something cold to put on her arm. He pulled out a glass container of milk.

"Put this on your arm." The burn was a pink mark the shape of the iron, but there was no blistering. "Stay here." He ran to the shed, filled a bucket with ice, and returned to the kitchen. "Put your arm in here." He went to the phone and dialed the operator. "Doctor Landry, please."

The doctor picked up after the third ring. "Jesus, boy," he said, after Nathaniel explained that his maid had been burned by the iron. Nathaniel could tell he had a cigar in his mouth by the way the words came out pinched. "How long you lived in these parts now? I don't know what you Yankees do up north, but down here white doctors don't treat colored folks. Take her out to her own people. I hear there's a colored doctor. Voodoo type."

Nathaniel hung up and glanced at Jeselle. "I could've told you he wouldn't see me, Mr. Nate," she said.

He leaned against the counter, trying to think what to do. "You want to see the other doctor?"

Her lips trembled. "No, I don't want any trouble. It's not that bad. I burned myself worse on the stove one time." She held up her other hand to show him a skinny scar across the top of her hand. "See, I got that taking Mrs. Greer's roast out of the oven."

Her unburned arm rested on her belly. Was she plumper than he remembered? She seemed bigger around the middle, especially compared with the slenderness of her arms and legs. And then it came to him: she was with child. From the size of her belly he guessed she was around five months along. That was around the time Frances had begun to show. He sank into the other chair. "Are you going to have a baby?"

She met his eyes. "Yes."

Frances's heeled shoes paced the floor in the other room. "Is that why your mother sent you here?" he whispered, indicating the door with his eyes.

She nodded, slumping forward. The clatter of Frances's shoes stopped. She listened at the door. "Get your things. I'll drive you home. You should rest this afternoon."

"But what about the work?"

"Don't worry about that. It'll still be here tomorrow." He pointed toward his parked car in the driveway. "Go wait in the car for a moment. I need to talk with Frances." Frances's shoes clicked away from the door. He waited for Jeselle to leave the house before he walked into the front room. Frances poured a whiskey from the glass decanter and pretended she didn't see him. He wanted to shake her, to make her teeth rattle, but he took a deep breath and turned her to face him, holding her arms firmly so she couldn't wriggle away. He spoke through gritted teeth. "Why? I simply want to understand what goes through your head."

She looked up through her lashes. "It was silk from India." She pouted.

"Frances, you burned her, for God's sake."

Frances waved her hand dismissively. "She should be more careful. She's a thoughtless, clumsy girl. First day here and already she's wrecked something."

"You cannot hurt someone in my house."

"Our house."

He let go of her and went to the window, pulling back the curtain to peer outside. Jeselle leaned against the car, holding her arm. "Your mother wrote to me about a place. A resting type of place that might be good for you. Maybe they could help you learn to control your temper."

Her voice was even, careful. "You wouldn't really send me to one of those places, would you, Nate?"

He turned to face her. She had rearranged herself into something pitiful, childlike, which angered him further. "I will do whatever is necessary. Do you understand me? You will never hurt another human being in my home again. Or so help me God, I'll send you away. As your husband, I have the right to do so."

She smoothed her hair. He noticed her hands shook, but her words came out haughty, unconcerned. "You don't have it in you."

"That was true once, but you've managed to suffocate most of my natural instincts." He moved closer to her, wanting to watch her answer his question. "The dean told me he thought he saw you coming out of Mitchell's Tavern the other afternoon. Were you there?" He paused and studied her face as it went from white to scattered with patches of red.

"Of course not. Why would I be at that dirty old place?" Sighing, she flounced onto the couch. "Anyway, I haven't felt well all week. You know that. I've been in bed. It's my nerves, Nate. Really, I'll behave. I promise."

"I want to believe that, Frances, I really do. But you lay another hand on this girl and I will take the necessary steps to have you sent away. Do you understand?"

She nodded, pulling on the front of her dress. "I understand."

*   *   *

Jeselle stood near Nate's car, cradling her arm against her chest, staring at the ground. The image of a fawn with a broken leg he'd once seen in the woods when he was a child suddenly came to mind. Jeselle's cheeks were hollow; she couldn't be more than a hundred pounds soaking wet, despite the pregnancy. "Let's go," he said, gently.

She darted a look at him. "Do I sit in the front or the back?"

"Where do you want to sit?"

"In the front." She met his eyes.

He opened the car door for her and held it as she slipped inside. "Careful of your head now."

Fifteen minutes later, per Jeselle's instructions, they turned down a dirt road from the road.

"You walked all this way to work?" he asked.

"Yes, sir."

They turned a corner and came upon a shack. Jeselle shifted in the seat. "This is it. Bess's place."

Bess's place was no more than some boards thrown together. How was a family living here? "Jeselle, does your mother know what it's like here?"

"I guess."

Nathaniel pulled a pack of cigarettes from his pocket and stuck one in his mouth, unlit. "There enough to eat out here?"

"You want the truth?"

"Of course."

"They have four children, and the landlord takes most of the profit from their crops every year. Doesn't leave them enough to live on. Doubt there's ever enough to eat. Especially to feed me."

He nodded, wrinkling his brow. "I see, tenant farmers. Cotton?"

"That's right."

"Where do you sleep?"

"Porch."

"No, no. This isn't right." He gestured with the unlit cigarette. "I'm sending you home. Your mother wouldn't want you here."

Jeselle gazed into her lap. Tears fell onto her folded hands. "Please, don't send me back. Mrs. Bellmont doesn't know about the baby, and we don't want her to. Please, I have no place else to go."

He reached into his front jacket pocket for his lighter. Oh, dammit. He'd vowed to quit smoking that very morning. A man of absolutely no discipline, he thought. Look at what this poor girl endures, and yet he couldn't quit smoking? He shoved the cigarette back in the pack. "Do you have a plan for the baby, Jes?"

She kept her eyes in her lap and spoke, barely above a whisper. "Mama arranged for me to give the baby to Reverend Young. She wants me to go to Oberlin."

"Is that what you want?"

"I don't know."

"Where's the father?"

She glanced up at the sky. "I don't know."

"Have you told him?"

"No."

"Best give him a chance to do the right thing. He might surprise you."

"No. It would ruin his life."

"A child could never ruin anyone's life."

She turned to him, a searching look in her eyes. "Do you think that's always true, Mr. Nate?"

"I do."

Her fingers clasped and unclasped in her lap. "Well, I best get on."

"Wait." He tapped a finger against the dashboard. "All right, here's what we're going to do for now. Make enough food for our meals like you're cooking for four hungry adults. Serve small portions to Frances and me. We don't eat much. Bring the rest of the food here. You eat at my house, whatever you like, however much you need."

"What will Miss Frances think?"

He kept his voice steady. "She won't notice." He stuck his elbow out the car window. "She doesn't understand practical things."

"Thank you."

Uncomfortable, he avoided looking at her by watching a sparrow fly from an oak tree to the top of the house. "When you're working, you've got to stay out of Frances's way. If she seems restless or if she starts in on the whiskey, make an excuse that you have to go to the market or something. Just get out of the house. Her moods usually pass once something else catches her interest."

Jeselle wiped her eyes. "I burned her dress. I'm clumsy lately. I'll work to pay for it."

"Don't worry about that. She has enough clothes." He turned to her, his concern for her outweighing his innate shyness. He attempted to sound stern but gentle. Was that possible? "You tell me if anything else happens with her. You understand?"

"Yes, sir."

He went around and opened her door, offering his hand. She stared at it for an instant before taking it. "Get a little rest if you can. Take care of your arm tonight. Put some butter on it." She nodded, though he realized there wasn't any butter inside that house, nor milk or cheese. "Well, anyway, try to get some rest if you can."

Looking up the dusty road, he imagined Jeselle walking in the heat. Unacceptable, no matter the circumstance. But pregnant and probably hungry was more than anyone should have to endure, especially sweet Jeselle. So many times in life we were unable to help others. But this time he could offer something that could ease another's discomfort. Unfortunately, this was all he could do—offer meals and transportation. For now, anyway. Perhaps something would occur to him to help Cassie's daughter. A quality in her eyes told him she had no intention of giving the child away. Hadn't he felt the same about John? No one could have pried him away from his baby. "I'll come get you in the mornings. You shouldn't walk in this heat." His eyes went to her stomach, and he felt himself blush. He walked around to his side of the car and said over the roof, "I'll be here at seven thirty tomorrow morning."

She smiled and nodded. "I'll be ready."

* * *

Not wanting to go home, Nathaniel drove downtown, parked near the deli, and went for a walk along Main Street and then down a side street he'd never walked before. He looked up to find a Presbyterian church, built in the spare and simple way of the Presbyterians that Nathaniel knew so well from his childhood. The doors of the church were open. He walked up the steps and went inside. It was a familiar sight to him: oak pews, a small pulpit, and an unstained wooden cross, similar to those of his home church in Maine. An older man with thinning white hair and stooped shoulders stood on a tall ladder perched in the frame of an open window. Nathaniel squinted in the dim light, making out a dark robe and black shoes.

"Hello?" Nathaniel called out, not wishing to startle him.

"Oh, hello." He held his robe up as he came down the ladder. "I'm Pastor Ferguson. Gillis Ferguson." Soft brown, kind eyes peered at Nathaniel. "What can I do for you?"

"Nothing, really. I just wandered in. I don't know why."

The pastor smiled gently and reached up to put a hand on Nathaniel's shoulder. "Welcome."

Nathaniel pointed at the window. "What're you doing there?"

"I've got myself an annoying woodpecker, I'm afraid. Won't shut up day or night. Pecks right through my sermons some Sundays. I'm aiming to get rid of the little bugger but have no idea how to go about it." He looked at his watch. "It's about my supper time. Lulu, my housekeeper, worries herself sick if I'm late. Hovers over me like a mother hen, that girl, when she's not thinking of ways to fatten me up. Care to join me?"

"Oh no, I wouldn't want to impose."

"No imposition at all. Be nice to have the company."

So Nathaniel found himself following the clergyman out the back of the church and down a narrow, brick path lined with camellia bushes, toward the parsonage. When they arrived at the house, they entered through the back door into a bright, if slightly shabby, kitchen. The housekeeper stood at the counter, cutting a loaf of crusty bread on a wooden cutting board. She had creamy white skin scattered with freckles and hair the color of copper. Nathaniel figured her to be no more than twenty-five, short and sturdily built, muscles running the length of her bare arms.

When Pastor Ferguson introduced Nathaniel to Lulu, she did a small curtsy, knife in hand. "Aye, good to meet you now." She spoke with a heavy Irish accent. "I hope you're staying for supper?"

"He is," said Ferguson. "Excuse me a moment while I wash up. That pesky bird's still at it, Lulu."

"Aye, that bloody bird'll be the death of him. Just pecks all day long. I can hear the obnoxious thing here in the kitchen."

Unable to think of a response, Nathaniel merely nodded.

She reached into the icebox and pulled out a mound of butter. "I've been with the pastor for five years now, since his wife died. I never knew her, but everyone says Rose Ferguson was the kindest woman you ever would meet."

The kitchen table looked out into a grassy, fenced yard shaded by an oak with moss drooping from its limbs. As Lulu talked, she set another place at the table, along with some bread and butter. "I take care of him now, but I know he's awful lonesome for her. He has two daughters that live up north, both married to preachers." She filled two bowls with bean soup that smelled of simmering tomatoes and onions, evoking an image of his mother's summer vegetable garden. She lowered her voice, glancing at the doorway. "Their youngest daughter, Caroline, died when she was only five years old. Just got terrible sick and died. There was nothing could be done. Such a terrible thing, to lose a child. Me own mum lost two babies when they were no more than two days old. Near killed her each time." She put her hands on her hips, surveying the table. "Well, that'll just near do it."

As if on cue, the pastor entered the kitchen, without his robe and dressed in a simple summer suit. His eyes lit up when he saw the table. "Looks delightful, Lulu."

"The pastor is awful keen on his supper, make no mistake." She grinned and then excused herself from the room, saying something about bringing in sheets from the clothesline. After she was gone, the pastor sat, indicating Nathaniel do the same. "Shall we pray?"

* * *

Twenty minutes later, the bowls were empty, and all that was left of the bread were a few crumbs at the bottom of the basket. The pastor sat back in his chair. "So why did you come in today? Are you searching for something?"

"Not sure. Felt a shift in the air or something." The smile of the woman at the train station came to Nate again.

"Do you like to walk?" asked Ferguson.

"I do."

"Come by tomorrow. We can walk together."

CHAPTER 31

Lydia

LYDIA PEERED at the name, Elden Hall, etched above the white doors of the music building, mustering courage. She stepped inside, blinking as her eyes adjusted to the cool and dimly lit room after the bright sunlit campus. She walked down the hallway, looking for Professor Nathaniel Fye's name on one of the doors. She found it at the end of the hall. Her stomach flopped over as she held on to her pocketbook, suddenly full of doubt. She might have stayed home and grown old gracefully instead of traipsing around a college campus like a kid, she thought.

She approached the door and knocked. No answer. Should she go in? Or wait in the hallway to be summoned? Down the hall, she heard the front doors open and then heavy footsteps coming toward her. She turned to look. A man dressed in a dark suit, carrying a small satchel and holding a hat, came toward her with long strides. He walked with his head down as if there were something interesting written on his shoes. Could this be the professor? Surely not? She'd imagined someone older, perhaps with a gray beard and a permanent scowl. But this man was tall and slender, with dark wavy hair slicked back from his forehead.

Several feet from her, he looked up and then came to an abrupt halt. She gasped. "It's you. From the train station."

"It's you," he repeated, staring.

"You're Professor Fye?"

"I am."

"I'm Lydia Tyler."

He blinked several times, peering at her as if he didn't believe her. "You're Mrs. Tyler?"

"Yes." She put out her hand. "Pleased to meet you."

He looked at her hand and then shook it quickly, like it was hot. "I imagined you as a little old lady with a tea cozy." His hand was strong and remarkably large, but his skin felt soft, like someone who hadn't done outside work. Her own hand appeared rough and freckled in comparison.

"I thought the same of you. Well, not an elderly lady with a tea cozy." She paused, laughing. "But rather an old man with a pipe and gray beard scowling at little children who run across your lawn."

His mouth turned up, just a slight curve, but there was a moment of merriment in his eyes. Balancing his hat under his left arm, he set his satchel on the floor before reaching into his jacket pocket and pulling out a set of keys. "Please come in, Mrs. Tyler."

As she moved past him into the small office, she held her notebook against her torso, feeling dowdy in her homemade dress. She should have listened to Birdie and bought a new dress or two.

She hadn't gotten a good look at the professor at the train station—the light was glaring, and she'd been anxious to get to campus. But now she saw that he possessed a considerable presence. His features were unremarkable except for their perfect symmetry. And his almond-shaped, brown eyes were sensitive, like they were working hard not to betray emotion of any kind.

"You're northern?" Why this was the first question out of her mouth, she couldn't explain. Sometimes her mouth just started moving of its own accord.

"Yes. Maine. The Northeast, like you."

She felt unreasonably pleased he remembered a detail from her letter. Or had she mentioned it at the train station? Well, either way, it was flattering. Warmth spread from her stomach out to her limbs.

He set his satchel on a modest wood desk and pulled back heavy curtains that looked out onto an oak and the lawn. The tidy office filled with light. He indicated she should sit. Once she settled in her chair, he sat at his desk.

He gazed at her, his forehead knit as if he were trying to solve a puzzle. "What do you hope to accomplish this summer, Mrs. Tyler?"

"I'm here to have an adventure and learn something new." She paused, glancing at a sparrow on one of the oak branches. "Really, to fight against the inevitable downward slide into old age, kicking and screaming and holding onto youth with the tips of my fingers." She paused. Why oh why couldn't she stop talking? "And, my youngest daughter said she wanted to stay at Auburn this summer and take classes."

"I see. I think."

"When I saw a notice about this program in the newspaper, I just decided then and there that, if you'd have me, I'd come." She sat forward in her chair. "My only worry was that this is a self-indulgent and vain decision, studying frivolously when the country is in terrible crisis." Again, the words simply tumbled out. Reticence? Not one of her gifts, apparently.

A shadow passed over his face as he shrugged. "Art is important, especially in the worst of times."

She tucked her hair behind ear. "Well, also, I thought of Eleanor Roosevelt."

"Excuse me?"

"I suspect she might say that it's actually noble to use the gifts God gave you, instead of languishing into old age, relics before our time. I wonder if it isn't the finest thing one can do, given the opportunity, to create beauty in the midst of chaos or despair. Can this perhaps be the highest form of worship to a good and merciful God?"

Watching her, the same guarded expression on his face, he reached into his jacket pocket and pulled out a cigarette. "It would be pleasant to think such a thing."

"Do you not agree, Professor?"

"I have no idea what pleases God." He put the cigarette back in his pocket. "I'm trying to quit."

"Excuse me?"

"Cigarettes."

"Oh, right. Why is that?"

"They make me feel terrible. I'm trying not to indulge in things that make me feel terrible, but I can't seem to stop." He stood, clearing his throat. "Would you play for me?"

His height and imperious, formal demeanor made her feel almost petite and oddly nervous, and something else. She shuddered, realizing.

Desire. So long dormant and now suddenly alive? Horror filled her. Desire for the professor? Five minutes into the adventure and she meets this? This man? This opposite of Santa? Why now?

He watched her with what she suspected was amusement. Had he read her thoughts? Her cheeks flamed hotter.

"Are you all right, Mrs. Tyler?" What a gentle way he had. A good teacher. She could see this already.

"Oh, quite fine. Thank you."

"Come on over to the piano. I'd love to hear you play."

She coughed into her hand, moving to the piano while he closed the door. He set her entrance composition on the piano and then moved to stand at her side, indicating that she should begin as he took a handkerchief from his pocket. "Hot in here." Mopping his brow, he grimaced. "Never have been able to adjust to the humidity down here."

Feeling overly warm herself, which she could not blame on the humidity but rather on the man at her side, she felt the impulse to fan her face with the sheet music but instead left it on the piano. She glanced up at him. "Play?"

"Please." He moved around to the left side of the piano and closed his eyes, resting his right hand on top. Feeling nervous, she willed her trembling fingers to move across the keys. When she finished, he opened his eyes and made a sweeping gesture across the top of the piano. "It's a lovely piece, in its simplicity."

"Simplicity?" She cringed inwardly at how childlike she sounded.

He nodded and looked at her with a kind of scrutiny that made her uncomfortable. "I'd like to hear you play something you haven't written." He shuffled around in his satchel, pulling out another piece of music and placing it on the piano. "This is one of my own. Would you play it for me?"

"Fine," she said, still stung and surprisingly miffed by his dismissal of her piece as she scanned the pages. It was untitled, and the markings indicated that it should be played at a rapid tempo in C minor. She took a deep breath and began, no longer nervous because of her anger. She'd show him how she could play, and he'd see she was not simple. A skilled sight reader, her hands found the notes with ease. The music was rich and varied, intricate in its composition. The mood of it felt melancholy, indeed almost dark. As she played, the drama of the music made her forget where she was or that she performed for her new teacher. She played for herself, just as she did at home, alone in her parlor.

When she was done, she gazed, unseeing, at the keys, lost in the beauty of the music and humbled. This was a man of immense talent—one who had indeed earned the right to call her piece simple. He was a musician of a caliber rarely seen and that she'd certainly never known personally. The professor stirred next to her. When she looked over at him, she wasn't sure if it was pleasure she saw there or boredom.

After a moment, he spoke, his voice gruff. "Your playing is remarkable, Mrs. Tyler. How did you learn to play like this?"

"I studied as a young woman. Before my marriage."

"Yes," he murmured. "So you said in your letter. But this music is complex, extremely difficult to play. Only the best can play it so well the first time."

"Thank you." She flushed. "I have a regimented practice schedule."

"Right. Your five hours a day." He paused, seeming to think out loud. "Discipline alone cannot take the place of talent. And please don't take this as an insult, but you have the largest hands I've ever seen on a woman."

Lydia felt herself turning what she knew from past experience to be an even deeper shade of pink. "Yes, I'm afraid so."

"Vanity aside, Mrs. Tyler, this is an excellent quality in a pianist."

"I suppose."

"Mrs. Tyler, had you never heard of me? I mean, before you applied to school?"

"No, should I have?"

"Not necessarily, but it surprises me, given your considerable dedication to your craft."

She stared at him, taken aback and unable to think of what to say.

"I was once called the best pianist in the world." He glanced at his hands. "I don't know if was true or not, but that's what they said. Most pianists your age would know that."

"I'm afraid I've been rather out of touch with culture. Atmore is small. And provincial. I've been raising children." A trickle of sweat ran down the small of her back. "Why do you no longer play professionally?"

He stepped back from the piano. "I had an accident. The nerves in my left hand are damaged. I can no longer play, which makes my former career as a concert pianist impossible."

Lydia, shocked, filled immediately with sympathy. "I'm sorry." I can think of nothing worse, except for the loss of a child, she thought to herself.

"Which is why I teach now."

She stared down at her own hands in her lap. "I see."

"Ah, well." He looked around the small office and spoke with a dismissive sigh. "One must rebuild from the rubble."

"Yes."

"And after many years of horrendous but well-meaning girls, I finally have a real student."

She felt her eyes widen. "You mean me?"

The professor's eyes lit up. "Yes, I mean you. Here, play this Schubert."

She did, and then he had her play a Chopin, and then an Albéniz.

He paced at the side of the piano. "What in God's name possessed you to give up a career to get married?" She couldn't decide if he was angry or excited. "With this kind of talent, how could you walk away from a career?" Now his voice was almost a growl.

"I did it on a whim, actually. A childish whim."

He massaged his left arm in an absent way that made her suspect he had a chronic ache there. He saw her watching him and dismissed her sympathetic glance with a sweep of his hand. "Never mind that, I'm having a bad day of it. That's all." He put his hands in his pockets and glared at her.

She pushed middle C three times, then glanced at the light fixture above the piano, which was full of dead bugs. "My mother died when I was nineteen, and three months later my father married a woman only a couple years older than I. It devastated me. I met William at a dance when I was on holiday, and, well, before I knew it I was a housewife." She paused, considering the truth of her next statement. "But I haven't regretted it for one instant. We had many good years together. He gave me my two daughters, which is better than any ambitions I once had. You must not have children, Professor Fye, or you would understand." She saw him flinch. "Do you have children?" she asked, meekly.

"I had a son. He died when he was only hours old."

"I'm sorry." She fidgeted, feeling awful and small. "I often say the wrong thing. I talk too much."

He glowered at her for a moment. Then to her relief he shook his head and laughed—more of a chuckle that seemed out of practice. "You are a surprise, Mrs. Tyler." He rocked back and forth on his feet. "With more instruction you could be really fine. Do you understand that?"

"A fine what?"

"Pianist. At the risk of sounding immodest, Mrs. Tyler, when you play, it reminds me of myself. Before my accident, that is." His face went dark again. "Will you allow me to mentor you?"

She stared at him for a moment before realizing that he expected an answer. "What does that mean, exactly?"

"When I was a young man, sixteen, actually, I went to New York and studied with a French master named LaPlante. His tutelage changed my life."

"But why me?"

"Because teaching is what I do." He shrugged, speaking casually, as if it was neither here nor there, and she suspected suddenly that he was embarrassed. "And your talent is worthy of a teacher."

She could think of nothing to say.

He tapped the top of the piano with his good hand. "I'm saying that with some hard work and dedication and more than a little boldness, we could turn you into a virtuoso."

"But aren't I too old?"

"I don't know, Mrs. Tyler. How old do you feel?"

"I feel the same as I always did."

"I imagine the work it took to raise children without a spouse would prove too much for most people, but you managed a practice regimen at the same time. That, Mrs. Tyler, is most unusual." He peered at her like she was a fascinating oddity; his pupils contracted as if he were staring at the sunlight.

"Should I go now, Professor?"

He rocked on his heels again, looking like a boy. "Yes, but you must come to my home sometime. Play on my baby grand. There's no finer instrument."

"Your home?"

"My wife will be there, too, of course."

"Oh, right, of course." She tried not to stutter as she accepted his invitation, feeling both dread and excitement. Wife. Well, of course, he had a wife. He wore a wedding ring. It wasn't a surprise, but it deflated her, nonetheless. "And your wife? Is she happy here in Montevallo?"

His eyes turned hard as his voice deepened. "My wife's a southerner, but she misses the city. She's found small-town life to be somewhat stagnant, I'm afraid." He glanced out the window. "Her health is fragile."

"I'm sorry. May I ask what's wrong?"

He pulled the same cigarette from his pocket that he'd abandoned earlier. "Frances suffers from what the doctor calls sad moods." He lit his cigarette with a small silver lighter and took a deep drag.

Wanting to ask more but knowing it was not appropriate, she nodded in what she hoped was a polite way. "I'm sorry to hear that."

He went to his desk and opened a notebook where he obviously kept his calendar. "What day next week would you like to come to the house, then?"

"Friday?"

"Good. I'll see you tomorrow, here at the office."

CHAPTER 32

Nathaniel

A WEEK HAD PASSED since Lydia Tyler had come to him. They'd worked together every day except Sunday. Nathaniel and Pastor Ferguson, during these same days, had established a pattern of walking in the early morning hours before he picked up Jeselle. During their walks, Nathaniel slowly told the pastor of his life, including his tribulations with Frances and the death of their child. To his surprise, he admitted to the reason for their marriage and then described the rapid decline of their relationship after John's death and his subsequent career-ending injury. All of which the pastor met without judgment or criticism. This wasn't the kind of pastor Nathaniel had ever met before.

Today they began at the parsonage and made their way out of town, to walk alongside the creek, warm despite the early hour. The sun slanted through the trees.

Ferguson pulled his hat farther down over his forehead. "You're smiling to yourself this morning, like you're thinking of something else."

He smiled. "I have a new student. Lydia Tyler. She's a middle-aged widow, but you'd never know it by the way she plays. She's on my mind this morning."

"You're excited to teach her?"

"More than I can say. More than anything in a long while."

Ferguson swatted at a fly hovering near his head. "Tell me, Nathaniel, what do you do for fun?"

"Fun?"

"Yes, y'know, something that amuses you."

Nathaniel slowed his pace, thinking. "I don't know." They reached the grassy bank where they often stopped. "It was just music. All my life, music. And then, Frances and music. And then, nothing." He motioned toward a wooden bench. "Let's sit."

Ducks waddled by on their way into the creek.

"Frances likes the moving pictures. She sees everything that comes to town."

"But what about you?" asked Ferguson.

"I like books. Yes, that's something. Novels mostly." He leaned down and picked up a pebble, tossing it into the creek, near the gaggle of ducks. A female dove under the surface, thinking it was some kind of food, brown tail feathers wriggling above the water. "And I love fishing with Whitmore. Frances's brother. After John died, Whitmore was a solace to me."

"My littlest daughter died when she was only five years old. Did you know that?"

"Lulu told me. I'm sorry."

Ferguson took off his hat and scratched the back of his head. "No worse pain than losing a child. You think you won't ever breathe again, and then, you find you have. But the pain never goes away, despite being able to breathe." He put his hat back on, adjusting it with both hands. "Do you see Whitmore often?"

"Not enough. He's at Princeton. He's a gifted artist and a wonderful boy. I'm hoping to make connections for him in New York when he's ready." He tossed another pebble into the water. "Truth is, I don't find I look forward to much these days."

"Well, perhaps this new student will help."

"I think she will." He felt a flash of happiness at the thought of teaching Lydia Tyler. "And you, Gillis. And our walks. I haven't had a friend since Walt. I've missed it."

Ferguson smiled and patted Nathaniel on the shoulder. "I couldn't agree more. But we better go. Lulu hates it when I'm late for a meal."

PART FIVE

From Jeselle Thorton's journal.

June 9, 1934

My birthday is tomorrow, the first I will have without Mama and Mrs. Bellmont and Whit there to usher me into a new year.

The memories come to me at night. Memories of home, of those I've loved, of moments that shaped me. I lay in the dark on this makeshift bed under the stars, the sound of the pines rustling, the small creatures scurrying behind boards, and the smell of decaying wood, and I remember. Is it that one can only understand something through memory? Is it only later that we can examine it and see how it changed us?

It is Mr. Nate practicing the Gershwin piece I remember tonight. The rest of the house rested that afternoon except for the two of us. As he played, I sat outside the music room, behind the open door, listening in my surreptitious seeking of beauty. I listened as a writer with my journal in my lap, wanting desperately to describe with words this divine sound.

The piece began with notes like repeated drops of tears into a tin pail from three different sets of eyes, a man's and two women's. Then the thud of a large tear, saved up behind that man's eye for years until it pushed itself out, despite his efforts to keep it inside, accompanied by the higher pitched plink from the women, who let their tears flow without restraint.

I thought, all is possible when there's beauty such as this.

Yes, it is this I remember under the starlit sky tonight. That music, played by a master.

We could not know then what would happen hours later. Would either of us have loved it more, knowing it was the last time?

Where did it go, this moment of beauty?

CHAPTER 33

Whitmore

WHITMORE'S CLASSES were over for the year, final exams completed, and bags packed. The summer loomed before him. Warm, he slid out of his sweater as he walked to the campus mailroom, trying without success to keep his mind from Jeselle.

The tenth of June. Jeselle's birthday. For the first time in their lives he would not be with her to celebrate. He understood, finally, that he was not going to hear from Jeselle. Her silence was an answer to the question he posed in his last letter. "Do you still love me? Just tell me one way or the other, and if it's no, I will give up and stop writing you." That was more than two weeks ago, and still no answer. His mother had written about Jeselle's acceptance to Oberlin College. Why hadn't she written to tell him herself? He couldn't fathom what her silence meant except that she no longer loved him. Had she met someone else? Or was it that college would create a whole new life for her? A life with no room for him?

His roommate, Reggie, had invited Whit to join the King family in Cape Cod for the summer, and Whit had resolved to accept. He'd lingered after classes were over, hoping for some word from home that Jeselle wanted him to come back to her, but finally he wrote to his mother of his intention to join the Kings. He hated to be away from the lake house for the summer and knew that his mother would be disappointed. But seeing Jeselle each day with this separation between them would be too difficult. Yes, he'd go to the beach with Reggie and paint, try to forget about the past. Which he knew was nearly impossible.

Now, he went into the post office. The kind postmistress sorted mail into boxes behind her counter. Whit made an effort to square his shoulders and keep the wobble from his voice. "Anything for Bellmont today?"

"Let me look. Yes, here's one."

"Thank you." It was from his mother. Of course it was. How could he have thought differently? How long would it take before he gave up hope? A week, a year, or the rest of his life?

"Have a good day, Mr. Bellmont."

"Yes, you as well." Once outside, he sat on a bench near the large magnolia tree and opened the letter. His mother wrote of her work with the Salvation Army, that his father was rarely home, and that she missed him terribly but that, of course, he could go to Cape Cod for the summer. But the next paragraph stunned him.

Jeselle was at Nate and Frances's.

He sat, dazed, holding the letter in his lap. Jeselle was with Nate and Frances. But why? The fine hairs on the back of his neck stood up. There was either something his mother didn't understand or didn't know. He was certain of this. He searched his mind, trying to come up with a reason, but nothing came to him. There was only one way to find out.

He sprinted back to his room, ignoring the stares of other students strolling along the green paths of campus. In his room, he gathered his belongings and stopped only long enough to cash his mother's check at the bank before making his way to the train station, where he purchased a one-way ticket to Montevallo.

It was late afternoon by the time he boarded the train. He took a seat across from a tired looking woman and a boy with sunken cheeks. Both were clean, with neatly combed hair, but the woman's dress, so thin he could almost see through it, and holes in the boy's shoes told their story. Still, the woman had perfect posture—the same proud carriage his mother had taught Frances when they were young. "Where you headed?" he asked.

"Birmingham. My husband's been down there, trying to find work." She looked at her hands before clasping them on her lap. "We've been staying at my sister's." The boy stared listlessly out the window as the conductor came through to take their tickets. This surprised Whit.

When he was a child he'd been fascinated by the conductor. This child was hungry, he thought.

Remembering the sandwiches he'd purchased from the cafeteria, Whit pulled them from his bag and offered one to them. The woman began to protest, but the boy grabbed a sandwich before she could stop him. "Please, Miss, take one. They'll spoil before long."

She reached out with a bony arm and took one, smiling shyly. "You aren't hungry?" she asked.

"I've got plenty."

"Thank you kindly." She watched him with veiled eyes for a brief moment before taking a bite of the sandwich. She reached for her son's hand and held it in her own while they finished their sandwiches. It must hurt to have a hungry child.

The car bumped along the track in a rhythm, and after a time the boy and his mother drifted to sleep. The sky turned dark, and a quarter moon appeared, hovering above his window, following them, as the train traveled farther and farther south. Whit longed to be lulled to sleep, wished to escape from his restless and disjointed thoughts. But slumber eluded him. He slumped against the window, staring unseeing into the night sky, his sketchbook open to a new page. If only his mind were as blank as the sheet of clean paper, he thought, before pulling a pencil from his bag and beginning a sketch of the sleeping mother and son.

CHAPTER 34

Lydia

A WEEK AFTER her first meeting with Professor Fye, Lydia walked the short distance to his house, thinking of how much had changed since she'd left home. Nathaniel Fye had come into her life, and nothing was the same and, she suspected, never would be. It was the hottest part of the day, and she was limp and overheated by the time she reached the shade of his front porch. Taking a deep breath, she tapped twice with the metal knocker on the front door. A black maid answered.

"Good afternoon, I'm Mrs. Tyler."

"I'm sorry, Mrs. Tyler, but the professor isn't home as of yet." The girl had a refined quality to her speech and a proud carriage. "But Mrs. Fye is waiting for you in the sitting room." She escorted Lydia into a spacious room decorated in shades of burgundy and green fabrics, plump cushions, and dark walls that made Lydia think of a coffin. The baby grand took up a large corner of the room, next to shelving filled with books.

Frances Fye was beautiful. She wore a white silk dress with a light pink sash tied in a perky bow at her waist. The skirt of her dress fell gracefully below the knees, displaying slender ankles. She stood as Lydia came into the room, offering her a soft, slender hand in greeting. For the second time that week, Lydia's own hands felt immense and calloused.

"Good afternoon, Mrs. Tyler. I'm Frances Fye." Her voice had a silky southern lilt. "I apologize. My husband's uncharacteristically late. Can't imagine what's gotten into him. He positively can't stand it if he's more than a minute late."

She indicated the armchair next to the couch and waved her bone-white hand at the maid. "Jeselle, bring us our refreshments." Frances's eyes narrowed as she gazed at Lydia. Lydia looked down at her practical cotton dress and walking shoes. Why had she worn this? And her hair was a mess, falling flat and damp against her neck.

"We simply must call each other by our first names and be best friends if you are to be my husband's protégé." Frances continued without seeming to take a breath, "I hope you like your tea iced and sweetened. That's how we drink it in this house." She nestled farther into the cushions. It occurred to Lydia that her mournful gray eyes made her appear almost tragic.

"My late husband preferred it sweet as well."

"And you, Lydia. What do you prefer?" She smiled, reminding Lydia of a cat looking at a grasshopper, wondering if it was worth the energy to pounce upon and chew through its crunchy exterior.

"It's fine for me as well."

"Nate didn't tell me you're a northerner."

"I've lived in Alabama for almost twenty years." What was this? Feeling defensive? What a ninny, she thought. I'm a middle-aged woman. No need to feel ridiculous next to this girl, who was ridiculous. And vapid. Obviously vain. *Stand up tall the way God made you.* Her mother's voice echoed in her mind.

Frances gazed at her. "Are you wondering how old I am?"

Lydia smiled. "On the contrary, I was just admiring your beautiful skin."

Frances flushed slightly at the compliment. "I'm twenty-six years old. My husband is twelve years my senior." She sat up slightly as the maid came into the room carrying a tray with iced tea and biscuits the size and shape of a quarter along with a dish of strawberry preserves. Lydia moved to assist the girl but hesitated when she felt Frances's hooded eyes on her. She met Frances's gaze for a moment and saw faint disapproval. Lydia folded her hands on her lap. "I understand you're from Atlanta?"

"My father's family has lived in Georgia since the early 1800s. Before the war we had a thriving plantation, sugar, tobacco, and cotton, but afterward, well, we all know the ending of that story." She did a quick dart at the downward-gazing maid, who for all appearances seemed absorbed in the task of placing two of the biscuits with a teaspoon-sized dollop of strawberry preserves onto the delicate china plates. "Jeselle, you're as slow as molasses. Do serve our guest before the sun goes down."

Lydia accepted the plate from Jeselle. "Thank you."

Frances drank from her iced tea and then made a choking sound, fanning her face as though she'd tasted a bitter root. "No need to ration the sugar, Jeselle." She wiped daintily with one of the crisp white napkins that rested in her lap. "Needs at least three more tablespoons."

Jeselle murmured. "Yes, ma'am."

Lydia stifled a shiver and put her not-yet-tasted glass of tea into the outstretched hand of Jeselle, who quickly disappeared from the room.

Frances turned to Lydia with a slight shake of her head, which she assumed was meant to convey an apology for her maid's behavior. "She's the daughter of my mother's longtime housekeeper. We couldn't find a soul in this town who understood how to properly take care of a house. It's bad enough I had to move to this godforsaken town, but to be alone all day while my husband works and not have decent help. Well, it's positively awful." She widened her eyes and moved her white hands in a flutter at her neck and then back again to her lap. "I don't know if Nate told you but I suffer from poor health. Our town physician is Doctor Landry, and he's the best there is, I mean, the very best." She elongated and emphasized each word before continuing. "But the poor man can't find a thing wrong with me. I'm a medical mystery, he said to me. And Lydia, it was terrifying the way his eyes looked at me, so tortured, like he would've given anything to save me, but for his own human weaknesses was not able to. He held his hands in mine and then wiped his brow, his distress apparent in every way. I believe he's a little in love with me, the poor man." She stopped speaking and looked toward the doorway. "I swear that child is an imbecile. If I weren't so completely worn out this afternoon I'd march into that kitchen and find out what could possibly be taking her this long."

As Frances finished the sentence, Jeselle entered, carrying the tray once more. Unabsorbed grains of sugar floated in the bottom of the glass pitcher.

After Jeselle left the room, Frances pinched off a small section of a biscuit and set it on the other side of her plate. "Mother sent three dozen of these jars of preserves when we first moved into this ridiculous elf house. This is the last jar. I begged Nathaniel to take me for a visit to Atlanta this spring, but he and Doctor Landry didn't think I could withstand the trip. My mother's unbearable and agitates my nerves no end."

"I'm sorry to hear that."

Frances's eyes became glassy, and she stared out the window with a sad look on her face. "It's been terribly difficult. And poor Nate, he worries so over me."

Lydia put her glass of tea on the table, unsure of what exactly had been difficult, but she nodded sympathetically nonetheless. "I can imagine."

"I've been awfully lonely in this sleepy ole town. When we lived in New York, before Nate's accident, gads, the parties we were invited to. My husband was never much of a conversationalist, but he's become downright somber in his old age. I swear there are nights when he doesn't say more than two words. And I'm afraid music doesn't much interest me. He plays after supper, but I'm more interested in reading magazines or listening to the radio shows."

Lydia put her half-eaten biscuit back on the plate. "He plays?"

"With one hand, yes." She pointed to the piano. "He'll sit for hours long after I've retired. The sound is enough to make a person mad after a time. Says he must keep the skill in his right hand, but for the life of me I can't understand why."

Lydia tucked this unexpected bit of information away to think about later and told herself to be kind. One must endure this tiresome woman if one wanted to study with the professor. "I understand perfectly. My husband worked very hard when he was alive. We had a small farm, and he was a banker."

"Were you lonely, then?"

Lydia thought it a strange question but tried to answer it honestly. "I don't remember being lonely, no. I remember feeling tired a lot. My daughters kept me busy, along with the garden and keeping house. I had my music. I played, still play, every day for hours."

"And your daughters, did they resent your devotion to something other than them?"

Lydia, again, was surprised by the question, for she had never thought about it. "I don't know. I believe they knew it was something I must do, like breathing or eating. And they never knew any differently. We don't have much choice in who our mothers are, I'm afraid."

"I'm afraid not." Frances looked at her with what Lydia could only think of as dislike. "You simply must come to dinner tomorrow night, Lydia."

CHAPTER 35

Nathaniel

NATHANIEL GLANCED at his watch for the sixth time in six minutes. He detested lateness. The dean had stopped by his office just as he was about to leave. Which he normally would have welcomed, since he enjoyed Dean Woodruff's conversation and company, but he was anxious to meet Mrs. Tyler. When he finally arrived at the house, slightly out of breath and dripping with sweat, he was a full fifteen minutes late. Jeselle stood at the stove, stirring something that smelled of onions in a large pot. He took off his hat, hanging it on the nail in the mudroom.

"Afternoon." Jeselle didn't look up from the pot.

Wiping his face with his handkerchief, he looked at her closely for any marks or tears. She seemed well enough. "How was it today?"

"Fine. She's in there with your student." She nodded toward the sitting room.

He loosened his tie as he went in. "Ladies. I'm sorry to be late."

Mrs. Tyler leapt to her feet. "There you are." She paused and smoothed the front of her dress. "I mean, your lateness is no trouble." She pulled absently on a lock of hair that fell over one eye and glanced at Frances. "Your wife was entertaining me." She turned to Frances. "The tea and biscuits were delicious."

Frances rose from the couch. "I'll take my leave then, now you've finally arrived. I've an appointment at the beauty shop."

He looked at his wife in surprise. "But it's not time for your weekly appointment, is it?"

"Darlin', sometimes a woman needs a change. I'll be back in time for a late supper. Lydia, a pleasure."

"You as well, Frances," Mrs. Tyler replied.

Mrs. Tyler found his wife ridiculous. Of this he was certain. He took off his jacket and tossed it onto the back of the couch.

Mrs. Tyler retreated toward the piano, resting her hand on its shiny surface as if it were an old friend.

"I'm sorry about Frances," he said.

"Sorry?"

"Well, most women find her difficult."

"Not at all. She's exceptionally beautiful. We had a lovely talk."

"Really?

"Well, sure, it was fine."

"There's no need to lie, Mrs. Tyler."

"I'm not lying." She looked at the floor, her cheeks red. "Not exactly."

He smiled. "I see." He motioned to the piano. "Shall we begin?"

*   *   *

Later that night, when he returned from taking Jeselle home, Nate found Frances sitting in her usual place on the couch, flipping through the same movie magazine she'd read earlier and sipping sherry. He looked closely at her hair. It seemed the same as when she'd left. Usually she came home from her weekly appointment in tight curls that loosened as the week went on. "I thought you went to the beauty shop?" he asked.

"I was supposed to, but when I got there the silly girl was nowhere to be found. She must have forgotten I changed my appointment. Honestly, Nate, this kind of thing would never have happened in New York."

"How did you feel today?"

Frances turned a page of the magazine, the flimsy paper making a delicate slice through the air. "Wrung out like a dishrag."

"Everything go all right with Jeselle today?"

She turned another page. "Did you see anything wrong with her?"

"No."

"Doctor Landry says to take a little sip of sherry when I start to feel that flare of temper." She drank from her glass. "See. Like now. It evens one right out."

"Doctor Landry's medical advice is to take a sip of sherry?"

She widened her eyes, looking innocent. "Darlin', does it ever get tiresome being so morally superior to everyone around you?"

He flinched, feeling the familiar anger before stifling it. Perhaps Dr. Landry's advice was good, he thought, reaching for the whiskey and pouring himself a four-finger measurement.

She held her magazine up, peering at something on the page, her eyes slightly squinted. "I do believe I look a little like Jean Harlow. Prettier, of course."

"I don't know who that is."

"How is it, darlin', that you know so much about music and so little about anything else?" She flipped a page and took another sip of sherry, wiping the glass clean of lipstick before setting it on the table. "There's a new Jean Harlow movie coming out soon." She put the magazine on her lap and then traced the outline of something with her finger. "Anyway, if I had a few extra pounds on me I think people would mistake me for Jean Harlow." She held up the magazine to show him a photo of an actress with bleached blonde hair and too much lipstick.

"She looks nothing like you, Frances."

She pushed her lips out in a pout. "How 'bout now?"

He didn't comment, placing his elbows on the top of the piano and folding his face into his hands, feeling like an old man. He ambled to the bookshelf, smoothing his hand over the books, which he had arranged in alphabetical order: Dickens, Fitzgerald, Hardy, Hemingway, Melville, and Shakespeare. He pulled *Great Expectations* from the shelf and opened it to the middle of the book, breathing in the dusty smell of the pages. He watched his wife, her delicate head bent over the ridiculous magazine, and then sat at his piano, closing his eyes, thinking of Mrs. Tyler.

"Doctor Landry told me his half-brother's visiting from Los Angeles. I didn't even know he had a brother."

"We hardly know Doctor Landry," said Nathaniel.

"I'm surprised you haven't made more of an effort. He is dear Walter's friend, after all."

"Frances, don't."

"What?" She raised her arms as if defending herself. "I didn't say a thing about your former leech. Anyway, I invited Doctor Landry to join us for dinner tomorrow. I also invited Mrs. Tyler."

He turned to her. "What? Why?"

Her eyes were slits. "You seem taken with her. Isn't that true?"

He turned back to the piano keys. "She's the most promising student I've ever had."

He heard her turn a page of the magazine. "They're both unmarried. Did you know that?"

"Who?"

"Mrs. Tyler and Doctor Landry. Perhaps they'll fall in love over roast beef."

"Don't be ridiculous." He breathed in this idea, feeling a sudden pang that he couldn't identify. He placed the fingers of his right hand on the piano keys and began to play the opening notes of Mrs. Tyler's composition, letting the music wash through him and out of his hand.

Over the music he heard Frances get up from the couch, then the pop of the sherry decanter and a splash of liquid as it hit the glass. "Doctor Landry's brother works in the moving picture business. He commented the other day that I have the face for the pictures."

"Who did?"

"Doctor Landry."

Nathaniel turned to look at her as she thrust the magazine onto the coffee table and began to stroll around the room with her neck elongated, sweeping her hand along the sway of her dress as if she imagined a camera followed her. "He said I move like a dancer, and I told him I studied as a child. He said, 'Well, it surely shows.'" She went to the window and placed her fingertips on the glass so that the curve of her arm was gracefully displayed. "Doctor Landry said he'd introduce me to his brother. Actresses work for studios; they have contracts and get to make a certain number of movies every year and pose for publicity photos and such. Doctor Landry didn't say so, but I got the distinct feeling he thinks I could be one of those actresses." She turned toward him, cheeks flushed and eyes wide. "Isn't that just the best news you ever heard?"

"Frances, the doctor in Atlanta said these fantasies about the motion picture business are not good for you."

She began to twirl, like a child performing for a room of adults. "I'm so lucky because I never seem to age." She ran her hands down her slight frame. "I'm the same as the day you met me. Mrs. Tyler commented how youthful I look. That's important if you want to be in the pictures. I can tell by all the studying I've done looking at these magazines that they like actresses to be young. I'm what they call an ingénue, you see."

He rose abruptly from the piano bench. "I'm going up to bed. Don't have any more to drink."

CHAPTER 36

Lydia

THE NEXT EVENING, Lydia rapped on the front door of the Fye home. She wore her blue dress, freshly laundered and ironed. She'd washed her hair and applied mascara and lipstick carefully, the reasons for which she chose not to examine too closely.

She heard footsteps, and then Jeselle opened the door for her, gesturing her into the house with the same silent nod from her previous visit. The sitting room smelled of talcum powder and roses. Frances sat on the couch while Nathaniel lurked near the piano, sipping a whiskey. There was a stocky, ruddy gentleman with a puffy face, dressed in a light gray suit that seemed a size too small, standing by the bar. The man rose when she came in the room.

"This is Doctor Ralph Landry," said Nathaniel.

"Pleased to meet you," said Lydia.

Dr. Landry kissed her hand, holding it for a moment in his own. "Pleased to meet you, Mrs. Tyler." She drew her hand away from the doctor's clammy, plump one, feeling the professor's eyes upon her. Without planning to, her eyes darted to his for a moment, and a bolt of energy surged through her. She quickly averted her gaze, feeling a flush begin in her chest and creep up through her neck so that she felt inflamed. Taking a shallow breath, she kept her hand from touching her neck by playing with the bow on the front of her dress.

Frances looked like a princess, dressed in a flowing, sleeveless gown, pinched at the waist and with a blossom-pink skirt that cascaded below her knees. Lydia instantly felt underdressed and oafish.

Frances glided to Lydia and squeezed her arm. "So good of you to come. We've been looking forward to hearing some delightful stories of your life in Atmore." Frances spoke with a smile in her voice, but Lydia knew she was mocking her by the way she emphasized the word Atmore like it was a flavor of cake.

Frances put her hand on Dr. Landry's arm. "Lydia, this is the wonderful doctor I was telling you about the other day. He's simply saved me. He was there the first night I ever spent with Nate. Do you remember, Doctor?"

"Sure. Seems like yesterday." Dr. Landry stepped back from Frances, stumbling slightly against the side of the couch.

Frances turned to Lydia. "I've suffered so, and this poor man has done everything imaginable to try and figure out what ails me." Her eyes glistened with tears.

"Would you care for a drink, Mrs. Tyler?" the professor asked.

"No thank you, Professor." Feeling damp with perspiration, she made her voice light. "I'm afraid I'm a teetotaler. My husband used to tease me that I was partly to blame for Prohibition."

Dr. Landry waved his empty glass at the professor. "Don't mind if I have another drop, now that you mention it."

Nate refilled the glass with whiskey and handed it to the doctor, who gave an appreciative glance at the copper-colored liquid. The way he smacked his lips together after the first sip made Lydia think of a pink frog. "This legal concoction is a hell of a lot better than some of the moonshine that came through these parts."

"Doctor, have you lived in Montevallo long?" Lydia sat against the back of the sofa, arranging her legs with a modest cross at the ankles in a way that Emma would have approved of.

"Born and raised. Here my entire life except for when I went away to school." He turned to the professor. "You heard from Walt lately?"

The professor nodded. "Just had a letter from him the other day. He's managing several projects for the government arts program in New York. And he married a woman from Mobile." He glanced over at Lydia. "Doc and my old manager, Walt Higgins, grew up together here in Montevallo."

"Really?" asked Lydia. "Is that how you ended up teaching here?"

"That's right."

Frances arranged her skirt in a circle around her on the couch. "Doctor Landry's a pillar of the community."

"Now, Mrs. Fye, that's just flattery on your part," said Landry. "Although, Professor, I've been meaning to invite you to one of my social clubs. Introduce you around."

"What kinds of clubs do you belong to?" Lydia asked.

Dr. Landry crossed a plump leg over the other. "I'm a Christian man, involved with people committed to preserving our Christian nation."

She felt a quiver of indignation in her stomach—she was sure he was referring to the Ku Klux Klan. She leaned forward in her seat. "Eleanor Roosevelt—" she began, but the professor interrupted her.

"Mrs. Tyler, won't you play for us?"

She looked at him in surprise. "Now?"

The professor spoke too loudly for the room, his voice sounding strained. "Something light to match the summer mood. Gershwin?" He pulled sheet music from a stack on the piano.

She moved toward him, feeling Frances's glare like a beam of light on her back. "Perhaps Frances and Doctor Landry would rather visit?"

Frances flashed a brilliant smile, rising from the couch. "That's awfully kind of you. I couldn't agree more. We'll take a turn in the garden while you play."

Dr. Landry followed Frances out the screened porch and into the yard. The professor stood near the bookshelf, hands in his pockets. "You must excuse my wife, Mrs. Tyler. She doesn't care much for music."

"It doesn't matter to me whether she listens or doesn't."

"Mrs. Tyler, I hope you won't mind some unsolicited advice."

"Yes?"

"Doctor Landry's a southerner. With southern ideals. Do you understand what I mean?"

"I most certainly do. That doesn't mean I have to like it. Or agree with it."

"Yes, but I do want you to be safe."

He was right. It was best to keep her opinions to herself. She'd certainly learned that by now, living in Alabama for twenty years. "Of course you're correct, Professor."

"I'm afraid I am." After pouring another whiskey, he went to the window, pulling the curtain back. Frances and Dr. Landry were strolling in the yard, arm in arm, pointing at various flowers. The professor let go of the curtain and turned back to her. "This Gershwin piece was the last piece I played in front of an audience. The same night as the accident." He gazed into his glass, his face pensive, speaking softly. "I've always thought it strange that I'd played such a happy tune just minutes before..."

She sat perfectly still, frightened.

"Something light. It was a summer party." He wandered to the piano, the drink still in his hand. "It's ironic really, when all my life my mother protected my hands, forbidding any kind of physical work, that I've ended up this way." He looked into space, his eyes far away. "I was something of a child prodigy. Have I told you that?" He took a sip of his whiskey. "I worked harder than anyone expected of a boy because I knew the sacrifices my parents made for me. And because I loved it and felt it was what God wanted of me. After the accident I asked myself and God a thousand times—why? But He never answered." He paused and examined his hands. "I felt forsaken."

"God never forsakes us."

He looked at her, smiling in a way that was almost a grimace, sadness in his eyes. "I've struggled a great deal with that particular idea, Mrs. Tyler." He finished his drink and put the empty glass on the bar. "Some works have been written for the left hand alone, you know?"

"Yes?" she said, startled by this turn in the conversation.

"But none for the right hand. Of course you know that."

"I, honestly, had never thought about it before."

He blinked and rubbed his temple. "I don't usually talk this much. Must be the whiskey. I apologize. What were we doing?"

"The Gershwin."

"Right, of course. The Gershwin."

"Frances told me you play at night with your right hand."

He looked surprised. "She told you that, did she? Yes, I play every day, just to remember the feel of the keys." Taking off his jacket and tossing it onto the couch, he came around to where she sat at the piano bench. "May I sit next to you?"

She nodded and moved to the far left end of the bench. He took the right side.

"One of my early teachers insisted on my practicing each hand separately so that one was not utterly dependent upon the other."

"Yes, of course. Mine as well," she said.

She detected the scent of fresh soap on his skin as he rolled up his right shirtsleeve. His long fingers hovered over the top of the keys. "I can remember my old exercises like it was yesterday." He began to play a scale. She found it impossible to move her gaze from his fingers.

He then scanned the Gershwin and took a deep breath before playing the right-handed notes from the first page. Her eyes filled with tears; his fingers blurred so that it was only the sound that remained. After he finished, the room, like a glass container, held the music.

"I miss it, Mrs. Tyler."

Her instinct was to take his left hand, which rested on the bench between them, and hold it against her chest, but of course she didn't. "I can only imagine."

She scanned the music. "I'll play the left hand if you play the right."

At first he looked as if he might refuse but then shrugged as if it was of no importance. "We could try it, I suppose." As she raised her left hand, he raised his right, and they began to play the opening passage. It felt odd, clunky. In tandem they took their hands from the keys and looked at one another.

"Let's match our breaths," said Lydia. "Like we're one body."

"Come closer."

She scooted several inches to the right, until their legs and shoulders almost touched, his left hand and her right resting on their own thighs. Together, they took a breath in and then out, several times, matching the other. She allowed her body to relax and felt his do the same.

"And one, two, three," he said. They began again, and this time, as if granted a gift by an unseen entity, they were one player.

After they were done, his eyes still on the music, he murmured, "Strange."

"Let's play another," she suggested, trying to keep her voice light so he wouldn't suspect how moved and inspired and excited she was.

He leafed through the sheet music on top of the piano and pulled out a Mozart. "This is a piece I have my students play from time to time."

When they had completed the Mozart, he looked at her with a teasing smile. "This is all well and good to play around with, Mrs. Tyler, but your right hand will go to nothing if we play together too often." His eyes were soft, his voice husky. "But thank you for indulging me."

Their conversation was interrupted by Frances's breathy laugh as she came in from the porch. Her arm was still linked with Dr. Landry's, but Lydia noticed that Frances's eyes skipped to where the two of them sat together on the piano bench. "What do we have here?" asked Frances.

The professor rose from the bench as Jeselle appeared in the doorway. "I was just showing Mrs. Tyler some scales."

"Excuse me, Mrs. Fye, dinner is served," said Jeselle.

The four of them made their way into the formal dining room, set with fine china and white linen napkins. Three shallow vases of cut lilacs lined the middle of the table.

Dr. Landry held Lydia's chair while the professor did the same for Frances. Nathaniel and Frances sat on either end of the table, with Lydia and Dr. Landry across from each other. Nathaniel said a quick prayer, and then Jeselle served a light green cream soup from a silver tureen. Lydia sipped a spoonful; it tasted of butter, cream, and fresh peas.

Dr. Landry lifted his eyebrows in appreciation and grunted as he dug into the bowl for his second spoonful. "Frances, did you make this delicious dish?"

"Frances doesn't cook," said the professor, chuckling. "This is Jeselle's soup."

Frances waved her hand in the air dismissively and pouted. "The Bellmont women most certainly do not cook." She dabbed at her mouth with the end of her napkin. "Doctor Landry has a brother in the motion picture business, Lydia. Isn't that interesting?"

"What does he do?" Lydia asked, genuinely curious.

Dr. Landry scraped the bottom of his bowl for a last taste of soup. "He helps run a studio. Other than that, I have no earthly idea. He was always the artistic type."

"Has the industry been hit as hard as the rest of the country?" Lydia asked.

"I suppose, but they keep making them pictures," Dr. Landry replied, putting a hand on his chest as if he might burp.

"I guess it helps people with their troubles, to watch a picture and escape from their own reality for a while," said Lydia.

The professor took a swallow of whiskey. "Do you like the pictures, Mrs. Tyler?"

"I've only seen one or two. My daughters love them, of course. I'm a relic, still thinking of the days when we had silent pictures and an organist to play the score."

"Well, those days are over," said Frances. "Now that we have talkies they need actresses to have beautiful speaking voices." She turned toward Dr. Landry. "I've been told I have a beautiful voice."

Dr. Landry turned a deeper shade of ruddy and glanced at the professor. "I suppose so."

Frances cocked her head, looking at Lydia. "Doctor Landry's promised to introduce me to his brother. See about getting me into a picture. I've been imagining it in my mind most every minute of the day since we talked last week."

"But now, Mrs. Fye, I didn't say he'd get you in a picture, just that I'd introduce you to him. I don't actually know that he makes those kinds of decisions." He spread butter on a biscuit and demolished half of it in one bite.

"But he helps run the studio, doesn't he?" Frances's face lost its rosy flush. Her hand shook when she took a sip of sherry. "Isn't that what you said?"

The professor sighed and spoke slowly, as if measuring his words, "Frances, Doctor Landry doesn't want you to set your expectations too high."

"But you said that he could do something for me."

"Frances, there's no need to get upset," said the professor. "I didn't remember you had a brother, Doctor Landry."

"Hadn't seen him for years when he showed up out of nowhere a couple weeks ago. He left town after his mother died. We had different mothers, both dead now."

Frances played with the stem of her glass. Her eyes glittered, focused on the professor. "The trouble with my husband, Lydia, is that he has no imagination. Isn't that right, darlin'? He thinks of nothing but his music all day, every day." She turned to Lydia in a conspiratorial wink. "Isn't that just the way with men? They think of nothing but themselves and let their poor wives wither on the vine."

Dr. Landry wiped his damp forehead with his napkin. "You're hardly withering now, Mrs. Fye."

Frances snapped her head up to look at the doctor. "Really? Is that your professional opinion, Doctor?"

Dr. Landry darted a look at the professor. "I simply mean, Mrs. Fye, that you're a beautiful woman."

Frances pushed away from the table. Her chair thumped against the wall. "What does it matter, if no one ever sees me? I'm condemned to this awful little town while my life passes me by." With tears in her eyes and lips trembling, she paced between the chair and table like a scared, trapped mouse. "I'm supposed to be something, someone important." Her voice was a high-pitched squeal that bordered on hysteria. "I can't just disappear into nothingness. I'm meant to be admired." She flopped back into her chair and buried her face in her hands, weeping.

Professor Fye went to her, kneeling by her chair and speaking softly. "Can't we just have a nice dinner?"

She lifted a tear-stained face. "I'm simply exhausted. I think I'll go to bed."

He spoke soothingly to her. "That's a good idea. This was too much excitement." He looked at Lydia and then the doctor. "Excuse me for a moment." He put his arm out to help his wife up, but she shrugged away, stumbling out of the room with him following.

From the other room Lydia heard him say, "You just need a nice rest, and you'll feel better tomorrow."

"I won't feel better, and it's all your fault," said Frances, in a loud, angry wail.

Dr. Landry buttered a second biscuit. "Quite a mess the good professor has here." He popped a piece into his mouth and chewed, the flesh of his face moving like raw dough.

"Does this happen often, do you think?"

"Oh yeah. I got a colleague in Chicago, specializes in mental disorders. He says it sounds like she suffers from hysterical personality."

"What is that?" The words were out of her mouth before she could stop them.

"Attention seeking, over-sexed, high opinion of themselves based in fantasy, and overly sensitive to criticism. I could explain in detail, but what you saw tonight was as good as any textbook."

"Can't you do something to help her?"

The doctor chuckled, leaning back in his chair. "What did you have in mind? Send her away to one of those nerve centers?"

She stuttered, embarrassed about her naiveté, "I, I don't know what that is."

"It's where they send women with her type of problem. But the professor won't even consider it."

"Do you know why?"

"Don't ask me. Professor keeps to himself. I met him once, before he had the accident. He was extraordinary back then, from what my friend Walt tells me."

"He's extraordinary still."

Landry spoke with a slight edge to his voice. "Yes, I've noticed how you seem to admire him."

The pulse at her neck thumped at a furious pace. She heard a stirring near the doorway and turned to see the professor, his expression dark. Had he heard Dr. Landry?

"Mrs. Tyler, get your things, I'll walk you back to campus." Without looking at him, he spoke to Landry, "Doctor, I'll let you show yourself out."

* * *

The dusk air had cooled since afternoon but was still warm and muggy enough that she walked without putting on her jacket. Professor Fye was silent, his head bent toward the ground. They crossed the street to campus. A bullfrog croaked.

They rounded the corner. At her building, they stopped, lingering at the steps.

"Mrs. Tyler, I'm sorry about this evening. I should have said no when my wife suggested the dinner party, but it's nearly impossible to discourage her once she has something in her mind."

"Professor, could I have the favor of one small thing?"

"What is it?" His eyes were soft, searching her face.

"Call me Lydia."

"Of course. Lydia." He paused and cleared his throat. "And you call me Nathaniel. If you want."

"Nathaniel." She let the sound of his name dwell inside her for a moment.

The crickets chirped in the thicket. He sighed. "Life's an endless loop, isn't it?"

"What do you mean?"

"Over and over, the same. Never any relief. Like Sisyphus with his boulder." Neither spoke for a moment. And then, like a confession, his voice hushed, "She does this sometimes—violent outbursts that seem to come out of nowhere. She has an incessant need for male admiration."

She didn't respond, waiting to see if he would say more.

"She's been sick for a long time now."

"Surely something could be done to help her?" she asked.

"I don't know what it would be."

"This is no life for you." She spoke gently, like she would to one of her daughters.

He turned to her. "My parents taught me that life is about duty. God, country, family. What would you have me do?"

"I don't know." That was the truth. What was to be done for this man? Life was particularly cruel sometimes. One's conduct, one's intentions, seemed to matter little.

"Let's meet tomorrow at my office. Say eleven o'clock?"

"Will have to be more like noon. I attend church in the morning."

"Fine."

"Good night, Nathaniel."

"'Night, Lydia."

They turned and walked in opposite directions. Strangely, she felt his eyes upon her even as she knew it was impossible to watch someone while walking away from them.

CHAPTER 37

Jeselle

JESELLE HAD BEEN in the Fyes' kitchen, taking the roast out of the oven when she heard the music. She cocked her head, listening. Despite the heat, she got goose bumps and the tiny hairs on the back of her neck stood up. What was it about the music? And then she remembered. It was the music Nate had played the night of his accident. Gershwin. Tear drops in a bucket.

She peeped through the kitchen door. He and his student sat together at the piano. She blinked, unsure of what she saw. And then she understood. They were each playing one-handed, making it sound like a single player. Making it sound like Nate—like he used to play.

How she wished for Whitmore then.

Later, after she'd served the soup, she tossed a spoonful of flour into hot lard and whipped it together to start the gravy. She was just adding some water when she heard Frances's voice, high pitched and loud. As she scraped drippings from the roaster into the pan, she heard Nate talking soothingly to Frances as he shuffled her past the kitchen door and up the stairs. A few minutes later Nate stopped by the kitchen. He looked at the roast resting on the fancy platter and the gravy already in the bowl and shook his head. "I'm going to walk Mrs. Tyler to campus, and then I'll drive you to Bess's."

"Yes, sir."

He waved his hand toward the food. "Take this with you."

"All of it?"

"Yes." He paused at the doorway. "Jes, sometimes I wish your mother or Mrs. Bellmont were here. They'd know what to do."

"Me too, sir," she said, fighting the lump her throat.

There was the sound of the front door opening and closing. Jeselle went into the dining room, anxious to have the cleanup done by the time Nate returned. Dr. Landry was still sitting there, helping himself to another biscuit. "Girl, wrap me up some of these here biscuits. You people sure know how to cook a biscuit."

"Yes, sir." She went to the kitchen. In a few minutes she came back into the dining room to give them to him, but he was not there. She looked for him in the sitting room and, sure enough, there he was, drinking more of Nate's whiskey. He finished it in a gulp, took the biscuits, and went out the front door.

Later, Nate's car, smelling of roasted meat and gravy, hummed along the country road. Dusk was a dusty purple. As they turned down Bess's dirt road and came around the bend to the house, fireflies appeared. Nate stopped the car. "You want me to help bring in the food?"

"No. Probably not a good idea."

"Jes, have you decided what you're going to do?"

"No, sir."

"You make sure and tell me if I can help you in any way. I know you don't want Mrs. Bellmont to know about the baby, but I believe this—she would want what was best for you."

Jeselle again felt the lump at the back of her throat that always seemed poised to choke her. "I know she would. That's what makes my shame all the worse." She reached for the door handle. "Mr. Nate?"

"Yes?"

"Mama and Mrs. Bellmont—they'd tell you to send Miss Frances away. If you told them how it really is."

"I know."

"They'd tell you this is no way to live."

"You're the second person to tell me that tonight."

"You're a good man. We all know that, too."

With that, she scrambled from the car, afraid she might cry, and went into the house.

Bess sat in her rocking chair, nursing the baby. Ben whittled something from a piece of birch branch at the table. Through the doorway to the bedroom, she saw the children were already asleep.

"I brought a roast."

"A roast?" said Ben.

"Mr. Fye sent it out. Their dinner party went awry."

"A righ?" said Bess.

Amiss, Jeselle thought. Askew, aslant, ruined. "Miss Frances threw a fit. The guests had to go home."

"And left all that food?" asked Ben.

The children, perhaps smelling the food in their sleep, wandered in, rubbing their eyes. "What is it?" Lizzie asked, pointing at the meat.

"A roast," Jeselle told her. "A big one."

Also, there were crisp potatoes and carrots and a dozen biscuits. They all sat around the table made from the side of a barn while Ben cut them all thick pieces of meat and covered them with gravy. The children gobbled like hungry puppies while the baby pitched forward like a bird to eat out of her mama's hands.

"Tell us the story, Jes," said Ben, stabbing a potato with his fork. "How did Christmas come to us in June?"

Jeselle told the parts they were interested in with great detail: Dr. Landry's big stomach and how he managed to eat a half-dozen biscuits washed down with a decanter of whiskey, and the white lady who cried and fussed instead of eating a delicious slab of beef. She left out the bittersweet sound of the music and how warm the kitchen was as she pulled the roast out of the oven and Nate's defeated eyes.

They all laughed and laughed at her story and ate until they lost their listless, hungry look. After they all had their fill, they put the rest in the icebox. Tomorrow there would be enough to eat. That's about the best they could hope for these days.

Later, from her cot, Jeselle searched the sky for answers. The night was a beauty, fireflies fluttered about, and a million stars surrounded a slivered moon. She felt small under the blanket of that night, wondering if she even existed in a universe so vast.

CHAPTER 38

Nathaniel

NATHANIEL SAT in his office at the college, expecting Lydia. He often came in on Sunday mornings, mostly to get out of the house, to catch up on paperwork or practice without the sighs and questions from Frances. Lydia wouldn't arrive for a few more minutes, but he couldn't concentrate, out of anticipation. He occupied himself by sorting through correspondence and half-written compositions until they were disorganized enough that they must be resorted back into neat stacks. All the while, waiting. Waiting for Lydia.

The various church bells rang, all in successive notes of five; the Baptist bell that clanged like an empty tin bucket, and the Methodist bell, pitched high like the jingles on the side of a sled. Then he heard a floorboard creak and looked up, expecting to see Lydia.

But it was Whitmore standing in the open doorway. Shocked, Nathaniel jumped to his feet, knocking one of the stacks of paper onto the floor. "Whit!" The boy looked older than at the Christmas holiday, haggard, with dark circles under his eyes. Nathaniel grabbed him, hugging him in a tight embrace. The kid felt thin and smelled of sweat. "What're you doing here?"

"I've come for a visit."

Nathaniel looked at him in amazement. "A visit?" He motioned for Whitmore to sit. "How did you know I would be at my office?"

"I hoped, given you said you often are on a Sunday, and I wanted to see you before Frances knew I was here."

Nathaniel sank into his desk chair. "How did you get here?"

"Train." Whitmore's skin looked gray.

"Are you sick?"

Whitmore closed his eyes and, despite looking worse than he had the moment before, said, "No."

"Does your mother know where you are?"

"She thinks I'm in Cape Cod." He visibly took a deep breath and looked Nathaniel straight in the eyes. "I've come to see Jeselle."

"What?"

"Why is she here?" asked Whitmore.

Nathaniel watched him sharply, feeling a rising fear in the pit of his stomach. He kept his voice even. "Your sister's worse. I needed help."

Whitmore glared at him now. "Why Jeselle?"

He shrugged, thinking through what to say. "Because she knows us." He crossed his arms over his chest, bracing himself for the answer to the question he had to ask. "Whit, why did you come to see her?"

"I needed to." His eyes glistened with tears. "I love her."

Nathaniel's heart pounded in his chest. Holy God, he thought. It was Whit's baby. "Whit, no."

"I know what you think. But it's her. No one but her."

Nathaniel simply stared at him for a long moment. Whit fidgeted in his chair, tapping his foot on the floor. "Whit, what I think doesn't matter. What you're talking about is illegal. Whatever you feel must be kept a secret."

"Why?" The boy continued to stare right back at him, almost belligerent in his stance, arms crossed and a challenging look in his eyes.

"Because it's dangerous. It's against the law, for heaven's sake."

"Not in the Northeast. You're from Maine. I could take her there and marry her. It's legal there."

"Whit, it's legal, but that doesn't mean anyone does it. Not out in the open, anyway." He paused, trying to discern if Whitmore followed what he said, but the boy's expression was unyielding. "They don't bother to change the law, because there's no need—no white person would dare marry a colored person even if the law allows it, knowing they would surely come to harm if they did."

Whitmore slumped over, hugging himself with his arms and rocking. "I haven't heard from her since Christmas."

He had to tell him. Nathaniel's voice came out hoarse, shaky. "She's going to have a baby."

Whitmore's gray face went white. "Oh, God."

"Cassie sent her here so your mother and father wouldn't guess the truth. It didn't occur to me that it could be—the baby's father, that is—that it could be you."

"At Christmas, we—"

Nathaniel nodded, putting up his hand. "Yes, I understand." He took in a breath, watching Whit closely. "Listen, Whit. Jeselle and Cassie intend to give the baby to a reverend and his wife back in Atlanta."

Whitmore stared at him with a look of disbelief. "She's agreed to give up the baby?"

He stuttered, "I, I think so."

Whitmore shook his head. "No. Not Jes."

"Whit, we could support her financially. You and me. Send her somewhere to live. But it must be kept quiet. As I'm sure you're aware, many white men do this."

"Do what?"

"Have secret relationships with colored women, families even, but in private."

Whitmore got up, placing his hands on the back of his chair, his knuckles white. "Jeselle's not a secret that must be hidden away. I want her to be my wife."

"Whit, do you know what could happen to you if you come out in the open? She's pregnant with your child. They call that illicit sex and will prosecute you under the fornication and adultery laws." He paused. "If they don't lynch you and Jeselle first."

"Where is she?"

"She's at her cousin's. On their farm. Sunday's her day off." He stood and spoke as sternly as he could. "But you cannot go there."

Whit pushed aside his chair and grabbed Nathaniel's upper arm, his voice raised. "Take me there."

"Absolutely not."

Whit shouted now, both of his hands gripping Nathaniel's shoulders, as if he might shove him. "Dammit, Nate, take me there."

A shadow behind them—someone was in the doorway. Freeing himself from Whit, he saw Lydia. Her breath was quick, as if she'd been running up the stairs. "Nathaniel, is everything all right?"

"Yes, fine. Lydia, meet my brother-in-law, Whitmore Bellmont. Frances's brother."

Whitmore stood against the wall, his arms crossed. He nodded toward Lydia but said nothing.

"Nice to meet you. I'm Mrs. Tyler. Nathaniel's student."

"Did you hear what we were arguing about?" Nathaniel asked.

Lydia took a step backward. "No, just shouting." She darted a look at Nathaniel and then back at Whitmore, plucking at the skirt of her dress. "Regardless, it's none of my business, of course. I only wanted to see if you were all right."

Nathaniel's words were out of his mouth before he knew what he was saying. "Whitmore thinks he's in love with Jeselle."

"The girl who works for you?"

He nodded.

A vein bulged on Whitmore's forehead. He looked at Lydia as if he were spoiling for a fight. "She's having a baby. My baby."

Lydia spoke without a hint of alarm, her voice pitched low, soothing. "I see. Well, let's all think this through." As if she were an old friend, she put her hand lightly on Whitmore's arm. "I have daughters, you see, just about your age. I'm well versed in matters of the heart."

Whitmore's combative expression lessened, and his shoulders slumped.

"Come, sit." She took Whit's arm and guided him into a chair, then closed the office door. "We might try and keep our voices low." She cocked her head to one side, looking at Whitmore. "How does Jeselle feel about this situation?"

"I, I don't know."

Lydia glanced up toward the ceiling as if she were thinking and then back at Whitmore. "You must ask Jeselle what she wants. This will determine everything."

"Yes." Whitmore said the word slowly. "I guess that's right."

"And what are you prepared to do?" asked Lydia.

"Anything."

Nathaniel stepped closer to Whit and put his hand on his shoulder. "This is an impossible situation. Please, Whit, think reasonably."

"I cannot," Whit said.

"You must be deliberate in your actions, not impulsive," Lydia said.

Whitmore nodded, never taking his eyes from Lydia's face. Nathaniel suddenly imagined how she must be with her daughters. She would rectify this situation—sort it through somehow. He was no match for this problem, but a mother, a mother would know what to do. Just as he was beginning to feel better, Lydia stood, brushing the front of her dress as if it were dirty. "Eleanor Roosevelt believes in freedom for all Americans, including marrying who you want, regardless of race. And I wholeheartedly agree."

Nathaniel came out of his seat. "Lydia," he said, almost shouting, "this has nothing to do with someone's ideals."

"No." She stood tall and crossed her arms over her chest. "This is about love."

"Nate no longer believes in love," said Whitmore.

Anger spread through Nathaniel's limbs. He spoke through clenched teeth, "I simply don't want you to give up your life for something that might prove to be false."

"Like you have, Nate?" asked Whit.

"Is that what you think?" His breakfast churned in his stomach. He wiped his face with his handkerchief, surprised by how angry he felt. "Whit, I'll be damned if I stand by and let you ruin your life."

"Nate, it will be ruined if I can't be with Jes. It's just that simple."

"Nathaniel, at least give him a chance to talk with her. We could go out and get her later."

"And bring her where?" asked Nathaniel. "It can't be here at my office. Someone might see."

"And I can't go to the house," said Whitmore.

"I have a friend who might take you in," said Nathaniel. "Stay here. We'll come back and get you if he says yes."

*   *   *

Nathaniel and Lydia walked to the parsonage. Lulu answered the pastor's door and, after introductions were made, they followed her into a sitting room. "Sit here now," said Lulu. "I'll get ye some tea and biscuits."

The biscuits were actually cookies. Although Nathaniel felt nauseous, he took one when Lulu offered. She stared at him, one hand on her plump hip, until he took a bite. It melted in his mouth, tasting of sugar and butter. "Very good. Thank you."

She beamed and poured them cups of steaming tea. "The good man should be back soon." A moment later, they heard the kitchen door open and close. "Ah, there he is now."

Pastor Ferguson walked into the room. "Nathaniel, what a pleasure to see you." Nathaniel rose to shake his hand. "And this is Mrs. Tyler, I believe? Front row, right side."

Lydia smiled. "That's correct."

"So good to see your face every Sunday. Perhaps Nathaniel could take a lesson from you on church attendance?"

"I'm afraid we have a problem," Nathaniel said.

"What seems to be the trouble?" Ferguson took a cookie for each hand. "Please, sit."

Nathaniel told Ferguson the entire situation. The pastor took another cookie and poured himself a cup of tea, then sat back in his armchair, looking thoughtfully out the window for a few moments. "This is certainly a complicated matter. A cookie, Mrs. Tyler?"

"No, thank you." Lydia stiffened next to him. Please don't start in on Eleanor Roosevelt, Nathaniel thought. Not now.

"Mrs. Tyler, I came to this country when I was a month old. My parents hailed from Scotland, where we had these same kinds of complications around clans instead of race. There is much fear in what we don't understand, in our misguided belief that if someone else has more, we somehow will have less. Unfortunately, I have to consider the current belief system within my community when I make decisions about my congregation. Whether I like it or not, this would be an explosive situation if it were to get out around town. I'm not sure you're aware of how strong emotions are around the separation of the races. My people will in no way understand nor support a white boy and a black girl. Do you see what I'm saying here?"

Lydia was at the edge of the couch now. "That you cannot help us. Isn't that it? Because you're afraid to lose church members?"

"This goes all the way up to the top of the national Presbytery. I have elders I must answer to."

Lydia sprang to her feet. "Tell me, Pastor, how exactly do you reconcile Jesus' teachings with the mistreatment of people because of the color of their skin?" She waved her hands in the air. "Are we not all equal in the eyes of God?"

Ferguson smiled gently, putting his half-eaten cookie back on his plate. "Mrs. Tyler, while I appreciate your point and happen to agree with you, this is a way of thinking that goes back hundreds of years."

"I'm not sure what that has to do with anything, Pastor," said Lydia. "Things will never change when the self-proclaimed righteous look the other way instead of taking stands against injustice."

Ferguson nodded his head, his face impassive before turning his gaze yet again toward the window. "I understand, Mrs. Tyler. And still, I must carefully consider things. Nathaniel, what do you propose to do about this situation?"

"Me? I'm not sure. My primary concern is that they're both safe."

The pastor murmured. "Hmmm, I agree. And they won't be, the minute this gets out." He sat forward and poured himself another cup of tea. "We all three must pray about it. He will provide us an answer." Ferguson took a sip of tea. "Until then, you'll have to put Whitmore up at the Rains sisters' boarding house."

On the way toward campus, Lydia was quiet until they were almost to his office. "Please take me with you to get Jeselle."

"Why?"

"Because I don't want you to have to do it alone."

"Thank you."

CHAPTER 39

Whitmore

WHITMORE WAITED with Nate on the wobbly front porch of the decaying Victorian for Sarah and Alba Rains to come down from their living quarters.

Hearing the women approaching, Whitmore held out his hand to Nate. "I know you're not sure about this. But, thank you."

Nate's eyes reddened, and he glanced toward the street. "Just get some rest. We'll sort it all out." Then, to Whit's surprise, Nate pulled him into a quick embrace before heading down the rickety steps of the porch.

Alba and Sarah were twins, both grizzled and gray, with identical whiskers growing out of their protruding chins. They took Whitmore down a dark hallway to a small room at the back of the first floor that smelled of dust and decaying wood; it held a twin bed against one wall, a desk with a chair, and a braided rug. A large glass window looked out onto a dry lawn. "Window opens if it feels stuffy," the sister in the plaid dress said.

"He won't want the window open," the other said.

"He surely will," her sister replied.

"The room's fine." He followed the women back to the desk in the foyer area near the front door.

"I'm Alba, and this here is Sarah. We live upstairs and only come down when absolutely necessary." Alba lowered herself gingerly into the chair at the desk.

"Sister's not as good on the stairs as she once was." Sarah stood at the side of the desk, scrutinizing him with eyes the same faded blue as her house dress.

Alba opened the guest ledger. "Sister's the one can't get up the stairs anymore. I'm as fit as a fiddle." As far as Whitmore could see, the sisters seemed to be in the exact same condition.

"We expect quiet after eight p.m." Alba wrote his name into the guest ledger.

Whit nodded politely. "Of course."

Alba continued, as if she hadn't heard him, "We have loaded shotguns we keep by our beds. We come down shooting if we hear any noises in the middle of the night."

"What my sister is trying to say, young man, is we expect quiet at night. No women or drink."

"I understand. I won't cause you a bit of trouble."

Sarah, still standing, crossed her arms. "We'll need at least a week in advance. That's two dollars a week."

"Fine." Whitmore took the money from his wallet and laid it the desk.

Sarah, continuing to watch him with distrusting eyes, wrapped a knobby hand on the back of her sister's chair. She raised a bushy, white eyebrow and said to Whit, "You don't look too good."

Alba looked up from putting the money in her dress pocket. "You sick? We don't want to catch anything."

"No, ma'am. I've been traveling for several days. I'm here to see about a girl."

"You best get cleaned up first," Alba said. "No sweetheart gonna kiss you looking like you do."

Sarah looked at her sister, shaking her head. "Sister, what do you know about sweethearts?"

"I figure more than you, sister."

Whitmore stepped back from the desk, muttering a polite farewell before heading toward his room. As he shut the door, he heard the women making their way up the stairs slowly, bickering over the price of bread. "I saw seven cents," one said.

"Surely it was eight cents. You don't see as well as you used to, sister," replied the other.

In his room, Whit sat at the desk, his hands between his knees, rocking back and forth, trying to conjure the right words to say to Jeselle that might shift her thinking, whatever it was. He moved to the bed, took off his shoes, and reclined with his hands folded behind his head. He counted fourteen bumps in the ceiling and one broken cobweb in the corner by the window. The glass panes were dirty and overlooked an old drooping oak tree. A child's rotting swing hung by a rope from a thick branch. Was it the sisters' swing from long ago? He tried to imagine the old women as children but couldn't envision them without their crepe paper faces, coiled white braids, and stooped shoulders. Had either ever had a sweetheart? Were their hearts broken once? Had they waited for someone who never came?

Ironic, he thought; he needed persuasive words now, but Jeselle was the writer. He closed his eyes, the pain there in his chest again, remembering Jeselle crouched in the butler's pantry at the lake house, scribbling word after word into the diaries his mother gifted to her every year on her birthday. It made him think, then, of his mother's bold decision to educate Jeselle all those years ago.

He'd never thought to ask his mother, or perhaps never had the courage to ask, why? He only knew his mother's choice to rebel against her husband, her upbringing, and every cultural norm of her time had set something in motion that was intertwined in every aspect of his life. Like the first hasty movement of a water bug on his beloved lake, the ripples of that one decision spread in wider and wider circles—a courageous move toward some equilibrium in a chaotic and unjust world.

He remembered the baby, again, with the same dart of shock. There would be a baby. And what world would he or she inherit? Would there ever be enough ripples of love set in motion to change humankind? He had to believe it started with one action, one movement toward love.

CHAPTER 40

Lydia

AFTER NATHANIEL LEFT with Whitmore for the boarding house, Lydia stayed in Nathaniel's office to await his return. It was nearing two in the afternoon, and she ate an apple she found on his desk, staring at Frances's photograph. Soon she was at the piano, her fingers flexed and lifted, tapping up and down the piano keys, practicing her assigned scales. She was on the second exercise when the idea came to her, so abruptly that she stopped playing. It was France. They must live in France. Whitmore and Jeselle could live there as man and wife, openly.

Just last month she'd read an article about the dancer Josephine Baker, a beautiful and eccentric black woman who had moved to Paris in order to live without the cultural constraints of America.

Later, as she and Nathaniel drove out of town to get Jeselle, she attempted to adjust her skirt to allow some air to reach her hot skin. What was this? Her skirt was stuck, caught in the car door. She'd closed the door on her own skirt. What an absolute oaf. It would be frayed and tattered by the time they reached Jeselle. She moved closer to the door, hoping to keep it from ripping.

Goodness, it was hot. Stifling actually. The inside of the car smelled of rubber with a hint of gasoline. Lydia rolled down her window, allowing the breeze to blow on her face, aware that this was the first time she'd ridden in a car without her braid. As they headed away from town, she glanced, with just a slight slip of her eyes, at Nathaniel's austere profile. In the afternoon light she saw that the rims of his eyes were pink and he was graying at his temples. He sat perfectly upright, elbow resting on the open window frame, looking straight ahead, his body moving only with the jars and bumps of the road.

As they drove deeper into the country, the smell of freshly plowed soil drifted in through their open windows. Beyond, as far as the eye could see, were rows and rows of cotton. The pickers were scattered among the rows, carrying sacks over their slumped forms.

"Does Jeselle walk all this way?" she asked, forgetting her vow not to talk too much.

"I drive her."

She blinked, surprised. "Why doesn't she live in?"

"We don't have enough bedrooms."

Not enough bedrooms? That model of kit home usually had at least two rooms upstairs. And then it occurred to her what that implied: he did not share a bedroom with his wife. She turned away, feeling embarrassed. Dust drifted in through the windows, sticking to their skin and clothes. Lydia glanced at Nathaniel. His face, pale, dripped with perspiration, and his eyes appeared unfocused. "You feeling peaked?" she asked, alarmed.

His voice sounded dry, almost raspy. "Something Jeselle said. Probably nothing."

"What is it?"

"She said Frances is gone in the afternoons." He wiped his face again with the handkerchief and slowed the car as they turned a corner. "That is not my understanding of how Frances spends her afternoons."

Lydia gazed at the giant oaks alongside the road. Moss hung from burdened branches.

"It's probably nothing," he repeated.

They drove in silence for several minutes until Lydia turned to him. "Have you heard of Josephine Baker, the entertainer?"

He nodded. "She's the Negro singer that sings and dances half-clothed?"

She chuckled. "Some might think of her as risqué, but I'm quite an admirer."

Eyes still on the road, she saw his mouth turn up in a brief smile. "Lydia Tyler, you're nothing if not unpredictable."

"She lives in Paris. Without cultural constraints."

He looked at her full in the face, and the car veered to the right, so that they were precariously close to the ditch. "You think they should move to France?"

"Exactly."

"What an idea." He yanked the wheel, straightening the car, his eyes focused on the road again. "How would we get them to France?"

"Ocean liner."

"No. Too dangerous. There's talk of war over there. Hitler wants to spread his power east from Germany. I can't imagine it won't include west—possibly France—at some point in time. He wants power, Lydia, and will try to get it however he can. No European country will be safe from war if the speculation is correct."

She paused for a moment, considering what he meant. "A second world war? Surely that cannot happen again?"

"Lydia."

"Couldn't be more of a risk than staying here," she said softly.

"We can't know that."

She turned and looked out her window, peeved that he hadn't seized on the idea. "Nathaniel." Her voice wobbled. She swallowed, hard. Why did this man evoke such emotion from her? "Think of the baby."

He took in a breath and shifted in his seat.

"In France there are others like them. I've read about it."

"What if he's miscalculated somehow?" asked Nathaniel.

"Miscalculated?"

"What if she's not the girl he thinks she is?" His eyes never left the road, but he jerked his head toward the window in a slight movement that reminded her of a yoked animal.

"Are you speaking about yourself, or are you thinking of Whit?"

They passed a creek. "I married Frances because there was a baby coming."

"Oh. Well." She opened her purse, pulling out a handkerchief, wiping a trickle of sweat that ran down the back of her neck. "No situation is exactly the same as another." She tried to keep her voice steady, but the shock of what he'd just told her made it difficult.

"Here it is," he said as he turned down a dirt driveway.

Tension made her sit up taller when they turned a corner and she saw Jeselle sitting in a rocking chair, knitting, on the porch of a ramshackle house. Nathaniel turned off the car just as Jeselle pushed herself up out of the rocking chair in the way pregnant women must and cupped a hand over her eyes, squinting. He moved to open his door. Lydia put her hand on his jacket sleeve. "Wait, what do we say?"

His eyes were sharp. "You're not saying anything. You're staying in the car."

She turned in the seat and faced him. "What's given you the idea that you can tell me what to do outside the practice room?"

He continued to stare at her for a moment, his eyes impatient. "I'm trying to keep you safe."

"That's not your job."

He sighed and shook his head. "Fine. Come along if you wish."

"I will."

As they approached, Jeselle jumped down from the porch and stood watching them, the ball of yarn unraveling. A black and white kitten leaped from under the porch and began to bat the yarn between its paws. "Mr. Nate? Mrs. Tyler? Is something wrong?"

"Whit came to my office today," said Nathaniel. "Looking for you."

Jeselle's lower lip trembled. "He shouldn't have come here."

"He knows about the baby," said Nathaniel.

"Did you tell him?"

"He says he loves you," said Nathaniel.

"You tell him to go home. Tell him nothing good can come of it." Tears rolled down her cheeks, and she brushed them away with ferocious swipes. "You tell him that for me."

"What if there was a place you could go where you could live together as man and wife?" Lydia asked. Lydia felt Nathaniel's gaze piercing through her.

"There is no such place."

Lydia kept her voice low. "What if there was? Would you go?"

Before the girl could answer, they were startled by a sound from the porch. Lydia looked over to see a black woman standing in the doorway, hands on skinny hips, scowling in their direction. Jeselle composed her face, but there was terror in her eyes. "Bess will wonder what you're here for."

Lydia's mind worked quickly. "Tell her we came by because Mr. Fye needs you to come into work."

Jeselle nodded and spoke quietly. "Whit's naive. He won't see it."

"What if we could figure a way?" Lydia asked her again.

Jeselle's brown eyes snapped. Nathaniel shuffled his feet. "Why do you care?" asked Jeselle.

Nathaniel put his hand on Lydia's forearm. It felt like a peace offering. Lydia softened. "She's a friend." He spoke gently. "Jeselle, answer her question."

"The answer would be yes, if I didn't know better." Jeselle's eyes darted to Bess, waiting on the porch, and then back again to their faces.

Lydia stepped closer, putting her hand on Jeselle's forearm. "Come with us. He's waiting for you."

Jeselle blinked, cocked her head. "Wait just a moment, please."

She turned and walked quickly toward the house, saying something to her cousin that Lydia couldn't hear before starting back toward them. Bess stood with her hands clasped together at her chest, eyes on the yard.

* * *

Nathaniel escorted Jeselle into the boarding house while Lydia waited in the car. She twisted her handkerchief between her fingers, looking out the window but seeing nothing.

When he slid behind the steering wheel again, Nate took off his hat and wiped his brow. "The sisters who run the place weren't at the desk, thank the good Lord. I said I'd come back for Jeselle after I drop you off."

They drove in silence. When they arrived at the edge of campus, Nathaniel slowed the car, parking next to the lawn. He took the keys out of the ignition and turned to face her. "Can Jeselle travel in her condition?"

"She needs to go within the next several weeks or not at all."

"All right then. Let's propose the idea to Whitmore. See if he's really willing to walk away from everything and go to France."

She studied him. "What's made you change your mind?"

"I don't see a safer option." He appeared to study his keys, moving them one by one until they looked like a fan in the palm of his hand. "I'm not the person you think I am."

"What do I think exactly?"

"That I'm small-minded." He continued to gaze at his keys. "I've been all over the world, you know." He cleared his throat, looking up and into her eyes. "I don't protest your ideals."

"Ideals only matter if you use them to actually do something."

He looked at her steadily. A magnolia blossom from a nearby tree drifted onto the car's windshield. "Perhaps." There was a slight flicker in his eyes. "I would've given anything for my baby son to have lived. I would've done anything. Anything. And I'll do anything for Whit. But I'm frightened to lose him. Sometimes I think he's all I have."

"I understand," she whispered. "Nathaniel, I'm sorry about your son."

"His name was John."

"John."

"My father's name." He dropped the keys into his lap. Shifting in the seat, he leaned closer and brushed the side of her face with his fingertips. "Lydia Tyler, I wish I didn't care so much what you think of me."

Her heart pounded. A roar started between her ears. "I couldn't think more of you than I already do." She put her hand on the door handle. "I have to go." She opened the door, blind and trembling, and put her feet on the ground. Steps from her dormitory, she turned to look back, startled to see him standing by his car, watching her. He lifted his hat, and she waved, feeling like a schoolgirl sneaking home in the middle of the night.

CHAPTER 41

Whitmore

WHITMORE SAT on the side of the bed. Jeselle stood near the desk, grasping the back of the chair. "You plan on giving this baby away?" he asked.

"It's what Mama wants. Doesn't mean I'm going to do it."

He got up from the bed and reached for her, took her hand between his own. "I knew it."

"Mama wants to give the baby to the Reverend Young. But I can't."

"Not even when you thought about Oberlin?"

"Even then. I've been saving every penny. I planned to go out west. I thought California, but lately I've been thinking Wyoming or Montana. Places with miles and miles of space where a person could get lost and never be bothered."

He moved away from her, trying to keep the pain out of his voice, but it was impossible. "Did you think at all of me?"

"Of course I thought of you. You're all I think of. I won't have you giving up your life or getting killed over me. Think of me living with that the rest of my life? Think about that, Whitmore Bellmont." She crossed her arms over her chest and winced. Was she hurt? He took her arm in his hands, gently. "What is it?" Then he saw it. A burn mark on her soft flesh. He knew instantly who had done it to her. "My God, Frances burned you?"

"Never mind."

"She burned you? With an iron?" He brought her into his arms and held her. "I'm sorry, Jessie."

She put her arms tighter around his neck, and he felt her chest moving up and down as she cried, her tears damp on his neck. After a moment he shifted so he could hold her face between his hands, catching the tears with his fingertips as they fell. "Do you love me?"

"You know I do," she whispered.

"Are you willing to go with me, wherever it is?"

"What about your life? Your daddy's plans for you?"

"My plan has been and always will be you."

"How will we live?"

"I don't know." He moved his hand to rest on her round belly, amazed there was a baby inside. "I'll find a way. Will you come with me?"

"Yes."

CHAPTER 42

Nathaniel

NATHANIEL WALKED OVER to the church early that evening, the sun behind a fat, ash-colored cloud dimming the landscape. He found Ferguson in the windowless pastor's office behind the sanctuary. The warm and untidy office smelled of dust and old books; piles of papers were scattered about the desk, and books stacked sideways and wrong side up looked as if they might collapse a rickety shelf on the far wall. An empty, chipped teacup was perched precariously on a tattered dictionary.

Gillis, writing, looked up and smiled broadly when Nathaniel knocked. "Nathaniel. Come on in. Excuse the mess." Getting up, he grabbed the pile of books off the visitor's chair and set them on the floor near the radiator. "This is the only place Lulu can't get to."

Nathaniel remained standing, too antsy to sit. "Lydia thinks they should go to France. To live."

"They could live in relative peace there, I suppose."

"Except for the war most believe is inevitable."

"Hitler. Yes." The room filled with a sound like someone beating a snare drum. "Ah, our friend the woodpecker, saying hello."

"If anything happened to Whit…" Nathaniel's throat tightened. "It would be the last thing I could take. I wouldn't make it through."

"How would they live?" asked Ferguson.

"I have money put aside from the old days. It's enough to get them started. Whitmore's talented. I could introduce him to some art contacts there and in New York City. He could paint portraits or something."

"The answer seems clear then."

"France?" said Nathaniel.

"France."

"I should get home, check on Frances. I haven't been home since I saw you earlier." At the doorway, he stopped and turned back to look at the pastor. "Jeselle says Frances is out most afternoons."

"Out? Where?"

"I don't know. Frances tells me she always rests in the afternoons. I mean, what would she do out all afternoon?"

"Do you suspect something?"

"What? No. I mean, suspect what?" The noise from the woodpecker ceased, replaced with the hum from a car on the street. "What would I suspect? A man?"

"Just ask her. Most folks tell the truth when asked."

"How do you remain so optimistic about people?" asked Nathaniel.

He chuckled. "Well, we're made in God's image."

"Yeah, but the mirror's awfully blurry for some of us."

* * *

When Nathaniel returned home he peeked into Frances's bedroom to find her at her dressing table applying lipstick. She met his eyes in the mirror. "Where did you get yourself off to?"

"Business to take care of." He leaned against the doorframe. "Frances, what do you do in the afternoons?"

"Rest." She turned from the mirror to face him. "Darlin', I've been thinkin' maybe we should move to California."

"What?"

"California. Los Angeles. I hear there are dozens of universities out there. You could get a post at one of them."

He sat on the end of her bed, sighing. "Frances, I can't leave my position here."

Her eyes filled with tears. "Why can't you give me one thing I want?"

"We're not moving to California. I'm sorry."

With that, she jumped up from the dressing table, swiping her arm across the top so that all the contents flew to the floor. "You're determined to ruin my dreams." She lunged toward him, wailing and pushing both of her hands into his chest. When she was in a fury, she had enormous strength, and he fell back onto the bed. She beat him with her fists until he managed to get his hands under her arms and toss her off him. Collapsing in a heap, she looked small and fragile and crumpled, her gown in a swoop around her as her small ribcage moved in wracking sobs.

I can't even look at her anymore, he thought as he left the room. I can't even stand to look at her.

CHAPTER 43

Lydia

THE NEXT MORNING Lydia made her way sluggishly across campus, through air that felt thick with heat, thinking even the bees that usually hovered and sucked luxuriously from the flowers were slower, as if the humidity made their wings heavy. Inside the music building it was cooler, and dim. She went to Nathaniel's office, where she knew he waited for her to begin their morning lesson.

He sat at the piano, spine straight, his face in shadow, his right hand playing the notes of an unfamiliar melody. She stood at the door, allowing herself to watch him for a moment before shuffling her feet to let him know she was there. At the noise, his hand stilled and hovered over the keys before he turned his gaze toward her. "Lydia."

Where had he been, she wondered? She opened her mouth to speak, but all that came out was a squeak that sounded like a question. Then, "Good afternoon." A trickle of perspiration meandered between her breasts. "Are you ready for me?"

He moved to stand behind the piano. "Please begin with the exercises I assigned you."

She played through the scales and arpeggios. When she finished, his eyes were hooded, unreadable. "Is it all right?" The walls of the room felt unusually close.

He blinked. "Yes, it was quite good."

She sighed, feeling limp from the warmth of the room and something else that hung in the air. She stirred on the seat. "I'm so warm."

"Yes, it's ungodly hot in here today." The vein on his neck above his shirt collar twitched. His skin was damp at the back of his neck. Her fingers twitched, wanting to feel his skin.

"Are you feeling poorly?" she asked.

"What? No, not all."

"You seem distracted."

"I am, I guess. Worried about the kids." He paused. "Lydia, how old are you?"

She moved from the piano bench and reached for her bag, attempting to sound lighthearted, teasing, like she'd observed in other women when they were asked a question that made them uncomfortable, but it came out flat and breathless. "My mother said never to tell a man your age."

He smiled. "Right, men and women don't discuss these things in polite society."

She rifled through her bag as if she were looking for something. "I'm forty years old, last month."

His voice was quiet as he rested his arms on the top of the piano, leaning over to peer at her. "I apologize if I've made you uncomfortable. You seem younger yet older, soft and hard, all harmonious."

"Is that how I appear to you?" She put her finger on middle C and tapped it, twice. The sound reverberated in the quiet room.

"Yes, it is." The tone of his voice was careful and measured, like he didn't want to alarm her.

She stared at his mouth. What would it feel like to kiss him? Put it aside, she told herself. No good comes from coveting a married man. Any imbecile knew that. Apparently her heart wasn't very smart.

"I have something for you." He rifled through his bag. "Yes, here it is. This is the Brahms *B-flat Piano Concerto*. I'd like you to begin practicing it. Might take you six months to learn, but I want you to perform it in public when you're ready."

Startled, she took the sheet music from him, scanning it quickly. "A woman can't play it."

"Small, weak women, perhaps not. But someone with the capacity of your large hands? I think you can." He smiled, teasing. "You're the perfect age. You should be at least forty to even attempt it."

"Did you play it?"

"Once. Publicly, that is. I was thirty, and it was only by some miracle it wasn't an utter failure."

"I would've loved to see you perform." Why had she said this? It would only make him feel worse.

"Performing made me feel powerful—to hold an audience's attention like I did. Does that sound awful?"

"Merely honest."

"You're either a performer or you're not. I believe you to be a performer, Lydia. I believe it with all my heart."

"Nathaniel." Pesky tears came to the corners of her eyes. "Thank you."

"It's selfish, you know, this mentorship. It feels a little like the old days, here, with you."

The old days? How unfair they couldn't play together. A world tour with her as the opening act for her teacher? It would have been splendid to be on the same stage as Nathaniel Fye. The same stage? Yes, that was it. And in that moment an idea came to her that seemed too grand and yet obvious all at once. In her excitement the words tumbled out before she could censor or evaluate the validity of the idea. "When I was in college I performed several duets with other students for recitals. One was a Mozart sonata. It was scored for four hands, and we found it difficult because one hand performed the melody while the other three hands provided accompaniment."

"Yes, it's difficult to get the balance right."

"Wouldn't it be easier for three hands? One hand plays the melody while the other two provide the accompaniment?"

His eyes widened. "For three hands?"

"Why not? If in combination we can play as one, with three hands we could play a duet."

His brow wrinkled, and it seemed as if he might dismiss the idea altogether. Seconds clicked by, and she could see him evaluating and then considering the possibility. Finally he spoke, casually, almost offhand. "I might take a look at the Mozart, see if it could work for three hands. It would be difficult. The music would have to be completely re-scored."

"Yes, but it could be done, couldn't it?"

He chuckled. "Yes, but this is not in our course work for the summer, Lydia."

"Well then, you'll have to take care of it yourself. I have the Brahms *B-flat* to work out."

CHAPTER 44

Nathaniel

THE NEXT MORNING, Nathaniel waited for Lydia on the cement bench outside the music building. The campus was quiet, resident life unfolding lazily within the dormitory walls. But Lydia, with her ferocious energy, had insisted they begin their tutoring session early so they might have time for the Mozart. Nathaniel had worked long into the still and sultry night until the arrangement was complete.

She came out of her residence hall, walking briskly with long strides, as she always did, straightening her hat, probably too impatient to have bothered securing it with pins. She spotted him and waved, her steps slowing for a moment before she continued her brisk pace. "Good morning."

"I've a surprise for you."

She looked taken aback. "Really?"

"Yes, in my office."

* * *

"Close your eyes," he instructed outside his office. She did so, and he opened the door, guiding her in with his hand on her elbow. "All right. Open now."

She gasped. "Oh, Nathaniel, how wonderful."

There were two upright pianos side by side, taking up almost the entire room. "For us," Nathaniel said. "To work on the Mozart. I had the janitors move it in yesterday afternoon. And I finished the Mozart arrangement."

"How did you finish it so quickly?"

"I couldn't sleep so I worked into the night."

"Well, it's best to get up and get something accomplished, I suppose."

"If you say so," he said with a smile.

And suddenly she lurched forward, throwing her arms around his neck and squeezing. "I'm so happy."

He stumbled backward, his arms stiff by his sides. She immediately moved away.

"I'm sorry," she said.

He cleared his throat. "We can work on the Mozart, after I hear your scales and the *B-flat*. I feel terrible pangs of guilt over this whole business." He looked at the pianos. "But, Lydia, to play again. The seduction is too great."

"To play with you, Nathaniel, is one of the thrills of my life. Don't ever doubt that."

"Enough of that. Time to get to work."

* * *

An hour later, Nathaniel yawned and rubbed his eyes.

"Are you tired?" Lydia pulled her hands from the keys and scrutinized him. "Or am I boring you?" She smiled.

"What? No, no."

"Let's do the Mozart."

"This is supposed to be your session, not our session."

"I'll work more on the Brahms later today. I promise."

"Fine."

Before they began, Lydia excused herself to use the ladies' room. While she was gone, Nathaniel looked over the Mozart arrangement until he heard rustling at the door. It was Walt! Thinner and with a hairline that had moved back an inch, but his eyes were the same: piercing, ever watchful.

"Professor, I have a question about my exam." Walt spoke in a high-pitched voice.

"I'm sorry, we only allow pretty girls at this school." They laughed, embracing. "What are you doing here?" A surge of happiness rushed through him at the sight of his old friend.

"Had some business close by and figured I'd come on over and see you."

Nathaniel shook his head. "Hard to believe you're here. I was going to write to you today. I have a student I want you to meet. Could be a potential client for you."

"That right? Pianist?"

"Yes. We have a session this morning, but maybe you could come back and we could have lunch. Get reacquainted."

"Sure. Great. I have some things to do anyway."

"It's awfully good to see you, Walt."

"You too," said Walt. "You too."

*   *   *

Shortly after Walt left, Lydia returned. Without a word, they sat at the twin pianos. They looked at one another and took in a collective breath, centering in the other. And they began to play. An hour escaped without their knowledge.

"We've almost got it," he said.

"I would say so," said Walt from the doorway. "Bravo."

Nathaniel jumped. "Walt, I didn't see you there."

Walt came over to Lydia and offered his hand. "I'm Walt Higgins. Used to manage Nathaniel."

"Nice to meet you." She stood. "I've heard a lot about you."

"All highly exaggerated, I'm sure," said Walt.

"Only the good parts," said Nathaniel.

*   *   *

Nathaniel and Walt walked across campus and then crossed Oak to Main Street. It was hot already, hinting at the stifling late afternoon heat that would settle in over the town like a greenhouse.

"Who is she?" asked Walt.

"Came to me through my summer composition program. Walt, she's remarkable." He pointed at the diner. "This all right with you?"

"Sure."

Inside, fans suspended from the ceiling on either end of the room moved hot air that smelled of coffee and grease and bleach around the room. In addition to a scattering of tables, four booths lined one wall. A well-dressed, white-haired couple sat in the second booth, eating fried chicken and butter beans. In the booth near the back, four young men played cards and sipped coffee. Out of work, Nathaniel thought.

The owner, an older man with a hump and shuffling feet, came forward to greet them and sat them in one of the middle booths. They both ordered fried chicken with a side of collard greens.

"My God, it was eerie, walking in and hearing that music," said Walt. "Would have sworn on a Bible it was you."

"I believe she could have a serious career. I have her working on the Brahms *B-flat*."

Walt nodded. "I noticed the size of her hands. Can she really play it?"

He smiled. "She might be better than I was."

"Not a chance."

"Needs several months' more work, but I think it could be concert worthy. You want a new client?"

"Maybe. But tell me more about this duet business."

"It was her idea we play three-handed. So I put the Mozart together for us." He kept his voice light, not wanting to betray the depth of his feelings for both the woman and the musician. But he felt himself growing hot. "Just for fun. Mostly we're concentrating on the Brahms."

Walt leaned forward, slapping his hand on the tabletop. "This is pure gold, Nathaniel. You playing again. We could book the two of you all over the world."

"No, no. Lydia has the talent to go all the way on her own. This three-handed thing is just a lark for the summer. I don't want to hold her back."

"A lark? Damn, it's inspirational, and we need that in these times."

"What? No. I have Frances to think of—can't be traipsing around on a tour. This is not a discussion about a three-handed duet. Matter of fact, I'd like to see Lydia study at Rochester, up with Hanson."

"Why not here, with you?"

"She needs the best."

"You're the best."

Nathaniel shrugged. "I hear Hanson's got the best music program in the country."

Walt surveyed him with those eyes that never missed anything. "This Lydia Tyler got some kind of hold on you?"

"Whatever do you mean?" Nathaniel kept his voice even.

"You in love with her?"

Nathaniel let several seconds go by in silence before quietly answering, surprising himself by telling the truth. "Yes." There it was. Yes. He loved Lydia Tyler. He hadn't fully admitted it to himself. He never could lie to Walt.

"You haven't acted on it?"

"Of course not. I'm married."

"Ah, yes. Frances." He adjusted his glasses, gazing into his drink. "How is Frances?"

"The same."

Walt scrutinized him with his eyes half closed and then made an all-knowing type of sound in his throat. "You worried you'll weaken, give in to temptation? Is that why you want Lydia to study with Hanson?"

Nathaniel gazed up at the ceiling and slowly nodded before looking back at his friend. "She's all I think about."

Neither man spoke for several minutes. Finally Walt leaned forward in his chair. "This three-handed duet could change your life, Nathaniel. It could give you back so much of what you lost. Do you understand that? Don't dismiss it too easily in the name of propriety. You've got to seize what's given to you on this earth. Anyway, all the great artists have mistresses."

"I was raised a God-fearing man, Walt. You know that."

Walt sighed. "Ah, yes, there's that."

*   *   *

Later that evening, after he drove Jeselle to Bess's, Nathaniel arrived home weary, ready for an early bedtime. But as he approached the back door, Frances swung open the screen, her face animated. "There you are." She wore a yellow dress in material that clung to her jutting hipbones, and her eyes had the feverish look they took on when she was in one of her manic moods.

"Darlin', hurry on in, we've got company."

"Company?"

Frances, hands fluttering, whispered, "Doctor Landry and his brother are here. You know, *the* brother."

"Terrific," he muttered under his breath, following his wife into their sitting room.

Dr. Landry lounged in the armchair, a tumbler of whiskey in his hand. As Frances made introductions, the brother stood and held out his hand to Nathaniel. "Michael Landry, but everyone calls me Mick." He flashed a broad smile that Nathaniel assumed was meant to be charming but gave him a shiver up his spine instead. Mick wore a well-draped, white linen suit over his tall, slim frame. Handsome, thought Nathaniel. Too handsome for his own good.

Nathaniel poured a whiskey and sat in the other armchair.

Frances and Mick sat on the couch. She had her legs placed so that one was angled toward Mick, with a slight hike of her skirt to show an inch or so of her thigh.

Mick took a drink from his whiskey, directing his gaze toward Nathaniel. "Your wife tells me she's interested in being in the pictures." His voice had a melodious quality and accent that reminded Nathaniel of someone from the radio.

"Yes." Nathaniel leaned back in the armchair and cocked his head to the left. Frances touched the tips of her fingers down her own arm and shifted slightly so that her dress moved several inches up her leg. Mick's eyes traveled to her thigh, and he licked his bottom lip before moving his gaze back to her face.

Nathaniel sat forward in his chair, his voice a decibel too loud. "Frances, perhaps you might fetch some pecans from the kitchen for our guests." He took a swig of whiskey, the liquid causing a fire down his throat.

Mick put his hand on his stomach. "I couldn't eat a thing. Ralphie and I ate before we came." He glanced at Dr. Landry. "Lord have mercy, I forgot how y'all fry everything out here." He spoke with a hint of an Alabama accent now. He chuckled, finishing his whiskey. "After a couple of whiskeys I start to sound like I never left."

"Oh, it sounds awfully nice." Frances turned toward Nathaniel as her hand caressed the outside of her bare leg. "Darlin', they were just passing by, and luckily I saw them on the sidewalk and invited them right in for a drink." She shifted her position so that she was more in the direction of Mick, and Nathaniel caught a glimpse of her panties, knowing that Dr. Landry from his position in the room would have as well. Nathaniel felt the pulse in his neck quicken.

"Frances, your dress." Nathaniel made the tone of his voice the same low and dead calm quality that he knew intimidated his students.

She held up her hands and pretended to look down at her lap in surprise. "Oh mercy me, excuse me, gentlemen." Laughing with a shrill tinkle, she tugged at her dress, managing to make it look attractive and flirtatious by crossing her legs at the same time. "I guess the drinks are going right to my head."

"What do you do in the movie business, Mick?" Nathaniel asked, keeping his tone cold.

Mick's neck flushed red above the collar of his white shirt. "I'm here and there, working for different studios. I'm a little between jobs right at the moment."

Dr. Landry cleared his throat. "You got another whiskey for me, Professor?"

Nathaniel rose from his chair and poured the doctor another tumbler of whiskey, setting the glass decanter down hard enough that the table shook. With his back to his guests, Nathaniel spoke to Mick, "You have any power out there in Hollywood, Mick? Why don't you just tell us straightaway so my wife can pull down her goddamned dress?" As much as he tried to control his voice there was a slight tremor to his words.

He turned to see Mick squirming as he stammered, wiping a bead of sweat from his forehead, "I, I don't know."

"You don't know what?" He spoke through clenched teeth now. "Because there's no telling what she'll do for a part, so if you have any power, I'd use it, if I were you."

Frances's eyes widened, and she stared at him open-mouthed. Nathaniel took a deep breath and looked at the floor.

Dr. Landry set his empty glass on the table. "It's getting late."

Mick jumped from his chair as well. "Yes, thank you for your hospitality."

Nathaniel held up his hand. "You didn't answer the question. What can you do for my wife?"

Dr. Landry put an arm on Nathaniel's shoulder. "Take it easy, Fye."

"No, I want Mick here to tell my wife the truth about what he can do for her."

Mick ran a hand through his hair. "Like I said, I'm kind of between studios right now."

Nathaniel turned to Frances. "Did you hear that, Frances?"

Frances's eyes were sparkling like an excited child's. "Don't get all riled up, darlin'. We're just having a few laughs. My husband finds fun so tedious."

Dr. Landry cleared his throat again. "I think we best be on our way."

"Professor, thanks for the drinks," said Mick.

Nathaniel merely nodded as the two brothers left his house. Without another word to Frances, he went to his room and slammed the door behind him.

* * *

The next morning, he found a note from Frances saying she would be gone all day, doing "woman things." Relieved that she would be away, he drove out to get Jeselle and then stopped at the inn and then the campus to pick up Whit and Lydia so they might talk through the logistical details about France.

"The ocean liner leaves for France in a couple of weeks. Nathaniel will cover the passage," said Lydia, after they were all settled in the front room.

"Thank you, Nate," said Whitmore.

Lydia pulled from a French-English dictionary from her purse. "Try to learn as many words as you can between now and then."

"I have money to get you started, too," said Nathaniel. Relief flooded Whitmore's face. Nathaniel scooted to the edge of the piano bench. "I have an old friend I met in music conservatory who now lives in Paris. He's rich and will let you stay for several weeks until you can find a place to live. Whit, you might try and do portraits, and Jes, you can find work as a cook or maid. I guess. Maybe. Actually, I don't know." He looked at Lydia for help. "What do they do with the baby?"

"It will all work itself out," said Lydia. "One day at a time."

Nathaniel heard a sound in the doorway. Frances stood there, watching them like a cat that's trapped her prey. Blood rushed to Nathaniel's head as he jumped to his feet. Jeselle moved away from Whitmore, but it was too late. Frances knew.

After the initial look of shock on her face, Frances put her hand on her throat, shaking her head and fluttering her eyelids like she might faint. Nathaniel rushed to her side. "Come sit."

She stumbled as he guided her to a chair. She looked at Whitmore. "This is going to kill Mother."

Whitmore's face was stony. "I can't think about that right now."

"How could you?" Frances whispered.

Whitmore leapt to his feet, shouting, "How could *I*? After all you've done to disgrace Mother and Father, you question me?"

Frances made a choking sound as if she were gagging. She indicated with a tilt of her head toward Jeselle, "They're not even clean. They're not the same as us. And a baby?"

Lydia moved to sit next to Jeselle, taking her hand. Frances turned to Lydia. "What are you doing here? This is a family matter."

"She's helping us," Whitmore said.

Lydia looked at Frances levelly, her voice calm and assured. "I notice, Frances, that you're awfully self-possessed this afternoon. When are your fake hysterics going to begin? I'd like to know so I can leave before the playacting starts." Nathaniel heard himself gasp.

Frances made a series of sounds like she was suffocating before looking over at Nathaniel. "Make her leave."

Lydia was on her feet, pulling Jeselle up with her and heading for the door. "No need." Whitmore followed.

"Whitmore, you stay where you are. I'm calling Daddy right now," said Frances.

Nathaniel put up his hand. "Frances, that's not a good idea."

Frances tossed her head, her blonde curls bouncing. "You can't stop me."

"Call him if you want," said Whitmore. "It doesn't matter because we're leaving town together, and nothing you or Father do or say will make a difference."

Frances's face went from white to purple, and her eyes darted to each and every one in the room and then rested on Nathaniel. "How could you do this?"

Lydia motioned to Whitmore as she pulled Jeselle out the door. "Whit, let's go."

After they were gone, Frances collapsed into the couch. "How could you be involved in this and not tell me?"

"Because I knew you would try to stop it."

"If decency won't dictate to you, think of Whitmore. This will ruin his life. Moving to France with a … I mean, it's simply too awful to think of."

"This is what he wants. There's no stopping him. When did you become so concerned for Whitmore, anyway? You've always acted like he doesn't exist."

"What kind of person do you think I am?"

He poured himself a drink. "It's Whit's life."

"I suppose that's true." She paused, motioning for him to give her his drink. "I won't call Daddy if you agree to something I want."

He handed her the drink. "What is it?"

"I want some money to go out to California."

"Frances, not this again."

"Don't dismiss me. You want to help Whitmore—this is the price. I want all the money you have in savings to take out there with me. I have a few ideas of how to get started, but I need money."

"You cannot go to California without me. And I have my work here. It's not safe for a woman out there alone."

Her eyes glistened. "That's what I want. Is Whitmore's freedom worth it to you?"

"Frances, you are not well enough for this sort of endeavor. These people, these Los Angeles people who run movie studios, they don't know you. You don't just arrive in town, and they immediately put you in front of the camera."

Her cheeks flamed pink. "You don't know everything." Her eyes turned hard as she rose from the couch. "Just remember that I gave you a chance to help me, and you refused."

"What does that mean?"

Her demeanor changed suddenly, the steely look replaced by her usual airy and delicate way of moving and talking. "Nothing, darlin'." She waved her hand in the air. "I won't say anything if you don't want me to. I suppose you know more than little ole me. I'm awful tired. I think I'll go rest in my room."

CHAPTER 45

Whitmore

AFTER THEY LEFT the house, Lydia, Nathaniel, Whit, and Jeselle agreed that Jeselle would walk back to Bess's and await word from Nathaniel while Whit and Lydia did the same in their respective rooms. After Lydia left them, Whit and Jeselle lingered for a moment in the privacy of Nathaniel's backyard near a rosebush with pink buds reaching toward the sun like young ballerinas.

"Do you remember the fireflies you caught for me on my birthday all those years ago?" Jeselle placed a hand on her belly.

Whit nodded, putting his hand over hers, imagining the baby growing under their clasped flesh, inside his Jes like a bulb buried in rich soil.

Of course, he remembered, each capture of brilliant light between jar and lid a token of his unspoken love. He gathered them for her, one by one, grinning with delight, knowing how they would please her, the anticipation of giving them to her was better than anything he could receive himself. But the fireflies, his gift, fluttered and shone in the enclosed glass world he'd created for them, and he became remorseful standing next to this girl, so like the fireflies themselves, full of life and light and beauty. They sparked to attract a mate, to attract love, he remembered, suddenly. His heart constricted, and the tightness came to his throat, the kind that made it seem as if he could not breathe. Nothing this beautiful should be locked away when the dark night awaited their spark, their love.

"We let them go. Do you remember why?" she asked, bringing him back to the garden and the smell of rosebuds and the unheard heartbeat of his child.

"Because they deserved to be free—to search for love." The answer came without a thought, and yet there was no need to say it out loud, this shared memory between them conjured in a second.

"Free to attract a mate."

"Free to attract the love they deserved. That every living thing deserves," he added.

He closed his eyes for a moment, remembering. When he took the lid off the jar, the fireflies immediately fluttered up and out, hovering for an instant before drifting into the night with the others. Nothing had seemed as lovely as that moment, knowing he'd restored them to their rightful place in the night. Once again, her words brought him back to the moment.

"Whit, their spark also attracts predators. Did you know that?" Tears tumbled from her eyes.

He wiped her wet cheeks with his thumbs. "Hatred is not the same as nature's predators. No matter how they try and defend it."

"They're winning, Whit. Hatred, bigotry, fear. They're all winning."

"They'll never win." He tapped his chest above his heart. "They can't touch us inside here. No amount of hatred can smother love, no matter how they try."

"You'll love me no matter how they try?"

"Until the end of time, no matter how they try."

*   *   *

When he arrived back at the boarding house, Whitmore paced the rickety porch, fighting a sense of dread and despair. Frances would be trouble. And unlike the escapades of their youth, this time her ill will toward him could have serious consequences. He'd had to send Jeselle back to Bess's instead of keeping her near where he could protect her and their baby. A man should not be asked to make such a choice, he thought as he went down the porch steps and wandered over to the abandoned wooden swing. Once held in place with a rope on each side, it hung now by only one end, the once flat slab warped into the shape of a child's sled. He held the decaying swing in his hands. Idle, helpless hands, he thought, brushing dirt from the swing.

He dropped the swing and went inside to his room. What to do in these futile, helpless hours while he waited to hear from Nathaniel? Without thinking, he went to his bag and reached inside for his Bible. Abandoned most days, he had remembered to tuck it in his bag before he left Princeton. A gift from his mother on his tenth birthday, which had surprised him because she did not speak much of God and attended church with more resignation than zeal. Yet, she'd insisted he have a Bible and reminded him to take it with him to Princeton. What would she say now, during this desperate moment?

Sitting on the bed, he opened it to somewhere in the middle, then placed his helpless palm on the soft page. His eyes, unfocused, did not read the words. Instead he prayed, silently. *Please God, let us be free to love.*

CHAPTER 46

Nathaniel

THE EARLY EVENING SUN glinted through the window of Nathaniel's office as he stood behind his desk telling Lydia of his conversation with Frances, including her asking for money for California. He came around the desk. "She wants to go to California, see about this actress thing."

"Really?" Lydia bit her bottom lip, her eyes scrunched up as if she were contemplating the idea.

"Of course I told her no."

"Why?"

He looked at her in disbelief. "She's not well enough."

"She isn't? Are you sure about that?" She sounded a little like a schoolteacher explaining the concepts of algebra to a student she thought capable but lazy.

"I can see you have an opinion. Why don't you tell me?" He watched her play with the collar of her dress. Outside the window he heard the buzz of bees drinking nectar from flowers. He spoke quietly, "Really, Lydia, what would you have me do with Frances?"

She shifted her feet, and he could see she was agitated. It almost amused him to see her struggling to keep her opinion to herself. "It's really none of my business," she said, clamping her mouth shut.

"No, say what you think. I'm asking you."

She stared back at him, moving her hands to her hips. "You might consider letting her go. You could hire a companion for her—a woman to look after her out there. Like you would for a child, like a governess."

"She's not a child."

"Nathaniel!" She threw her hands in the air. "You're impossible." She marched to his office door, as if to leave.

How dare she criticize his decisions about Frances? She hadn't been here, hadn't lived with her for all these years. His voice rose louder than he meant it to when he said, "She's ill. I have to look after her."

She swung back to look at him, her voice tight. "Of course you're right."

"A woman does not travel alone to a strange place."

She turned to face him. "I have."

"That's different."

"How is it different?" Her voice raised an octave, full of sarcasm. "I'm an old, dried-up widow, and your wife is young and beautiful? No harm could come to someone like me. Is that it?"

"It's not the same. Frances is fragile."

It surprised him to see the rims of her eyes turn pink, as if she might cry. But her voice was even when she spoke, "I'm sure you're correct."

"I know how to handle my own wife," he sputtered. "And perhaps you're right, it is none of your business."

She flinched. Her eyes flashed and then glazed over with a coldness that changed her entire face. "I couldn't agree more."

"We didn't ask for your help."

She stepped back from him like he'd moved to strike her. "Do whatever you think is best."

"My wife suffers, has suffered."

"We all suffer." Her voice was loud now as she gripped the back of the chair with both hands. "You have suffered, and I'm beginning to see it's of your own making. When is it exactly, Professor, that you say, 'Enough. I've had enough.'"

"It would be nice to have that luxury, wouldn't it? To denounce God and country and family whenever they inconvenience us. But that's not my way." He felt his words choke at the back of his throat and put his fingers to his forehead, suddenly weary. "The truth is, I'm being punished."

"Being punished? By whom?" Her face changed as the understanding of what he meant came to her. "You think God's punishing you?"

He nodded. "I wanted to divorce her. I wanted nothing more than to go off on my own, pursue my career once again without the constraints of this woman I'd grown to despise. And God took my fingers away because of it. So, as you can see, I am quite clear about what God wants from me. He wants me to take care of Frances."

She bit her bottom lip. "This is what you think of God?"

"It's what I know, Lydia." He closed his eyes and pressed at them with his fingers until he felt Lydia's hand on his shoulder, her skirt brushing against his thigh. When he opened his eyes, her face had rearranged itself into something kind and tender.

"This is not the same God I know, Nathaniel."

He breathed in her scent: lemons and violets. "Lydia, this can't work."

"What can't work?" she whispered.

"I spoke with Howard Hanson. He runs the program up at Rochester."

"I know who he is."

"He's agreed to take you as a student. Lydia, it's the chance of a lifetime."

"Rochester." She jerked away, as if he'd just slapped her.

"Lydia, there are so many reasons you should go."

"But I'm studying with you."

His face contorted in pain as he reached for her, but then he pulled his hand away. "Lydia, you're all I think about."

She squeezed her eyes shut as if she were about to crash a speeding car into a tree. She said in a ragged breath, "Yes. Me too." Her mouth trembled.

"I can't trust myself." He took a deep breath and went to the window, looking out. "It'll be better this way. Howard said you could come this week."

"So soon?"

"It's for the best."

"Yes, of course. For the best."

He heard her crying and moved swiftly across the room and grabbed her in his arms. "Lydia, please don't cry," he whispered.

She drew in a long shaky breath as she gazed up at him, her hands on the top two buttons of his shirt. A strong warm current like swift water pulled him under. He leaned over and kissed her, hard and desperate. At first her breath caught, and he thought she might pull away, but instead she moved closer, pressing against him and parting her lips. Nothing else mattered, everything faded, except for the feel of her next to him.

Finally, he pulled away, wanting to search her eyes, to see what was there. It was more tears, dampening her cheeks and making her eyes a bottomless blue. "I'm sorry."

She put her fingers to her mouth, shaking her head. "Please, don't be. I've felt invisible for so many years. And then there was you, and suddenly I was alive."

"All I want is to have you by my side." He reached for her, pulled her tight against him once more. She cried, with little sobs that heaved her chest. He felt sick to his stomach, ravaged with remorse and tenderness and guilt. "Do you see why you must go?" He loosened his arms from around her waist. "Do you understand?"

"Yes," she whispered. And then she fled, her footsteps fading down the hallway until he was alone, wrung out from shame and desire.

*   *   *

Later, Nathaniel trudged across campus. The grounds were the same as yesterday, same flower blossoms, same old oaks that dipped romantically over green rolling lawns. But now he saw the flaws in the landscape: the unevenly trimmed hedges and the patches of brown lawn. It was all ugly to him. The air suffocating.

Somehow he made it to the front row pew of the empty Presbyterian church. With his eyes shut tight, he prayed as hard as he could to a God he doubted. After a time, he didn't know how long, he smelled Pastor Ferguson's scent of cinnamon and yeast and aftershave.

"What's happened?" He placed a hand on Nathaniel's shoulder.

Nathaniel leaned back in the pew, studying the cross on the wall behind the pulpit and raking a hand through his hair. "I've asked Lydia to go. To Rochester. To study there."

Pastor Ferguson didn't react except to nod and tug on his ear. As if musing on a philosophical question, he asked, "And what prompted this decision?"

"I can't trust myself."

"Yes, I see."

Nathaniel studied him. "Have you ever lost your faith, Gillis? Has anything in your life ever caused you to think perhaps there is no God?"

The pastor hesitated, looking upward for a moment and then back at Nathaniel. "I've never questioned His existence, but my faith, once, was shaken."

"When your daughter died?"

"Yes, I'm afraid the pain of the circumstance was such that I was blinded to His wisdom, to His love for a short time. It seemed my crisis of faith came in the form of questions. Why her? Why me? As you know, I would advise any of my flock that, here on earth, we do not always understand His ways, and the glorious reunion in heaven will wipe away all questions, all fear. But when you're in the midst of the pain sometimes it's not possible to remember these things." He went on, "Five years ago when I lost Rose, after watching her suffer so, I didn't falter in my faith, but the pain of missing her was all consuming. But with God's help one can go on, you see."

"When will it stop for me, Gillis? I've been without pity for myself. I began again. I've given to others through teaching. I've stayed married to a woman I do not love, all for the sake of pleasing Him. And now I've walked away from a woman with whom I might find some peace. I've been righteous, Gillis. And still I suffer. And I cannot help but ask why? Why did God turn away from me?"

"He never turns away, Nathaniel. It's merely your perception."

Just then they heard the sound of the red-bellied woodpecker pecking against the building. Both men were quiet, the only sound between them the rhythmic drumming of the woodpecker's beak. After a moment, Gillis smiled in his tender way and gazed at the cross that hung on the wall behind the pulpit. "I've been wondering about that bird all these months, thinking of it merely as an irritant or interruption during my daily conversations with God. I imagined this bird was a sign the building was eroding with termites and that it would need repair with money we cannot raise from the downtrodden people of this congregation. Yesterday I did research on this bird, and do you know they eat mostly berries? They make their nests where sawdust already gathers, which means the hole he has slowly chipped away at was already there. He just made it bigger. I went up there last night to see this hole for myself. And inside were all these dried berries and acorns, food he's storing for later, I suppose, when hard times come for him." He stopped, smiling and scratching his temple. "It's made me understand something. Something important. Sometimes what we think we know is not so at all." He sat beside Nathaniel in the pew. "I have something I want to say to you. I've prayed on it for several weeks now, and I feel I can no longer be silent." Gillis looked him straight in the eyes. "Son, sometimes we need to know when to let go."

"What?"

Gillis's eyes were gentle. "You've done what you thought God wanted, but perhaps you were incorrect. The answers to our questions to God are sometimes difficult to discern. I ask you this—is Frances worthy of your loyalty? Is there any question in your mind about that? If there isn't, there should be." He reached over and put a hand on Nathaniel's shoulder. "Please give serious thought to what I'm saying to you now. You need to go home and ask your wife some hard questions about how she spends her time." He turned his gaze back to the cross.

"What do you know that I don't?"

"It's not my place to say. I'll say only this. Secrets will destroy you if you let them, but you must discover this for yourself. Go home, Nathaniel. Sort through your life and see it clearly without the constraints of the rules you've given yourself. Keep only that which is good, that which doesn't threaten to ruin you. This is what God wants for you."

"How can you be so sure?"

He smiled and rose from the bench. "Because He speaks to those who will listen."

* * *

Nathaniel walked blindly, not realizing he was home until he almost stepped on the neighbor's tabby cat asleep on the sidewalk. At his driveway, he leaned against the back of his parked car, trying to muster the energy to go into the house. A cigarette. That's all he wanted. Just one. Remembering a pack of cigarettes in the glove box, he took one and lit it, taking a deep drag and blowing the smoke into the sticky air.

The neighbor's young son Homer sat on the steps of his front porch, tossing pebbles into a bucket. Nathaniel lifted his hand in a wave, and Homer waved back, grinning and yelling over to him. "Hey, Professor, I lost another tooth."

"Good man."

Homer's mother appeared on the front porch, dish towel in her hand. Nathaniel nodded in greeting, but she stared through him. She said something in Homer's ear, a stern look on her face. Homer shrugged and kicked the grass. Without a word they both disappeared into the house. Despite the heat, Nathaniel felt an ominous chill run through him. Stubbing out his cigarette, he headed around to the back of his house.

He wiped his forehead with his handkerchief as he put the key into the lock, but then hesitated, steeling his resolve, one hand frozen on the doorknob, kicking at the dry grass that grew in yellow tufts near the stairs.

As he entered, the phone began to ring. "Hello?" he answered.

"Nate?"

"Clare?"

Her voice had the thickness of sorrow. "I've received a call from Frances."

He sat down at the table, hard.

"She told me about Jes and Whit." Her voice cracked, and then she cleared her throat. "She's threatening to tell everyone unless I send 15,000 dollars. Nate, why does she need money? Are you in trouble?"

His heart pounded in his chest, somewhere between rage and horror and worry. "Clare, it's not for us. It's for her. The actress thing. She's talking incessantly about California."

"That's what this is about?" He heard Clare crying softly into the phone, picturing the way she crossed her arms over her stomach when she was upset. "Why didn't you tell me about Jes and Whit?"

"Cassie wanted it kept secret. From everyone. Including Whit. She wanted Jes to give the baby away so no one would ever know."

"How did I not see it? Cassie never let on one thing. Nate, I can't help but think both their lives are ruined."

He spoke as gently as he could, "They love each other. And they'll have a chance in France."

"But Nate, we might never see them again."

"I'm sorry."

"Honestly, I couldn't care less what people think. Let all of Atlanta find out for all I care, as long as the kids are safe. But it's Frank. I can't get the money without him knowing what it's for. I'm afraid of what he'll do if I tell him the truth." Silence on the other end of the phone went on for what felt like minutes. When she spoke her voice was stronger. "We have to send Frances away."

"Clare, I don't know."

"Think of what she's done."

"But those places. I'm afraid of what they'll do to her there. And she's sick. This fixation of hers is nothing more than that."

"They'll cure her, and then she can come home."

He sighed. "Clare, I don't know if they can."

"I have to believe that." A pause. "Nate, I'm her mother."

Still, he couldn't bring himself to agree to it. "I don't know."

"I'll call her later and tell her I'm getting the money for her but that it might take a few days." The phone line crackled, and he thought he heard her sigh. "I'll make the arrangements for one of the resting homes I found. Until then, keep her away from Jeselle and Whitmore." Another pause. "And Nate, you need to file for divorce. It's been long enough. Frances is my problem from now on. You hear me?"

Before he could reply, she'd hung up.

Nathaniel still had his briefcase in his hand as he walked into the front room. He set it near the piano and poured himself a large tumbler of whiskey. He gulped the drink and played a D-minor chord. When his glass was empty, he went upstairs, the creak of the floorboards sounding loud in the quiet house. Frances's bedroom door was wide open. He stepped into the room. One of the windows was open and the screen removed. The bed seemed hastily made, the pillows askew, and the quilt folded over on itself in several places.

The room had an odd smell to it. What was it? A scent familiar to him. After a moment, a sick feeling washed over him. He was outside his own flesh now, hovering above, everything clear all at once. It was the smell of human bodies intertwined, the salty scent of sweat and sex and Frances's perfume. Frances, after lovemaking. He knew the odor like he knew certain pieces of music from his youth, deeply embedded in forgotten recesses of his mind. She'd been in this room only moments before with someone. Of this he was certain.

He moved to the foot of the bed, the image of her here with a man as clear as if he were watching as it happened. The only thing missing was the man's face, and then he realized it was his own face that he saw—the ghost of his passion for her all those years ago, the remembrance of her pale cool skin and how his obsession for her had brought him to this very moment.

She had never loved him and never would. He was a fool. Divorce her, Clare had said. He should have divorced her years ago. Why hadn't he? This he would ask of himself for the rest of his life, he figured, staring into the yard from the open window.

How had Frances and her lover gotten out of the house so quickly and without detection? He leaned out of the window, examining the side of the house for a possible escape route. That's when he saw slabs of wood nailed into the side of the house, hidden behind the magnolia tree so that they couldn't be seen unless one looked from this angle. Four footholds, just the right amount to be able to reach the ground safely. How many times had she sneaked in and out? Where did she go and to whom?

Reeling, he left Frances's bedroom, his legs shaking so hard he had to put his hand on the stairwell to keep from falling. He tried to think clearly, but nothing came, just numbness that seemed to extend even to the nerve endings of his lips.

Once downstairs, Nathaniel poured another drink, with trembling hands, and then sat down at his piano. This room smelled of fading roses. The vase near the couch was filled with them, cut a week ago, the stems bowed over. The petals, once lush pink, were now dull, shriveling, their sweet smell lingering even as they died.

His stomach was empty, and the whiskey made him feel like he was in a cloud. Who had been here? Had they really climbed out the window while he smoked in the driveway, thinking of how to dull the pain of sending Lydia away? He drank again from his tumbler of whiskey, staring at the keys of his piano.

His mind shifted, allowing this new information in. Was this the first time, he wondered? Or were there others? Had there always been men and he was too naïve or stupid to see it? Nathaniel had seen Frances's flirtatious behavior as part of her illness, as an extension of her compulsion to be noticed. But perhaps it reached further than that. He was a fool, he thought again. He understood it but could not fathom it at the same time. But no, perhaps this was all just his imagination—merely a lonely man's paranoia. And yet he knew in his bones, in his heart, that it was true.

He finished his drink in one gulp. The screen door in the kitchen slammed. A moment later, Frances stood near the doorway to the kitchen. "Darlin', I didn't expect you home." He heard a slight apprehension to her voice even as the lilt of her accent carried into the room like a jingle.

He couldn't speak. Stay at the piano, he thought. Feed upon it as a source of power and comfort, as it had always been. She looked lovely—lovelier than he'd ever seen her. She wore a soft green dress that flowed softly around her thighs, and her hair was tousled, her cheeks flushed. No lipstick. No purse.

"I've had a call from your mother." He stood, pouring himself another whiskey. "She told me of your phone conversation."

Frances's face drained of color. "I'm surprised. I thought she'd keep it from you. She's always afraid you'll run off and leave me."

"I've been sitting here wondering how you could do such a thing." He moved toward her, the whiskey sloshing in his glass. "Why, Frances? Why couldn't you just leave it alone, let Whitmore go?" He waved his hand around the room in a way that he meant to be dramatic but was only a small, tired flutter. "What does it matter to you?"

Frances's eyes flickered, and her chin moved slightly toward the ceiling, like a small child trying to assert a stubborn independence, her eyes blazing. "Because I asked you to give me the money for California, and you dismissed me like I was a silly girl." She calmed suddenly, putting a finger through the curl next to her ear. Her voice was smooth and detached now, almost sounding playful. "And Whitmore ruining our bloodline that way makes me sick." She lowered her eyes to the floor, speaking softly. "And the way you look at Lydia Tyler."

"What did you say?"

She raised her chin. "You heard me."

His voice was raw and hoarse when he managed to speak. "That's pretty amusing, Frances, considering."

She twitched and put her hand on the back of a chair but didn't say anything.

"What did you plan to do? Just leave if you got the money? Without telling me?"

"I hadn't thought that part through yet."

"You're a liar. Everything you do is calculated. I see that now." He swallowed a gulp of whiskey, and it burned down his throat and into his gut. "Where have you been?"

Her eyes widened as she took a step backward. "Out. For a walk."

She swallowed hard; he saw her neck muscles move. He moved closer. Right next to her now, he felt her breath on his neck. "Who is it, Frances? Who was here?"

She took another step backward, her fingers at her neck. "No one was here. Just me."

"I saw the makeshift ladder." He put his hands on the sides of her face, wanting to scare her, to feel her tremble under his hands. The rage pulsated like something alive in him. He spoke through clenched teeth. "Who was here?"

"No one."

He slid his fingers around her neck. "Tell me who." His voice was louder this time. "Now." He shook her by the shoulders. "Tell me the damn truth."

He felt her tremble. "You're frightening me."

"Am I? Good, I think that's right after all this time. Because after all these years, all this time I've devoted to you and your health— getting repaid with this." He tossed her from him with force, seeming to have no control over his own body. She slumped against the wall, staring at him with big, frightened eyes. It did not soften him. "You let me think all these years that it was the horror of that night that kept you from wanting a man's touch. And yet you've betrayed me." He paused, shaking his head. He felt himself crumpling, turning from rage to despair. He grabbed her about the shoulders once again, shaking her. "Why, Frances? I want to know why."

She spit out the words, "Because your touch repulses me. I cannot, could not, stand the thought of you anywhere near me after that child we made together."

A wail escaped from somewhere inside him. "He was our son."

"See there. Just that. You think it's been easy for me living with Saint Nathaniel? I've pined for a new life, a chance to start over, a chance to be with a man I can actually stand to be in the same room with. A man who has something, anything, to say or do besides sit at that ridiculous piano day and night. A man who will give me what I want."

He felt his legs start to give way beneath him. Stumbling, he sank onto the piano bench. "Have you found that, Frances?"

She came toward him, her arms crossed over her chest like armor. "For now."

"Tell me who it is."

"I don't know why it matters to you. But it's Mick Landry."

He stared at her before an abrupt, scornful laugh escaped from inside his dry throat. "You can't be serious. Frances, he's a fake, a con man. What could you possibly think he could offer you?"

Her eyes were haughty, but her voice betrayed the smallest edge of doubt. "At least he can fuck me properly."

Her cruelty took his breath away. He shook his head in disbelief. "Get out."

Her face turned from sorrow to contempt and then rebellion, all within seconds. "There was no other way to get away from this life that's killing me. I'm a woman with nothing to rely on but my beauty and my wit. He's offered me a way out."

"With what? The man's obviously broke." The truth came to him suddenly. "So that's it. You want money so you can run off with Landry? How can you love a man like that?"

She had a drink in her hand now. A brief smiled passed over her face before her eyes turned cold. "That's the problem with you, Nate. You don't understand anything about me. He sees opportunity in everything. Including in me. You see nothing, like a man already dead." She paused, the drink hovering at her mouth. "And he provides what I want."

"And I never could. Is that it?"

"No, you never could. Others provided what you couldn't."

New rage welled in him as he realized what she meant. "There were others?"

"So many I can't count."

He knew then how much she wanted to hurt him. And the truth came to him, the horrible truth that he'd denied to himself all these years. "The man at the lake, was he your lover?"

She whispered, her face dark, "He was no one to me, but yes, I went up there with him. I didn't mean for anyone to get hurt. I've been sorry for it."

"I lost everything that mattered to me when he stabbed me." He began to sob. "Everything."

"You never loved me like you love the piano. I knew eventually you'd divorce me. I'd be a divorcee with no prospects but to live with my parents. And all the time—everyone fawning over you. I was barely discernible to anyone, and I went looking for something, for someone, who could see me."

He stared at her, trying to get control of the rage that made him want to crush her in his hands, to make her suffer.

She continued, her voice soft now, "Don't pretend like you've been happy or that you haven't wished to be rid of me and start over. The only difference between you and me is that I'm brave enough to go get it."

"Then go get it, Frances. By all means, go get it." He stood, holding on to the piano for support. "Your mother wants to put you into one of those rest homes. But I don't want you there, sucking up funds when you're not sick. I don't want to ever see your lying face again. You have two hours to get your things and get out. Expect divorce papers in the mail." He moved toward the front door without looking at her. "And don't expect a dime from me. Or your mother."

She ran after him, her voice a screech, "I'll make you sorry for this. I'll tell everyone in this town what you and Lydia Tyler did for Jeselle. They'll lynch you all. Don't think I won't do it."

"Goodbye, Frances."

He heard a crashing glass hit the front door. But by that time he was already down the steps.

PART SIX

From Jeselle Thorton's journal.

June 20, 1934

I think of Mrs. Bellmont tonight. Did it occur to her that treating Whit and me the same in regard to our studies might indicate to us that we were equals in all ways? Was it a conscious decision, knowing that it would begin a chain of tolerance in the mind of her son? Or was it just her instinct to teach, no matter who it was, her inclinations toward learning dwelling so deep within her character? I might never know.

But I know this: every moment of our childhood led us to this very moment. Her kindness changed the trajectory of my life and of Whit's life. It was Mrs. Bellmont's day-to-day decisions that taught Whit and me there was no difference between us. He does not see the color of my skin as an indication that I am his lesser. He simply does not see it at all. He sees only me.

CHAPTER 47

Whitmore

WHITMORE SLEPT HARD, dreaming of the lake house. He and Jeselle were young and unencumbered, scampering up the wishbone stairs. Their footsteps made a thudding sound on the dark wood floors. They laughed, and the air smelled of steamed peaches and dried sunshine on their skin.

He was jarred from sleep, a smile still at the corners of his mouth. The thud in his dream was really a pounding at the door of his boarding house room. It was deadly dark, and he fumbled to turn on the lamp. There was a sound of splintering wood, and the door swung open, giving the room partial light. Whit squinted in an attempt to understand what he saw. Spilling in from the hallway were five men in white hooded robes, slits for eyeholes, bringing the smell of whiskey and men's sweat. He didn't know where to look; they all came at him at once. Rough hands grabbed him, tossed him to the floor. A boot came down on top of his head, pinning him there, the heel pushing into his ear. He cried out in pain as another boot crashed into his gut and then his spine. The boot lifted from his head, and Whit put his hands over his face and tried to curl into a ball, but it was too late. The same boot smashed into his nose. Hot, red blood gushed out, tasting of metal down the back of his throat. The smell of gasoline. Oh, God, help me, he begged silently. Someone poured something cold on him. Gasoline. They were going to set him on fire. He felt his bowels begin to loosen. He called out, "Please, no." Then he heard shouting from outside the room. The deafening sound of a gunshot. Something crashed to the floor behind him, near some of the men. Maybe it came from the ceiling or from somewhere high, like a shelf. The men's boots were moving away from him. He moved his head to look up and saw the sisters, both holding shotguns. "I'd sure love to blow one of you idiots to kingdom come," said Alba.

"You ladies go on back upstairs," a gravelly male voice said.

"While you burn up our family home? I'll shoot you all dead before I do that."

Sarah pointed her gun at them. "Get out, or I'll gladly take your heads clean off."

"We grew up hunting wild boar and pheasants when we were the only house for miles. If you think we can't do it, you're sorely mistaken," said Alba.

"We'll just take the kid, Miss, if you don't mind." This was a raspy, indolent voice, like someone used to getting his way.

Whit heard both guns cock and then the roar of another gunshot.

"Holy shit, she just about took off my ear," a man said, almost squeaking.

"C'mon boys." This voice sounded like he held a toothpick between his teeth. "Let's get out of here."

Someone kicked him in the gut. He cried out, the pain in every part of his body.

"We'll get him some other time," the raspy voice said.

Unable to lift his head now, Whit saw only the men's heavy boots tromping out of the room. After they were gone, the two women, their feet in heavy socks bunched around their ankles, came toward him. Alba got on her knees, joints creaking, and peered at him with every crinkle and crease on her face gathering into worried folds. "We need to get the doctor," she said.

"That won't be possible," said Sarah.

"I suppose you're right about that. Doc Landry's probably along for the ride."

"That's right, sister. How're we going to patch this poor child up?"

"I surely don't know. What's this boy done that's got the Klan after him?" asked Alba.

Whit tried to move, tried to answer, but the pain in his ribs was unbearable. "Get Jes," was all he managed before everything went to purple and then black.

CHAPTER 48

Nathaniel

A SOOTY, ACRID SMELL drifting in from a partially open window awakened Nathaniel from his whiskey-induced sleep. For a moment he was a child waking to his mother's early morning fire. He imagined she knelt before the open door of the wood stove, stacking thin, dry pieces of kindling around the last hot ember, her mouth in a circle, blowing to make a flame that would warm and feed them. After the room lost its chill, she would summon him from his narrow bed and set cooked oats with a teaspoon of maple syrup at his place near the stove. His stomach full, he would practice on the upright piano until it was time to go to school.

But then the scratching of his shirt collar against his neck reminded him that, hours before, he'd fallen onto his bed in his clothes and shoes, his half-empty glass of whiskey discarded on the table. He'd thought, in his drunkenness, that sleep would give respite from the pain and confusion; he would know what to do in the morning, he had told himself as he put his weary head upon the pillow, his heavy eyelids closing to dreamless sleep.

Now, head aching, he bolted upright, everything rushing back to him. He looked over at the clock. It was almost midnight. His dry mouth held a bitter, sour taste. This nonsense with the whiskey hadn't helped him. The liquor gave him a few hours of senselessness, but it was all still here, waiting. He was awake now, he thought, after years of being asleep—days and days of acting like the dearly departed. No more. He would brush his teeth and then go downstairs to drink all the cold water he could hold. It would soothe his body, perhaps heal the pain in his head and heart. Then he would come back to bed and sleep off his hangover. And in the morning he would sort through all his muddled emotions and concoct a plan for the rest of his life.

Then he realized something in the room was different. There was an eerie glow to the walls, a flickering of orange light. He went to the window.

Something burned in the middle of his lawn. In his shock, his mind grappled to make sense of the image, to name it.

It was a burning cross. He stared into the blaze, unable to look away.

His shirt was damp with sweat. He shivered. His pounding heart seemed large in chest.

Somehow they'd been exposed. Frances. It had to be Frances. But the idea of that kind of betrayal was too much for him to understand. He must collect the others and get them all out of town. He'd take them all to Maine. To his mother. She'd fold them all into her simple house where there were no burning crosses, no hatred. He thought of Whitmore and Lydia, alone and unprotected in their rooms and pregnant Jeselle on her cousin's farm. He remembered, with a terrible jolt, Bess and her family.

A memory came of a painting above the pulpit in his childhood church: a depiction of Jesus on the cross in the last moments before death, in physical agony, questioning His father, crying out, "Oh God, oh God, why have you forsaken me?"

He thought of his own cries in the dark of night to a God he felt had abandoned him. And then, the Lord's Prayer came to him. He spoke it out loud, like he had so many times as a child.

He threw a change of clothes and a few toiletries into a bag. A gun. He needed a gun. There was a small pistol, a wedding gift from her father that Frances kept in her bureau, hidden in her vanity for safekeeping. The moment he opened his bedroom door, a cloud of smoke rushed into the room, drifting up from the first floor. Peering over the railing he saw the sitting room encased in flames. A rush of adrenaline seized him. He ran to the white, ornate vanity in Frances's bedroom. In his haste he couldn't remember which drawer held her underclothes. He yanked open the top drawer. It was full of lipsticks, hair combs, and perfumes. He pulled open the second and saw undergarments of various colors: eggshell, pink like apple blossoms, lemon yellow. He felt toward the back of the drawer, searching for the gun. Gasping for air, he put his hand past and through his wife's garments to the farthest corner of the drawer until he felt cold metal.

He shoved the pistol into his pocket and went to Frances's bedroom window, sliding the glass pane upward as high as it would go. He threw his bag out first. It opened when it hit the grass, spilling his few material remnants onto the lawn, illuminated in the light of the flaming cross. Holding tightly to the window frame, he climbed out feet first and found the topmost foothold so carefully positioned by Frances. Once he reached the ground, he gathered his things and ran to his car. The flames engulfed the entire first floor as he backed out of the driveway.

He imagined his piano, ablaze, intense heat snapping strings and devouring the keyboard, flames creeping up the graceful legs and spreading until the only steadfast item in a house made of grief and deceit was finally destroyed, too.

CHAPTER 49

Lydia

LYDIA DREAMT of gunshots, waking out of the edges of the dream to the realization that someone was pounding on the door of her room. Alarmed and shaking from being startled out of sleep, she opened it a crack. It was Nathaniel in wrinkled clothes, his hair disheveled.

She opened the door all the way as he slumped against the doorframe. "Nathaniel, what's happened?" He smelled of smoke.

He swayed slightly. "We have to go."

"What is it?" She moved to where he stood in the doorway, wishing to put her hand on his forehead.

"Pack your things." His forehead was dotted with perspiration. "Please, hurry. We have to get the others."

Something terrible had happened. She reached out her hands, and he took them in a way that was like a desperate grip on life itself, as if he might not make it without the gesture. When he was inside the room, he said her name three times, like a chanted prayer. She guided him to the armchair, but he remained standing, clinging to her hands as if he might not let them go.

"There was a cross. A burning cross. In my yard."

She couldn't speak.

"And they've burned down my house. It's gone. We have to get the kids and go."

"Where?"

"To Maine. To my mother."

She nodded. "Yes, Maine."

"I cannot let anything happen to any of you."

"Where's Frances?"

His face went dark, his eyes clouded, the words deep in his throat. "She's gone."

She wanted to ask more, but words failed her. Reaching under the bed, she pulled out her suitcase, tossing her few belongings into it while he stood at the window, peering into the darkness.

"I can't tell if anyone followed me or not."

Shaking, she held her dress against her chest, so frightened she wasn't sure what to do next.

He turned from the window and looked at her, his face rearranging from focus to concern. In one stride he was in front of her. "Lydia, I know you're frightened, but you must get dressed at once."

His words jarred her from her stupor. "Yes, yes, of course."

He backed out of the room. "I'll wait for you right outside the door. Please hurry."

She shivered as she pulled her dress over her head, shoved on her shoes, and grabbed her suitcase. They ran across campus to the car, where he opened the trunk and tossed her bag inside. As they pulled away she saw him search the darkness for movement, but it was quiet. Neither spoke. Lydia looked at her hands in her lap, praying silently.

"We'll get Whit first," he said.

* * *

They found Whitmore collapsed in a pool of blood on the floor of his room. The two sisters, holding shotguns, stood over him.

"Some white hoods beat him pretty bad," Alba said.

"We heard the noise, but it took us a few minutes to get down the stairs," said Sarah.

"They'd had a good go of him before we got here," said Alba.

The room reeked of gasoline. "They poured gasoline on him?" Nathaniel asked.

"Yep. Just about to set him on fire when we showed up," said Sarah.

"Had to shoot out a lamp to get their attention," Alba said.

Nathaniel stooped, gathering the boy into his arms. "We've got to get to Jeselle," he said.

Whit opened his eyes and murmured, "Jeselle."

"Lydia, find him clean clothes. These are soaked." Lydia opened the small dresser and found a stack of clothing inside. She grabbed a shirt and pants and tossed it to Nathaniel as he pulled the wet clothes from the boy's bruised and battered body. While she threw his remaining clothes into the open suitcase near the bed, Whit opened his eyes briefly, moaning, and then closed them again.

Nathaniel carried him to the car, putting him gently in the backseat. "We'll get to the next town," Nathaniel said. "Get him medical attention then. But first we need to get Jeselle."

It was almost four a.m. as they sped from the boarding house, making their way through a sleeping town. At the entrance to the highway, Lydia turned to look into the backseat. Whit was curled into a half circle, making occasional whimpers. Just as Nathaniel turned onto the highway a dark car appeared behind them, following so closely that the cab of Nathaniel's sedan filled with light. She watched his face closely, as his eyes darted between the road and the rearview mirror.

"You think the car's following us?" she asked.

"I don't know." He shifted on the seat, reaching into his pocket and pulling out a small pistol. "Here, keep this on your lap."

She took the gun without mentioning she had no idea how to use it. The other car continued to follow closely until they reached the turnoff for Bess's dirt road. Nathaniel slowed, preparing to turn left. The other car slowed, too, inches from them now. Nathaniel jerked the steering wheel, making a quick dart across the highway onto Bess's road. Lydia turned to see if the other car would follow. To her surprise, it did not. It simply sped away down the highway. Lydia sighed, feeling some relief but afraid to speak.

"Trying to scare us," Nathaniel said.

"It worked."

"Sending us a message that we're being watched."

They were halfway down Bess's road before they saw another car. This one was parked, waiting. As they approached, two men got out, fedora hats low over their foreheads, and stood in the middle of the dirt road, forcing Nathaniel to either stop the car or run over them.

"Lock your door." He took the pistol from her lap and rolled down his window. "You boys need something?"

One of the men, young, clean-shaven, and lean, came over to the window and leaned down, looking into the car. "Evenin', Miss." He tipped his hat at Lydia before taking a flask from his shirt pocket. "Kinda late to be out for a drive, isn't it, Professor?" The other man came around to Lydia's side of the car, glaring at her before perching on the right side of the hood.

"Couldn't sleep," said Nathaniel.

"That right? How 'bout her?" He pointed at Lydia. His dialect had a harsh, uneducated quality.

"I couldn't sleep either." She sat with her back straight and looked him directly in the eye.

"You picking something up?" The man sneered and wiped his mouth with the back of his hand.

Nathaniel shoved the pistol near the man's face. "We're on our way out of town."

"That right?" He stepped back, raised an eyebrow, and took a swig from his flask, ever so casual, like he didn't see the gun. But Lydia saw his left cheek twitch. "From what I hear, you best be staying out of town."

"Says who?" Nathaniel sounded eerily calm and sat perfectly still.

The boy shrugged and took another swig. "That's the word around town. No one wants you here. You'd be watching your back everywhere you went."

"You tell your friends I'll do as I please. If I decide to stay, I'll stay."

The boy raised his eyebrows, shrugged again. "I'm just trying to help you. We heard the Klan's got word of it."

"We have to go." Nathaniel cocked the pistol, still pointing it at the boy. "Now."

The boy backed away and said something to his companion, who nodded as they slid into their car. Its headlights came on, and the car turned around and headed down the dirt road back toward the highway. Lydia realized she'd been holding her breath. She let it out in one, long sigh.

Nathaniel gave her the gun. She held it in both hands, pointing it straight at the windshield. They continued on, around the bend in the road, until they saw Bess's shack. He came as close to the porch as possible before turning off the car. "Stay here. I'll get her. Be ready to shoot that gun if you see anyone."

"Maybe you should take it." She couldn't keep the quiver from her voice.

"No," he said, his voice firm. "Keep the lights on."

She watched him run between the beams of the headlights to the house. Jeselle popped up from a cot on the porch. Nathaniel said something to her, his head bowed. Jeselle put her hand up to her mouth and nodded her head in apparent agreement. Then she disappeared inside and a few moments later came out with a small bag over her arm.

They were halfway between the porch and the car when a dozen men came out of the woods carrying lit torches, white hoods covering their heads and upper torsos. Two of the men broke out of the circle and took hold of Nathaniel and Jeselle, putting guns to their temples. Lydia held the pistol in both hands, trying desperately to think what to do. Just then one of the men yanked open the car door, grabbed the pistol out of her hands, and dragged her out by the neck. She gagged as the man's hand dug into her windpipe. He loosened his grip on her neck, moving his arm to hold her tightly at the waist. His breath smelled of whiskey as he put his gun to her throat.

Nathaniel struggled against the man who held him. "Get your hands off her."

The man smacked Nathaniel on the side of the head with the butt of his gun. "Shut your mouth, Yankee." Nathaniel's knees buckled, and he crumpled to the ground. Lydia wanted to scream, to run to him, to make sure he was alive, but she couldn't move. The man held her tighter.

Jeselle, too, remained trapped. Her captor had one arm around her neck in a choke hold, and her brown eyes, big and scared, darted from Nathaniel's limp body and back to Lydia. Then, Lydia thought she heard a low hum that sounded like another car approaching. Was she imagining it? No, there it was, louder. Yes, it was a car, coming fast. After a moment, it lurched to a stop next to Nathaniel's car. The motor went silent, but the lights remained on, matching those of the other car, like four eyes shining in the dark. It was eerily quiet. No one made a sound. Everyone waiting.

The door of the car opened. Lydia had to blink twice to make sure what she thought she saw was real. Yes, it was indeed Pastor Ferguson. He wore his pastoral robes like he did at Sunday service. She almost expected to see a Bible in his hands, but they were empty. He looked around the dirt yard, seeming to survey the situation before noticing Nathaniel on the ground. "What have you done?" He directed the question to the man standing next to Nathaniel's limp body. The man took a few steps back as the pastor knelt and put his fingers gently on Nathaniel's neck. He whispered something that Lydia assumed was a prayer.

Nathaniel stirred, groaning, and sat up, looking dazed. "Gillis?"

The pastor rose to his feet, looking around the yard. His quiet, steady voice drifted into the night air. "You boys put down your guns. I'm escorting these folks to their car."

"This is none of your concern, Pastor," said one of the men in the group behind Lydia. "This here is town business. Has nothing to do with the church."

As if he hadn't heard him, Pastor Ferguson continued, "You boys all need to get on home to your beds. These folks have a long trip ahead of them."

The man who held Lydia tightened his grip. His breathing turned heavier next to her ear. "No, that's not how it's gonna be." He spoke hoarsely, his breath hot against her cheek.

Ferguson put up his hand, like he did sometimes to make a point during Sunday sermons. "No one needs to get hurt tonight. These are good people."

"They've gone against God," someone shouted.

Ferguson turned in a semicircle, appraising the clusters of men. "I know who you are, even as hide your faces. More importantly, God knows who you are. Go home, take care of your families instead of causing harm to the innocent."

"These ain't the innocent," someone shouted.

The man holding Lydia started shaking, like he was becoming more and more agitated. He muttered under his breath about the righteous and God's will and false idols. He thrust her away from him and raised his rifle, aiming it at Pastor Ferguson. A single shot exploded out of the rifle and into the pastor's chest. Ferguson put his hand to the wound and, as if his body had become too heavy for his feet to hold, fell to the ground. The shooter retreated backward at first toward the woods, then turned on his heel and ran full force into the trees. Behind her Lydia heard someone shout, "He shot the preacher, he shot the preacher."

Another voice shouted in equal volume, "Get out now. Go, go, go." The man holding Jeselle flung her aside and followed the other men into the woods.

Nathaniel and Lydia, in tandem, rushed to Pastor Ferguson. Nathaniel immediately ripped open the front of Ferguson's robe to see the wound. Blood everywhere, soaking through his robe and undershirt. His eyes fluttered and opened, searching their faces until he found Nathaniel. Nathaniel leaned close. "We'll get the doctor. You're going to be fine."

Ferguson's voice was barely a whisper, "The doc's just been here. He was one of the first to retreat to the woods." He shook his head slightly, and his mouth turned up in a peaceful smile, his eyes glowing bright in the headlights of the cars. Strangely, in the dark, they heard a bird chirping. "Ah, do you hear it, Nathaniel? It's my friend the red-bellied woodpecker."

"Are you in pain, Gillis?" said Nathaniel.

"No." Blood had seeped through Ferguson's robe, and Lydia felt it on her own hands as she clasped his other arm.

"We've got to get him to a doctor," Lydia said. "Nathaniel, let's lift him into the car."

"Won't be necessary," Ferguson said, closing his eyes like he was taking a nap. "I'm glad to hear his song once more before I go." He opened his eyes, smiling at Nathaniel.

Nathaniel glanced at Lydia, his eyes frightened, before turning his gaze back on his friend. "Gillis, don't talk."

Ferguson made a sound in his throat like he was choking. Nathaniel's face contorted, and his hands covered the spot on the pastor's robe where the wound gushed more and more blood. "Please no, Gillis, you're going to be fine." Nathaniel tore off his own jacket and pressed it into pastor's chest.

Ferguson spoke with more strength. "Don't fret. Tell my daughters I love them. As for you, Nathaniel, you must let go." He smiled as he reached for Nathaniel's arm. "Take the love that's right in front of you." Then he stared upward at a starless sky before the life drained from his eyes and he was still.

Nathaniel cried out, his hands now helpless in his lap, his head bent over his dead friend. "They've killed him, Lydia." He rocked back and forth on his knees, his eyes blank. "They've killed him."

She put her arms around Nathaniel, and he leaned into her, burying his face into her neck. In the light from the headlights Jeselle ran toward the car, letting out a cry when she saw Whitmore's wounds, and she moved quickly to stand in front of Nate and Lydia. "Please, Mr. Nate, we have to go."

"We can't leave him here," said Nathaniel.

Remain calm and firm, Lydia ordered herself. "I'm afraid we'll have to. Whitmore needs a doctor. We'll have Lulu send someone to collect Gillis." Lydia stood and took Nathaniel's arm, tugging him to his feet. Bess had come out of the house, carrying a blanket, and hovered beside them.

"I'll wait with him." Bess knelt in the spot Nathaniel had just vacated and covered the pastor from head to foot with the blanket.

"Bess?" Jeselle's voice cracked.

"Go on now, Jessie. You need to get somewhere safe." Bess smoothed the edges of the blanket. "We'll be all right here."

"What about the children? The food?"

"We always manage, somehow," said Bess.

"When we're settled and are able, I'll send money." Jeselle rested her hand on Bess's shoulder. "Whatever we can spare."

Bess looked up at Jeselle. "I'm grateful." Her eyes skirted to Nathaniel. "To both of you."

The women embraced as Lydia took Nathaniel's hand and led him to the car. He sank into the driver's seat, staring at his lap. She put her hands on his shoulders, forcing him to focus on her face, and, with that, he appeared to come back to the current moment and to the task they had in front of them.

"I don't know if I can drive," he whispered.

"You have to," said Lydia. "There's no one else. You have to get us to safety."

Jeselle appeared at the driver's side window. "I can drive. Whitmore taught me how. You get back here with him."

Nathaniel did as he was told, sliding in beside Whitmore and taking the boy's bloody head into his lap. Lydia got into the passenger side, and Jeselle turned the car and sped down the dirt drive.

Whitmore was more alert now but still groggy, peering around as if he didn't know where he was.

"What hurts, my boy?" asked Nathaniel.

"Around my middle." He took a breath that sounded painful. "And I think my nose is broken."

Lydia sighed with relief as they got out to the highway. There were no cars in sight.

*   *   *

When they pulled into the parish driveway, Lydia saw Lulu in the kitchen rolling out biscuits for Ferguson's breakfast, unaware of the moment about to come, thinking instead of the mundane, the ordinary—biscuits and the making of beds and shopping for a pound of bacon later, with no idea that everything she thought was important for the day ahead was about to be shattered. It occurred to Lydia as she watched Lulu tossing the biscuits into a pan that life was like this. Tragedy was always around the corner, with no warning. She remembered the day of her husband's death, of the moment when she understood he was gone, how she wondered over and over how a person could be there one moment and gone the next.

Nathaniel stared out the window, seemingly at nothing. "I don't know if I can do this."

"You can," Lydia said. "You must."

He nodded and opened the car door, gazing for an instant at the ground before getting to his feet and moving toward the house. She watched him knock at the kitchen door and saw Lulu's surprised greeting. Through the window she saw Nathaniel's mouth moving until Lulu fell into a kitchen chair.

Whit moaned from the backseat. Nervous, Lydia glanced at Jeselle. "Mrs. Tyler, we have to go," Jeselle whispered.

"I'll get him." Lydia jumped from the car and sprinted toward the house. Without knocking, she threw open the door. The kitchen smelled of coffee, bacon, and baking biscuits. "Nathaniel, Whit needs a doctor."

Lulu's face seemed to have sunk into itself with the news. Now her eyes flashed determinedly as she stood. She wiped her cheeks of tears and indicated the door. "Well then, best be getting on. The fine man wanted you to get the lass on the boat." The freckles on her face stood out against her white skin as she pushed a strand of hair behind her ears. Lulu's Irish accent seemed stronger. Grief does that to a person, Lydia thought. Peels off your layers until you're nothing but the soft flesh you were when you were a child skimming your mother's hemline, holding on to her legs as she moved about the house.

"Professor, it was Mick Landry who warned the pastor. He told Gillis where to go. You all might be dead if he hadn't."

Nathaniel flinched and stepped backward. "That can't be."

"Landry heard his brother on the phone planning the whole thing," said Lulu. "Excuse me for saying so, but it was your wife who set the whole thing going."

"Frances did this? And Mick saved us?" Nathaniel asked.

"Sometimes we can't understand the ways of others. Gillis always said it was up to God to judge, not us." Lulu pushed them toward the door and handed them a basket of biscuits. "I started baking the minute he left as a way to keep my mind busy. Was hoping against hope he'd be home to eat them before the sun came up."

CHAPTER 50

Jeselle

NATHANIEL INSISTED on driving from then on out, and Jeselle was grateful to take the backseat. She wanted to be by Whitmore, where she belonged. The skin around his eyes was black and blue, and his face was covered with dried blood. Occasionally he opened his eyes but then seemed to fall back into a deep sleep, moaning when they went over bumps in the road.

Jeselle prayed silently, closing her eyes and pretending to sleep.

"Nathaniel, where is Frances?" said Lydia from the front seat.

"On her way to California, I suspect. She'd been carrying on with Mick Landry. And others. So many others. The man, the gardener that night, she went up of her own free will."

Lydia gasped.

"Mick Landry did the right thing at the end. He was a smarter man than me when it came to Frances," said Nathaniel. "I've been a fool, Lydia."

There was nothing but the hum of the car for a long moment. "What will you do?" said Lydia.

"Learn to live again."

They came to a town named Longview. Near the edge of town, they spotted a roadside motel and stopped, renting two rooms.

Nathaniel left to take Whitmore to a doctor, while Jeselle and Lydia went into one of the rooms to bathe. Afterward, Jeselle curled up on her side and closed her eyes. But the images from earlier played before her eyes. From the bed she saw Lydia in her slip leaning over the bathtub, washing both their dresses.

"You shouldn't be washing my dress," Jeselle called out to her.

"Why's that?"

"Doesn't seem right."

"Must get the stink of those awful men off." Lydia hung the dresses over the tub before coming to stand at the side of Jeselle's bed. "Can't sleep?"

"Can't turn off my mind," Jeselle said.

"Me either." Lydia disappeared into the bathroom and came back with a cool, damp cloth. She set it on Jeselle's forehead. Then she lay on the other bed. "I'll never forget the moments when my babies were born. To see their faces for the first time—there's nothing like it." Her voice was soft and reassuring, reminding Jeselle of Mrs. Bellmont.

"What did you name them?" But she fell asleep before she heard the answer. She awoke later to Nate tapping her arm. "Jes, we're back," he said.

She sat up, rubbing her eyes. Whit was on the other bed, awake and smiling. "Jessie, I made it. They patched me up, but the doc says my nose might be slightly crooked. Will you still love me?" He reached out his hand. Jeselle took it, kneeling at the side of the bed.

"Will he be all right?" Jeselle asked Nathaniel.

"Yes. He has a broken rib and a concussion, so we have to take good care of him. I'm taking you all to my mother's up north. To Maine. And Whit's going to sit by the ocean and let the saltwater mist heal his wounds."

"We're going to the ocean?" said Jeselle.

"Yes, Jessie. We're going to stand by the ocean," said Whitmore.

"And we'll feel small," she said.

Whitmore smiled at her and then shifted to look at Nate. "I can't ever repay this."

"No need," said Nate.

"So you say."

Nate, smiling, started for the door. "Get some sleep. Both of you."

"Where's Lydia?" Jeselle asked.

Nate fidgeted with his shirt collar. "She's resting next door."

After Nate left the room, Jeselle lay down next to Whitmore on the bed, gently so as not to hurt his ribs.

He placed his hand on her stomach. "You feeling well?" he asked, soft.

"I'm fine."

"When those men came to get me, I thought of you, Jes. First and last."

"Me too. Always."

CHAPTER 51

Nathaniel

NATHANIEL KNOCKED on the other motel room. Lydia answered at once, as if she'd been standing at the door, waiting. She wore her blue dress, the one that matched her eyes. He wondered, absently, if the blood had come out of the yellow one.

She motioned for him to come inside, which he did, shutting the door behind him and leaning against it, feeling liberated finally to gaze at her in her entirety, to take in every detail without guilt. Her hair looked clean and soft, and pink flushed her cheeks. She'd had a bath, he realized, imagining her long legs in the water of a tub. But the whites of her eyes were red. He felt a pang like the tapping of a pointed object against his chest. He did not want her to cry. Not ever again, most especially because of anything he'd done.

The room held the odor of stale cigarette smoke, embedded in the carpet and the white paint, but when Nathaniel approached Lydia, he smelled nothing but her freshly washed hair.

She sank onto the edge of the bed with her knees pressed together, like a schoolgirl.

"Have you been crying?"

She nodded, and her chest rose and fell in hiccups, like a child after a long cry. "All this ugliness. The pastor. He was such a fine man."

"Yes, but think of the kids. Next door, together. It's what the pastor wanted. He came around, Lydia, to your way of thinking. After years of thinking one way, you see, we both came around, which should give you great hope for the lot of humanity. It's possible to change our minds about what we think we know."

"Yes, there's that. Yes." Her neck flushed red, and her eyes flashed as she jutted out her chin like she did whenever she was angry. "I don't want to go to Rochester." She took a long, deep breath. "I don't want you to leave me there. Without you."

He smiled and knelt on the floor, near her feet. For such a tall woman she seemed small to him just then. "Lydia."

"Yes?" In what he suspected was an attempt at defiance, she wiped under her eyes with her forefinger and looked toward the door. A lock of her hair was stuck to her damp cheek, and he pulled it away with his thumb, holding it between his fingers for a moment, thinking that the dampness made it the color of honey.

"I thought perhaps you might like to come to Maine. We could stay with my mother. Work on the Brahms and our three-handed duet. Ready ourselves for a tour in the spring. Walt's agreed to manage us."

"And would this arrangement be purely professional?" she asked, looking at her hands.

"That depends."

"On what?"

"On how you feel. About me."

She peered at him for a moment. "Don't you know?"

"Not entirely." His knees made a popping noise as he sat next to her on the bed. He placed the fingers of his left hand on the pulse at her neck, feeling that the blood pumping there could just as easily have been from his own surging heart. Perhaps the pulse might heal his hand? And yet, knowing nothing could restore the movement he at one time relished more than anything else, he realized, at least in this very moment, that it mattered less, because of the woman sitting next to him. Nothing felt as important as the warmth of her body next to his or the way she leaned toward him, inviting his touch, her eyes peering without reserve into his own. When he gently kissed her, her mouth softened, and he drew her to him, like she'd been there all his life.

It was joy, the feel of her skin underneath his fingertips. He moved to the buttons of her dress, undoing them one by one, until he was able to slide it from her torso. Then he paused and, without taking his eyes from her, tugged his wedding ring from his finger and placed it on the bedside table.

CHAPTER 52

Lydia

IT HAD BEEN so long since a man had touched her that Lydia assumed it would feel strange. But it hadn't. The sensations were as she remembered and different, too. She was older, her body softer, perhaps more yielding than it had been in the years with William, more willing to accept pleasure. Nathaniel was rougher, more demanding than her husband had been, more consuming of her, less worried about hurting her, as if she were his equal, and she relished this. He pressed into her as if it were an act of redemption, of triumph, in a way that made her unable to think clearly, rattled her teeth, and made her cry out.

It also surprised her that she didn't think of the morality of it, that they weren't married or that he was not divorced. No, she was merely there in the moment, taking all the pleasure she could, knowing the sweet things of life were fleeting and uncertain. And, in that knowing that only comes from age, she opened to him with ease and without restraint, feeling bound to him in a way not dictated by conventions of society or a slip of paper, but through their fearless choosing of one another.

Afterward they lay together, at ease, the tension between them spent. She felt weary and yet wide awake, wanting to drink in his form just as it was in that moment.

"What will your mother think, with you still married?" she asked.

He shrugged, and she understood that he wasn't sure. "I'll tell her I'm divorcing Frances." Then he rolled over to look at her. "Can I tell her that we're going to marry?"

She felt her eyes get big. "Are you asking me?"

"Are you saying yes?"

"I suppose I am."

"Then I'll tell my mother I'm going to marry you the minute I'm able. Until then she'll have to live with our untraditional arrangement." He pulled her closer. "It's quite impossible to describe how I feel about you."

"And I you."

They talked for a while longer. She told him details of her life in Atmore, of her children, of her friendship with Midwife Stone. "How small my life must seem to you," she said.

He shook his head. "Not small. Nothing could be small with you in the center of it."

When she told him how she'd taken to wearing William's boots and clothes for the outside work after his death, she expected Nathaniel to laugh, but instead his eyes had softened as he pushed a stray piece of hair from her face. "I know it's been harder than you let on, and I'm sorry for it."

"Isn't that true for most of us?" she asked. "We just make do with what we have without complaint, always hopeful tomorrow will be better."

"Most, not all." His face darkened, and she knew he was thinking of Frances. "I have to tell Frances's mother what happened."

She nodded, smoothing her fingers along his cheekbone. "Sleep first. Call her when you wake up."

He agreed and closed his eyes. She watched him drift toward sleep until his face was slack, and he breathed in and out with even repetition. He was both new and yet familiar—her family she had not known existed. After a few minutes she began to drift off to sleep, thinking about Birdie and Emma. Her daughters must be attended to as well. Emma would be beside herself over the news. But Lydia took her own advice and slept first.

CHAPTER 53

Whitmore

WHIT WAS DREAMING. He was on the lake, rowing. His mother called out to him from the back door of the lake house, waving her arms over her head. "Come inside," she said. He increased his pace toward her, and his strokes were smooth and easy, but then the water turned thicker, the texture of blood, and the boat was stuck. A hand reached up to pull him under the dark water. He tried to scream, but no sound came.

He woke to Jeselle, stroking his face. "Whit, it's just a dream." His eyes fixed to her. "Jes, we need to go to the lake house, see our mothers. Say goodbye properly."

CHAPTER 54

Nathaniel

NATHANIEL DIDN'T WAKE until early evening. Lydia was still asleep, curled up like a cat, her hands clasped at her stomach. He took in her long, lean limbs, the callouses on the sides of her big toes, made, he was sure, from the man's work she had been forced to take on after her husband's death. He watched her for some moments, thinking about the events of the day, wishing only to stay and gaze upon the flush of her cheek.

Instead, he rose from the bed and bathed and dressed in clean clothes, quiet so as not to wake her. Though unsure how to explain the events of the last several days to either woman, he must call Clare and then his own mother. He walked to the motel's office, his mind reeling. After giving the attendant a dollar for use of the phone, he called Clare first. She answered on the first ring. Waiting, he thought.

He began to tell her everything, first with trepidation, until the truths unfolded from him in a steady succession, sorrow and relief combining, knowing that his words whittled away at the soul of this good woman. He understood she did not deserve the grief that would ultimately possess her after hearing of everything Frances had done. But he knew, too, that it was important for the facts to be told, that it mattered more than anything that at last they all understood the truth.

Finally, he told her about the horrible night when the gardener died and he'd lost his career because of Frances's voracious appetite for attention. Clare cried then, in sobs that were nearly unbearable to hear. He pushed onward, wanting it to be over. "I'm filing for divorce, Clare."

"I'm glad for you, dear boy. You deserve a chance at happiness," she said, sounding defeated, dull. And then almost without pause she went on, "I've known, or suspected, that Frances went up there that night of her own volition. I never outright asked her because I didn't want to know the answer. I couldn't stand the thought that her carelessness, her disregard for others, would've caused you to lose your career. I'm so terribly sorry, Nate. Nothing I do can ever make up for it or change the fact that she's my daughter. I raised her. There's no one to blame but me."

"Clare, you also raised Whit." He paused, hating her grief, hating Frances.

"Do you remember the doctor we took her to, years ago? Do you recall how angry he made me?"

"Yes, of course."

"I knew it was true, what he said, but I couldn't accept it, couldn't look at it."

"Clare, it's all done now. There's nothing to be done except for us to move on."

"Yes, I suppose. Nate…" She paused. He heard her take in a shaky breath. "Since the first day you came into my family I've loved you like my own."

"That's your way."

She chuckled in a mournful way. "What good has come from it?"

"Oh, Clare, Whit has come of it. All his goodness, his generous spirit, it all comes from you and the way you've been all his life." Then he told her his plans for Maine, and then of France for Jeselle and Whit.

"Nate, could Cassie and I take the train to Maine?"

"Not all the way to where my mother lives. You'd need a car."

He heard her sniffling. "I don't know how to drive. Neither does Cassie."

"Clare, what do you mean?"

"Cassie and I should go with you. To Maine. To look after our children."

"What about Frank?"

"Would you believe me if I said I didn't care?" Without a pause she continued, "We could take one of our cars. But you or Jeselle or Whit would have to drive us."

"We could come for you." He hesitated before speaking—knowing once he said Lydia's name that Clare would know it all. "The kids and Lydia."

"Lydia?"

"My friend."

Silence, and then Clare in a wobbly voice said, "I see."

"It was her idea about sending the kids to France. She has progressive ideas. She's northern." As if that explained everything.

"She helped Whit and Jes?"

"Yes, with everything. It was all her." Crackling on the other end of the phone was the melody to his beating heart as he struggled to find the right words. "I didn't look for it. I've been loyal all these long years. I want you to know that. But I love her."

"I can't think what to say."

"Say it's all right, Clare." Suddenly he knew he wanted her to release him, that he needed absolution from her in a way that didn't make sense, given everything. But it was there nonetheless.

"You must go, Nate, if it's toward happiness, which is what I want for you above all else." She sniffed; he heard her crying. "I'll miss you terribly."

He felt his own tears coming, breathed into them, his voice shaky now. "Thank you, Clare." Then, "We'll come get you. Tomorrow."

CHAPTER 55

Whitmore

WHITMORE'S RIBS ACHED by the time they approached the lake house. He'd been in the front seat while Nathaniel drove, trying not to cry out when they hit bumps and potholes as they wound through the pines. He knew professing pain hurt Jes, so he kept it to himself.

When they turned the corner and saw the familiar sight of the lake house, he glanced at the backseat where Jeselle sat, huddled in the corner, her face tight, brown eyes darting back and forth like they did when she was nervous.

Nate stopped the car in front of the house and looked over at Whit. "Ready?"

Whitmore didn't need to glance in the mirror to know how horrific his face still looked. Because of the broken nose, his face was black and blue, especially the skin under his eyes and over his cheekbones. His eyes were bloodshot, and he couldn't walk without wincing. "I'm afraid Mother might faint at the sight of me."

When they slid out of the car, Lydia hung back, looking unusually uncertain. Nate went to her and whispered something in her ear. She nodded and slipped into the front passenger side of the car. Whit took Jeselle's hand. "Stay close."

They walked to the door, hands clasped. Jeselle reached up and used the knocker as if they were strangers. Nate hung back, near the gate. "You two go on," he called out. "We'll be here. Waiting."

Clare yanked open the front door, with puffy eyes and uncombed hair, dressed in a plaid cotton housedress. Her eyes darted between their faces and then to their intertwined hands. Something went across her face—he could not discern if it was pride or rebellion or sadness. Then she held out her arms, wide enough for both of them. They both leaned into her, and she wrapped an arm around each of them. She smelled as she always did, of talcum powder and French perfume.

"Mother, I've missed you."

"Me too, darlin'. I'm so happy you came home."

His mother withdrew from the hug and peered at Jeselle's stomach. She put her hand softly on its roundness. "My goodness," was all she said. She looked at Whit and touched his cheek gingerly with the tips of her cool white fingers. "Whitmore, your face. Does it hurt much?"

"A little, but I'm alive."

"Thank God." She reached in her pocket and pulled out a handkerchief, wiping the corners of her eyes.

"Mrs. Bellmont, where's Mama?" Jeselle asked.

"In the kitchen." Clare backed up and motioned for them to come inside. "She's fixed something for y'all to eat. Where's Nate?"

"Outside."

"You two go on in. I need to talk to him."

CHAPTER 56

Nathaniel

NATHANIEL SAW CLARE coming toward him. She looked years older than when he'd last seen her. His heart constricted. Damn you, Frances. May you rot in hell.

"Nate." She reached out and pulled him to her. "Thank you for bringing them to me." Taken aback by the gesture, he stood stiffly for a second before softening into the embrace.

"Let's walk. I have some rather upsetting news. I don't think I can tell it without walking."

She seemed unsteady on her feet, and he offered her his arm, which she took as they walked to the lakeshore and then to the end of the pier. At the edge, he felt her shiver despite the June heat. Something mimicking physical pain moved its way across her face.

"Frank called me from Atlanta. Frances showed up at the house. She was alone." Clare paused, and her gray eyes that matched the dark smudges underneath her bottom eyelashes looked away from him, toward the hazy sky. "It'll rain later." At first he took this as an afterthought, but then she continued, "Like that night you were hurt. Do you remember?"

"Yes," he said.

"Frances showed him photos. Dreadful photographs the young man had taken of her. Apparently he's a photographer of the risqué variety. Postcards and such."

He covered his eyes. "Oh, God." Bile rose in his throat.

"She threatened to send the photos around to everyone we knew unless Frank gave her money, knowing he'd rather be penniless than have society see those photos of his daughter."

"Did he?"

"He had no choice. He said goodbye to her. Forever. Frank told her to never contact any of us again."

"She's gone to California, then?"

"I suppose." Her eyes had turned a dull gray and were hooded with downcast lashes.

He turned away, looking at the lake. Dozens of water bugs made rings on the water. A jay called to its mate.

"Nate, it's nearly impossible to explain to a man what it's like to be a woman in this time. I don't excuse her behavior, but I know what it's like to feel trapped in your own life. God knows I've been trapped in this life for so long now that I can't even remember who I once was. Or who I wanted to be."

There was a pebble near his foot. He kicked it into the water. "Clare, I mean no disrespect, but no one could've felt more trapped in his life than I."

"Yes, I know, Nate. I know." Tears were falling down her cheeks and onto the collar of her dress. "Nate, there's something else. Frank went crazy after Frances left, with grief and disappointment about her, and about Whit's choice. Frances told him. I don't know which felt like the worse of the two betrayals. That's how he saw them, you know, as betrayals to a southern lifestyle he spent his life trying to preserve.

"After she left with the money in her pocketbook, he called me, slurring his words the way he does when he drinks, ranting about Whitmore and Jes, saying it was all my fault, that if I'd been a better mother none of this would've happened. He told me he was headed up here in the morning, that he planned on giving us what we deserved." She wiped her face, words choking in the back of her throat. "But I got a call later from the police." Her voice sounded wooden now. "He crashed his car into a tree, that silver flask of his in his lap. He's dead." She paused and looked toward the sky. "A witness to the accident told the police it was like watching someone driving blind."

CHAPTER 57

Jeselle

MAMA STOOD at the stove, frying up eggs and hot cakes. She crossed her arms over her chest, looking at Jeselle's belly. "You got big."

"Yes. I've missed you, Mama."

Mama reached out and folded Jeselle into her arms. Her sinewy frame felt like home. "Baby girl," she whispered. Jeselle looked up and saw tears running down Mama's face. It was the first time she'd ever seen her cry.

Mama motioned for Jeselle and Whit to sit at the table. "Got some food fixed for you." She put a plate of hot cakes in front of Whitmore. "It's foolish, Mr. Whitmore. What you've done. But brave too."

"I guess I don't have to tell you I'd die for Jes."

"You've done proved that, sure enough." Mama sniffed and moved back to the stove. "Don't mean I think it's right. None of it."

Jeselle glanced out the window and saw Mrs. Bellmont on her knees at the end of the pier. Nate was kneeling beside her, a hand on her back. Whit and Jeselle exchanged glances.

"Go out to your mother," Mama said to Whit. "She has something to tell you."

They watched him hobble out. As Whit came upon his mother, Nate helped Mrs. Bellmont to her feet, and she held out her hands to Whit. "What is it?" Jeselle asked.

"Frank Bellmont's dead. Drove his car into a tree."

"Drunk?" asked Jeselle.

Mama continued to look out the window toward the lake. "No. I did it."

"What do you mean?"

Silence.

"Mama?"

"Remember when the birds kept up and dying?"

"Yes."

"I figured what berry was doing it, months ago. So I gathered some and snuck down to Atlanta. Ground them up and put them in his flask. Made it so it'd look like drink that done it."

"Mama. No. Why?"

"He told Miz Bellmont he was coming to kill both of us and you and Whitmore too." She turned toward Jeselle, tipping her chin between her calloused fingers. "You'll learn this, Jessie, once you hold that baby in your arms. No one will ever harm her if you have any say in the matter. Mama bears, that's all we are."

"What if you get caught?"

"I won't. But it don't matter if I do because you'll be safe, and that's all I care about. All I've ever cared about."

"Oh, Mama, I'm sorry."

"Don't be. You're the best thing ever happened to me, and don't you forget it."

"Does Mrs. Bellmont know?"

"No. And Mr. Whit can't know either. Do you understand?"

"Starting a marriage with secrets, Mama?"

"It's better they don't know. When you love someone like we do Miz Bellmont and Whit, well, sometimes you have to protect them from the truth when it would hurt more than the lie. You understand?"

"I think so."

Jeselle sank into the window seat, watching as Nate walked toward the car.

Her eyes shifted back to Whit and Mrs. Bellmont. Mrs. Bellmont gazed at the ground, holding on to Whit's arm. Her mouth moved, surely telling him the dreadful news. As if someone punched him in his aching ribs, he flinched, stepping away from Mrs. Bellmont, like an animal anticipating a trap but jerking away at the last moment. A shudder went through his body. He stooped over, his back rising and falling. Then, he stood to his full height, peering back at the water, his hand hovering over his forehead to shield his eyes from the blazing sun.

After a moment, he turned and took Mrs. Bellmont into his arms and held her against him. Whit's mouth moved, and Jeselle imagined he said something of comfort—a mention of the future that she could cling to with all her might, as they had done. And in that posture, that gesture, Jeselle saw both the past and the future. Standing there was both the man he'd become and the father he would be. Perhaps feeling Jeselle's eyes upon him, he turned toward the house. When he saw her at the window, he placed his hand over his heart and, like so many times before, they anchored to one another. He tucked his mother's arm into his own. And they walked together, toward the house.

*   *   *

The supper Mama put out for them of cold fried chicken and slices of fresh bread slathered with Mama's butter and cold cider from the cellar tasted better than any meal Jeselle could ever remember.

"I hope there's fried chicken in France." Whitmore grinned.

Mrs. Bellmont put down her piece of chicken and wiped her hands delicately with a cloth napkin, ironed so carefully by Mama. "Some southern traditions need to come with us. Fried chicken being one. And your mama and I. We've discussed it, and we're coming too."

"Mama, really?"

"Well, Miz Bellmont needs me."

"I surely do."

"And we don't want to be an ocean away from our babies," said Mama.

"Will you have us?" asked Mrs. Bellmont.

"Mother, of course," said Whitmore, rising from the table to embrace her.

Jeselle put her hand on her belly, feeling the baby move, as if reacting to the news too. It was then that she first realized what Frank Bellmont's death meant. Whit and Mrs. Bellmont were free to do as they pleased with the family's fortunes.

When Mama put out a peach pie, the discussion turned to the future.

"I think you should buy land in France's southern region, where grapes grow," said Mrs. Tyler.

"How do you know about that?" Nate asked her with an amused expression.

"I read it in a book. And it's nothing to tease me about, Nathaniel Fye."

They all laughed, even Mrs. Bellmont, who had watched Lydia Tyler all evening with a curious yet reserved expression.

"You will visit, won't you, Nate?" asked Mrs. Bellmont.

"Yes. Lydia and I would love to," said Nate.

Jeselle glanced over at Whit. He saw it too. Finally Nate had found happiness with the right woman. They fit, just like us, she thought. Now her eyes stung. She went to the sink to hide her tears and put her hands in the soapy water, thinking of every dish Mama had washed, every meal made, the mountains of laundry washed and ironed. The room fell silent. It was all there, between them, like a photograph of a troubled time: the injustice of inequality, the reality that money had the power to change circumstances.

Then, quietly but with a firm resolve, Mrs. Bellmont spoke, "Cassie, wherever we live, you'll have a room of your own, upstairs. Next to mine."

Mama raised an eyebrow. "Won't have none of that unless I continue to look after you. I take care of folks and their homes. That's what I do."

"I defer to your good judgment, Cassie Thorton," Mrs. Bellmont said.

"I might like to learn to read," said Mama.

Jeselle stared at her. "Mama? After all these years?"

"Well, Miz Bellmont needs a new student," said Mama.

Mrs. Bellmont clapped her hands together. "I surely do."

*   *   *

The remnant of the pie was nothing but sticky sauce on the bottom of the dessert plates when the conversation turned to Europe, of the troubles there: Hitler's quest for global power, his hatred of Jews and belief that white Germans were the supreme race. To Jeselle, the descriptions of this by Mrs. Tyler sounded eerily familiar. The crease between Mama's eyebrows deepened. "Surely the hatred we know is better than moving halfway round the world to hatred we're ignorant of," Mama said to Nate.

"I understand your fears," Nate said. "But there's no better place for you now, with the way things are. Someday it'll be different."

"Not so sure 'bout that," Mama said, gathering up the supper dishes. She muttered to herself at the sink, scrubbing the plates and silverware like they'd been rolling around in cow manure. Nate and Lydia exchanged worried glances, but Mrs. Bellmont motioned for them to stay silent as she took a sip of her tea. Jeselle understood; Mama might fuss all the way to France, but nothing would keep her from getting on that boat.

"Clare, I wonder if you might allow me to play at the piano one more time?" asked Nate.

Mrs. Bellmont looked startled. Her teacup clattered as she put it back on the saucer. "Play?"

"Lydia and I play together, Clare," he said, a tiptoe quality to his voice. "Three-handed on two pianos. But tonight, two-handed on one."

Mrs. Bellmont suddenly seemed quite concerned with smoothing a nonexistent wrinkle from the tablecloth.

"We might have a tour in the future." He spoke in the same soft voice.

Mrs. Bellmont raised her chin, gazing at him with sorrowful eyes. "Oh, Nate, is it possible?"

"It is, Clare. After all this time, a second chance," said Nate.

"I'm so pleased." Mrs. Bellmont reached across the table with her delicate hand that always made Jeselle think of fine bone china and patted Lydia's broad hand. "It would be lovely to hear you play together." The women smiled at each other, shy almost, like two children meeting for the first time.

*   *   *

The two musicians sat straight-backed on the piano bench, his right hand and her left hand poised over the keys, their free hands resting between them, almost touching. Nate whispered the time as their torsos moved together in preparation. And then, as if one player, they began. It was the Gershwin piece—music of their collective story, their shared pain. Jeselle shivered and reached for Whitmore's hand. Mrs. Bellmont, a lace handkerchief neglected on her lap, let tears roll down her cheeks unhindered. But as the music continued, Jeselle detected something else enter the room, almost a physical entity that moved about, loosening the ache they all held and replacing it with a tenderness that only comes from forgiveness of the past and acceptance of the now and hope for the future.

*   *   *

Mrs. Bellmont and Jeselle walked with linked arms in the twilight. The birds were quiet, asleep for the night so the only sound was of water lapping against the shore, bringing a sense of tranquility. They stopped at the roses, in full glorious bloom. The petals seemed to drip fragrance, having warmed in the afternoon sun. Mrs. Bellmont held a yellow rose in the palm of her hand, caressing the petals between her thumb and middle finger.

"I'm sorry about Oberlin," said Jeselle.

"We'll find another college for you. Over in France. We'll find a way for both you and Whit to go."

"Whit might prefer an apprenticeship with an artist."

Her eyes turned serious. "I suppose you're right. We can do that now."

"What about the baby? How will I attend college with a baby?"

She laughed. "Don't worry about that. I'll be surprised if either one of us has a chance to hold the child with your mother around."

Jeselle laughed, too, as they walked across the lawn toward the lake. At the water's edge, they paused. Jeselle moved some pebbles in a circle with her foot. "Mrs. Bellmont, why did you do it? Why did you educate me?"

She glanced out toward the water. "It was selfish, really. Teaching you made me feel important. Each time I saw the light of new knowledge appear in your eyes, I was significant." She smiled, turning toward Jeselle. "I've made a lot of mistakes in this life, Jes. Only God knows how many. But, everything else aside, I'm a teacher." She smiled and touched the side of Jeselle's face. "When I looked into your eyes and saw that natural curiosity, that yearning for knowledge, I would have walked to hell and back to give it to you." She paused. "I saw myself in you, too, and I wanted you to have a chance for a better life. Once I saw how gifted you were, I set about trying to figure a way for you to keep going."

"I don't understand why you call it selfish," said Jeselle.

"Because you were my accomplishment, my something that mattered. Someday, when you're an author or a doctor or a teacher, I'll think—I helped make you." She plucked a wilted petal from a yellow rose. "I loved you, too, Jes. You and Cassie are family to me."

Jeselle looked away, pretending to slap a mosquito.

"When Frank wanted me, all those years ago, I told my grandmother that I didn't love him, that I'd rather stay in that shell of a town and be a teacher. For the only time in my life, she lashed out at me, scolding me for what she called my romantic view of things. Told me life wasn't like the books I read."

"Mama said that to me once," said Jeselle.

"A proposal from a rich man was the best it got for girls like me, my grandmother said, and I best take what the good Lord offered. She shamed me. So I did it. I said yes. And I've suffered some and profited some. Every choice is this way." She paused, like she was searching for the right words. "Jes, your mother, she's like my grandmother. Things have been hard for her all her life, and it causes a person to be afraid of change because in their experience change usually brings something worse. She's been holding on tight, hoping you wouldn't start dreaming of something better only to be disappointed and bitter when it didn't come."

"But if you don't wish for more, how can things ever get better?"

"That's for you to teach your child."

Jeselle looked at the grass, trying not to choke on her words. "That's what you gave to me—a chance to dream bigger."

She pointed toward the house. "Let's go inside. Whit's waiting for us." She brushed her fingers on the roundest part of Jeselle's belly. "To think there will be a child where there was once an empty space."

Once inside the house, Mrs. Bellmont motioned toward the study. "You write in there tonight. At a desk, where you belong."

EPILOGUE

June 22, 1934

Night has come. Fireflies dance over the lake. It's quiet except for the steady chirp of crickets. The rest have gone to bed, all exhausted from these trying days.

And, like the other firsts of this new life that Whit, Nate, and Mrs. Tyler forged for me—that Mrs. Bellmont began the first day she opened a book and taught me to read—I sit at a desk only white men have used. Every so often I look up and see myself in the picture windows, an educated black woman, pen in hand.

Tonight, I have more questions than answers. How do two such divergent people as Frank and Clare Bellmont coexist in the world, let alone marry? How do they have both a child like Frances and a child like Whitmore? How does a time and place hold both the men in the white hoods and Pastor Ferguson? How do the men of the Klan claim they are the chosen people of God and not see that their hatred is in direct opposition to the teachings of Jesus? How can all of this be of the same world? I suppose I won't know until the end, when I face my maker.

How did Mama find the courage to do what she did? Risking it all for those she loved? Perhaps someday I'll understand how, but I hope I never have to be that brave, that self-sacrificing. But perhaps none of us gets through life unscathed. Perhaps, most especially, mothers.

Still, I search for meaning in our suffering, for understanding of this world so bursting with contradictions. Whit finds hints in the beauty of nature, splashing what he sees upon a blank canvas. Nate and Lydia hear it in the music or perhaps between the silences. Mama pours her energy into the practical care of others, while Mrs. Bellmont and I seek enlightenment in the books that line her library. And me, on this page, where I write and write—seeking clarity. But, as Virginia Woolf says, perhaps meaning can only be found unexpectedly, like matches struck in the dark.

Whit tells me all good begins from one bold move that spreads like ripples on a still lake. But I think of it as coming in flashes, which, when combined, make a dazzling light—like the fireflies outside this window. Their small sparks are reminiscent of the brave moments of kindness, of compassion, the giving of one's self to another that ordinary men and women did for me, that made me who I am. These fireflies in the night sky are a flicker of hope, a minuscule miracle, a fighting for love over hatred. I bask in their collective, speckled light, knowing I am here because of them. For in the radiant flashes we see that love remains to conquer the dark night.

ALSO BY
TESS THOMPSON

Riversong Sometimes we must face our deepest fears to find hope again. A redemptive story of forgiveness and friendship.

Riverbend A woman finds her life in danger when her abusive ex-boyfriend gets out on parole, leaving her no choice but to accept help from a cold and wealthy recluse hiding a dark history of his own.

Riverstar A feisty Hollywood makeup artist bands together with the beloved River Valley characters to prove the innocence of the man she loves in this romantic and suspenseful tale.

Caramel and Magnolias A former actress goes undercover to help a Seattle police detective expose an adoption fraud in this story of friendship, mended hearts, and new beginnings.

Tea and Primroses Money, love, power and loss – a mother shares the truth about them all with her daughter, but is it too late to help her shape her life differently?

Blue Midnight Searching for her road not taken, Blythe uncovers the unexpected in the foothills of Blue Mountain. With a second chance on the horizon, she must face the complexities of trust and vulnerability that come after betrayal and believe in her destiny.

MORE GREAD READS
FROM BOOKTROPE

Just Friends with Benefits by **Meredith Schorr** (Contemporary Romance) Stephanie resolves not to let her old crush Craig slip away again, but surprises and self-discovery await. A warm, hilarious tale for those who've wondered about the path not taken.

Pulled Beneath by **Marni Mann** (Contemporary Romance) When Drew unexpectedly loses her parents, she inherits a home in Bar Harbor, Maine along with a family she knew nothing about. Will their secrets destroy her or will she be able to embrace their dark past and accept love?

Seasons' End by **Will North** (Contemporary Romance) Every summer, three families spend "the season" on an island in Puget Sound. But when local vet Colin Ryan finds Martha "Pete" Petersen's body in the road on the last day of the season, he uncovers a series of betrayals that will alter their histories forever.

Starting From Lost by **S.K. Wills** (Contemporary Romance) Does that first heartbreak ever truly heal? Starting from Lost is a new contemporary romance that answers the question. In this turbulent journey about self-discovery, forgiveness, and love, some second chances aren't worth taking, but others have their own rewards.

The Inn at Laurel Creek by **Carolyn Ridder Aspenson** (Contemporary Romance) Hurt by her ex-boyfriend's pending marriage to a virtual stranger, Carly escapes to a beautiful bed and breakfast to heal her wounded heart. At the inn, Carly meets struggling musician Ben, and suddenly feels her heart is home. Can Carly's feelings survive when she discovers Ben isn't who he seems?

CPSIA information can be obtained
at www.ICGtesting.com
Printed in the USA
FSOW01n0442170715
8914FS

9 781620 157183